Moskva

Moskva

JACK GRIMWOOD

MICHAEL JOSEPH
an imprint of
PENGUIN BOOKS

MICHAEL JOSEPH

UK | USA | Canada | Ireland | Australia
India | New Zealand | South Africa

Michael Joseph is part of the Penguin Random House group of companies
whose addresses can be found at global.penguinrandomhouse.com.

First published 2016
001

Copyright © Jack Grimwood, 2016

The moral right of the author has been asserted

Typeset in Garamond MT std by
Palimpsest Book Production Limited, Falkirk, Stirlingshire
Printed in Great Britain by Clays Ltd, St Ives plc

A CIP catalogue record for this book is available from the British Library

Hardback ISBN: 978–0–718–18155–0
Trade paperback ISBN: 978–0–718–18156–7

www.greenpenguin.co.uk

MIX
Paper from
responsible sources
FSC® C018179

Penguin Random House is committed to a
sustainable future for our business, our readers
and our planet. This book is made from Forest
Stewardship Council® certified paper.

Red Square, Christmas Eve, December 1985

In the same hour that a sergeant in the Moscow police threw a tarpaulin over the naked body of a boy below the Kremlin Wall, a missile pulled by a diesel train a thousand miles away jumped its rails approaching a bend and killed everyone on board. Faced with such a disaster, the local soviet took the only decision it could.

Military bulldozers began gouging a 200-yard trench in the dirt.

In the weeks that followed, any evidence that the track had not been properly fixed was buried, along with twisted rails, the wreckage and the bodies it had contained. Fresh track was laid along the edge of a lake and fixed properly this time. The accident simply ceased to exist.

In Moscow, the truth was harder to hide.

It was six in the morning, not yet dawn, and the old man using the short cut behind Lenin's Tomb was old enough to remember when Resurrection Gate still guarded the entrance to Red Square; back in the days before Stalin had it demolished to make it easier for tanks to parade.

The old man was unkempt, shaggy-haired. He'd been born to peasants and fought beside Trotsky in his teens. He would be happy to resign his seat on the politburo if only the USSR had someone to replace him.

That fool Andropov, dead after fifteen months. Chernenko didn't even last that long. Now Gorbachev, practically a child . . .

How could he possibly step down?

The man only realized something was wrong when a torch momentarily blinded him. It was lowered quickly, lighting trampled snow. The sergeant was apologetic, abjectly so. 'Comrade Minister. Sorry, Comrade Minister . . . I didn't realize it was you.'

'What's happened?'

'A car crashed into a bollard.'

'What kind?'

'Sir?'

'A Zil, a Volga, a Pobeda?'

'A Volga, sir. A new one.'

The old man frowned. The waiting list for a Volga was so long it could be resold instantly for double the original price. Even in a country where vodka was often the only way to keep out the cold, crashing a new one would be more than unfortunate.

He watched the sergeant shift nervously from foot to foot.

How long would it take him to realize the obvious? There would be tyre tracks in the snow if he was telling the truth. He didn't blame the man. He'd obviously been ordered to lie.

'Tell them I insisted on seeing for myself.'

'Yes, Comrade Minister. Thank you, Comrade Minister.'

They should have been around when Stalin was alive. Then they'd know what real fear was. Ahead, lit by uplights on the Kremlin Wall, a major of the *militsiya*, Moscow's police, stood bareheaded before a politburo member the old man had never liked. The man's preening idiot of a son was on the far side.

'Vedenin,' the old man said.

'Comrade Minister? You'll catch cold.'

That was Ilyich Vedenin for you, the old man thought sourly. Always willing to state the obvious. At their feet, falling snow turned a tarpaulin white.

'Well, aren't you going to show me?'

Vedenin's son yanked back the cover to reveal a boy of twelve or thirteen, apparently asleep. He was naked, his head and any body hair shaved clean. His mouth was very slightly open and his genitals looked tiny. The jelly of his eyes was milky white and he stared so blindly that for a second the old man looked away.

The little finger of the boy's right hand was missing. The cut was clean, no blood on the snow beneath. Kneeling, the old man touched the boy's chest and then his face, almost gently. The flesh was hard as ice.

'Strange,' he muttered.

'What is, sir?'

'He can't have been here long enough to freeze.'

The old man was readying himself to stand when he paused and covered his action by tapping for a second time the white marble of the frozen boy's chest, pretending to listen to its dull thud. Then he checked that he'd seen what he thought he'd seen.

Almost entirely hidden in the boy's mutilated hand was a tiny wax angel.

That was unnerving enough. What was more unnerving still was that the angel had the boy's face. Glancing up, to make sure he wasn't being watched, the old man palmed the angel and pocketed it.

There was a message in the whiteness of the wax.

As there was in the frozen state of the body placed so carefully in front of the Supreme Soviet's centre of power. The old man had to admit he was slightly shocked that the dead boy and the figurine should come together. Not least because the latter could only have come from someone he knew to be dead.

2

New Year's Eve, December 1985

The British embassy on Maurice Thorez Embankment was across the river from the Kremlin. As the ambassador was fond of reminding people, the sight of the flag on its roof once so upset Stalin that he demanded the building back. When the British refused, Stalin had curtains put up to hide the view. Anglo-Soviet relations were better these days.

But not by much.

The last man to arrive at that night's party was a major in British Army intelligence, recently seconded to Moscow at short notice and with the kind of ill-defined job that annoyed Sir Edward intently. The ambassador liked people who knew their place. He also liked to know what that place was. It might have reassured him to know the major wasn't a whole lot happier.

The place, the people, the party . . . none of them fitted Tom Fox's idea of a perfect New Year's Eve.

He'd arrived five days earlier to discover that barely anyone at the embassy knew he was coming and those who did seemed bemused by the fact. Only Sir Edward had been unsurprised, and he'd been disapproving without bothering to say why.

Tom managed fifteen minutes before heading for the nearest balcony and an emergency cigarette. Standing in a chill wind, with snow splattering on to his dinner jacket, he looked resignedly at the icy flatness of the Moskva River and wondered how soon he could head back to his flat.

4

He'd been in the Soviet Union less than a week.

It was already too long.

If Caro were here, she'd say go and make friends. She'd know what to say and who to say it to. His wife's talent for socializing had rubbed off for a while; until things soured between them and he'd stopped bothering. When the balcony door creaked, he refused to look as a figure came to stand beside him, leaning against the cold balustrade.

'Got a cigarette?'

He passed his packet across without comment.

'I'll need a lighter.'

Tom put his Bic on the balustrade where it wobbled in the wind until the girl closed her fingers around it. As it flared, and she put up a hand to shield the flame, he noticed a jade ring on her engagement finger and a graze on her wrist.

'These are foul.'

He nodded.

With the tiny stub of tobacco only half gone, she flicked her papirosa over the edge and they watched the wind whisk it away, darkness taking it long before it hit the snow below. 'It's bloody cold out here,' she said.

Tom nodded.

'You don't say much, do you?'

Shaking his head, he kept his gaze on the red brick of the Kremlin Wall, which was lit from below. He'd been told how many kilos the red star on top of Spasskaya Tower weighed, how much power it took to make it glow. Like most of what he'd been told in the past week, he'd forgotten. He had a sense though, as the balcony door shut, that he'd remember the girl. If only because she'd been wearing black jeans and a dinner jacket of her own.

Then he blinked, and the moment was gone, and he forced himself back inside, heading for the floppy-haired young military attaché whose job it was to help him settle in. Gold cufflinks, signet ring, a dinner jacket he looked as if he'd been born to . . . Tom sighed; he should give the boy a chance.

'Do the Soviets usually attend these things?' Tom asked.

'The Russkies? We always extend an invitation. Mostly they turn us down. Prior engagement. You know the kind of thing. This year . . .'

'What's different about it?'

'They accepted. Well, a few of them did.'

'No, I mean, what's different about this year?'

'Who knows with them?'

'It's my job to know.'

'Is it now?' The young man looked interested. 'We were wondering what you did. "Visiting analyst" sounds a bit American. You know, cubicle offices and fountains in the foyer. Some of us thought you must be a treasury spy.'

'You don't approve of efficiency drives?'

'Only if they improve efficiency.'

'Believe me,' Tom said, 'I'm not a treasury spy.'

The young man excused himself, pleading necessity. Tom watched him head through a crowd of uniforms, dresses and dinner jackets towards the loos, wondering if he'd return, and if he did, how to politely ask his name for a third time, and maybe even remember it.

'You all right?' the man asked, when he got back.

'This isn't really my thing.'

'Nor mine. But it comes with the territory.' He caught the eye of a black woman in a long white dress, who swerved around a Russian colonel, nodded apologetically to the group she'd been about to join and strode towards them.

'Impressive, isn't she?'

Tom wondered whether he'd say that about any other woman there.

'First at Oxford. Good school too.' As she reached them, he said, 'This is Mary Batten. She knows things.'

'Tom,' said Tom. 'Tom Fox.'

'I know,' Mary said. 'I approved your flight. How's the flat?'

'Bug-ridden, most probably.'

For a second she looked surprised, then laughed loudly enough to make a young Russian in a flashily cut velvet jacket glance across. He held Tom's gaze and nodded politely.

'Who's that?' Tom asked.

'See the thickset man smoking cigars by the window? That's Ilyich Vedenin. Newly made minister. He's the highest-ranking Soviet in this room. Vladimir's his son.'

'And the man he's talking to?'

'A general,' said a voice behind Tom. 'Recently recalled from Afghanistan . . .' They turned to find Sir Edward Masterton, the ambassador, looking every bit as languid as Tom remembered from their introductory meeting. 'It might be best,' Sir Edward said, 'if the three of you mingled. We have slightly more shows than expected. We did ring round, didn't we?'

'Yes, sir.' Mary Batten nodded.

'So what happened?'

'Everyone came.'

'Typical. I'd love to know why Vedenin accepted.'

'I'll find out,' Tom said.

Sir Edward raised his eyebrows. 'And how will you do that?'

'I'll ask him, sir.'

Minister Vedenin shook the hand offered and glanced at the crowd over Tom's shoulder. For a moment Tom thought he was looking for someone more interesting, then he realized the real reason.

7

'Your son's over there.'

They looked towards an alcove where the young Russian was deep in conversation with the girl who'd begged the cigarette earlier. As they watched, the girl stopped glowering and almost smiled. The minister sighed.

'He's a good-looking boy,' Tom said.

'And knows it, unfortunately. You have children?'

Tom hesitated. 'A boy,' he said finally. 'With his mother for Christmas.'

'Who is not here?' Opening a silver case, Vedenin offered Tom a cigar. 'These things happen . . . Life is invariably more complicated than one wants. Especially family life. Of course, in my position, the whole of the USSR is my family.'

'That must make for a headache.'

'You have good Russian. For a foreigner.'

'I have terrible Russian.'

The minister shrugged. 'I was being polite.'

The man smelled of cigars and brandy, and a faint whiff of what could be cologne or schnapps. If it was schnapps, it came from a hip flask. He looked like the kind of man who might carry a hip flask for when his hosts kept insisting on offering champagne long after everyone stopped tasting it.

'You went to Sir Edward's school?'

The Russian watched in amusement as Tom half choked on his champagne.

'I doubt they'd have let me through the door . . .'

'Ah, you're . . .' Vedenin smiled. 'Salt of the earth? That's a Rolling Stones track, isn't it? From *Beggars Banquet*. My son has the album.'

'Should you admit that?'

'Times they are changing. That's Dylan.'

'He has that album too?'

'I do. Vladimir bought it for me in America . . .'

The man looked over to where his son now stood talking to an Indian woman. 'I was born in 1923,' he said. 'Two-thirds of Soviet boys born that year didn't survive the war. My hope is Vladimir never has to go through the same.'

Together, Tom and the Russian examined the crowd.

Two hundred and fifty guests filled a ballroom that probably looked just as it had back in the days when the embassy was a rich sugar merchant's mansion. All those uniforms, all that braid, all those dinner jackets. Caro would have been entirely at home.

'Would it be rude,' Tom said, 'to ask why you're here?'

'I was invited.'

The two men stared at each other and Tom wondered whether Vedenin dyed his hair or if he wore a wig, or if his hair really was that dark and wiry. The man lacked his son's good looks, and as a young man would have had an earthiness missing from the boy.

'My wife was an ice skater. Famously beautiful. She died young.'

'How did you know what I was thinking?'

The minister smiled. 'You looked at me, you looked at him, you looked momentarily puzzled. It wasn't hard to follow.'

'I'll remember that.'

'I'll remember you knew I was looking for the boy.' Vedenin hesitated. 'She's young, that English girl you keep staring at. Pretty, admittedly. But young. You know whose stepdaughter she is, of course?'

'I take it you do?'

'What do you find so interesting?'

The dinner jacket, the shaved sides to her head, the irrationality of my anger at the graze on her wrist . . .

'It's hard to say.'

9

'You mean you won't. "A riddle wrapped in a mystery inside an enigma." You know who said that?'

'Churchill. About Russia.'

The minister smiled. 'What are you doing in Moscow?'

'I've been exiled.'

'Really?' Vedenin looked intrigued.

'Well. Someone thought it would be useful if I was out of the way.'

The Russian laughed. 'Your queen offered Ivan the Terrible refuge once. Did you know that? He wanted to marry her. She refused but said if he ever got into trouble at home he could come to live in England. So you see, the ties between our countries are historic and strong. If a little fractious, in the way of all families. Especially those where the members haven't been talking for a while. And that, to answer your question, is why I'm here. Now, if you'll excuse me . . .' The minister swept the ballroom with a sharp gaze, looking for more than his son this time.

A Soviet colonel in dress uniform nodded and slid across to a general, who glanced at Vedenin and nodded in turn. The man the minister didn't look at, the one not in uniform, the one who'd been watching Vedenin's son earlier, didn't catch anybody's eye. He still managed to disengage himself from an elderly Indian diplomat though. And he reached the door ahead of his principal. He was the one who'd checked for the exits, windows and light switches earlier. The one Tom Fox recognized as a younger version of himself. The one he'd have worried about, if worrying about these things was still in his job description.

With the Soviets gone, the party relaxed.

Someone turned the lights down and the music up and a woman began chivvying couples on to the dance floor. Most were embarrassed but well aware there were still two hours to midnight. Abba gave way to Rod Stewart. Rod Stewart to Hot Chocolate . . . Not really Tom's kind of music. He was thinking about going back to the balcony when he saw the ambassador lean in to the woman and mutter something. There was a manicured look about her as if she'd wandered in from Chelsea, and now found herself living in a Georgian rectory somewhere in Wiltshire and regretted the move.

She frowned but headed for Tom all the same.

'It's always hard,' she said, 'when you first arrive. If you don't know anyone. We're a friendly bunch really. Edward says your family will be joining you later.'

'Possibly.'

Her smile faltered.

'My wife's having Christmas with her parents and Charlie's back at school on the seventh. I might try to get back for half-term if I can.'

'Charlie's your son?'

Tom nodded.

'Anna,' she said, putting out her hand.

'Lady Masterton?'

'I prefer Anna.'

Her grip was as strong as her gaze was unfocused. 'I couldn't help noticing you glancing at my daughter earlier.'

'Her dinner jacket is an interesting touch.'

Anna Masterton winced. 'She's cross with me.'

'You in particular?'

'Everyone really. It's a difficult age.'

'Seventeen?'

Anna Masterton didn't know whether to be amused or appalled. 'Is that what she told you? She's sixteen next month.'

'What's she furious about?'

'Lizzie went to Westminster for sixth form and Alex wanted to go too. Lizzie's her friend. My husband wouldn't let her. So now it's a battle. An East German girl she met at the pool was having a party tonight. Edward said she had to come to this. Now he wants to drive out to Borodino, stay a few nights and walk the battlefield. Alex says he can't make her. You can grin, but it's bloody tiring.'

She spoke with the fierce intensity of the quietly drunk.

'I'm sure it is,' Tom agreed.

Anna Masterton shook her head, quite at what Tom wasn't sure, and forced a smile more appropriate to an ambassador's wife at an official function. 'You're a Russia expert, Edward says.'

'I wouldn't go that far.'

'But you did lots of preparation for your visit here?'

'I rewatched *Andrei Rublev*.'

She looked at him quizzically. 'Isn't that the strange black-and-white film with naked peasants in a forest setting fire to everything?'

'Tarkovsky. 1966. It opens with a pagan festival.'

'I thought Russia was Christian by then?'

'Double faith,' said Tom. 'It's called *dvoeverie*. Think of it as dual nationality for the unseen kingdoms.'

'This is your area?'

'That, and recognizing patterns in things. I'm here to write a report for the Foreign Office on religion in Russia.'

'Isn't that rather academic?'

'If faith can move mountains, why shouldn't it bring down a government?'

She looked round, realized her Soviet guests really had gone and lifted another glass of champagne from the tray of a passing waiter.

'Do we want to bring their government down?'

'Your husband's more likely to know that than me.'

It wasn't the real reason he was here, of course. He was here to keep him out of trouble. How much trouble he was in was being decided back in London. Meanwhile, to give his bosses a break, he was here.

Having made enough small talk to give him a headache, Tom pleaded the need for air and another cigarette. Skirting the dance floor entailed endless 'excuse me's as he made his way round the edge of the chocolate-box ballroom, with its white panels and gilding. As he went, he wondered what Caro was doing, then wished he hadn't.

It would be teatime back home. She'd be on the sofa between her parents most likely, a fire already blazing in the hearth. The black-and-white portable wouldn't be turned on until later. And even then it would have the sound down so no one had to pay it any attention until the chimes. Charlie would be getting ready for bed.

A brief protest at not being allowed up, then sleep and, with luck, no dreams.

A year from now . . . ? His boy would still be in bed come New Year's Eve. Probably still protesting, but not fiercely enough to make a difference. And Caro? Whoever's bed she climbed into, Tom doubted it would be his. So why not give her what she wanted? It would be best for the boy. That was what she kept telling him. *Charlie needs to know where he stands.* 'Bitch,' Tom muttered.

'Hey, that's rude.'

It was the girl who'd begged a cigarette.

Tom blinked, 'I'm sorry?'

'I said that's really rude.'

'I wasn't talking about you, obviously.'

'*Obviously* . . .' She did a passable imitation of Tom's irritation.

'People are watching,' he said.

'You think I care?'

'No, I think that's what you want.'

Her hair was wilder than before, her dinner jacket too tight to button. She'd folded up both sleeves since he last looked. Close to, he could see she was younger than he'd imagined. Her gaze found Sir Edward in the crowd and she smirked. 'I'm going to tell my stepfather about you.'

Tom grabbed her as she turned.

The bones in her damaged wrist felt frighteningly fragile. Out of the corner of his eye, Tom saw the black woman he'd talked to earlier heading towards him and let the girl's wrist drop. Her mother wasn't the only one drunk around here.

'Roll your sleeves down,' he said, stepping back. 'Or roll them up, let your parents see and have the damn argument. You're obviously desperate for a fight.'

'He's not my parent.'

'Whatever.'

Beneath her cuffs, not quite visible and not quite hidden, raw welts crossed both wrists. A blunt knife would do it.

'What's it got to do with you anyway?'

'Nothing.'

'Exactly.'

'Wrist to elbow,' he said. 'Wrist to elbow. If you're serious.'

3

Sadovaya Samotechnaya

Shrugging himself into his Belstaff, Tom left the party through high gates between wrought-iron railings mostly hidden by frosted trees. He made a point of nodding to the *militsiya* sergeant stamping his feet on the pavement outside. Brown coat, peaked cap, cheap boots, Makarov in a brown-leather holster.

Same poor sod as earlier.

Taking the metro would cost five kopeks, and the stations had such elegance they put London to shame, but Tom wanted to walk and if the little Russian assigned as Tom's KGB shadow had to walk too, that was his bad luck.

From his pocket, Tom pulled a rabbit-fur cap bought that afternoon. It was second-hand and split along one edge. Cramming it on to his head, he lit a Russian cigarette and checked his reflection in a car window, flattering himself that he was safely anonymous, as drably dressed as those around him.

Just north of the Bolshoi and south of the Boulevard Ring that ran round inner Moscow, what Tom thought was a scraped-together mound of snow on the steps of a church shivered, and he stepped back as the mound shook itself from white to black, recently fallen flakes scattering to reveal an old woman.

A red scarf was tight around her head. She looked for a moment puzzled at where she found herself and then shrugged and examined the man in front of her with bright eyes. 'American,' she announced.

Tom shook his head.

'Ah, he speaks Russian. Well, perhaps he knows the odd word.' She looked beyond Tom to the crossroads, which was empty except for Tom's shadow a hundred paces away, pretending to tie his shoe. Early twenties, skinny and rat-faced, he was putting in time as a pavement artist on his way to a nice warm desk from which he could order others to trawl around in the cold. Tom waved and received a scowl in reply.

He'd expected Soviet tradecraft to be better.

'Here.' The old woman offered Tom what looked like a sliver of ivory.

It was an angel carved from wax. Squat and moon-faced, unnervingly ugly, with a bent wing.

Distractedly, Tom dug into his pocket for change. He shook his head when she pushed the figure at him. 'Sell it again,' he suggested.

'That would be bad luck.'

Her accent was hard. She might be southern, to judge from her leathery face and the sharpness of her cheekbones. Georgian? Azerbaijani? Tom's Russian was too rusty for him to place her. He was pleased enough to understand the words.

'So,' she said, 'what's your name?'

'Why?' Tom demanded.

'I was being polite.'

Despite himself, Tom grinned.

'See. That's better. Can you spare one of those?' She nodded at the burned-out papirosa in his fingers. And taking one for himself, Tom gave her the packet. As he was leaving, she called after him.

'If not American?'

16

'English . . .'
'Covent Garden. The Royal Ballet. Sadler's Wells.'

Hard walking on slippery pavements brought him to the Garden Ring and the Sadovaya Samotechnaya block for foreigners that stood in its shadow. As he approached, a black cat hurried between ruts in the snow, dodged round the KGB man guarding its entrance and mewed for the gate to be opened.

'He lives here?' Tom asked the guard, who did his best not to be shocked that Tom spoke his language.

'I'm not sure he has papers.'

Tom laughed.

The man couldn't help glancing beyond Tom to his shadow, who was now pretending to admire a bronze statue of a Soviet youth in gym shorts holding the hand of a girl in a summer dress. When the boy felt he'd admired the statue for as long as was believable, he knelt and tied his shoelace for the fifth time that evening.

Tom could lose him easily.

But the Committee for State Security would assign someone better. Then, when Tom really needed to shake free – if he ever really needed to shake free – it would be harder.

'Where's a good place to drink?'

'Everywhere is closed.'

'It's New Year's Eve.'

'In Moscow, bars close at eleven.'

'*Tovarishch*. Comrade . . . Don't be ridiculous. It's New Year's Eve. There must be a bar open somewhere in this city.'

The KGB man sighed.

Lights still shone in at least half the flats overlooking the bleak street, but its cafes and shops were firmly shut. He'd just decided he must have overshot the address he'd been given – along with a warning about foreigners not necessarily being welcome, New Year's Eve or not – when a man shouted from a concrete walkway above, and a familiar noise brought Tom up short.

He knew the sound of a door being kicked open.

He'd heard enough of that in Northern Ireland. Usually, though, the kick came from outside. This time . . . Tom heard the door slam into a wall and saw a man's body tumble down the concrete stairs to land in a sprawl.

Behind him stamped a broad-shouldered man in his twenties, his torso bare except for a stained singlet. What Tom noticed, though, was his leg. It was missing, its replacement constructed from the leaf spring of a vehicle. Having dragged his victim to his feet, the man hurled him into a bank of snow and finally noticed Tom watching.

'What are you looking at?'

'You,' Tom said.

The man considered that.

'Do I look like I play Abba?' he asked furiously. 'I mean, really? The Beatles, if you must. The Stones, back when they were good. New York Dolls. The Cramps. The Ramones. But Abba?'

'Always hated them,' Tom said.

'You lost?'

'Who isn't? No. I'm looking for a bar.'

The man jerked his head towards the stairs down which the drunk had been thrown. 'There are worse ones than mine. Not many, mind you . . .'

'I'm not that choosy.'

The upstairs bar had a long length of battered zinc against which a dozen men leaned. Another four formed a queue behind a fifth, who stood in front of a computer monitor with a filthy screen. The fifth man was battering a keyboard as he tried to twist the shapes that rained from above. When he mistimed a move, falling blocks built up and his screen filled. Cursing, he stepped aside for the man behind to take his place.

'Tetris,' the bar owner said sourly. 'Worse than heroin.'

'Where did the computer come from?'

'The army.'

'Do they know it's gone?'

'They've probably replaced it.'

The man who'd just lost his game yelled a food order.

Instead of answering, the one-legged man took himself behind the zinc and vanished through a curtained gap in a wall of records. Mostly albums, although a row of 45s sat high up. He returned with a bowl of red cabbage, which he thrust at the loser with a shrug that suggested personally he wouldn't eat it. Then he headed for a battered turntable on a shelf attached to the record wall.

'Any requests?'

There was silence from the room.

'Yeah,' Tom said. '"Sympathy for the Devil".'

The barman stared at him.

'Could have been written about any of us,' said Tom. 'Apart from the bits about wealth and taste.'

Straight after came 'Stray Cat Blues'.

'To Behemoth,' said the one-legged bar owner. 'Sadly absent.'

Then the man put away *Beggars Banquet*, pulled out *David Johansen* and played 'Frenchette' twice before lowering the needle on to a badly scratched 45 of The Damned's 'New Rose'. In between, he served flasks of vodka and iced bottles of Zhigulevskoe lager to a slowly dwindling crowd that finally comprised only a hard core of drinkers and those too drunk to find the door.

There were no seats in his bar, no tables.

His customers were restless and cheaply dressed and stank of the vinegary cabbage ferried endlessly from the kitchen. Sweat, vodka and cigarette smoke soured the room. Anyone who believes vodka doesn't smell hasn't sweated it out. After a flask and a half, Tom finally cracked and asked for a bowl of whatever everyone was eating.

The bar owner shouted and a whey-faced teenager came in from the kitchen. She scowled at the owner, looked over at Tom and her eyes flicked towards the papirosa he was lighting. Tom realized it wasn't the cigarette that attracted her.

It was the flame . . .

The cabbage she dumped at his elbow was sweet and sour and tasted of raisins. Its welcome warmth reminded him of hunger. Of being cold and fed up, cold, fed up, wet and hungry. Without thinking, he went to the window and stared down at his KGB shadow. The man was stamping his feet in a doorway, his donkey jacket wrapped as tightly round him as it would go. Cold nights in dark doorways.

Worse nights in the wastes of a Belfast multi-storey.

The wind blowing through him, whistling between his ribs, while he pissed in a milk carton and shat in a supermarket bag, waiting for a man who didn't show and men who wanted to kill him, who did.

There'd been women over there. When the nights were darkest, they'd put warmth in his bed. Only one of them had realized it wasn't the sex he needed. She'd cradled his head as he cried through a long December night, and never referred to it again. That was ten years ago. Her man came out of prison eventually. Around the time her son went in.

'Who is he?' the bar owner asked.

'KGB. My shadow.'

'You American?'

'English.'

The bar owner looked doubtful.

'Promise you,' Tom said. 'English.'

The man brought Tom another beer and a fresh flask of vodka, waving the payment away. 'What brings someone like you to a bar like this?'

'I like this bar.'

'So do I. I own it. That doesn't answer my question.'

'I was at a party . . .' Tom hesitated. 'I left.'

'You didn't like the other guests?'

'I wanted to punch them.'

The man smiled sympathetically.

'Ivan Petrovich Dennisov,' he said, putting out his hand. '*Tovarishch.*'

'You call me Dennisov.'

'Tom Fox,' Tom said. 'Major Tom Fox.'

Dennisov grinned. 'David Bowie. "Space Oddity". Also "Ashes to Ashes", "Scary Monsters (and Super Creeps)".' He put a fresh flask of vodka in front of Tom, helped himself to a glassful and raised it in salute.

'Major Tom.'

Tom looked at him.

'You have to say "Ground Control".'

A copy of that day's *Pravda* had been dumped on the zinc and Tom read it, as much to keep his Russian sharp as for any information it might contain. Victories in Afghanistan, a new dam beyond the Urals, advances in Soviet computing. The police in the Yakut autonomous republic were investigating a spate of horrific murders with all diligence. An arrest was imminently expected.

A famous dissident had been rehabilitated. A poet had

been unbanned. An amnesty granted state-wide in five categories for politicals jailed before 1953.

'Things are getting better?' Tom suggested.

'They could hardly get worse.'

Later, as dawn threatened, while the teenager clattered around her tiny kitchen, the man came out from behind his bar with a mop to rid the floor of spilt beer. Seeing Tom glance at his leg, he said suspiciously, 'You sure you're not American?'

'Quite sure. I have friends who'd be impressed by that.'

'Friends who crashed helicopters?'

'Who tripped wires on mines. Met bombs beside the road. Bombs in bins.'

'You never met bombs in bins?'

'No,' said Tom. 'I just got shot.'

'Me too,' the man said. 'But by a missile. An American one. Three friends died instantly. One man lived. One died later.'

'What happened next?'

'Me? Airlifted to Kabul. My countrymen? They went in with gunships and lost another Mi-24 reducing some shithole to rubble. Now . . . It's time you went home.'

What home? Tom wanted to ask. The man was right though. Looking around, Tom realized the room was empty; he was the last.

4

Wax Angel, 6 January 1986

She'd danced once. Danced the greatest roles by the greatest composers in front of the greatest men in the Soviet Union. In Moscow at the Bolshoi. In Leningrad at the Kirov. She'd looked after the young ones on the beautiful and perfect and disastrous tour where everyone danced wonderfully at the Palais Garnier in Paris, and the orchestra were at their finest, and Nureyev defected to the enemy, and the tour and everyone else's careers fell apart around him.

Her body was old and battered now.

Not as old as her face made her look. Not as old as those who swept past her on the street with families and flats and places to go imagined. But older than she liked and battered certainly. She hurt from sleeping in doorways and the crypts of those few churches still open at night. It was nothing to the pain of training though: the blood-soaked points to her ballet shoes, the agony in her groin where she stretched and split and twisted her body in a way no man had dared.

They had doctors at the Bolshoi.

She could remember the relief morphine brought when her injuries threatened to prevent her going on stage. The strong hands of the physios kneading the knots from her locked muscles. She'd lived on champagne, caviar and the admiration of her lovers, male and female. No prison had been more luxurious.

It was a different kind of hard on the street.

No fun in summer and worse in winter. A new pair of boots would have made all the difference but who would give new boots to an old parasite like her? There'd been the year she wanted to hang herself but didn't have a rope. When she eventually found a rope, she decided to cut her wrists instead. Broken glass wasn't good enough. It had to be a knife. When she found one and still didn't kill herself, she decided she must want to live after all.

The old woman begging on the steps of the Church of Our Saviour always told the police she bought the candles she carved from an Uzbek in the market near the motorway. She couldn't say where the Uzbek got the candles. That wasn't her business and you never knew with Uzbeks . . .

It was only new recruits who questioned her.

Bumpkins in uniform.

There was no crime in Moscow. At least, very little.

That was the official version. No crime, and what crime there was was the fault of gypsies and Jews. Occasionally a good Russian got drunk and killed his wife in a temper, and wept in remorse come morning. Mostly he simply turned himself in. Every imperfect society had recidivists, of course. And the Soviet Union was not yet perfect. It would be in time but until then the *militsiya* were here to help keep it honest. She didn't really buy her candles at the market by the motorway. How would she get up there with her poor legs and how could she afford the sort of prices an Uzbek would ask? She was given the candles by a priest she'd known when he was a boy. He probably rationalized the candles as Christian charity. She knew it as guilt for something forgotten by everyone except them.

She didn't carve wax angels either.

At least, not as far as the *militsiya* were concerned.

If, after explaining where the candles came from, the old

woman was asked why she carved angels, she was careful to correct the questioner. Angels were religious, and although freedom of religion was enshrined in Soviet law, belief itself could lead to complications. In her view, belief in anything led to complications, but she kept that thought to herself. She carved the Spirit of Moscow. Wouldn't her questioner agree the spirit of a city as great as Moscow deserved wings?

They didn't believe her.

They weren't required to believe her.

She was simply required to tell the lie.

She denied that she carved angels so often that Wax Angel became what they called her among themselves, and how she started to think of herself. It wasn't as if anyone remembered her real name anyway.

The *militsiya* left her alone, mostly. In return she told them things now and then. For all she knew, everyone in Moscow told them things. The secret was to tell them as little as possible and very definitely nothing they needed to know.

5

Telephone

Tom Fox woke a week into the New Year to the sound of a telephone. He was grateful for its ring. He'd been in the Bogside on a dark and unwelcoming street, with light in pools from the few street lamps not yet broken and republican songs echoing from a pub on the corner. Before that he'd been on the hills near the border, with a cottage in flames behind him. In the Bogside, he'd been plastering an upstairs wall. Plastering was his cover but this was for himself. He was skimming a false wall beside a fireplace. Behind it was the L96A1 he'd used to kill the man in the cottage.

For all he knew, the rifle was still there.

It took Tom a moment to recognize his flat, to shake away one world and acknowledge another. The telephone was on a table by the front door and he went there naked, freed by waking alone and not bothered by the sight of himself in a mirror in the tiny hall. 'Fox . . .'

'Is my stepdaughter with you?' The voice was imperious.

'What?' Shutting his eyes, Tom squeezed away the last of his nightmare and focused on the receiver in his hand.

'This is Edward Masterton. Is my stepdaughter with you?'

'Of course not . . . Sir, this is an open line.'

'I know it's an open line. There's a car on its way and I want you here now. Apparently you're the last known person

26

to talk to her. I want to know what she said. I want to know if she told you where she was going.'

'She's vanished?'

'Obviously she's vanished.'

Alert now, and shivering in the chill hallway, Tom said, 'Did she leave a note?'

'What makes you ask that?'

'Isn't that what teenagers do? Leave notes.'

'Here, Fox. Now.'

The line went dead, followed a moment later by a second click and then silence. Tom put down his receiver, picked it up again and listened to the lazy tone. Whichever KGB clerk had the job of transcribing his calls would pass that up the line the moment he realized the significance of what had just been said. Tom imagined that the Soviet Committee for State Security operated like every other intelligence agency he'd ever come across. Rule One was cover your back.

The ambassador's response shocked him, though. Either Sir Edward believed the Soviets already knew, or he was too angry to worry.

When Tom's phone rang again, it was to say a car was waiting. Leaving Sad Sam, he stepped over the stray cat that spent its days guarding the gate, passed the bored KGB man in his little box and opened the rear door of a blue embassy Jaguar. In the back, on the shiny leather seat, sat Sir Edward's head of security. First glance would have told you he was an ex-serviceman. Second glance might have suggested he needed to exercise his body less and his mind more. A flint-like sharpness suggested that second glance would be wrong.

'Morning,' Tom said.

The ex-serviceman stared at him.

'Here to make sure I don't abscond?'

'Something like that.'

The man nodded at the driver's mirror and the V12 purred into life. As the Jaguar turned south, a sleek Volga fell into place behind it.

'Subtle,' Tom said.

'There's a hierarchy. Sir Edward merits a Volga. I merit a new Moskvitch. You merit an old one. That's also how you tell the services apart. The KGB drive Volgas, the police Moskvitches.'

'I had a Volga the other night.'

'You must have got that wrong.'

Tom shook his head. 'I don't get things like that wrong.'

The man looked at him. A long considered stare until Tom glanced away. He had no wish to get into a pissing contest with an ex-paratrooper. Unless he wanted to go home, of course. Because that's where the Second Secretary could send him. 'Do you know where she is?' the man asked finally.

'Why the hell would I –'

'Do you know where she is?'

'No,' Tom said. 'I have no idea where she is.'

The man sat back and considered his next question carefully. When he spoke, his voice was less clipped and there was a trace of an accent. Something northern, Yorkshire maybe. 'Any idea why Sir Edward thinks you might?'

'Because he's clutching at straws?'

'There has to be more to it than that.'

Tom shrugged. 'What happens now?'

'You see Sir Edward.'

'Have we told the Soviets?'

'Sir Edward's rather hoping she'll come back on her own.'

'Does London know?'

'Fox. You don't seem particularly concerned.'

'For the kid? Of course I'm concerned.'

'For yourself. When I left, Sir Edward was raging. Apparently you gave his stepdaughter a lesson in how to commit suicide.'

Tom inhaled sharply. 'Oh, bloody hell.'

The car trailing them stopped outside, as if the embassy's high gates and wrought-iron railings were enough to make its engine fail. In a way they were. Inside was Great Britain. Outside, Soviet Russia.

'He's in his office,' a woman at the reception desk told the head of security, who nodded and headed for the stairs. Across the hallway, two guards were watching, but casually. They knew something was going on. They didn't know what. Ex-soldiers, possibly still serving. One caught Tom's eye and shrugged.

Sir Edward's office was as big as Tom remembered.

The desk was impressively huge and largely empty. There was the obligatory Annigoni portrait of the Queen as a young woman on the wall behind it. On a side table sat a photograph of Sir Edward with the PM. Before the door had even shut, the woman at Sir Edward's side strode over and slapped Tom so hard his head jerked sideways.

'*Anna!*' Sir Edward protested.

'How could you?' she shouted. 'How could you be so stupid? What kind of monster says *Wrist to elbow if you're serious*?'

'Did you know?' Tom asked. 'Did you know what your daughter was doing?'

For a moment Anna Masterton's face was hollow as a mask and, as the anger went out of her, Tom knew that she had.

'What's this about?' Sir Edward demanded.

'Your stepdaughter had dragged something sharp across

her wrists. Not for the first time from the look of it. I told her to roll her sleeves up or roll them down. Have the fight or . . .'

'Not?' Sir Edward asked.

'Was there a fight to have, sir?'

'With Alex there's always a fight to have.'

'What did her note say?' Tom asked.

'There wasn't one,' Sir Edward said crossly. 'We went up to her room when we got back from Borodino to see if she was still sulking and half her things were gone. She'll be back,' he added. 'We've barely been out here six months. She's spent most of those at school. Not to mention half this holiday moping upstairs. Where's the wretched child going to go? Anna just needs to ring round Alex's friends . . .' Running his hand through silvering hair, Sir Edward looked at the pen on his desk and then at files piled in his in tray.

Lady Masterton caught the glance and her face tightened. Now was when Tom should leave. If he was wise, he'd simply ask permission to go, but a question needed answering. 'Where was the party?'

Husband and wife turned, as if they'd forgotten he was there.

'The one she wasn't allowed to go to.'

'Who told you about that?' Sir Edward demanded.

Catching Lady Masterton's eye, Tom lied. 'Your stepdaughter, when we were talking on New Year's Eve. She seemed upset about it. Actually, she seemed upset about everything.'

'So you taught her how to cut her wrists?'

'I wanted to shock her into thinking about what she was doing, sir.' Tom hesitated. 'Before she did something really stupid and it was too late.'

'I don't see what it had to do with you.'

'Nothing, sir. It had nothing to do with me.'

'Quite so.' Sir Edward sat back as if he'd won a debating point.

'I'll ring round,' Lady Masterton said. 'Although I doubt she's with anyone we know. One of the mothers would have called me by now. Whether Alex wanted her to or not. And yes,' she added, before her husband had done more than draw breath, 'I'll sound everyone out as discreetly as possible.'

Tom watched her go.

'Fox, I have reports to check.'

'Yes, sir.'

'Wait outside. I'll call for you if I need you.'

Lady Masterton looked surprised when Tom joined her.

'Important papers,' Tom said.

Taking a *Country Life* from a side table, he buried himself in the ads at the back. He could buy a two-bedroom mews house in Cheyne Walk, Chelsea for £98,000. The same sum would secure a small island in a Scottish loch with a shooting lodge ripe for conversion. If he didn't like that, there was a cottage in Hampshire with a hundred yards of its own bank and fishing rights. He'd be fifteen miles from Caro's parents if he bought that.

Good for seeing Charlie.

Mind you, being able to afford any of them was only slightly more likely than finding money for the castle in northern Spain, 200 hectares, a vineyard and its own stables. Offers around £500,000.

When Tom closed the magazine, he realized that Anna was still making calls. She was explaining that Alex had had a sleepover while they were away and like an idiot she'd forgotten where. She didn't suppose ... Anna Masterton was a convincing liar, at least to anyone not looking for the panic in her voice.

6

Kisses for Mayakovsky

A stark black-and-white sticker on the girl's bedroom door announced *Parental Advisory: Explicit Lyrics*. A smiling sun below it declared *Atomkraft? Nei Takk*. Inside, posters were plastered so thickly they overlapped. A huge fishing net hung from her ceiling. It had been spray-painted black and silver. A poster of a vaguely familiar movie star claimed pride of place on the biggest wall.

His collar was up, a slash of light lit his eyes.

'Bela Lugosi,' Anna Masterton said.

A flyer for Killing Joke, The Pale Fountains and Heist at the Hammersmith Palais rested under the glass sheet that topped her bedside cabinet.

Anna sighed. 'We didn't let her go.'

Of course you didn't, Tom thought.

'And that?' he asked.

A postcard of a wolf peering through wire with fir trees behind.

'She got it from an East German girl at the swimming pool. The one having the party. We're caged, you see. It's free . . .'

Turning it over, Tom found a cartoon from *Krokodil*, Moscow's satirical magazine, pasted to the back. It showed a Soviet tank exhibiting a bad case of brewer's droop. The card was made in Leningrad, not East Germany; Tom wondered if Anna realized that.

'You don't mind Edward asking you to help with this?'

That wasn't the question she wanted to ask.

Even upset, Anna Masterton was far too polite to put the question she really wanted answered. *Why the hell would my husband suggest I show you round my daughter's bedroom?*

'I've done a certain amount of investigative work,' Tom said carefully. 'While seconded to Intelligence. Sir Edward thought I might find something to indicate where this party was held.'

Anna nodded doubtfully.

Yanking back a black curtain, Tom found himself staring towards Vodootvodny Canal, with Gorky Park to the right. A purple-haired gonk smirking at the recently revealed view was the first babyish thing he'd seen.

Alex's books sat in a row against the skirting board.

Mostly Stephen King or Virginia Andrews, with a battered copy of *Lace* defiantly on top. It had been read so often page 292 fell out. Tom didn't need to look to know it was the goldfish scene. 'Lizzie's,' Lady Masterton said. 'So, I can't bin it.'

'Whose?'

'The girl who went to Westminster.'

A black vinyl box revealed a Russian-language Linguaphone course: a row of well-used cassettes and a tatty paperback full of instructions on how to order a coffee, ask the way to the library, or tell someone you needed a lavatory and could they point you in the right direction please . . .

'She's fluent in Russian?'

'Better than me, but that's not saying much.'

'"To speak another language is to have a second soul."'

'I'm not sure I find that idea reassuring.'

The only large-format book was a stained copy of *When the Wind Blows*, with an elderly and ordinary-looking cartoon couple on the front. Flicking through, Tom discovered it took them forty-eight pages to die of radiation sickness.

'Edward hates that book,' Anna said.

'That's why Alex owns it?'

'No. She really likes it. It makes her cry.'

An advertisement for *The Company of Wolves* torn from *Cosmopolitan* had Sellotape scars to say it had been up somewhere before. Beside it, a poster for *Legend* showed Tim Curry painted red and wearing horns.

'What are we looking for?' Anna asked.

'A photograph of the East German girl would be good. A note of where the party was being held would be better. Do you know if your daughter kept a diary?'

'Not that I'm aware.'

On the bedside cabinet was a tiny cardboard box; Tom opened it without asking, feeling Lady Masterton bridle slightly.

'What should be in here?' Tom asked.

'A jade ring from Lizzie. It's ghastly. And not jade, obviously. Luckily it's too big and keeps falling off, even when we tied cotton round the back. Alex must have decided to wear it after all.'

Tom wondered if maybe her friendship with Lizzie wasn't over. Or perhaps Alex had another reason for taking the ring. The only photograph on display was a Polaroid of a busty teenager in a tight pink top and purple ra-ra skirt, her hair teased to the point of bullying.

'Lizzie?' Tom asked, and Anna nodded.

'And that?' He pointed to a television and keypad.

'Alex's computer.'

'*Her computer?*'

'It works like a fancy typewriter. Alex expressed interest and Edward thought . . .' Anna shrugged. 'Who knows what he thought? Perhaps that anything was better than hiding up here sulking.'

'Lady Masterton . . . would you mind if I did the rest alone?'

She did mind. She minded very much. Forcing a smile, she said, 'It's Anna. And that's fine. There are things I should do. I'll tell Edward you're still up here.'

The silent precision with which Anna Masterton shut the door almost shamed Tom into calling her back.

Stripping back Alex's duvet, Tom checked the bottom sheet, then stripped that back too and examined her mattress. Then he stood the mattress against the wall and examined the bed's base. It had its original stitching; its springs moved as they should. The mattress ditto. Recently stained from an unexpected period but otherwise original. Nothing hidden inside. No evidence of anything ever having been hidden inside.

Remaking Alex's bed, Tom sat on it and emptied her bedside cabinet.

The drawer at the top held two kohl pencils, sharpened down to stubs, three tampons, a metal comb, nail clippers, black nail varnish, purple nail varnish and pearl . . . A handful of British change had been pushed into one corner.

The only letter was from Lizzie.

She complained about Alex not writing.

At the back, behind the nail varnishes, Tom found an empty packet of Rothmans with a disposable lighter inside. The shelves below held old copies of *Smash Hits*, *Jackie* and *NME*. The *NME*s were recent. The *Smash Hits* stretched back to 1983, which meant Alex had brought them with her. The *Jackie*s were even earlier.

No hidden letters or photographs fell out when he riffled their pages.

Behind the stack of *Smash Hits* he found condoms, the Durex packet unopened and still in its cellophane. The lack of a price sticker suggested it had come from a slot machine. Tom put the packet back where he had found it, and replaced Alex's magazines. So she liked pop music, smoked in secret and had, at the very least, considered sex. Nothing to suggest she wasn't like most kids her age.

Except this was a girl who'd been feather-bedded and wrapped in cotton wool. Boarding school from God knows what age, holidays undoubtedly spent with her family. No street smarts at all. Tom knew what he'd been doing at fifteen. He knew what easy prey he'd have found a girl like Alex.

Nothing was taped to the cabinet's rear. Nothing but eye shadow, mascara, blusher and moisturizer occupied the dressing table. A bottle of *Babe* by Fabergé stood on its glass surface, unopened.

A Walkman balanced against it.

First and Last and Always, Love, Power, Corruption & Lies, Hyæna.

The cassettes inside the boxes matched their titles.

Nothing was taped to the underside of any of the drawers, nothing hidden in the dead space below the lowest. Bare hangers showed where clothes had been taken. The last thing Tom did was drag a chair to Alex's wardrobe and step up so that he could check the top. It was dusty, but nothing like as dusty as it should have been.

In the space below the detachable top were Alex's secrets. Some of them anyway.

A new edition of *Yevtushenko* and a *Complete Andrei Voznesensky*, both collections of poetry in the original Russian. *Kisses for Mayakovsky* was English, by Alison Fell. Loved obsessively from the look of it. The book had been published only the year before and was already falling to pieces. Inside,

Tom found a postcard of the wedding-cake monstrosity that was Moscow University:

You will hear thunder & remember me & think: She wanted storms . . .
Dxxxxx

'Dxxxxx'? Five kisses?

Immediately, Tom wondered if D was the East German girl and all of this was more complicated than Sir Edward and Anna were prepared to admit. Perhaps Alex's old school friend's sulk was about more than her lack of letters. How careful need he be in how he asked about that?

By the way, do you know if your daughter is a lesbian?

Oh, you're right. Of course. It's probably just a phase she's going through.

Beside the books sat three Soviet pin badges and a gothic cross on a chain. Tom wasn't sure if the last was cheap or expensive. His wife would know. Caro was good at things like that. Two computer disks sat underneath.

Amsoft WordProcessor, LocoScript.

Tom had decided this was his lot when he saw a cassette box at the back. It was empty, the insert homemade. A photo-copied Soviet Star coloured in with fluorescent highlighter. *For Alex* said the spine.

He wondered if she'd taken the tape, then had a better idea.

Putting the chair back where it belonged, he flipped open her Walkman and found a C60 ferrous-oxide tape, American made, no writing either side. Hitting play, he heard drumming so precise it had to be a machine, followed by a few bars of intro from an electric guitar and then a voice dark enough to come from deep inside a cave.

A second track followed, then a third.

It was the third Tom recognized. The words of 'Comfortably Numb', familiar and frighteningly true. But this version was darker and stranger and altogether more anguished than any he'd heard. The hissing of the tape told him that Alex had played it half to death. Looking round her room, Tom read what he saw.

The purple-haired gonk on the window ledge, the photograph of her friend, the copy of *When the Wind Blows* said fragments of an earlier Alex remained. But they were fragments. The sense of a newer, more complex, more adult Alex was overpowering. Tom ran through the options.

She'd run away. She'd been enticed away. She didn't want to come back. She wanted to come back and couldn't . . .

There was no her to come back.

7

Meeting Anna on the Street

Tom was heading down the steps from the embassy on to Maurice Thorez Embankment when he spotted Anna Masterton standing by a low wall, staring at the frozen river. She was huddled in a sheepskin coat, and carried leather gloves in one hand. Her surprise at seeing him was so overdone he wondered how long she'd been waiting.

'Find anything useful?' she asked.

'Not yet.'

Her smile faded at his answer. 'Edward says you served in Ulster.'

Tom nodded, face carefully neutral. 'Both sides of the border.'

'Do I ask what you were doing?'

'Best not. I have to ask. Might Alex have gone home?'

'Home?'

'To the UK. To her father?'

Anna looked as if she'd just been slapped. 'He's dead,' she said flatly. 'And this is her home, for now. For better or worse.'

'I'm sorry. An accident?'

'Cancer, prostate. Alex took it badly. Well, you would.' Anna tried to smile. 'Do you have time for a coffee?'

Tom pretended to glance at his watch. No one senior would read the report he'd been sent to Moscow to write. At least, no more than the necessary skim through to confirm he'd written the bloody thing. 'The Resilience of Religion in Soviet Russia'.

Maybe he was misjudging his bosses. Maybe he was meant to find a magic lever to bring the whole Soviet state to its knees.

Personally, he doubted it.

You are required to present yourself at the Palace of Westminster on 14 February at 3.45 p.m. Please use the Cromwell Green entrance . . . You may, if you wish, make a written submission in advance of the hearing.

He didn't wish. He didn't wish at all.

Tom was in Moscow to keep him out of the clutches of a parliamentary select committee on Northern Ireland, who'd whine at his absence and note their displeasure and move on to safer matters. Much safer. Safer for everyone.

'I should probably get back to work,' he said.

'You have a deadline?'

'Oh yes.' He did too. Although he couldn't remember what it was.

'I'd better let you go then.'

'Anna . . .'

She turned back.

'What did you really want to ask?'

'Oh God, look, between us . . . All right? Alex was keen on an American boy at the university here. Nineteen, so a bit old for her. They met at the swimming pool. I've been trying to leave David messages but they're not getting through.'

'That's where Alex is?'

'That's what I'd decided.' Anna bit her lip. 'Hope against hope, really. Anyway, after I left you up there, I cracked.'

'You're driving out there?'

'Dear God, no. Edward would want to come. I called the American ambassador's wife. We get on well enough. The thing is, our embassy keeps a list of British exchange students at Moscow University. We're their post office. They come in now and then to check on mail from home. The Americans run the same system.'

'So you got a message to him that way?'

'He doesn't exist. At least, there's no David Wright.'

'Your daughter told you about this boy?'

'I lied about Alex not having a diary.' Anna Masterton coloured slightly. 'He must have given her a false name.'

'Or she suspected you were reading it and used a false one.'

That thought obviously hadn't occurred to her.

'Where's her diary now?' Tom asked.

'Gone . . . Along with half her clothes.'

'Boy trouble is good,' said Tom. 'Certainly better than your other options.' Anna looked so sick he regretted his words immediately.

'Ask your husband what Alex said in her note.'

'There wasn't . . .' Anna stopped. Her face hardened, and Tom was glad not to have her as an enemy. She'd make a bad enemy. 'Bastard,' she said. 'That's why he's so bloody calm, isn't it? She didn't simply vanish. She left a note.'

Tom imagined so. There usually was.

Her glance was sharp. 'How long have you known?'

Since your husband looked shifty when I asked, would be tactless even for him. So Tom shrugged and said it was just a hunch. He doubted she believed him.

'Do you have a photograph I could borrow?'

'Of Alex? Probably. Why?'

'I'll go out to the university first thing tomorrow.'

8

Hunting for David

The storm was already in him when Tom opened his eyes. It didn't need some passing slight or cruel memory to birth it. The damn thing was there and waiting as he rolled out of bed, took a second to balance and knew he was going to do what he'd told Anna Masterton he'd do.

Hunt down David Wright or whatever the little shit was really called.

'Foreigners will come to Moscow, walk around, and find no skyscrapers . . .' As the Great Patriotic War came to a close, Stalin fretted that Moscow was not sufficiently grand for the capital of a victorious world power. His response was to order the construction of the Seven Sisters, huge tower blocks known locally as Stalinskie Vysotki.

The Kotelnicheskaya Embankment Building, built as elite flats but re-designated as *kommunalka*, communal apartments, was the third highest. The Hotel Ukraina, until recently the world's tallest hotel, was the second highest. Top of the list was Moscow State University at Lenin Hills.

The tallest building in Europe, it was unmissable and owed its position on Moscow's south-west edge in equal parts to Stalin's paranoia and historical common sense. He didn't trust the intelligentsia, and Russian history recorded numerous student riots against tsarist policy when the university was in the centre.

What Tom's *Guide to Moscow* didn't mention was that

Europe's tallest building had been built by slaves from the gulags, several thousand of them, housed in the later stages on the twenty-fourth and twenty-fifth floors to reduce the chance of escape and avoid transportation costs.

Putting the guide away, and hoping he looked suitably academic in a scruffy tweed jacket with elbow patches, Tom tucked a fat hardback under his arm, swung a tatty briefcase he'd scrounged from a man in the embassy comms room and headed not for the main tower, which housed the lecture theatres, but for the furthest of the four wings flanking the tower.

Like the others, it housed students.

A *deshurnaya* at a desk looked up and Tom nodded sharply.

She might have stared after him but she didn't call him back as he strode towards the stairs. He'd already decided not to use the lifts. If they were anything like the lift at Sadovaya Samotechnaya, he stood a good chance of getting stuck between floors.

A group of Russian boys heading down parted to let him through without noticing. They smelled of damp coats and bad aftershave. Their scarves were home-knitted, their boots stained to the ankle by yesterday's snow. The strip lighting did nothing for their complexions, their clothes or their expressions.

The student cafeteria on the third floor stank of disinfectant and was spartan even by Soviet standards. Formica tables and moulded orange chairs filled an expanse of plastic tiles. The view over the Moskva was striking, though.

So striking that Tom stopped to admire the ice before heading for the counter, where he ordered a tea, dropping a few kopeks into the gloved hand of a babushka, and then chose a chair that let him watch students enter and leave. Someone had left an issue of *Krokodil*, which Tom discovered was a month out of date. He read it anyway.

Private Eye with worse cartoons and better jokes.

Factory management were mocked for their inability to deliver fridges that worked, enough cars to fill showrooms, clothes anybody might actually want to wear. What was most shocking about the shiny new amnesty for political prisoners was that everyone was so shocked. The old guard were dinosaurs, Gorbachev a breath of fresh air.

When it went for political targets, it went for those at a safe distance from Moscow. The head of police in Yakut was too drunk to capture a murderer who'd flayed a teenage boy upriver from Yakutsk, and another approaching Olyokminsk. It had to be obvious even to an idiot the perpetrator was making his way along the River Lena, probably looking for casual work. Tom suspected it wasn't as simple as that.

He could tell the Western students. They moved in little shoals.

Half a dozen was their preferred number.

And while they might be as damp as the Russian students, their clothes were more expensive, they were better fed and their hair better cut. They mostly stuck to speaking Russian, but Spanish, French or German would creep in, the conversation flipping languages for a sentence or two. When a group of three boys and two girls broke into English, Tom wandered over.

'Are you from the UK?'

'Who's asking?'

'I am,' Tom said.

A boy in a leather Lenin hat glanced away, then looked back and made himself hold Tom's stare. He sucked his teeth theatrically. 'So,' he said, 'what are we meant to have done this time?'

'What did you do last time?'

One of the girls laughed. Late teens, maybe early twenties.

44

The boy with the leather cap didn't like that; his scowl said so.

'Whatever it was,' Tom told him, 'I don't care.'

The girl said, 'You aren't from the embassy?'

'In a way . . .' Tom slid his ID on to the table and took it back before they'd done much more than glance at it. When he had their attention, he sat.

'Are we in trouble?' the girl asked. She sounded Welsh.

'Not yet,' said Tom, passing Alex's photograph across.

'Pretty. Who is she?'

'Someone who's missing. You haven't seen her?'

'No,' the Welsh girl said.

'You sure? Her boyfriend studies here.'

'Quite sure. I'm Siân,' she added, as if this was something that needed to be said. 'I thought I knew most of the girls from the UK. What's she studying?'

'She's home for the holidays.'

'From boarding school?'

Tom nodded.

'Tacky.'

Tom glared at Lenin Cap.

'Not her,' he said hastily. 'Whoever's boffing her.'

Siân peered at the photograph carefully. 'Upper sixth?'

'Lower,' Tom said.

'Even tackier,' the boy muttered.

'What's her boyfriend's name?' That was Siân again.

'David Wright. I'm told he's American.'

The friends glanced at each other. The other girl shook her head very slightly. A warning, Tom imagined. Unless she was simply suggesting they stay out of it.

'Spit it out,' Tom said.

Only the first girl met his eyes. She looked embarrassed.

'Mr Right. Davie Wong. It's a pun.'

45

'And a play on Dr Jekyll and Mr Hyde?' Tom asked.

She nodded gratefully. 'He's Canadian, not American, and I very much doubt he's going out with . . . What was her name?'

'Doesn't matter. Where do I find him?'

'I'll take you.'

'Siân . . .' Lenin Cap said.

'It's okay. Davie knows me.'

'Davie knows you?' Tom asked, when they were on their way out.

He left the others convinced they'd got off lightly, without knowing for what. Moscow probably did that to you after a while.

'The students halls are self-policing,' she said. 'Elected representatives, Komsomol committees. You know, the youth organization of the Communist Party. Every corridor has a *deshurnaya*, one of those old women who sit at a desk and spy on who comes and goes. Some of them have been here for ever. We should be okay. I know most of those in this block.'

Concrete stairs led to a swing door with a corridor beyond. A hard-faced woman looked up from a desk and barked a question when she saw Tom. It was Siân who answered. 'I told her you were from the embassy.'

'I speak Russian,' Tom said.

He watched the girl assess that.

She knocked at a door and waited. There was a sound of scurrying and then silence, as if someone was pretending not to be there. 'Davie,' Siân said, 'it's okay. It's me.' Very slowly the door opened a little and a slim boy peered through.

'Who's that?'

'He needs to talk to you.'

'About Alex,' Tom said.

The door opened as wide as its little chain would allow. 'I haven't seen her,' a soft voice said. 'She only came here twice. Now go away and leave me alone.'

'She's disappeared,' Siân said.

'Maybe she wanted to disappear.'

'Maybe she did,' Tom agreed. 'Her family are still worried.'

'You're family?'

Tom knew the chain would snap with a single kick. All the same, he pulled his ID from his pocket and held it up so Davie could examine it. 'I'm from her embassy.' The door closed a little, but only so the boy on the far side could slide the chain free and open it properly.

'I'll find my own way out,' Tom said to Siân.

She nodded, glanced once at the nervous boy in the doorway and kept whatever she'd been about to say to herself. She left without looking back.

'Friend of yours?' Tom asked.

'She's nice.'

He said it so sadly Tom wondered if he was simple.

The room stank of piss, and shit stained one wall. The window was wide open despite it being less than zero outside. A torn copy of Pushkin lay face down on a locker, the shredded halves touching as if the boy hoped they'd heal. A Praktica SLR sat on the windowsill with film ripped from its back. The front of its leather case had been torn off and the Zeiss lens cracked.

'Christ. Who have you upset?'

Davie Wong said nothing.

His eyes were huge and brown, and fearful behind the tiny wire spectacles he put on to examine Tom. His lashes were long enough to make a girl jealous. He wouldn't have lasted a day at Tom's school.

Remembering the postcard, Tom wondered if the 'She' in

'You will hear thunder & remember me & think: She wanted storms' had been referring to Alex at all. Perhaps Davie had been talking about himself.

'Anna Akhmatova,' the boy said when Tom fed him the line. 'You've been through Alex's things then . . .'

'As I said, her family are worried.'

'Bit late now.'

'When did you last see her?'

'A few days before New Year.'

'You didn't fly home over the holidays?'

'My parents can't afford it. The university let me stay.'

'Ask them for the money and go home. Don't stay here. If the Russians are being this nasty, there's little point. It'll only get worse.'

'The Komsomol keep an eye on us, you know? One Uzbek boy wanted to be friends. I didn't dare.' Davie reddened, realizing he shouldn't have said that. 'It's not the Russians though. They're not my problem.'

'Who is?'

'I thought you wanted to talk about Alex?'

'I do. I'm just getting a picture of how things work here.'

'Has Alex really run away?'

'I'm told that her note said she'd be staying with a friend. I was hoping that was you. She's not your girlfriend then?'

Davie Wong looked so shocked Tom smiled.

'Didn't think so. How did you meet?'

'At the swimming pool.'

'The big one opposite the Pushkin?'

The boy nodded. 'She was smart and funny and suggested we get a coffee after we got changed. So that's what we did. We met a few times. Nothing happened.'

'Not your type.'

Davie Wong glanced at him sharply.

'My uncle was a stoker on destroyers,' Tom said. 'These days he lives in Portsmouth with a P&O steward he met in Singapore in the sixties. They're just friends, obviously. Two bachelors sharing a small mews house outside the dockyard because it's easier than living alone.'

The boy grinned.

'So, if you weren't going out with Alex, who was? I mean, she's smart and pretty and about to turn sixteen. There has to be some boy on the horizon. Unless her tastes don't run in that direction.'

'They do,' Davie said.

Seeing Tom's look, he added. 'We used to ogle Russian boys at the pool and in the cafe afterwards. She likes brooding and dark or blond and angular. I'm a bit less *dramatic*. It's difficult here though. I mean, it's not just illegal, it's an illness. Did you know they put you in a mental hospital?'

Yeah, Tom did know that.

The wrong politics. The wrong public pronouncements. The wrong kinds of religion. The wrong sexual orientation. They put you in a mental hospital for a lot of things in the Soviet Union, although these days it was getting better.

'There was a Russian boy at the pool,' Davie said suddenly. 'Thin, good-looking, very intense. He came over and introduced himself. I thought . . .' Davie hesitated. 'I thought he was interested in me. We went out as a group for a coffee and he took us to Patriarch's Ponds to sit on the bench from *The Master and Margarita*. I didn't see him again. Alex might have done.'

'Might have done?'

Davie blushed. 'She cancelled me the next week. She was nice about it but we both knew why. She was going swimming with K.'

'What does the K stand for?'

49

'Kotik. But that's just Russian for . . .'

Little cat. Yeah, Tom knew.

'Did Alex mention a New Year's Eve party?'

Tom watched the boy wrestle with his conscience and the good angel win. Looking round the ruins of his room, the boy found a paperback of Cocteau sketches that had escaped destruction and flipped towards the back, extracting an address not that far from Tom's flat.

'It was going to be great, Alex said. She said I should go. Her new friends were cool, they'd like me.' Davie shrugged, looking briefly puzzled. 'The thing is,' he said, 'Alex didn't *do* friends, not really. She hated school. Things were horrid at home. Her mother drank. Her stepfather hated her. I'd never met anyone so lonely.'

Tom wondered if Davie realized that he kept referring to Alex in the past.

The student room Tom wanted was right at the end.

'Who is it?'

He knocked again.

'I said, who is it?'

A third knock produced swearing, more swearing and the clatter of someone stamping to the door. It was thrown open and filled with the bulk of the sneering jock who'd been persecuting Davie for being different.

Tom's punch was low, fast and dirty.

The boy was twenty, maybe twenty-one. Not used to being on the wrong side of the equation. Not used to being the one on the floor. Once the Texan had his breath back, Tom hooked two fingers into his nose, yanked back his head and gripped his throat. The list of nasty things he promised to do if the boy trashed Davie Wong's room again, or indeed went anywhere near him, was long and very detailed.

The boy believed every word.

Tom left him curled on the floor and found his own way out of the overblown concrete cake, Stalin's idea of how a skyscraper should look. Outside, an old woman sat in the shelter of its steps being ignored by students, a black scarf tied tightly round her head to protect her from the wind. He wondered how many old women there were in Moscow selling wax figurines.

Tomorrow he'd have a new shadow, one better suited to dealing with someone trained in tradecraft. Tom didn't regret losing the rat-faced little KGB man. He had an address for the party and, anyway, it was worth it for a morning of walking free.

Snow glittered on the distant roofs of the Kremlin, and the ice on the Moskva had been broken and healed so often that shards lay scattered across its surface like shattered glass. The balustrades of the bridge he used were glazed with virgin snow. Tom barely noticed. His thoughts were locked tight inside.

Alex was sad and lonely? He knew that already. She hated school and had problems at home? He could tell that by looking round her room. If he could do that for a teenager he'd barely met, why hadn't he been able to do it for his own daughter?

Why hadn't anyone?

9

Party Address

'No work today . . .?'

'This is work,' Tom said.

Narrowing his eyes, Ivan Petrovich Dennisov put a flask of vodka in front of the Englishman without being asked, shouted to the kitchen for some food and found a cold can of beer that left a ring on the zinc.

'What's this?' Tom asked.

'The produce of our wonderful democratic neighbours.'

Picking up the can, Tom examined it. East German and past its drink-by date.

'Drink up,' said Dennisov, punching holes in the top.

It was eleven in the morning and Tom had already eaten borscht at a stall by the metro but he took the bowl slapped down in front of him by the lumpy teenager in her badly fitting knitted dress, knocked back his vodka, glugged from the can and offered Dennisov a cigarette.

They smoked in silence for a few minutes.

The hours the bar kept were written by the door. Six a.m. until nine thirty. Eleven until two. Seven until eleven at night. It could be local regulations. It might simply be Dennisov. 'How's the leg?' Tom asked.

'It got blown off.'

'You've got painkillers?'

'Morphine,' he said. 'Reserved for glorious veterans.'

Behind them the teenager who'd slammed down the bowl muttered something.

'Yelena,' Dennisov said, sketching an introduction. 'Ignore her. She blames me for going. Also for losing my leg. At least she didn't blame me for coming back. There are those who do . . .'

The girl looked ten years younger than Dennisov. But pain had etched so many lines into the helicopter pilot's face it was hard to say how old Dennisov really was.

'You found coming home hard?' Tom asked.

'You never come home,' Dennisov said. 'You know that. A little bit of you always gets left behind.' He regarded his leg sourly. 'Sometimes a big bit. You know how many alcoholics we have in our glorious state? Forty million. Those are just the ones we admit to. I tell Yelena it could be worse, I could be an opium addict.' He squinted at Tom. 'What's this about work?'

'My boss needs a favour.'

Dennisov dragged harder on his cigarette, winced as he hit its cardboard filter and ground it underfoot. His face was oily, he sweated vodka and a tightly wound unhappiness tightened the sinews in his neck. 'Let me guess,' he said. 'He wants to buy icons? Preferably old ones?'

'Not icons.'

'Foreigners always want icons.'

'Not this one.'

'If he wants roubles for dollars, I'm the wrong man.'

'Britain doesn't use dollars.'

'No wonder you're fucked. Not drugs. He'll get into trouble for drugs. Unless he's got a doctor like mine. That's the secret. Then you can have anything. I'm not sure my doctor's allowed to treat foreigners though.'

'Not drugs either. I'm looking for a girl . . .'

Before Dennisov could do more than grin, Tom pulled a 5x4 from his pocket and put it on the counter, wiping up spilt beer with his sleeve first.

'Young,' Dennisov said.

'Too young.'

The picture had been taken, according to Lady Masterton, the day her daughter turned fifteen. Alex was silhouetted against an English sky. Scowling, inevitably. A shaggy pony munched grass beside her. A large white-painted rectory stood behind. She looked as self-conscious and uncomfortable in her own body as she did in her brand-new body warmer, jodhpurs and shiny riding boots.

The teenager from the kitchen stopped at the sight of the photograph.

'This girl,' she said, 'she's missing?'

Tom nodded.

'In Moscow?'

He nodded again.

'Your boss has gone to the authorities?'

'I imagine they know. But until he asks for help officially, they can't approach him. He won't ask unless he has to. He feels he should handle it himself.'

Dennisov appeared to believe this. At least to believe it as much as Tom did, which was not at all. There had to be deeper reasons than not wanting to lose face for Sir Edward's refusal to go to the Soviets.

Tom intended to discover them.

'Handling it himself meaning asking you?'

'Yelena . . .'

'It's a fair question. Anyway, how do you know he's telling the truth? What if he's hunting the girl for other reasons? He's a foreigner. What if it's a trap?'

'Her mother's worried. Wouldn't your mother worry?'

'My mother's dead.'

'*Yelena!* Enough.'

Helping himself to what remained of Tom's vodka, Dennisov shooed the girl towards the kitchen and reached for the photograph, examining it carefully. He seemed to be paying particular attention to the grandness of the Georgian house behind.

'There's a reward?' he asked.

'Dollars if you want.'

Dennisov spat on the floor. 'That for dollars.'

'He'll help you anyway.' Yelena was back with a mug of black coffee, which she put in front of Dennisov, removing Tom's glass. Before Dennisov could open his mouth to protest, the girl took the photograph, peered at it intently and then placed it in front of Tom, keeping her fingers on the edge. 'You like her?'

'It's not like that.'

'All the same, for you this is personal?'

The girl's scrutiny lasted another few seconds, then she nodded as if Tom's silence was answer enough, lifted her fingers from the photograph's edge and tried to smooth where it had curled. 'I hope you find her.'

Tom produced the address Davie had given him.

'Who's meant to live here?' Dennisov asked.

'A boy she met at the swimming pool.'

Dennisov slid the address along the zinc to the girl.

'You're sure this is the place?' She sounded worried.

'There's a problem?' Tom asked.

She shrugged. 'As you know, there's no crime in the USSR. If there was, this is where it would live. Even the *militsiya* walk in pairs.'

'You don't mind me borrowing your husband?'

Yelena scowled. 'I'm not his wife.'

'Your man then.'

'I'm his sister.'

'I'm sorry. I didn't mean . . .'

'His wife left him when he lost his leg.'

A dead bullfinch lay at the edge of an overpass with an illegal car lot beneath. The small bird was frozen solid, eyes closed, orange breast glazed pink by frost. Seeing Tom's gaze, Dennisov pointed to the corpse of a sparrow.

'Happens every winter,' he said.

The overpass was crumbling concrete with squat pillars, and the taxi that Dennisov had ordered and Tom paid for had left them in the shadow of an office block built around the same time. The car lot offered a handful of Ladas, a couple of Moskvitches and a single sleek Volga. The Moskvitches and Ladas were dented and rusting while the Volga looked new.

Tom couldn't help wondering what had happened to its owner.

When he voiced that thought, Dennisov smiled. 'Bought new, sold for a profit next day. There's a five-year waiting list. You know that old fridge Yelena uses? I can get more for it than it would cost me to buy a new one. You know why? Because I can't buy a new one. You know what else?'

Tom dutifully shook his head.

'If I could, it wouldn't work.'

A dark-skinned man, with the collar of his fur coat turned up against the sub-zero temperatures, looked briefly hopeful before losing his smile when he realized they weren't buying. Dennisov showed him the photograph.

When that produced no flicker of recognition, Dennisov asked about the address and the man jerked his head towards the far side of the lot, indicating a concrete slum beyond. As they were leaving, he said something Tom missed.

'What was that?'

'She's probably already been sold.'

A bulldozer driver in a puffy orange anorak cleared rubble on a building site, a half-finished cigarette between his lips. He was lost to the scratch of steel on grit and the slow curl of icy rubble his blade drove ahead of him.

When the man glanced up, Dennisov waved.

The driver knew the block well enough, but when Dennisov showed him Alex's photograph he shook his head, both to say he'd never seen her and at the state of the world. Climbing back into his machine, he clamped his noise-protectors firmly to his ears and returned to scraping rubble.

'Your boss is important?'

Tom nodded.

'He might not like what we find.'

When they finally reached the right place, the apartment blocks were even more ruined than Tom had expected. Five-storey Khrushchevkas backing on to a railway track, jerry-built, thrown up in the 1960s as part of a five-year plan to solve the housing shortage. According to Dennisov, the five-year plan never ended, and nor did the housing shortage. Khrushchevkas kept being built. They were still prefabricated, still low-ceilinged and they still leaked.

'Okay,' Dennisov said. 'Now keep your mouth shut.'

An old woman protested as they pushed through a front door reinforced with sheets of blue-painted steel. A crop-haired boy in the hallway took one look and turned for the stairs. Dennisov grabbed him, shook his head and jerked his thumb towards the door. The boy took himself outside.

Inside the communal kitchen, an old Georgian in a string

vest sat by a saucepan boiling beef shank. A red onion stood on a butcher's block next to three carrots and the air was thick with sour steam. He stood when he saw Dennisov, and then sat again. A teenage girl, breastfeeding a newborn, with a toddler at her hip, turned away to cover herself and then shrugged.

Dennisov showed her the photograph.

She shook her head firmly. '*Nyet*.'

The man boiling meat reached for the picture, examining it carefully. He too shook his head. Without being asked, he went to the door and shouted into the stairwell. A minute later, two Tartar women came down. Neither had seen Alex. Nor had the old Russian woman who appeared after that, grumbling about her husband's shouting.

It was the crop-haired boy outside who gave Dennisov the lead.

One of the men in the block had been having a New Year's Eve party. The boy couldn't say it was the right party. It didn't seem the sort of party a girl like that would go to, but all the same. It had been quite near here.

What did this man do?

Military. Kept himself to himself.

What time did the boy think he'd be home?

Who could say? He hadn't been seen for two days.

Dennisov asked if anyone else had come looking for him and the boy's face closed down for a second, then he realized he was too far in to back out and he'd already said too much, or not enough.

'The police came.'

'*Militsiya*. Here?' Dennisov looked around him.

'Different police. They took everything. Even his bedding.'

The boy took the packet of papirosa Tom tossed across and gave them the address for the party he'd mentioned.

There were no Khrushchevkas there. Only a smoking warehouse beside a shop selling second-hand water heaters. The shop was a scorched ruin, still smoking in places; half the warehouse had fallen in, taking the party wall with it.

A *militsiya* man stood at the corner, staring uninterestedly at a half-broiled rat that had made it to the road before dying.

'You'd better wait here,' Dennisov said.

Taking up position by a fence, Tom tapped a Russian cigarette from its paper packet and glanced casually in both directions. His new shadow was threading his way between an oil drum and a doorless fridge. He stopped the moment Tom looked at him and dipped to tie his shoelace.

Then Dennisov was back, his face grim.

'There's a body,' he said.

Tom was moving before Dennisov could stop him, heading for the door into the smoking ruin. When the *militsiya* man moved to stop him, Dennisov barked something and the policeman hesitated, shrugged and stood back.

'What did you just say?'

'I told him you were KGB.'

The ground under their feet was sodden and the walls damp. There were patches of smouldering rubble but the fire itself was out. The ceiling had fallen in halfway along, leaving a cathedral-like gap to stone beams.

The warehouse was far older and better built than the buildings around it, and its brick walls had helped keep the flames in check. There'd been a party, according to the *militsiya* man. A three-day party no one had dared ring in to the police.

'The body's at the back,' Dennisov said.

On the floor, almost against a wall, a carbonized figure twisted in agony. Tom knew its apparent anguish was down to muscle contraction but he looked away just the same and had to make himself look back. Fire had eaten eyes, ears, lips and hair. The head was thrown back, the mouth open in a teeth-baring scream.

If there had been any clothes, and Tom's instinct said not, they'd wicked fat from the body as it burned and long since turned to ash. Even given the state the corpse was in, Tom could see there was something wrong with its arms.

Dropping to a crouch, knowing that he was contaminating a crime scene, Tom supported himself on the wall, finding the brick still warm to his touch.

The figure's wrists were tied with wire.

Fire had eaten the hands and finger bones had fallen away.

As Tom sat back, a circle of metal caught the daylight coming in from above. Tom shook it free from bone, knowing he shouldn't, and a half-circle of jade dropped away from the cheap steel beneath.

He was holding Alex's ring.

He *knew* it was Alex's ring. It was the one she'd been wearing on New Year's Eve . . . Retrieving the half-circle of burned jade, Tom looked for the other half and realized it would take several hours and a sieve to sort through the rubble on which he knelt. Dennisov was waiting behind him.

'You think it's her?' Dennisov said finally.

Tom did, but he made himself look again.

Then, before he could give himself time to reject the idea, he lay down in the dirt beside the body to judge its height against his and felt relief sweep through him so fast he had to fight back tears. He'd been wrong. It wasn't her.

'You all right?' Dennisov asked.

Clambering to his knees, Tom brushed off his trousers and brushed half-effectually at his coat. 'Can you find out when the fire started?'

Dennisov vanished to ask.

Tom had regained control of himself by the time Dennisov returned.

'The coroner's van's on its way,' Dennisov said. 'I'll tell you the rest when we're out of here.' Without waiting to see if Tom followed, he limped for the street, not wanting to be found at a crime scene, and nodded as he passed the *militsiya* man, who watched him go with interest. Dennisov might have changed his metal leg for something more discreet but his limp was still noticeable. Tom passed by without acknowledging the man at all.

As he imagined a KGB officer might do.

'It was called in yesterday by a passing police car,' Dennisov said. 'The fire brigade were here until an hour ago. They put out what was left of the fire, called in the body and left.' He shrugged. 'This area falls between three districts and is full of undesirables. Our friend back there imagines everyone hoped someone else would deal with it.'

'How do I find out if it's Kotik, a teenage boy who liked swimming?'

Dennisov shot him a sideways glance.

'I was given the name,' Tom said hastily. 'By the person who gave me this address. Well, the last address. Kotik is a friend of the missing girl.'

'Who had enemies.'

'Someone did, definitely,' Tom said. 'Now, how?'

'Your boss will have to ask the authorities.'

'What are his other options?'

'They'll cost.'

'Of course.'

'The KGB don't drink at my bar. Not that I know. The ordinary police, on the other hand . . .'

Tom pulled out his wallet.

'Not here! Your shadow will think I'm changing dollars. America is our enemy. Changing dollars is a crime. Also, their president is a shit who sells missiles to savages.' Dennisov headed into an alley so overhung with balconies that snow barely reached its floor. 'I'll give back what I don't use.'

'Keep –'

'I'll give it back,' Dennisov growled.

They parted at a metro station and Tom headed for Red Square, walking the last leg across a bridge over the frozen river. The sun was lower than ever, the horizon darkening and lights were coming on around him.

In reception, Tom asked to be put through to the ambassador, feeling pompous as he added that Sir Edward would want to take the call. It was the kind of thing his brother-in-law would say. Tom was halfway up the stairs when he met Anna Masterton coming down. 'Any news?' she demanded.

'I'm on my way to see your husband.'

'You can't tell me?'

'I should probably tell both of you.'

Anna turned on her heels and headed upstairs before Tom could say that it wasn't as bad as it could be. She rapped on the inner door to her husband's office before his secretary had time to do more than look up. The noise of her golf-ball typewriter stuttering to a halt sounded like the dying throes of a small revolution.

The knock drew a tight-lipped 'Come in'.

Sir Edward looked no happier to see her than he did Tom, although he took off his spectacles and put down what he was reading.

'You found the address?'

'Alex wasn't there.'

'Told you,' Sir Edward said. 'She's sulking with some friend.'

He sounded so relieved that Tom glanced sharply across and Sir Edward looked away, checking the time on a wall clock against the watch he was wearing as if that had always been his intention.

'No one else knew anything?' Anna asked.

'We went to a warehouse too. But it was burned out. The police recovered a body . . . Not Alex,' Tom added, as Anna threw a hand to her mouth.

'How do you know?' she demanded.

Tom prayed he had remembered right. 'How tall is your daughter?'

'Five foot three.'

'Then it definitely wasn't her. Burned bodies shrink, but even shrunken this one was taller.'

'Anna . . .' Sir Edward sounded as if he was trying to be soothing. 'It's going to be fine. She probably wasn't even there.'

'I'm afraid she probably was, sir. I found this in the rubble.'

Tom put the remains of the jade ring on Sir Edward's desk, the half-circle of burned stone coming loose and falling away.

Anna Masterton vomited.

Tom left, having decided not to mention that the body might be Alex's boyfriend. He'd find a way to tell Sir Edward later, or maybe he'd tell Mary Batten, who would find her own way to let the ambassador know.

Neither Mary nor Sir Edward would need telling that anyone who could wire a boy's hands behind his back and burn him to death was not someone you wanted to have hold of a fifteen-year-old English girl for long.

10

Not Enough Room to . . .

Something in his flat was wrong. Tom knew it the moment he opened the door.

It wasn't the smell, although that was metallic and flat, a slight odour underpinning the sourness of unemptied bins and sheets that needed washing. He'd been planning a bath, hot water allowing, to rid himself of the stink from the warehouse that infected his clothes. But the stench of something older and darker made hairs stand up on the back of his neck.

Later, with a whiskey in his hand and his back to the wall in the living room, sitting on the floor in the dark, he came up with a logical explanation for his split second of atavistic fear of what he'd believed an ancient evil.

He recognized, without realizing it, the smell of blood.

That thought held for the time it took him to sip dry his whiskey, time he spent going back over what he'd found on returning home. If you could call a top-floor flat in a Moscow block reserved for foreigners home.

His living room had been undisturbed.

The ashtrays still overflowed. The cactus he'd inherited looked as miserable as ever. His briefcase, with its combination lock, lay exactly where he'd left it. His bedroom was a mess, but no worse than when he'd dragged himself from sleep and rolled out of bed that morning.

Pillows adrift, duvet thrown back, greying sheets.

Tom knew, because his flat at Sad Sam was tiny, and its

bathroom door was open and nothing looked different in there either, that what awaited him must be in the kitchen.

He was right.

A dead cat hung above his sink.

It was suspended by its back legs from a string tied to the fluorescent tube above. Tom knew it was Black Sammy, the cat he'd seen the night he came back from the New Year's Eve party, because whoever had skinned it had left its pelt on the worktop.

Thinner than blood and thicker than lymph, the liquid that pooled in his sink told him the animal had been alive when the torture began. Rigor was well set in though, stiffening the carcass. Tom cut it down with scissors.

He used scissors because his only kitchen knife rested on the folded skin, where it had been placed after it had been used to flay the animal. Under the knife was a photograph of Tom on the corner by the Khrushchevka, with his shadow away to one side and an old woman he didn't remember huddled in a doorway.

Picking it up, Tom took the photograph into the hall where the light was better.

The depth of field was so flat it had to have been taken with a telephoto lens. From high up, looking down. If it was taken from the top of a block of flats, then the photographer must have been there waiting, which meant he had known where Tom was headed. Someone didn't want questions asked about Alex.

For all Tom knew, that same someone was watching his flat now to see how he'd react. Would he call his embassy? Would he simply wrap the poor bastard cat in newspaper and dump it in the communal bins? He could imagine the children of one of the journalists who lived in a bigger flat below finding it.

Returning to his kitchen, Tom took down the chopping

board left by the previous tenant and ran the cat under cold water to make it less slippery. Then he began with the head, which he removed by putting the knife on the back of its spine and smacking the blunt edge of his blade. It was the most noise Tom would make that evening and the action he found hardest.

Dealing with the carcass was easy enough after that.

Having split the head down the middle, he rinsed and flushed both pieces, before filleting the rest and jointing it cleanly, running each piece under the tap before flushing it down the loo. He opened the ribs with scissors, washed the contents of the stomach down the sink, and flushed out the viscera.

Tom thought he was beyond shock. But unfolding Black Sammy's pelt, he discovered he had exactly half of it. That was when he realized the pan he'd left dirty had been neatly washed up. As had a spatula and fork. Plus, his olive oil was out, along with his salt and pepper. A neat little threesome on the countertop.

Like a small family.

Tom took care not to clog the lavatory with flesh or fur and to leave long enough between flushes to keep what he was doing from being obvious to those below. What had happened never happened. He wanted anyone watching to know that.

When he was finished, Tom scrubbed the board and hung it back on the wall, washed the knife and the scissors, rinsed out the sink, put away his olive oil and salt and pepper, and poured himself another whiskey, taking it through to the darkness of his sitting room.

The alcohol would help, but it wasn't enough to dull the rage at what some bastard had done to the poor bloody cat, and he knew he'd still be seeing its carcass hung above his sink as he tried to sleep.

Cross Hairs

He'd looked lonely in the cross hairs. So lonely that Wax Angel wondered if he'd welcome a bullet. When it came to it, people often did.

'You . . .'

'Me what?'

The *militsiya* man had looked sharply at her dishevelled state. So she'd glanced sharply back and made a point of buttoning the front of her dress. Only when he'd turned away did she return to the ancient Zeiss F-4 sniper's sight she kept hidden in her clothing. It had been black once but in the last ten years its paint had begun to peel away in scabs. She still had the leather caps that fitted on either end though.

She'd watched the foreigner and his friend move through falling snow, his head down and his shoulders hunched, his thoughts a black cloud above him.

One hundred paces.

Two hundred paces.

If the snow had been heavy, she'd have lost him by now.

If the snow had really been falling, she'd have lost him before he travelled the distance of his own arm. At four hundred paces he'd begun to blur, vanishing at five. And Wax Angel realized the snow settling on her was camouflage. No need now for the white uniforms they'd worn and the sniper rifles wrapped in rags they'd carried through the smoking ruins of Stalingrad.

After the Englishman and his friend had gone, the coroner's wagon had arrived. The woman driving had glanced over, made to turn away and then headed in Wax Angel's direction. 'Are you all right?' she'd asked.

'Yes, thank you,' Wax Angel had said. 'Are you?'

'You must be freezing.'

'This is nothing,' Wax Angel said. 'This is practically summer.'

'Here.' Digging into her jeans pocket, the woman had found a rouble. 'Buy yourself something hot. You'll buy food, right?'

She meant food rather than vodka.

Wax Angel was impressed that she left that part unsaid.

After the coroner's office took the body, the *militsiya* man abandoned his post without sealing the ruin, or even putting tape across its door. How could Wax Angel not go to investigate? She found the burned-out building to her liking. There was something familiar, almost comfortable about its ruin.

Even better was a smouldering pile in one corner, with enough embers at the bottom to restart the fire once the rubble smothering it was dragged away.

Wax Angel spent a happy hour feeding the growing flames with every unburned scrap of wood she could find and then settled back to enjoy the warmth while snowflakes fluttered down in the sections of the warehouse where the roof had fallen away.

She could remember real blizzards, God wiping the face of the earth until everything was white.

She'd been younger then, of course. Much younger than the girl who'd given her money . . . And it was a long, long way from here. She'd been a campaign wife, but with a difference. Other 'campaign wives' were clerks or signallers. She was a sniper in her own right, dozens of kills to her record, her photograph in the army newspaper.

He was different too.

A political officer with actual battle experience.

He wasn't one of those red-badged fools who screamed through a megaphone from the rear that everyone had to advance, that the Motherland was counting on them. He expected everyone to advance, right enough; he expected them to die. He just found that the walking dead fought better if talked to properly.

Not softly but firmly.

He'd been matter-of-fact about shooting anyone who tried to retreat.

It was the woman by the road Wax Angel remembered most.

They were beyond Breslau, with snow piled high against the hedges and a vicious wind ripping across the German fields and through the ruins of farmhouses destroyed in battle or burned by their owners before fleeing. She was young, the woman by the road. Her hair, in a thick blonde plait, was covered by a scarf too expensive to be any use against the cold. When Wax Angel found her she had her back to a hedge. Her skin was marble and her flesh as hard.

The baby at her frozen breast had died of cold, not hunger.

The men – heroes all – said what you'd expect.

All the houses were huge, palaces that turned out to belong to doctors and lawyers. Everyone had fridges. Most people had cars. More cars than anyone could imagine. At first their letters home were censored. Then they were burned in front of them. Finally, they'd been told that writing home would be forbidden if they kept exaggerating what they saw.

There'd been another nursing mother after Breslau.

Young and clear-skinned. Very German.

That had been later, after they'd won another battle.

The girl had been dragged into a church and raped throughout the day, the same men coming back hours later to take another turn. In the end, her grandfather had gone in tears to Wax Angel's political officer. He'd begged him to make them stop; not for good, he knew that wouldn't happen. Simply for long enough to let his granddaughter feed her child, which was hungry and wouldn't stop crying.

Wax Angel shot the girls she saw after that.

The pretty ones first.

Such things happened because of Stalingrad.

Life expectancy for a new conscript was a day. Three days for a seasoned officer. Half a day for a junior lieutenant. She'd survived Stalingrad's full seven and a half months. The lifespans of over two hundred men.

I2

A Knock on the Door

For Soviet citizens, a knock on the door at four in the morning traditionally indicates trouble for whoever quivers behind it, wondering whether to answer. But a knock on the door of an apartment in a block given over to foreigners? Tom took a Tokarev from his bedside cabinet, jacked the slide noisily enough for whoever was outside to hear and kept to one side as he undid the bolt.

As the door swung open, he grabbed the figure outside and hauled it into the apartment. Flicking on the overhead light, he found Anna Masterton glaring at him. Releasing the Tokarev's clip, Tom dropped it out and would have put it in his dressing-gown pocket if he hadn't suddenly realized he was naked. Squeezing the trigger, he supported the hammer with his thumb while it fell into place. He put the sidearm on the table beside the telephone, which began glowing red.

'Why are you here?' he asked.

'Why are you naked?'

'Anna, why are you here?'

'You're having an anxiety dream.'

The knock came a few minutes after Tom woke, as he stood in the flat's tiny kitchen, boiling a kettle and staring at empty Carlsberg cans, filthy coffee cups and a slick of Vesta curry dried to a crust across the only unchipped plate in the place.

'At least this time I'm wearing a dressing gown.'

Anna Masterton's glance was wary.

'I wanted to thank you,' she said, 'for letting me know the body was definitely not Alex. Your note said male, early twenties. Do I ask how you found out?'

'A *militsiya* major from the investigator's office south of the river on Novokuznetskaya Street lives locally and we drink in the same bar. I bought him a flask of vodka and he told me what I wanted to know.'

'You make it sound so obvious.'

There was more, facts that Tom hadn't put in his note.

The boy's hands had been bound so tightly that his wrist fractured. Also, wounds exposing body fat burn at a different rate. In the coroner's opinion the boy had been castrated. Given that his genitals had been cut away and his wrists bound tightly enough to crack bone, the balance of probability was that he'd been burned alive . . . Further tests could have proved that. But resources were tight, the department overworked and no one knew who he was anyway.

'That's the official version,' Tom had said.

The *militsiya* major had stared at him, shocked.

'That's the truth,' he insisted.

'The Moscow prosecutor cares so little about crime victims that he doesn't even investigate arson, torture and murder?'

The major hesitated. 'That building was used by deviants. Homosexuals,' he added, in case Tom hadn't understood his meaning. 'I talked to the case officer, who objected to the prosecutor's decision. It was suggested that his department has more pressing priorities.'

'Who would suggest such a thing?'

'The KGB,' said Dennisov, abandoning all pretence of not listening. The *militsiya* major didn't agree, but then he didn't deny it either. He simply finished his vodka, thanked Tom for the flask and cut his evening short.

72

'Lose me customers,' Dennisov said, 'why don't you.'

Yelena sighed.

'Aren't you going to ask me in?' Anna said.

'Is your entourage downstairs?'

'They let me out of my cage now and then.'

'All alone?'

'Moscow's one of the safest cities in the world.'

'Provided you're not Russian. Then I imagine it's different.'

'Soviet,' Anna Masterton corrected. 'Provided you're not Soviet. Even then it's safer than London. Far safer than New York.'

'If you believe their crime figures.'

'Do you believe ours?'

'Lady Masterton. What are you doing here?'

'Anna, for God's sake. I wanted to talk to you.'

'About Alex?' Tom asked.

Obviously, her expression said. *What else?*

'You'd better come in then.'

'Hallelujah . . . It's smaller than I expected,' she said, looking around.

'There's only one of me.'

'So your family aren't . . .?' Something in Tom's expression killed the rest of her question. In daylight, without full make-up, she looked older, more tired. There were lines beside her mouth, dark rings around her eyes. 'My jewellery's gone.'

'Alex?'

'Who else?'

'Your jewellery box was locked?'

'I keep the key in a Wedgwood pot on my dressing table.' She caught Tom's glance. 'Yes, I know. But it's a bloody embassy, for God's sake. And what does a girl of fifteen need pearls for?'

73

'To sell.' Tom listed the reasons Alex might want money.

Drugs, drink, an abortion, blackmail, greed, a very long stay, somewhere very far away . . . Anna wasn't keen on any of them. He was in the kitchen, putting two slices of black bread into his toaster, turning them round and grilling them again by the time she reached the end of her reasons why he was wrong.

'Have you told Sir Edward?'

'I daren't.'

Nothing as strange as other people's marriages. Nothing as strange as his, come to that. Tom decided to pass on asking why. If Anna wanted to tell him, she would.

'I'm going to eat,' he said. 'Then take a shower. You sticking around long enough for that?' He hadn't meant it as a challenge but her look told him she took it as one. When he got back, she'd done the washing up.

'In here,' she called. She was in his living room, flicking through a week-old copy of *Time*. 'Vesta curry?' she said.

'What's wrong with it?'

'Even students don't eat Vesta curry.'

'I don't like Pot Noodles.'

'My daughter does . . .'

'Does your husband at least know you're here?'

Her gaze sharpened. 'Have you any idea how that sounds?'

'I'd have thought it was an obvious question.'

'Which,' she said flatly, 'says more about you than the question.'

She's probably right about that, Tom thought. 'Unreconstructed' was the word his daughter had used. Reaching into her bag, Anna Masterton pulled out a pack of B&H and flipped the lid.

'You don't mind?'

Tom gave her the cactus saucer as an ashtray.

Then he picked up something else he'd inherited from the

previous occupant and shook the child's toy, hearing tiny beads rattle inside a tatty plastic case as they cleared its grey screen. Twisting the wheels at the bottom of the Etch A Sketch, he wrote: *You realize this place is bugged?*

She nodded.

So they know you're here.

'I was followed. Obviously they know I'm here.'

You want them to know?

'My daughter is missing,' Anna said. Her matter-of-factness contradicted the hurt in her eyes. 'She's fifteen. Sixteen next week. Adrift in a strange city. I want her back. I will do *anything* to get her back.'

'Did I tell you I tracked down David?'

'Why the hell didn't you say?'

'That's how I got the party address. The boy himself is a dead end. Canadian, not American, and their friendship is strictly platonic. He hasn't seen her since before New Year. He has no idea where she is now. I'm sorry. This must be really hard.'

For a moment, he thought she'd slap him.

She had agate eyes, he noticed. Tiny speckles like flaws in stone caught the winter light. Her daughter had those eyes too.

'It's unbearable,' she said finally. 'If this was London, we'd have called the Met. We'd be getting hourly updates. Edward has friends at the Yard.'

The man probably had friends everywhere.

'I know you don't like him.'

'He's the ambassador. It doesn't matter whether I like him.'

Anna sighed. 'Do you mind if I make coffee?'

'I'll make it,' Tom said.

'I'll help.' Pushing herself out of her chair, she headed for the kitchen. Tom followed, stopping in the doorway while she filled the kettle, found his jar of Maxwell House, rinsed a soapy cup and left the tap running . . .

Tom's hovering in the doorway had more to do with the extreme smallness of his kitchen than any wish to let Anna do the work.

Gesturing him in, she stepped so close he could feel her body heat and smell Dior and something altogether more animal beneath. For a second, possibilities flared and then died as she stepped back a little, looking rueful.

Whatever might have happened didn't.

Leaning across her, Tom turned off the kettle, which had long since stopped being able to turn itself off, spooned instant coffee into the mugs and poured on boiling water. When he stood back, Anna reached round to turn off the tap.

'Sir Edward's not losing sleep over this?' Tom asked.

'I wouldn't know.' Looking suddenly embarrassed, she fell silent.

'You have separate beds?'

'Rooms,' she said. 'We have separate rooms.'

'This is recent?'

Her glare asked what business that was of his, and Tom had no real answer. Except that something about Sir Edward's reaction to Alex's absence worried him. The man was too controlled, too buttoned down.

'Yes,' Anna said tightly. 'This is recent.'

He almost asked how long things had been like that and caught himself in time. If he had to put money on it, he'd guess since Borodino. Since Anna returned to find her daughter missing. 'Would you like a biscuit?'

When she shrugged, he opened a Tupperware box and took out a half-empty packet of Hobnobs, not bothering with a plate. 'I thought you meant Russian biscuits,' Anna said, helping herself.

'Do you know if the KGB are already searching?'

Looking up, Anna opened her mouth . . .

'I mean,' Tom said, 'I know Alex is embassy. But the Soviets must realize she's missing. And she's foreign. So that makes it a KGB matter, doesn't it? Even if she ran off with a Russian boy, they're hardly going to leave something like this to the local police. I imagine they're looking already.'

'Without us having . . .?'

'Not officially, obviously. But I wouldn't be surprised.'

Fetching the Etch A Sketch, Anna turned its plastic knobs to and fro. *Please tell me you mean that.* Her writing was shaky. Everyone's writing is shaky on an Etch A Sketch. Hers was shakier than most.

'You should probably see these.'

Tom pulled the three books from his briefcase, handing her *Kisses for Mayakovsky* first. Opening the tatty paperback, Anna found her daughter had written her name in precise and tiny letters. She'd been equally neat in the *Complete Voznesensky* and the *Yevtushenko.*

'I didn't even know Alex liked poetry.'

Taking out a plastic disk, Tom slotted it into the Amstrad. 'She writes the stuff.'

He waited for software to load and green lettering to appear on the television-like screen. *Drive A: 163k used. 10k free. Six files.* Choosing the first of them he waited for the file to open and one of Alex's poems to appear.

'A Room With No View' was as overblown as its title.

Alex's bedroom at the embassy, her life and her family were all prisons. The view south to Gorky Park was no view. Her window, like her life, simply opened on to places she couldn't go. When Tom looked up, Anna was crying. Silent tears dripped on to the cheap keyboard. He felt ashamed for dismissing Alex's feelings so glibly. Without a word, he found the brandy he'd brought from Dennisov's and topped up her coffee. After a moment's thought, he topped up his own.

'Now this one,' he said.

'Do Not Talk with Strangers' was less indulgent.

The poem's setting was a wooden bench outside the swimming pool opposite the Pushkin. The voices were those of a boy and a girl separated by race, language, religion and politics. Different in every way except for looking at the world through the same eyes. They fell in love while waiting for a cat. They'd been waiting for the cat their entire lives. The cat never appeared.

'You don't think that's David?'

'Canadians are hardly different in every way. How interested is she in . . .'

'Boys?' asked Anna, before he could put another word to it.

Tom watched her take a large mouthful of coffee, then another. She winced at the heat, or maybe the strength of the Georgian brandy.

'Obviously more interested than I imagined. You've read them all?'

'There's only one more.'

'Show me.'

'If you insist.'

Alex's last poem was religious.

'Born Anew' spoke of life and death and unity. Of sensing the sinews under the skin of her lover as he hovered in the dark above her, her own nerves lit by lightning.

'Thank God,' Anna said.

It was hardly the reaction Tom expected.

'Come on. No one who's actually had sex could write that.'

Sex, underage or not, wasn't the worst thing that could

happen to a missing girl in Moscow. Maybe it was the mention in Alex's poem of a cat that never appeared, but Tom couldn't help remembering the brutalized animal hung above the sink in the kitchen where they'd just made coffee.

He decided not to mention that.

One of the badges was Komsomol, these days little more than the Soviet version of the Scouts; one had been issued the previous year to celebrate the fortieth anniversary of the USSR's Second World War victory. It was the Lenin badge that made Dennisov pause.

Tom had seen dozens like it. At least he thought he had.

'What's different about this one?'

Dennisov glanced around.

A dozen men swayed and sweated in the warm fug of his bar. The floor was slippery from melted snow and the windows steamy enough to reduce Tom's shadow to a shivering memory. Having checked that everyone who needed vodka had it, Dennisov poured Tom a large shot, poured himself an even larger one and dragged Tom through the wall of records to the kitchen.

Flames blazed from a naked gas ring, the flames dancing high and yellow. At the sight of Tom and Dennisov, Yelena slammed a pan filled with soup on top. A yellowing fridge, its handle replaced by a loop of rope, was clattering in the corner like an old car. A sack of potatoes beside the stove meant Yelena had to step over it every time she used the sink.

A door was open to a tiny box room beyond. Clothes were folded into piles along one wall, two camp beds occupied most of the floor. A small window with an ill-fitting frame had a bird feeder on the far side. The only decoration was a tattered poster of a blonde Komsomol girl with braids wrapped tightly round her head. Full-breasted and blue-eyed, she raised her face to the sun as she stared enthusiastically into the future.

Dennisov said, 'A childhood present from the general.'

'The general?'

'Our dear father,' Yelena said.

She stamped across and shut the box-room door, muttering darkly as she returned to her saucepan and turned off the gas. Dennisov and Tom watched as she slopped soup into two bowls, cut thick slabs of dark bread, dumped the lot on a tray and headed for the curtain. 'Call me when you're done.'

'Yelena . . .'

'Talking to foreigners is dangerous.'

It was hard to tell what Dennisov was thinking as he watched the curtain fall into place behind her. 'She and the general don't get on.'

'Any particular reason?'

'She burned his dacha down when she was ten.'

'Good God, why?'

'He was inside.'

'You've served,' Dennisov said. 'Haven't you?'

Tom thought of long nights watching darkened windows, dawns when he'd witnessed uniformed men smash down doors to extract people who thought they were safely hidden. He thought of firefights in glens so beautiful they belonged on postcards, and pushed his hands into his pockets, noticing Dennisov notice.

'After a fashion.'

Dennisov grinned sourly. 'Me too,' he said. He repeated Tom's 'After a fashion' back to himself. 'Yours was not a clean war?'

'As filthy as it comes.'

'Mine too. The generals want it ended. The Kremlin

refuses. So year after year, TASS tells the people we're winning, when everyone knows we're not. Once the Americans
started giving the mullahs missiles . . . You think these wars
are winnable?'

'What do you think?'

'I think you shouldn't answer a question with a question.'

'I think we should talk about this another time. But no, I
don't think those wars are winnable. It's hard to win against
people who want their country back.'

Dennisov gulped his vodka. 'Too many dead children.'

Tom looked at him.

'Once you start killing children, how do you stop their
families wanting to kill you? . . . War, what is it good for?'

'Absolutely nothing.'

The Russian laughed. 'You have LPs?'

Tom's own vodka stopped halfway to his mouth.

'You know? Edwin Starr? The Who? Led Zeppelin?'

'Those are old.'

'New bands would be better. Good bands.'

'I have this,' said Tom, pulling Alex's cassette from his
pocket. 'And yes, I've got a few LPs somewhere. I'll dig them
out.'

'This is a bootleg?'

'Home-taped. It's killing music.'

Dennisov stared at him blankly.

'Do you have a tape recorder?' Tom asked.

'Of course I have a tape recorder. All Russians have a tape
recorder.' He pulled a bulky brown slab from one of Yelena's
kitchen drawers. 'East German.' Dennisov's expression was
sour.

'What's it doing in there?'

'It lives in there.'

'Where do you live?'

81

'In the room you just examined. You saw the beds.'

'No perks for returning veterans?'

'None that I'd want. And Yelena is not good on her own.'

Tom spread his hands to admit defeat, perhaps incomprehension. His own sister was six years older, already a mother several times over and quite possibly a grandmother. 'Haven't seen my sister in years.'

'I would miss Yelena.'

When the snare drum and guitar started up, Dennisov grew still. 'This is good,' he said finally. 'This is very good. You find any more like this, you bring them to me, right?'

'If I do,' Tom agreed.

'These badges have to do with that girl?'

'No. I found them on the street.'

'Show me the last again.'

Dennisov took the Lenin badge, turning it over in his hand.

'The others are tat. This is gold and reserved for senior Party members. These days they're platinum, so this is at least twenty years old.'

'You're saying her boyfriend was older?'

'More likely his father is important.'

It looked like any other Lenin badge to Tom, although perhaps the great man's head was a little finer, the enamel a little brighter. This wasn't good. He'd been hoping they were all tat, the kind of thing a foreign student out at the university might give a younger girl to impress her.

'You're sure?'

'My father has one. It goes nicely with his silk suits.'

Stubble, gym shorts, rusting prosthetic leg . . . Dennisov really didn't look like someone whose father was *nomenclatura*, important.

'He lives in Leningrad with my sister.'

Tom glanced towards the bar.

'Not Yelena. My other sister. Yelena's our housemaid's daughter.'

'Your father has housemaids?'

'He calls them something else.'

13

Beziki

The call came first thing next morning. A brisk five or six rings, put down at the other end and then, almost immediately, the phone rang again, and kept ringing until Tom rolled out of bed, grabbed his dressing gown and slumped on to a tapestry-covered stool beside the telephone table. 'Fox,' he said.

'This is Masterton.'

'Sir?'

'Thought you must have left.'

'I was still asleep, sir. Hard night.'

'You're not out here to enjoy yourself.'

'Believe me, sir, I'm not. I went drinking with the son of a KGB general. Ex-Spetsnaz. Ex-pilot. Wounded in Afghanistan and invalided out. He's of the opinion that killing civilians is self-defeating. Also, that Afghans are fanatics. Like all religious fanatics, the more you attack them the worse they get. The Red Army have been begging the Kremlin for years to bring the troops home.'

'Any of that true?'

'Every word of it.'

Sir Edward was silent for a moment.

'You realize he's probably reporting everything you say? So take care not to compromise us. As long as you don't do that, and get more out of him than he gets out of you, I suppose it's fine. This is for your report, I imagine?'

'Yes, sir.'

'Want a word. I'll send a car.'

'Probably quicker if I take the metro, sir.'

'Quick as you can then.' Sir Edward began to put the phone down, then his voice was there again, suddenly loud in Tom's ear. 'I gather my wife visited you yesterday. Is that correct?'

'She wanted to know what I found on Alex's computer.'

'And what did you find?'

'Nothing, sir. I'm not sure Alex even turned it on.'

'That's what Anna said.' The telephone clicked, and a second later there was another click and then static and a sudden sense of distance. In part, that had to result from the magnitude of the gulf between Tom and the man he reported to. Tom was closer to Dennisov, a crippled Soviet pilot, than he was to the ambassador, in every way except being on the same side.

The last thing Tom did before leaving his flat was pin two of the three enamel badges he'd found in Alex's room to the collar of his Belstaff. The Fortieth Anniversary of Victory badge on the right, the little circle with Lenin's head to the left. He left the Komsomol badge on the side.

Tom really did intend to take the metro. But the Muscovites flowing down the steps into the underworld had clothes the colour of smog, and their cheap aftershave, bad haircuts, dour expressions and stink of cigarettes and wet wool reminded him of Belfast. So he let himself be caught up in the tide flowing past the entrance, with two men in heavy coats behind him and a woman with a wobbly pushchair up ahead. When she suddenly stopped, Tom stepped into the road to avoid her, raising his hand in apology to a black Volga.

The crop-haired driver wound down his window.

'Foreigner,' Tom said. 'Sorry.'

It took the men in coats moving in for him to realize this wasn't about him stepping into the road. An arm went round his shoulder a split second before a blade touched his side. 'No one would see a thing,' one of the men said.

The other nodded towards the Volga.

'Your choice.'

Three of them. Two outside, one in the car. Four, if you included the woman with the pushchair, who once again blocked his way.

'I have diplomatic immunity.'

'Not with us.'

A hand touched Tom's head to force him into the back and he tensed, feeling the blade jab slightly. You could survive a stab to the side . . . All those shit-filled tubes, though. You could die from it too.

'I demand to talk to my embassy.'

'Later,' the man said. 'Perhaps.'

'Perhaps?'

'Perhaps not.'

It was the driver who made up Tom's mind.

Instead of worrying about how this would unfold, he reached into his glove compartment for a packet of cigarillos, took a lighter from his leather jacket and lit up, sweetish smoke drifting through his open window.

It was magnificently 'fuck you', the action of someone who already knows how a scene will unfold. Tom too knew his part. The rules said stay alive as long as possible.

Until dying became preferable.

One of the two men slid in beside him.

As the Volga pulled away, the other turned back towards the metro, shrugging to Tom's shadow. Only the woman with the buggy stared after them. Up ahead was what passed for a Moscow traffic jam: a handful of cars edging past a broken lorry. A *militsiya* car, siren off, lights flicking lazily, was parked behind. Tom's driver didn't even glance across as he pushed his way through. He was younger than Tom had thought, less confident than his display with the cigarillo had suggested. Discreetly checking the door, Tom found it locked.

'I have a gun,' the driver said.

'I'm sure you do.'

The problem with the young was that they had things to prove.

Tom certainly did back then. Thirty-eight wasn't old but it mostly wasn't reckless either. These two had been entrusted with delivering him. They wanted to live up to that trust. The IRA worked on the same model. Young men sent out by men far older. All forces worked like that, Tom's included. Of course, his didn't have black Volgas, black glass office blocks or famous jails.

'Where are you taking me?'

The man beside him looked over, his expression flat. 'You talk too much.'

Heading south, they passed Red Square, crossed the Moskva and a canal beyond, then joined a long loop of the Boulevard Ring that carried them back over the river and round the east side of Moscow. Finally, they turned back towards the centre and stopped a quarter of an hour later outside a row of houses fronted by spindly trees. They sat for a moment, the engine ticking to itself.

Tom began sliding for the door the moment he heard it unlock, only for a thickset pedestrian on the far side of the road to unbutton his coat, show Tom his holster and walk across and open the door for him.

'Am I under arrest?'

'You have immunity. Who could arrest you?'

The driver, who was happily lighting another cigarillo, smiled.

The house had curtained windows and stone steps up to a shiny black door. The door looked freshly painted and the steps had been scraped free of snow. But Tom was shown to cellar stairs at the side.

'Take care,' the thickset man said.

Tom looked at him.

'The brickwork is icy.'

'What now?' asked Tom, when they were in the cellar, where a single chair stood in the middle of a stained concrete floor, under a bare bulb on a fraying flex. The walls were splashed with God knows what. A coil of rubber hose hung from a nail. A tap below it dripped repeatedly. At the far end was a steel door.

'What now? You strip.'

'No chance.'

Stepping back, the man folded his fingers round his Makarov and lifted the weapon from its holster, jacking back the slide to put a round in the chamber. The action was unthinking, effortless. Close to instinct. 'Those are my orders.'

No noise came from beyond the steel door.

No screams. No raised voices. No pleas for mercy.

Tom scanned the room for CCTV but the cellar was clean. A swept expanse of concrete, splashed walls scabbed with ancient paint. The ceiling was supported on beams as old as the walls. Perhaps the space beyond was soundproof. Perhaps it was simply empty.

'What then? I tie myself to this chair? Torture myself?'

'Who said anything about torture?'

'Why am I here?'

The man sighed. 'I have no idea.'

'And after I strip?'

'You go through that door and I go home to a brandy. And, unless the boss calls later, maybe I get to fuck my wife or go to a card game. Or perhaps we go to the movies, if there's something worth watching. Have you any idea how long it's been since there was something worth watching?'

Tom shook his head.

'Fucking years. You know what's on this week? *Come and See*. About the Great Patriotic War. Just for a change. Only this time they used live ammunition to make the battle scenes realistic. A country can have too much realism, you know . . .?'

It was the pub-like nature of his conversation that threw Tom, the way his words contrasted with the filthy cellar and solitary chair. The man really did look as if all he wanted was to get home to a drink, his wife and maybe a movie.

'What was the last film you liked?' Tom asked.

'*Solaris*. She had good tits . . . Think about it,' the man said. 'If you don't strip, how can my boss be sure you're not carrying? That you're not wearing a wire? He has to be careful. You can't blame a man in his position for being careful.'

Placing his trousers over the chair, Tom put his socks inside his shoes, his pants under his shirt and his Belstaff over the chair's back. The concrete was like ice under his feet and goose pimples covered his legs.

'Through there,' the man said.

They looked at each other. When Tom knocked crossly on the steel door, it was the man with the gun who sighed with relief.

'Welcome, Major Fox.'

The young woman who handed him a bathrobe was dressed in a short skirt and a slightly too tight white blouse. Despite his nakedness, she was the one who blushed when she caught Tom staring.

'If you'd follow me?'

She led him along the edge of a pool, past bentwood chairs and between squat palms in terracotta pots. White marble pillars held up porphyry arches that supported a domed ceiling above. Steam from the pool made the chairs on the far edge look further away than they were. 'In here, sir.'

Tom was slapped by a wall of heat.

'Come in, Mr Fox.'

A huge man sat on a marble bench, his back to the green tiles of the steam room, a white towel the size of a sheet worn like a toga. He had the broken nose and heavy brows of a boxer, but his gaze belonged to someone altogether more complex. When the door slammed, Tom knew the girl was gone and they were alone.

'So,' said the man, 'tell me about your daughter.'

'My daughter?'

The man surveyed him silently for several seconds. 'Start with how she died.'

14

Chacha *Over Ice*

Steam rose through grills in the floor, condensed on the ceiling and ran down the walls into gutters that edged the room. The man watched Tom look around him and smiled. 'A wise man always gathers his thoughts.'

Tom snorted. It was instinctive.

'Although you haven't always been wise, have you?'

'How do the KGB know about Rebecca? What interest could she be?'

'KGB?' The man looked amused. 'They'd be very upset to find I'd been mistaken for one of them. The KGB are the pillar of the state. Good Party members.' He tossed his huge towel aside, revealing eight-pointed stars at his knees and shoulders. 'I, on the other hand, am *vor v zakone*, a thief in law. What you would call mafia. Entirely undesirable. A very successful undesirable, admittedly. When one becomes this successful, it leaves the state with two choices. Reach a compromise or kill.'

'Why haven't they killed you then?'

'Like your one-legged friend, I have influence in all the right places.'

'You know about Dennisov's father?'

'A bitter little fool who'd crush me underfoot if he could. He survived Stalin by feeding his superiors to the machine.'

'Why didn't he get fed to the machine in turn?'

'Because the Boss died. You know there are those who say

he was murdered? Think of that. Besides, Dennisov was good at picking patrons. You've heard of Golubtsov? Beria's deputy? Dennisov took Golubtsov's son's place after the boy died in Berlin. Such a stroke of luck . . .'

'You were in Berlin?'

'We all were.' The man patted the wooden bench beside him. 'Gabashville,' he said, offering his hand. 'Erekle Gabashville.'

When Tom's hand stayed by his side, he smiled.

'A wise man is always cautious. You may call me Beziki.'

'Why would I do that?'

'Because we're going to be friends. Perhaps.'

Reaching for a plastic box, Erekle Gabashville opened it to reveal a bottle on ice, and two tiny shot glasses. He handed one to Tom, filled it to the brim, smiled and poured one for himself. '*Chacha*,' he said. 'Clear brandy. Stalin gave a bottle to Churchill and Roosevelt at Yalta. Now, drink. Before it gets warm.'

The alcohol went down in one.

'Right,' Gabashville said, 'tell me about Rebecca.'

'This has to do with Alex?'

'Do you imagine either of us would be here otherwise?'

'You have me forced into a car at knifepoint, brought to a basement in the middle of nowhere, told to strip by a man with a pistol . . .'

'Petrovka is hardly the middle of nowhere. And it would be absurd to enter a steam room dressed. As for the pistol . . . sidearms are illegal for private citizens in Moscow. Since my employees have no attachment to any official body, you must be mistaken.'

'I'm meant to be seeing the ambassador.'

'He will do nothing. He hasn't even reported his step-daughter missing.'

'There are diplomatic reasons.'

'So his wife tells you.'

Tom tensed and felt Beziki tense in turn.

'I've been watching you. Well, my men have. I'd be a fool not to discover all I could first, wouldn't I? It has to be obvious I want to talk.' Dipping for the box, he refilled both glasses. 'Alcohol,' he said, 'makes the truth more bearable.'

'How do you know about Becca?'

'I asked a man I know to ask a man he knew to find out everything there was to know about you. A dead daughter is what I was told. He's a journalist. One of yours working for us. I mean the USSR, obviously. Or maybe working for you while pretending to work for us. I'm not sure even he knows.'

'What does Becca have to do with Alex?'

'I'm told it's only six months since your daughter died. I imagine one reminds you of the other.'

'And your interest?'

For a moment the man looked too furious to answer. But the sudden flare of anger in his eyes was for something else. Something so dark that the fat man held it inside and examined it in the few hot seconds that passed.

'Edvard's dead,' he said finally.

Should Tom know who Edvard was? He made himself wait.

'I have twins. Had twins. One may still be alive.'

Beziki swept his hand across his skull, wiping sweat from his hair, and as his forehead uncreased and his jowls lifted Tom caught a glimpse of the man he'd once been: fiercer, outwardly harder, less considered.

'What happened?'

'They left my boy dead below the Kremlin Wall.'

Opening the cooler box, Tom refilled the man's glass, watched him drink it down and refilled it again. Then he drank one down himself.

'Who are *they*?'

'I'll tell you when I know. First, Rebecca.'

Last night's hangover already tainted the sweat rolling down Tom's chest to gather in his navel, before dripping between his balls to splash to the floor. He could feel the next wave of alcohol flushing his veins. Eat more and drink less. It was an easy thing for a doctor to say.

'Sometimes it helps to tell,' Beziki said.

'Have you told anyone?'

'I'm telling you.'

Leaning back, the thickset man settled his bulk and closed his eyes as if intending to wait him out. Tom didn't make him wait long. He was shocked to discover that he wanted to talk. He had things to say that he couldn't begin to say to Caro. Things he couldn't say to the police, his friends, what passed for his colleagues. And Beziki was right. If it weren't for Becca, he'd never have spoken to Alex in the first place. 'We had her young,' Tom said. 'It was complicated.'

'You married because of it?'

'I was training to be a Catholic priest. "*Tu es sacerdos in aeternum.*"'

'What does that mean?'

'You're ordained for ever. Only, not quite. I admired the car in the window, got the brochure, booked a test drive but I never took Catholicism on the road. I was twenty-two, Caro nineteen. Her mother was furious.'

'And yours?'

'Mine died shortly afterwards. My dad was in jail.'

Beziki opened his eyes with the laziness of a fat cat hearing the scurrying of mice. 'He was *vor v zakone*?'

'He was a thief. And he was in the law. But nothing so grand. Bent copper.'

'Copper?'

'Military police . . .'

Beziki's nod was carefully neutral. 'Let's get back to your daughter. What happened?'

'Her car hit a tree. She was seventeen.' Tom no longer cared that Beziki knew. He simply wanted to tell someone the truth.

'A traffic accident?'

'The police wondered if she'd been drinking. I told them no way. She was too careful to drink and drive.'

'Another car was involved then?'

'Maybe she swerved to avoid an accident? That was one of their suggestions. There was no paint from another vehicle on the Mini we'd bought her. No skid marks to say she'd been braking when she went off the road.'

'She was racing?'

'The police suggested that. Perhaps, if she'd been a boy . . . But not Bec. She was quiet. Stubborn as hell but a nervous driver, not the racing kind. The police wondered if someone had been tailgating her, or maybe she was being chased. Did we know of any reason someone might have been chasing her?'

'Did you?'

'She was seventeen and three months. A model student. She'd had the same boyfriend since she was fifteen.'

'The weather was good?'

'A clear night and a full moon. The headlights were working. The tyres were good. We'd insisted the garage give us a new set. The Mini was MOTed, taxed, newly serviced and insured. The police asked if she took drugs, if she'd been acting strangely, how college had been going, if we knew of any reason she might be upset . . .'

'And the answers?'

'Her marks were great. She occasionally quarrelled with

her boyfriend but it was never serious. She didn't seem any different. She certainly didn't seem upset.'

'What do you think happened?'

'I know what happened. She killed herself.'

'Why would she do that?'

'I don't know.' Tom chewed at his lip. 'I've asked myself over and over. The answer is . . . *I don't know*. But she put her Mini into a tree at eighty miles an hour on a straight dry road. She died instantly. So the police were careful to tell us.'

'What aren't you saying?'

They'd got to the bit Caro didn't know.

Taking a deep breath, Tom said, 'We'd already told the police she barely drank and said dope made people stupid, but they had to be certain. My father-in-law arranged for a pathologist he knew to do the autopsy. His report . . .' Tom paused, then kept going. Safer that way. 'His report was to the point. It consisted mostly of a list of broken bones and ruptured organs. Like the police, he said that she died instantly. Unlike with the police, we believed him. There was no alcohol in her blood. No drugs. Nothing to suggest an aneurism. Her blood count was down, her haemoglobin low. A few other clues suggested she'd been tired at the time . . . So the coroner recorded his opinion that she'd dozed off at the wheel and only woken at the very end.'

'You don't believe him?'

'Becca was three months' pregnant. That was what was left out of the report my wife was given. I thanked the pathologist for his discretion, went straight round to Bec's boyfriend and put him through a wall. When his dad tried to stop me, I punched him out. With his mum screaming that I'd got it wrong, I dragged the little shit into the garden and began hurting him. By the time the police arrived he'd pissed himself. It took three coppers to pull me off.'

'How old was this boy?'

'Nineteen.'

'Old enough. You have friends in the police?'

'My father-in-law does. The family agreed not to press charges in return for a promise I'd never go near them again . . . Wounded in Northern Ireland. Back on leave from Belfast. Hush-hush work. Distraught at the tragic death of his daughter. The police suggested they let the matter drop. My marriage was in ruins by then. Charlie off to boarding school. My wife decided it was the best place for him. I moved into a hotel a week later.'

'So you're divorced?'

'Temporary separation while we see how it goes.'

Beziki opened one eye. 'And how is it going?'

'As badly as you'd expect.'

'In Russia, your daughter would have had an abortion.'

'In the UK too. We'd have stood by her. We'd have been unhappy about it. Furious even. But we'd have stood by her.'

'And the boy . . . Would his family have helped?'

'He wrote to me. He wanted me to know he'd told the truth. He never slept with Becs. As far as he knew she'd never slept with anyone. He was sorry she was dead. He'd loved her. He always would.'

'Who was the father?'

'I've no idea. I sorted through her record collection afterwards. Caro couldn't bring herself to do it. "All Cried Out", "Tainted Love", "King of Pain". It was as if Bec wanted to tell us something.' Tom shook his head.

There was no *as if* about it.

Reaching for the cooler box, he refilled his glass and tossed it back. *Chacha* burned his throat. A burn to match the sting in his eyes. It was true that he had no idea who the father was, no idea what had happened in the last six months of his daughter's life. Since Becca's death, he'd come to wonder if he'd known her at all.

'My wife died young,' Beziki said.

'And left you with two boys?'

'You know how precious boys are.'

'Bec was precious.'

'Girls are different.'

Tom couldn't argue with that. Bec was very different. He'd seen no trace of himself when he looked at her, and precious little of her mother. Bec was bright, studious, stubborn. She'd intended to go to Oxford. She'd found herself work in a greengrocer's for the holidays. When Caro said shop work was vulgar, Tom pointed out Bec could be pulling pints in the village pub.

That hadn't helped Bec's case.

'You're remembering her?'

'Yes. She was very beautiful. Very clever.'

Beziki sighed. 'Edvard was very beautiful. Not so clever.'

'What do you want from me?' Tom asked. 'Why am I really here?'

Erekle Gabashville leaned forward and settled his bulk like one of those huge Japanese sumo wrestlers preparing for a bout, his weight balanced, his hands over the eight-pointed stars on his knees. 'There was a letter.'

He held up his hand to halt Tom's question.

'After the boys were taken . . . It should not have been possible to take them. I want to say that. They were at my dacha. There were guards. The guards died.' He shrugged. 'Just as well. I would have had to kill them otherwise. They were good men and I would have disliked that.'

Beziki dragged his thoughts back to the letter.

'Russians don't trust Georgians but we're useful and Stalin trusted us, obviously enough, which is maybe why others don't now. As a boy, I found a rifle and shot Germans. The partisans could have killed me but they made me their mascot instead. Later, the Red Army gave me a uniform and a family. We were young. Very young. We drank, we shared German women, we stood in Berlin's ruins and took photographs. We did good things, bad things. Bonds like that bind you. I'll show you the photographs one day.'

'This has to do with the letter?'

The man nodded heavily. 'It demanded money for the return of my sons, a huge amount in American dollars. If that was all, I'd have paid. Maybe made them wait a little while I tried to find out who had the balls for this. Although the fact they dared should have been warning enough. It wasn't about dollars though. They also wanted information, information they had already, they said. Sending it would merely confirm what they knew.'

'You didn't send them the information?'

'I said I needed a week to think about it. Their answer was to leave Edvard naked below the Kremlin Wall. He was frozen like ice.'

'It was that cold?'

'No. I have men asking questions in factory units and food-processing plants all over Moscow. Anywhere with industrial freezers. No one's seen or heard anything suspicious.'

'You've sent the information since?'

'How can I?' Beziki said. 'It risks betraying my oldest friends.'

'How long do you have to comply?'

'I don't know. That's what worries me. Since Edvard died, I haven't heard a word. No contact. No notes left. I have the dollars ready. Twice the amount they asked for, in case that's enough. And nowhere to send it.'

'You intend to kill them, of course?'

'I would say yes. However, I ask myself, who would dare do this? And I don't like any of the answers. So I ask myself what was being said when his body was left by the Kremlin and I like that answer even less. It was a warning, obviously. I'm just not sure it was a warning for me.'

'For who then?'

'Those inside? Except who else has the power to do this? No one outside the Presidium, the high command, would dare.' Beziki shook his head. 'That worries me. What do you know of Andropov?'

'Little enough.'

'KGB. He died after a year. Chernenko. Also KGB. He lasted a year too. Give Gorbachev a year and he'll probably be gone, nothing more than another plaque on a wall TASS can't be bothered to report properly.'

'You're saying Andropov and Chernenko were killed?'

'Would it matter?' Beziki touched his forehead, his heart and his balls in a weird parody of crossing himself. 'They were dead here already.'

15

Drunk Again

He was very drunk when she found him. Drunker than most foreigners manage, lacking the liver, determination and soul of the average Russian. Drunk enough to be a Muscovite. And *found* wasn't really the word. She'd been waiting for him on a bench in a little park on the corner. She was Wax Angel, carver of the guardians. It was her job to keep an eye on what was going on.

She put being in the right place to see him abducted down to having once been in such a wrong place – and at such a wrong time – that God had spent most days since making it up to her. As for finding the man now . . .

If he went in that door, he'd come out the other.

She knew he would. Even men like Erekle Gabashville didn't abduct victims in broad daylight if they later intended to dump their bodies . . . Now, the KGB, they'd have no trouble with that at all. Wax Angel shivered with more than cold and gripped the edge of her bench. There'd been two office workers sitting here, collars up and heads down, smoking their cigarettes and reading books when she arrived. But they'd been kind enough to let her have the seat to herself.

She liked this park and she liked this bench.

She'd seen the Boss himself sitting here one Saturday, about ten years after he died. Few others seemed to notice. Although the black cat from the cafe on the corner had refused to come when she called. She'd wondered since what

Stalin was doing back in Moscow and decided hell must have been having an open day.

'So there you are,' she said.

The Englishman stared at her, owl-eyed.

'No,' she said, when he dug his hand into his pocket for change.

He looked even more puzzled. He wasn't safe to be let out in daylight really, never mind after dark.

Her husband had been like this for a while, in the bad years. So drunk he didn't know what to do with himself. It had been a clever move. Better to be a drunk than to be suspected of being a conspirator or traitor. Alcohol had never worked for her. The insides of her head were messy enough already without making them worse.

'This way,' she said.

He tried to free himself when she took his arm.

'No,' she said firmly. 'You need to come over here.'

She led him down a slippery path to where bushes behind low metal railings wore snow like torn blankets, more holes than warmth.

Wax Angel knew how they felt.

'Careful now . . .'

When he missed his step, she decided that was far enough.

Since, conveniently, he was now on his hands and knees, she walked round to his side and booted him lightly in the stomach. He vomited so fluently that snow melted, the grass beneath steaming like a spa bath.

The sight of it made him throw up again.

'Well done,' Wax Angel said.

She watched him struggle to his feet and helped him the last of the way.

'Now . . . you'd better get yourself home.'

'Embassy,' he said. 'Taxi.'

Wax Angel looked at him doubtfully. He was sweating alcohol, his knees were sodden from the snow and he had the shakes. She wouldn't trust him not to throw up in her taxi, and she didn't have a taxi.

'Come with me,' she said.

Tom's cab to the embassy wasn't actually a cab. It was an old and rotting mustard-yellow half-truck, stinking of the onions its owner had been unloading when Wax Angel led Tom into the car park. There was a queue in front of an empty stall, so word must have got out. That was one of Moscow's basic laws. If you see a queue, join it. If you don't want what's being sold, someone will.

The stallholder told Wax Angel to join the line.

'He needs a lift into town.'

'Tell him to take the metro like everyone else.'

'He's a foreigner.'

'Dollars or roubles?'

'Which would you like?' She hoped the Englishman had dollars. But he was foreign. All foreigners had hard currency of some sort.

'I'll just dump these.' Hefting his sack, he headed for his stall, dropping the sack at the feet of a woman.

'Follow him then,' Wax Angel said.

Tom nodded. A few minutes later, it occurred to him that he should have thanked her but when he looked back she was gone.

The Niva was rusty, with broken lights, and looked like the bastard offspring of a Jeep and a Landrover designed by someone who'd seen neither.

'Where to?' the man demanded.

'How much?'

'Depends.'

Tom chose the route.

He had intended to be dropped on the corner where the Embankment began but the Niva was warm and he was fighting sleep, so he had the driver pull up outside the embassy instead. Both the *militsiya* and the British guard inside watched with interest.

Dragging a five-rouble note from his pocket, Tom handed it to the man, who opened his mouth to protest and shut it again when his passenger pointed at the floor. Ten dollars lay in the footwell of the Niva, held down by the rubber mat.

The man scrawled a number on an old copy of *Pravda*. 'Any time,' he said. 'Ask for Pyotr. Say you're the foreigner.'

The snow-covered cobbles between the gate and the steps were as unsteady as a ship's deck in a storm. Climbing the steps was even worse. Having reached the top, Tom was terrified that if he let go of the doorknob he'd fall over.

'Christ, you look bad.'

He peered at the man who came out to meet him.

'Andrew,' the man said. 'I'm helping you settle in. Are you drunk, sir?'

'In the line of duty.'

His mouth twitched. 'Can you prove that?'

'Yes,' said Tom. 'Probably.'

'Just as well. You're not popular at the moment.'

'Sir Edward?'

'More all the people he's been shouting at since you weren't here to be shouted at yourself. It's been a bit of an afternoon. This morning wasn't great either. He's demanded to be told the moment you arrive.'

'Is the medical officer around?'

'You mean the doctor? Yes. Usual place.'

When Tom just looked at him, the young attaché sighed.

Tom left the surgery an hour later, having confirmed there was nothing worse than Georgian *chacha* in his system. He'd drunk what felt like his body weight in soda water, napped for forty minutes, had a partial blood transfusion and swallowed tincture of *Hovenia dulcis*. He'd also washed his face, brushed his teeth and rinsed his mouth with Listerine. The embassy doctor was ex-medical corps.

He'd been in Belfast too.

Andrew was coming out of the ambassador's office when Tom appeared in the outer doorway. The woman with him looked away. 'Ah, I'd heard you were still in the sick bay.'

'How is Sir Edward?'

'Incandescent.'

'No, I mean confident, worried, reticent?'

Tom realized the ambassador's secretary was listening. She looked back down at her work when he looked over.

'He's the ambassador,' Andrew said.

'I assume you have a good excuse, Fox.'

'What did the note say?'

'I'm sorry?'

'The note, sir. What did it say?'

'We've had this discussion. You know what Alex said.'

'I'm talking about the other note.'

For a second, Sir Edward hovered on the edge of denying there had been another note. Tom watched it happen. Then the fight went out of the man and he sat back, his anger deflating like a ruptured balloon.

'Who told you about that?'

'A Georgian. May I ask what the note said?'

Tom knew it was the wrong question the moment the words left his mouth, for all he'd guessed right about there being a second note. A flintiness returned to Sir Edward's face and his gaze hardened. 'No,' he said firmly, 'you may not.'

'Too personal?'

The man almost rose to the bait. Then he caught himself and bit down on his anger at Tom's impertinence. When he sat back, he was in control. 'What it said is none of your business.'

There were two ways to read that.

The note was personal and Sir Edward was damned if Tom was going to know the contents. Or it was beyond Tom's competence and pay scale. Either way, the man had known for a while his stepdaughter hadn't simply run away to sulk.

'Have you told London, sir?'

'Not yet.'

'Who here knows?'

'About the second note? Nobody.'

'Who knows about the first?'

'My wife, and Mary Batten.'

'With respect, sir, perhaps you should tell Mary Batten about this one.'

'Wait there,' Sir Edward said.

He vanished into his outer office and shut the door. All Tom could hear was muted conversation. How much of the embassy was bugged by the Russians? How much, if any, by us? The Americans had found a Soviet bug behind their great seal, that damn eagle in a circle behind their ambassador's desk.

There was something fitting in that.

On a side table was a photograph of Anna and Alex. Anna looked younger and Alex untroubled, barely into her teens. Both were smiling in the shadow of the Colosseum and their smiles seemed real, despite the tourist backdrop.

'Rome,' Sir Edward said. 'They liked Rome.'

He retook his place behind his desk and said, 'Mary will join us.'

There was an awkward silence. Sir Edward picked up a file and hid himself in whatever was inside. Mary Batten entered without knocking. She was wearing a blue skirt suit that looked almost mockingly smart. Her dark eyes met Tom's, and some question was asked that Tom failed to answer, because she looked at him coldly and waited for Sir Edward to put down his file.

'Thank you for dropping by.'

Her face tightened at the ambassador's careful politeness.

'Major Fox has something to say.'

That wasn't the way Tom would have put it. All the same, he sat back in his chair to order what thoughts he had and looked up to find Mary Batten watching him.

'This is about being forced into that car?'

'You know about . . .?' Of course she did; she'd just mentioned it. 'You've been having me followed?'

'We're following the man following you.'

Sir Edward stopped reading his memo.

'You were told about that, sir.'

'If you say so.'

'The question,' Mary Batten said, 'is why do the Soviets have a KGB colonel shadowing a British major? One who, without wishing to be rude, is expected to retire as a result of recent difficulties.'

'Difficulties?' Sir Edward asked.

Tom had an instant picture of two men dead on the floor of a Boston bar. One was an IRA commander, the other black ops for army intelligence and so far under cover Tom doubted even he remembered where his true loyalties lay.

Tom could still hear the crack of his own Browning and the sudden shocked silence of the customers, with only the commentary to a Red Sox game and the rise and fall of a distant cop siren to break it.

Then the breeze from the door as he left.

'The best that can be said,' said Mary Batten, 'is that nothing can be proved. It's probably wise not to go into it now. Still, I can see why London decided to park you here to decompress. What did Erekle Gabashville want?'

'You know him?'

'Of him, certainly.'

'His sons were kidnapped. One was left dead at the Kremlin Wall, the other is still missing . . .' Tom watched Sir Edward glance at Mary, who shook her head. Obviously neither had heard about the body. 'Gabashville wants his revenge. But mostly, at this point, he simply wants his other boy back.'

'Who is this man, Mary?'

'*Vor v zakone*, sir. Mafia, with connections.'

Sir Edward kept his gaze on her and waited to see if she had anything else to add. When she didn't, he said, 'By connections, I'm assuming you mean high-level protectors. Why would anyone murder the child of a gangster with connections?'

'Maybe his protector's no longer so powerful,' Tom said. 'Perhaps it's revenge, and the killer's been waiting for this moment. Apparently the Politburo's at war with itself. The Soviets are big on fighting wars through proxies. Beziki's definitely a proxy. Maybe whoever killed his son is too . . .'

'Beziki said that?' Mary's gaze sharpened. 'About the Politburo?'

'As good as.'

'Interesting choice of location for the body.'

'Very, sir.' Mary Batten agreed.

'You'd better tell Mary how this connects to Alex.'

From the look on her face, Mary was already busy joining the dots between the ambassador's stepdaughter being missing and Beziki's son being dead, and not liking where those thoughts led her at all.

'What Sir Edward's been keeping private,' Tom said, 'is that he received a second note. Not from Alex this time. It contained . . .' Tom glanced at the ambassador. 'I'm not sure what it contained.'

'When did this one arrive, sir?'

Sir Edward looked worried. 'Just after Tom told Anna and me about the fire.'

Tom thought of Black Sammy, the Sad Sam cat, hanging flayed in his kitchen, felt the bile rise in his throat and decided he should tell these two about that too.

Mary looked grim.

And Sir Edward . . . Tom spent the rest of that evening replaying Sir Edward's reaction. The blood drained from his face. There was no other way to describe it. The man went pale, and he gripped his desk so hard his knuckles turned white.

For a moment, Tom thought he might cry.

'You don't tell my wife,' he said finally. There was a quiet fury in his voice. A steeliness, as if a blade had just been unsheathed. 'This isn't something Anna needs to know. You keep it to yourself.'

'Sir . . .' Tom protested.

'I'm serious, Fox.'

'But at least tell me what the note said.'

'It's secret. I mean that. As in, I don't know your security clearance off the top of my head, but I very much doubt this is something you're authorized to know.'

To Mary, the ambassador said, 'Get me a line to London.'

He nodded towards his door and his secretary beyond. 'Don't leave it to Grace. I want you to place the call yourself. Fox, you can go. Mary, you'd better stay behind.'

Tom left. Fury at being cut out of the conversation followed him like a cloud.

16

Supper with Beziki

In the three days that followed Tom heard nothing from Sir Edward, had his request to see Mary Batten turned down and was invited to supper by Beziki on the afternoon of the third day. Partly out of bloody-mindedness, mostly because he was fucked if he was going to be condescended to by Sir Edward, he asked Anna Masterton if she'd like to come too. He didn't mention the cat, though.

The place Beziki suggested was shut for refurbishment, according to a sign outside. The shutters were closed, right enough. And the scaffolding on Gorky Street had made Tom wonder if he and Anna had come to the right place.

They had. Inside, chandeliers glittered, candles flickered and the tables were laid with cloth and silver. On the wall, an engraving showed three hunters cross-legged on grass. They wore muted robes, heavy beards and criss-crossed cartridge belts. The man who handed Tom a wine list could have been their grandson.

'Has Alex's relationship with Sir Edward always been difficult?'

'She took her father's death badly.'

'So you mentioned. It was recent?'

'Alex was six. We were divorcing anyway.'

Empty Shampanskoye glasses stood in front of them. These had been hurried across the moment they entered.

But no one had offered a refill and Anna was jumpy enough to leave if Erekle Gabashville didn't arrive soon.

'More wine?' Tom asked.

At her suggestion, he ordered a Tsinandali, which arrived in an ice bucket with a crisp napkin over the top. Tom sniffed the dribble he was poured and nodded to say it was fine, waiting for Anna to take the first sip.

'How polite,' she said.

'Shouldn't you be somewhere?'

She hesitated on the edge of taking a second sip.

'I mean . . .' Tom looked at his Omega, a present from Caro, as were his cufflinks. As was his shirt come to that. 'Seven thirty on a Wednesday night. Isn't there bridge, or something? An embassy wives' committee to attend?'

'Don't be a shit. Edward's in meetings. Everyone's in meetings. Well . . .' She shrugged. 'Everyone who matters.'

'I'm not.'

'There you go.'

'He'll ask how your evening was and you'll say fine?'

'Something like that. I won't lie. But I'm not going to volunteer information unless he asks for specifics.'

'Tell me again . . .'

'I had a call from a *militsiya* major. Svetlana something. Her English was perfect. Her manner less so. She said she'd heard my daughter was delinquent. And a foreign teenager answering Alex's description was shoplifting in GUM.'

'Why didn't they stop her?'

'Alex has embassy credentials, for God's sake. She isn't even officially missing. Edward won't tell the Soviets and he won't tell me why. Maybe the major was just being kind and thought I should know?'

'What did you do?'

'Went straight to GUM, obviously.'

Three hundred yards long, a hundred yards wide, three storeys high and roofed in glass, the department store had a hundred and fifty shops selling nothing very much and four hundred thousand people a day looking to buy it. Finding someone in there who didn't want to be found would be damn near impossible.

'Any sign?'

'Nothing,' Anna admitted. 'I'd just got back when you called to ask if I wanted to go to supper. You didn't say we'd be meeting someone else.'

'Did you get the major's number?'

She scowled as if he was the one changing the subject. 'No. I should have done. But I was so excited someone had seen Alex ... I know it's stupid. It'll be the first thing my husband asks.'

Alex in GUM? Shoplifting?

If she'd simply run away with her boyfriend and they were both at large, then possibly. But Tom figured her boyfriend was dead, killed in that fire. And Alex, well, wherever Alex was, he doubted very much she was wandering department stores. Although the shoplifting was a nice touch.

It's what delinquent Western girls would do.

Tom wondered who was winding Sir Edward and Anna up and why. He'd barely done more than consider the question before the manager hurried from behind his counter and headed for the door. He helped Erekle Gabashville out of a full-length sable and folded the fur coat carefully over his arm. Tom rose to meet him.

'What's she doing here?'

'You should meet her.'

The man's eyes flicked to Anna, who sat very still and looked so serene she had to know she was being discussed.

All signs of her earlier jumpiness were gone. Tom couldn't help being impressed.

'How should I name her. Lady Anna?'

Tom nodded. It would do.

She was Anna, Lady Masterton.

Tom didn't believe it mattered. Caro would though.

But then Caro was Lady Caroline Fox, daughter of an earl. She wouldn't revert to her maiden name when they divorced. She'd regard that as common. She'd remain Lady Caroline Fox until she became Lady Caroline Someone-Else.

At various times Caro's father had been minister for education, minister of defence and home secretary. These days, his own father being dead, he sat in the Lords and on a handful of committees.

Invariably committees that mattered.

He'd decided early on that Margaret Thatcher might not be 'one of us' but she was going places and only a fool would stand in her way. It was a good call and the last few years had been kind to him. He'd begun to talk about his legacy.

After the recent riots in Brixton, Orgreave and the Beanfield, Tom wondered if his legacy would be what he thought it was.

Beziki asked Tom to say he was delighted to make Lady Anna's acquaintance.

Anna Masterton said how sorry she was to hear of Edvard's death and she hoped his other son would be returned safely.

'You told her about that?'

'I thought the two of you should talk.'

The manager stood squirming on the periphery of this. He knew who and what Gabashville was, without knowing what made him suddenly furious.

'What matters,' said Tom, 'is that we save the children.'

'Bit late for you though, isn't it?'

'Yes,' Tom agreed, feeling pain wash over him like lava. 'It's too late for me. It's not too late for you, though. It's not too late for her.'

Beziki gripped him by the shoulders.

'You're a good man.'

'There are many who would disagree.'

Letting go, the Georgian laughed. 'You and me both.'

Turning to the manager, he reeled off a list of dishes and the order in which they should be brought and the length of time to be left between each. Then he nodded politely to Anna, pulled out a chair and seated himself. She winced and he shrugged as it creaked under his weight.

'You've eaten here before?' Anna asked.

'Often,' Beziki said. 'Never with someone so beautiful.'

Leaning across, he took Anna's hand and kissed it, then sat back and nodded as dish after dish was delivered from a kitchen that must have half guessed his order in advance.

'Of course,' he said, 'we all know God doesn't exist. And Georgia is part of one big happy union. All the same, it was hard work making the world and God was exhausted by the time he finished Russia. That's why it's so flat and boring. Being hungry, he told the angels to bring him food. The food was so good he forgot about improving Russia and sent for more. In his hurry to eat it, scraps fell from his plate on to Georgia. That's why Georgians still respect God. Also why our food is the finest.'

'I'll be sure to include that in my report on religion.'

'It's a good story,' Anna said.

'A true one.'

Having finished his wine, Beziki suffered Tom to pour him another glass and downed that just as fast, then he put his wine firmly aside and a flask of *chacha* appeared without him asking. Anna had just put her knife and fork neatly together when a massive silver dish of shashlik chicken was carried in.

'Dear God,' she muttered.

Beziki scooped half of it into his own bowl.

Then he produced a snapshot from his pocket and put it in front of Anna. 'These are my boys.' He seemed pleased that she examined the photograph carefully, before passing it to Tom.

'Tell her,' Beziki said, 'that what I'm about to say is for her alone. Not you. Not her husband. If I could say it without needing you to translate, I would. Tell her I know what it is to have a child vanish. Tell her I have good connections. The kind of connections that should be able to discover who would dare do such a thing. They have discovered nothing about my child or hers.'

The fat man waited for Tom to put it into English.

'I have no idea what her husband has been asked for. It is not my business to know. Apparently, since you don't know, it is not yours either. He will, however, have been asked for something . . .'

Beziki stopped.

'Please translate that exactly.'

Tom did.

'What they wanted was for me to betray my friends, old comrades from the darkest days of the war. These are not people I can give up. They are not people it is safe to give up. They also asked for money. I collected double the amount requested. I intended to offer it in place of my friends. The kidnappers never made contact. They didn't need me to tell them my decision. They already knew.'

'So now,' Anna said, 'you don't know who to trust?'

'So now I talk to you.'

Anna ate and drank very little after that and Beziki conceded defeat and signalled to the manager that pudding should be skipped. He sat while Anna sipped coffee the consistency of silt, and stood the moment she pushed back her chair. 'My car is at your disposal. Or a taxi is waiting if you prefer. The driver knows where to go.'

Glancing between the two men, Anna's eyes narrowed.

'Major Fox is staying here?'

'It would seem so,' Tom said.

'Perhaps a little highly strung,' Beziki said, after the taxi pulled away, 'but charming. Now, this husband of hers . . . He tells you Alex wrote a note but can't produce it. He admits things were *difficult* between them. He asks you to find her. Then he tells you to stop. Teenage stepdaughters can be tricky for some men. I imagine that's occurred to you?'

17

Dennisov's Bar

'Where are your customers?'

'I threw them out.'

'You're closing early?'

'It's late. Even cripples need sleep.'

Dennisov shook out a rag with a snap like gunshot and fragments of bread flicked over the counter he'd just cleaned. Sneering at the mess, he tossed the rag on to the zinc and reached for a vodka flask. It was empty.

'Are you all right?'

The Russian glared at Tom. 'No,' he said, 'I'm not. And Yelena is terrified. You should know I've been offered a lot of money to kill you. Real money.'

'Sterling?'

'Dollars.'

'Are you planning to take it?'

Grunting, Dennisov gestured around his bar, which looked shabbier than ever under the brightness of its cheap strip lighting. 'Why would I need American money? Now, if they'd offered me a bootleg of The Clash in Victoria Park ...' He reached for a Stoli bottle, not bothering to decant the vodka first.

'Who offered you this money?'

'People came.'

'Ex-service? Maybe still serving?' When Dennisov didn't contradict him, Tom said, 'Perhaps you should accept.'

'They accused me of disloyalty.' Dennisov tapped his leg with the Stoli bottle and it rang like a cracked bell. 'I told them to get out and come the fuck back when they could do this.'

'Who'd accuse a one-legged veteran of disloyalty?'

'Russia's changing.'

'Says who?'

'Those who want it to stay the same. If you don't throw scraps at the dogs, they bite you. To survive requires compromises. Gabashville's dangerous, remember that. These people, they don't like Gabashville. They like what you're doing even less. If I were you I'd start worrying about why they don't want this girl found. Whether Gabashville is really helping.'

'You think he's behind her kidnap?'

'Who says it's kidnap?'

'You did,' Tom said. 'Just now. Tell me about these men.'

Dennisov shook his head. 'I knew Gabashville when I was a child. He is an old friend of my father's. He would stay at our house in the Crimea. He is not a nice person.'

Did that make General Dennisov Beziki's protector? From what Tom could gather of the relationship between the two Dennisovs, anyone the general liked his son was bound to hate. 'These men,' Tom said, 'did you recognize them?'

Dennisov didn't nod but he didn't shake his head either.

'What do they have over you?'

Tom followed Dennisov's gaze towards the curtain and the box room beyond where Yelena slept. 'What do you want this time?' Dennisov asked.

'Besides vodka? I want to know if a tattoo of a wolf's head wearing a cap means anything . . . I forgot to ask last time.'

'What colour cap?'

'That makes a difference?'

'It might,' said Dennisov. 'And it's probably a bear.'

'All right. A bear's head. What does it mean?'

'This has to do with that girl of yours?' Dennisov sucked his teeth. 'Of course it has. If the cap's blue, whoever has the tattoo probably served with the Airborne. That doesn't look like it makes you happy.'

'It doesn't . . .' Tom ended up telling Dennisov about going out to the university. About a call that afternoon from Davie to say he'd remembered that the Russian boy Alex liked had a wolf's head tattoo.

'You have no proof Kotik and the girl saw each other again.'

'I have no proof they didn't.'

'You think he was the boy who died in that fire?'

Tom nodded. 'Someone must know.'

Taking a record from a stack, Dennisov slid it from its sleeve and set his deck spinning. Music blasted from the speakers. 'Nautilus Pompilius,' he said. 'We played this before battle. They tried to kill us. We tried to kill them. I liked it when life was simple.'

'Me too,' Tom said.

They clinked glasses.

At a shout from behind the curtain, Dennisov turned the sound down slightly, then shrugged and clicked it off. 'My turn,' Tom said. He pulled an LP from his bag and put it on the zinc, first wiping away scraps of food with his elbow.

Dennisov slid the record from its sleeve, holding it at an angle to check for scratches and wear. 'This is punk?'

'Irish folk music.'

Dennisov snorted. But as soon as Moya Brennan's haunting voice echoed from the speakers Tom stopped regretting bringing the record and felt a shiver run down his spine, his eyes fill with unexpected tears. He turned away.

'Your enemy's music?'

'And their language,' Tom said.

'What does it say?'

'The obvious. In a war like this no one will stop fighting. In a war like this no one can win, everybody will lose . . . It's from a poem.'

'You're allowed to own this?'

'It's very popular. Well, it was. They still play it on the radio. Of course, most English people don't understand what it says.'

'What a country.'

Reaching into his bag again, Tom said, 'We also produce this.'

'And what's that?'

'A great British tradition.'

'Selling slaves? Persecuting workers? Sucking up to America?'

'Bacon. For sarnies.'

Pulling a pan from under a pile of plates, Tom slopped in oil already used to fry something else, flicked on the gas and lit the ring. While the oil smoked, he hacked slices from a Russian loaf the consistency of sawdust, spread it with Anchor butter and fried four rashers of bacon until almost burned.

Tipping the rashers on to the bread, he slathered Heinz ketchup over the top, sealed the sandwich and handed it to Dennisov.

'Eat,' Tom ordered.

Yelena came through to see what the smell was, took one look at the packet of bacon, found herself a knife and began slicing away the rinds, which she piled like worms into a saucer.

'For the wild birds,' her brother said.

Tom nodded.

'I still don't like you,' Yelena said.

He made her a sandwich anyway.

'My brother likes you. But then he's a fool.' She shrugged. 'You've seen our customers. When they first come in, they mournfully try to match him glass for glass, then stagger home. Some don't even make it that far. They never try again. You keep coming back. You keep drinking. Of course he likes you . . .'

'We've seen the same things.'

She looked at him, surprisingly severely. 'I hope not.'

Tom wondered which of them she thought had seen worse.

Her brother sent her back to bed two sandwiches later, the bruise on her cheek unmentioned, and Tom put the remaining bacon, butter and tomato sauce in her fridge.

'Bribery?' Dennisov asked.

'Soviet butter isn't better?'

'We have butter?'

'You look dreadful,' Sir Edward said.

'Insomnia, sir.'

'Have you seen the embassy doctor?'

'He suggested sleeping pills, sir. I don't like sleeping pills. They can cost you your edge.' Tom was amused by how hard Sir Edward had to work not to ask, 'What edge?'

'He's a doctor, Fox. You should take his advice.'

'I will if it doesn't go, sir.'

Sir Edward nodded doubtfully.

Even after Tom arrived twenty minutes late, he got the feeling the ambassador couldn't decide whether to be irritated or grateful that his unshaven underling had turned up for the meeting at all. Tom had spent forty-five minutes under the shower at Sad Sam trying to turn into something vaguely human. He was clean if not shiny, his suit almost uncreased. He even had a razor in his pocket in case the chance arose.

'I'm told you want copies of Alex's photograph?'

If nothing else, he couldn't fault Sir Edward's spider's web. The other reason Tom was late was because he'd wasted time in Photographic trying to persuade a technician that turning a Vivitar enlarger over to making copies of Alex's photograph came ahead of any other embassy business. That information had reached Sir Edward's office before Tom did.

'Can I ask why?' Sir Edward said.

'Your stepdaughter was seen in GUM.'

That wasn't his real reason, but it would have to do. Tom's real reason was he wanted Dennisov to try to find anybody who'd admit to seeing Alex arrive at or leave the warehouse where the body was burned.

'Unlikely, as it turns out,' Sir Edward said. 'Although Anna told me that too. Unfortunately, she forgot to get the number of the *militsiya* officer who told her. What were you planning to do with them?'

'The obvious, sir. Take them down there, go round the stalls and ask them to notify us if she returns. It might help if we can offer a reward.'

'No need, Fox. The Soviets have found her.'

'We're talking to them now?'

'Yes,' Sir Edward said. 'We're talking to them now. Mary called London and London talked direct. Calls were made. Ground rules set. You know how it works. Alex has been traced to some kind of commune. We have that from Vedenin himself. He wanted to know if we'd like help retrieving her.'

Tom had thought that the ambassador was looking more relaxed than he'd seen him in a while. It wasn't relaxed, he realized. It was relieved.

'A commune, sir?'

'More of a cult really. Didn't know they had them here. But, as Mary says, these are the people who produced Rasputin.'

Becca's voice was in his head before Tom could stop it, followed by the memory of discovering her dancing round the kitchen to the radio, how she'd frozen on being caught and retreated into silence as the joy went out of her, becoming the stiff, controlled little thing he remembered. Nothing as simple as a cult for Becca. Nothing so comprehensible.

'What happens now, sir?'

'What do you know about the . . .' He looked at a sheet of paper. 'The Vnutrenniye Voiska?'

Tom searched his memory.

'Soviet equivalent of the French Gendarmerie Nationale,' Sir Edward said impatiently, 'but better armed. They deal with internal unrest. Riots. Terrorist outrages. Religious problems. Also cults, apparently. They report to the MVD, the Soviet Ministry of Internal Affairs.'

'We're involving the Internals?'

'Yes, Fox. The Internal Troops are involved.'

From what Dennisov said, the VV kept an eye on the mullahs in the south, pretty ruthlessly from the sound of it. There'd been a Muslim riot outside Volgograd, Stalingrad as was. When the thing was done and dusted, there hadn't been enough ringleaders left to put on a show trial. The VV kept an eye on the madder Orthodox sects, too. The ones dedicated to poverty, free love and the establishment of Christ's Kingdom on Earth, once the Soviet Union was overthrown.

'Isn't that overkill, sir?'

'Not at all. Vedenin fixes their budget or something. He's sending an English-speaking major across to talk to us. We have a deal. The minister will give us the major as a liaison. You'll be the major's contact. In return, we'll help with your gangster, if we can.'

Sir Edward sat back with a satisfied smile.

'My what, sir?'

'Your gangster.' He checked the paper. 'Erekle Gabash-ville. The Vnutrenniye Voiska have been after him for years. The man's a separatist, thinks Georgia can go it alone. Georgia gave the USSR Stalin and Shevardnadze, their current foreign minister. Why the hell would they want to go it alone?'

'How exactly do we *help* with Gabashville?'

'You're friends, aren't you? More or less? Just tell Mary anything interesting he says and she'll pass it through.'

18

Major Milova

The elderly Zil parked beyond the gates of the embassy had the profile of a slightly bloated shark and the chrome smile of a limousine escaped from the sixties. Tom thought the woman climbing from the front was a chauffeur until he registered the braid on her shoulders and her peaked hat. Her uniform looked new. Although Tom doubted if anything straight off the peg would come with creases quite that sharp. Her shoes were sensible, though, stretched across the instep and slightly down at the heel. They were polished to a high shine.

She stared at him doubtfully.

'You're late.'

'I was shaving.'

'Not well, from the look of it.'

Putting his hand to his ear, Tom felt a sticky patch where he'd nicked himself with the dry blade. He should have been another ten minutes late to see the ambassador and done it properly. Did he look as English to the Russian as she looked Russian to him? Not slight like a gymnast, or thickset like a shot-putter, but compact and stern, her fair hair folded into a complicated braid.

'At the gate. What did that woman say?'

'Mary? She said not to trust you.'

'Good advice. We won't be trusting you.'

Tom grinned despite himself and the woman looked

offended. 'Tom Fox,' he said, offering his hand. Her shake was every bit as firm as he had expected.

'Svetlana Milova, Major.'

'How do you do.'

'We should go.'

'How far is it to your office?'

'We're not going to my office.'

'You're *militsiya*?'

'I'm Vnutrenniye Voiska.'

'But you are the officer who telephoned Lady Masterton to say her daughter had been spotted shoplifting in GUM?'

'Telephoned who?'

She lied badly and drove well.

'Why,' said Tom, 'would a *militsiya* major tell a missing girl's mother that her daughter had been seen in GUM if it was untrue? Hypothetically speaking.'

'To see if the mother knew where the girl really was.'

Major Milova ran a red light and hit her horn when a truck threatened to pull out from a side street ahead. Glancing across, she checked to see whether Tom had another question, and when he didn't, she added, 'For example, if she dropped everything in hope of finding her daughter, you'd know she didn't.'

At Sad Sam, the major came up with him, looking around his flat with open interest, and hovered in the bedroom doorway while Tom dragged on heavyweight jeans and a warm leather jacket. When she stepped in after him it was to straighten the trousers he'd just hung on his wardrobe door.

'Now we should go.'

'Is it far?'

'Further than foreigners are usually allowed.'

Since that was sixty kilometres from Moscow it didn't tell him much. Climbing into the car, Tom winced as Major

Milova pulled out in front of a truck, which obediently braked to let her in.

'They say you're army,' she said after a while.

Tom nodded, realized she was too busy negotiating the city's outskirts to register his answer and left the reply unspoken. She knew anyway. They drove on in silence, until the roads got rougher and the fields bigger, the sky darkened and the Zil turned on to a dual carriageway with signs for Leningrad.

'You've been shot?'

'Twice,' Tom said.

The major snorted. 'Five times.'

She looked as if she meant it too. Her eyes were on the darkness beyond the window, and her cap was low, making an angle with her cheekbones. Tom found it impossible to guess her age. Younger than him. Her blonde braids were so neat they looked artificial.

'Afghanistan?' he asked.

'No. The only women there are nurses, cooks, support staff. They do their duty on their backs comforting our glorious troops. No woman but a fool would go to Afghanistan. These are campaigns you won't know about.'

'Why not?'

'Because we don't talk about them.'

It took Tom a moment to realize she'd switched to English, and very good English at that. 'Where did you learn?'

'London. Where did you learn Russian?'

'School, then a refresher course before I came out.'

'Your schools teach Russian?'

'Mine did.'

'One of those expensive ones for aristocrats?'

'State-run, boarding school. For children from problem families.'

The car's headlights revealed a town ahead. Falling snow

reduced its main street to shapes glimpsed through fog every few seconds, when the wipers scraped the windscreen clear. The heater gave off little heat and a stale, bar-fire smell. After a while, the major reached without looking to turn it off. The Zil grew chillier.

'You're shivering,' she said after a while.

'I'll survive.'

At a roadside stop – little more than an awning over a cart, with a brazier up front to warm patrons – she halted long enough to let Tom stamp his feet, eat a baked potato, drink harsh coffee from a tin mug and vanish behind a canvas screen to piss. It was too dark for Tom to see how yellow he made the snow. Very, from the size of his headache. It was always the dehydration that got him.

'I'd like to ask you something,' said Major Milova, once the huge black Zil was back on the road. 'Why didn't you tell us sooner about the girl?'

'You're telling me you didn't know?'

'That's not the point.' The major hesitated. 'Although I personally didn't know until yesterday.'

'Should you have done?'

'Only if the cult element is true. You realize she could just be hiding out in the countryside with her boyfriend? Young girls do that. Especially spoilt Western ones. We have people watching the building. They'll be able to tell us more.'

'Who told you yesterday?'

'The minister briefed me himself.'

'Vedenin?'

'He had it from the local *militsiya*. They found the location when looking for something else.'

Tom spent the next ten minutes trying to work out what Alex or anyone else would get out of joining a cult, while the road became a ragged twist of rapidly unfolding hedges on either side. A sense of belonging, maybe? It was easy to see what cult leaders got out of it: money, sex and power. The things everyone wanted. They just got more of them. Tom's thoughts stalled there. Largely because Major Milova glared at a lorry blocking their way and overtook it on the first clear stretch, her wheels bouncing on pitted tarmac at the road's edge. Adjusting for black ice on a bend without seeming to notice, she settled back, the headlights of her Zil revealing the now empty road.

'You stink of alcohol,' she said after a while.

'Last night's. You don't drink?'

'My grandfather drank. You need to stop for vodka?'

Tom shook his head.

'That's something.'

Her words left Tom wondering when one beer had become three, and three five. At what point had drinking in bad bars stopped being part of his cover and became his preferred way of life? When the cracks with Caro appeared? The first time he realized she'd taken a lover? It would be easy to blame her for what he'd become. It was always easier to blame someone else. Dennisov was his perfect drinking partner. Next to Dennisov, he was practically teetotal. And Becca . . . He'd been absent for half her life and back just in time for her death. He'd been drunk for a week after that.

'Did your grandfather ever give up?'

'After my grandmother was arrested.'

'What happened?'

'He lived. She died.'

The set of Major Milova's mouth and the intensity with which she stared at the darkened road made it clear that further questions were unwelcome. *So much hurt compressed into so few words,* Tom thought.

He knew he was guilty of that.

Half an hour later, when the snow finally stopped falling and the night sky cleared, and the moon suddenly became visible, and lights of a lorry they'd overtaken were so far behind they appeared only occasionally, looking like the single headlamp of a distant motorbike, she asked how he had met Gabashville.

'He asked me to dinner.'

'You met him before that,' she said firmly.

'If you know, then why ask?'

'To see how much we can trust you.'

'I thought you said you didn't?'

She sucked her teeth in irritation and drove on.

She drove fast, using all of the road, taking the middle line through corners and overtaking anything in their way. Tom had been told a Zil produced insane amounts of torque but this was tuned to a higher spec than he'd thought possible.

'BMW,' she said, when he told her that.

'You swapped the blocks?'

'Of course not. 7695cc, 315 hp, 120 mph. The Zil has an excellent engine. However, 0 to 100 km in 13 seconds. A West German diplomat was caught . . .' She shrugged. 'Being indiscreet in his choice of friends. He went home hurriedly and left his car. It was a nice car. We borrowed a few parts.'

She took the next corner so fast Tom braced himself as the snow tyres skittered, although she pulled out of the skid before it really began. 'Combat driving?' he asked.

'You did the same course?'

'Something similar.'

'You use live ammunition in training?'

'Thunderflashes and blanks.'

'I don't know why we haven't overrun you yet.'

Villages, a town and then a lone garage loomed out of the

darkness and Major Milova pulled on to its forecourt without indicating, edging her way to the head of a five-vehicle queue and parking diagonally across the front of a Moskva that had been about to reach the pump. The young man inside didn't even seem surprised.

'You want cigarettes?'

Tom dug in his pocket for roubles.

'It's fine,' she said. 'The Soviet Union will pay.'

Clambering out, she tramped to a hut lit by a dangling bulb. Through the wide window, Tom watched her point at a phone, say something and pick up its receiver without waiting for an reply. She listened, talked a little, then listened some more. When she came back she looked thoughtful.

'You know Dennisov?' she said.

'I thought your interest was Gabashville?'

'I'm told you drink in his bar. You're friends.'

'We share a taste in music. He's a good man.'

'Did this good man tell you he killed his commander?' The stiffness of her shoulders told him she expected a reply.

'What should I call you?' Tom asked.

She glanced over at his question. Waited.

'Just, if we're going to be working together . . .'

'Since I have more combat experience, you could try "sir".'

Tom couldn't tell if she was joking. 'If Dennisov killed his CO, why isn't he under arrest? Come to that, why is he still alive?'

'You know who his father is?'

'That's the only reason?'

'It helped. His father is a Soviet Hero. Dennisov hates the man. For some people . . . serious people . . . that's more valuable than any patronage his father could give.' Major Milova hesitated. 'Also, his CO was not a good man. He was not even a good CO. Dennisov's report said the man died on impact. Dennisov and his sergeant survived, the sergeant dying of his wounds soon afterwards.'

'Then how do you know he killed his CO?'

'Before he died, the sergeant told a nurse.'

'What does she say now?'

Major Milova's mouth soured. 'She insists she didn't hear anything like that. As for the colleague she confided in . . . there was an unfortunate incident involving some of Dennisov's troop who thought she talked too much. They decided to fill her mouth for her. She's retired. Gone back to the Crimea, I believe.'

'I've worked with COs who should have been killed.'

'Mine have always been outstanding . . .'

He couldn't tell if that was a joke either.

The major went back to positioning her car for corners and sliding through bends at speeds that had Tom discreetly gripping the door and wondering about the state of her tyres. It wasn't malicious. He wasn't even sure it was conscious. She was simply enjoying herself.

'Svetlana,' she said finally. 'You call me Svetlana.'

'Tom.'

She took her hand from the wheel and they shook awkwardly.

The major's fingers were so close to frozen Tom turned on the Zil's heater without asking. The thing still stank like an electric fire but the interior was almost warm by the time she flicked the car on to a side road and hugged a tight turn that took them on to a narrow track up a hill. The track had been gritted, which was just as well given the black rock rising on one side and the ditch on the other. She brought the Zil to an abrupt halt at a barrier, winding down the window at a gesture from a guard who stepped from the trees.

'Major Milova,' she said.

A torch played across her face while a second guard stood directly in front of the Zil with his SLR at the ready.

'And him?'

'Major Fox. He's with me. We're expected.'

They knew that already, because the bar came up and the first guard rolled away a cement-filled barrel to let the Zil through. The snow banks beyond were pristine and the birches ghostlike. Neat wooden houses stood amongst the trees, each one a hundred paces from the next. The further they drove, the bigger the dachas and the wider the gaps between them. By the time the road turned to climb again, the dachas had high fences and heavy gates protecting wide snow-covered lawns. The last of them had its gates open.

'Vedenin's?'

'Of course. He's expecting us.'

The door opened just as they reached it, and it took Tom a second to recognize the grinning young man standing there. 'Come in,' Vladimir Vedenin said, opening his arms as if he intended to embrace them both. 'The old man's waiting.'

Stepping hurriedly aside, Svetlana indicated that Tom should go first.

Vladimir Vedenin led them through a cluttered hall, past a wall hanging that seemed to show a squat Viking couple standing side by side, and into a kitchen, where Minister Vedenin stood in the middle of an admiring crowd.

Tom recognized three men from the minister's group at the embassy party. A woman whose face he recognized from *Pravda*, astronaut-turned-politician, if he remembered rightly. What he couldn't see was the young man who'd been running Vedenin's security on New Year's Eve. 'Dmitry left us,' Vladimir said.

His father shot him a sharp glance.

Vladimir grinned. 'Look what I've found you.'

'Welcome to my humble holiday home,' said Minister Vedenin.

His heavy fingers gripped Tom's hand for just longer than was comfortable, then his arm came round Tom's shoulders and he began steering him through the crowd and towards a door beyond. 'Vladimir will look after Svetlana. You come with me. We should talk.' They went out on to a small wooden terrace with white painted rails. 'Valentina doesn't like me smoking indoors.'

'Your wife?' asked Tom, watching the man shake a Cohiba Robusto from a branded leather case. The minister lit the cigar and shook his head.

'My wife's dead, sadly. Valentina's a friend.'

He offered Tom a cigar and winced when Tom held up his papirosa. The back door opened behind them. Vedenin scowled, until he saw it was his son.

'We're just having a quick word.'

'I thought our visitor might like a drink.' Vladimir held up a goblet of mulled wine. 'He must be cold after the drive.' Smiling, as if he'd only just noticed Tom was there, he added, 'It was my mother's recipe . . .'

'My son makes it every winter,' said Vedenin.

Vladimir smiled again. 'Every year since she died.'

The wine was hot and sweet and spiced with cloves. There was brandy in there somewhere. Some kind of spirit certainly. The overwhelming taste was of honey though. Tom could feel its stickiness on his lips.

'You like it?' Vladimir asked.

'Very much,' Tom told the young man.

'I'm glad.'

The door to the kitchen closed on the noise inside and left Tom and the minister to the creak of firs, the slight whistle of the wind in the bushes and the sudden hoot of an owl. The minister laughed as Tom froze. 'Sometimes,' he said, 'a cigar is simply a cigar and an owl is simply an owl. You should have called us earlier, you know. When her trail was still warm. We could have acted before this.'

'It wasn't my decision.'

'All the same. You must start thinking of us as friends.'

'You knew, though? You must have done.'

'Not officially.'

The man drew deep on his Cuban cigar, held the smoke for a second and let it trickle into the chilly air. 'Officially I don't know now. The KGB knows the ambassador's step-daughter has run away. The local *militsiya* know delinquents are squatting a deserted house twenty miles from here. The Vnutrenniye Voiska know they have to clear a house of cult-ists using minimum force. I alone know these things are linked. I would be delighted if you'd join me. The others will stay here.'

'The others?' Tom asked.

'It's my son's birthday,' Vedenin said. 'How could I break up his party? We'll be back soon enough and most of my friends are so drunk on *sbiten* they'll barely notice we're gone. How did you find Major Milova?'

'Impressively professional.'

The minister smiled. 'Good. She can drive us.'

19

Night Attack

White trucks parked in the depths of a lay-by, a bank of Scots pine screening them from the road. An empty stall with its back to a ditch showed where someone local sold provisions in the summer to lorry drivers on the road between Moscow and Leningrad. Major Milova pulled in and parked behind the last truck.

The drive from Vedenin's dacha to the lay-by had been slow to the point of sedate and conducted in absolute silence, on her part at least. Vedenin had talked non-stop, pointing out landmarks, roadkill and types of local tree. She'd opened her window only once, when smoke from her boss's cigar had made it briefly impossible for her to see the road ahead.

Suddenly Vedenin said, 'We're here.'

Major Milova took it as a question instead of a statement of the obvious. 'Yes, sir. We're here.'

'You should know,' Vedenin told Tom, 'these men aren't aware that one of the cultists they're retrieving is English. Let's leave it that way.'

A knock on the major's window made Tom jump.

The ghostlike figure's uniform was entirely white, down to his facemask and goggles. He held an AKSU-47 wrapped in pale sacking. What little showed of its barrel was wound with white tape.

Tom got the minister's door.

The ghostlike figure's report was brief and to the point.

A ruined house stood a quarter of a mile back from the road, hidden by forest. His men, an elite force of Spetsnaz within the VV, had it surrounded on all sides. They'd been in position since mid afternoon without being spotted. There had been no movement since dusk and no lights currently showed. Delinquents or gypsies would have lit lamps or built a fire. Since none were visible, they were obviously dealing with those intent on staying hidden.

The man stared at Tom once. He ignored Svetlana.

'Very good,' Vedenin said. 'Now, what's your plan?'

The first part seemed to involve asking the comrade minister if, once they neared the ruined house, he'd be prepared to stay back as he and his guests weren't in camouflage. Tom didn't hear the second part, because the man took Vedenin to one side. Their conversation was short but intense.

Ice made climbing the path difficult, and the hundred yards through firs and dead brambles had Comrade Vedenin gasping. They followed the glow of the Spetsnaz officer's torch, which had been taped to leave only the narrowest beam. The minister slipped so often that Tom ended up taking his elbow. The man was trembling by the time he reached the edge of a frozen lake.

'Where do you want me?'

'We've prepared a hide, sir.'

White netting had been thrown over a frame. Inside, fold-out stools, a huge Thermos flask and heavy night-vision binoculars waited on a tarpaulin that was acting as the floor. The makeshift hut felt like a shooting hide of the kind Tom's in-laws used. The Spetsnaz officer looked relieved when Vedenin slumped on to the nearest of the stools.

'As little fuss as possible,' Vedenin said.

'We understand, sir.'

'Go, then.'

The air inside the hide was clean and cold and tinged with smoke trapped in the minister's jacket. Tom was reminded of Guy Fawkes Night and the last time he'd seen Charlie. Then it had been back to boarding school for the boy and a refresher course in Russian at a country house in Surrey for him. A quick telephone call on Christmas Day, cut short because lunch was beginning, had been their only contact since.

Tom had written, of course. Charlie had asked him to write. But Tom's own letters were stilted and Charlie's read as if a housemaster checked them first.

Picking up the binoculars, Vedenin stared across the lake. 'Hope they're right,' he said. 'That place looks deserted to me.'

He handed the glasses to Tom, who looked in turn. The house was wooden and had three storeys. An octagonal turret rose from one corner. Several windows were smashed. Darkness and the night-vision lenses of the glasses made it impossible to tell what colour the walls had originally been.

The front door was open and slightly off its hinges. The turret had an intricately carved fascia hung below cedar tiles. The fascia had slipped in two places. One bit hung down like a tongue.

It was, even in ruins, an impressive building.

'I'm surprised it hasn't been repaired,' Tom said.

The minister shrugged as if he wasn't surprised at all.

Sweeping the binoculars along the edge of the ice, Tom saw mounds that might be camouflaged men or simply banks of snow. Except for slowly falling flakes there was no movement out there at all. Everything suggested the house was deserted. To Tom, that probably meant it wasn't.

'How will they approach this?' he asked.

'Depends,' Svetlana said.

Five minutes became ten. A lorry on the road below lit the

sky with double headlights as it began cresting a hill. It could be seen several minutes later as a slowly receding glow. An owl hooted from an oak, and a rabbit froze in the moonlight, then bounced away. Reaching for the glasses again, Tom found tight scars in the snow marking its departure.

'What's holding them?' Vedenin muttered.

It was Svetlana who answered. 'I imagine they're waiting for the moon to go in, sir. From the position of the clouds, it won't be long.'

She was right. The moment the moonlight vanished, a snow-mound became a man on the move, white against white, except where his helmet showed against the dark house beyond. He began a slow and steady military crawl towards the half-open front door. He'd have made it too, if the cloud hadn't suddenly thinned.

Flame flashed from the turret.

The snap of a rifle and the crawling man's shout filling the same second.

Welling blood stained the man's uniform, and streaked the snow as he began to retreat. When Tom glanced over, Svetlana's face was frozen. He passed her the glasses without being asked. She grabbed a look before pushing them at the minister.

'This is not good,' Vedenin said.

'No, sir.'

Watching the man crawl put Tom back in the stony fields of a hill farm beyond Enniskillen. There'd been no snow, just the sodden dirt from a fortnight's rain. When the wounded Russian dragged himself half-upright and zigzagged for a tree, reaching safety, Tom sighed with relief.

'Why didn't they fire again?' Vedenin demanded.

Tom said, 'Limited supply of ammunition?'

Svetlana shrugged. 'Possible.'

Out on the lake, nothing moved. The mounds, some of which might simply be mounds, stayed where they were. The next shot came from a different window and a snow mound quivered and remained simply a mound. No cursing man and no blood to stain the white. A third shot came half a minute later from a window beside the turret. This time a mound rolled over and curled into a ball.

The next shot stilled it.

'Minimum force,' Vedenin said. 'Remind them.'

Svetlana put down the binoculars. When Tom opened his mouth, Vedenin waved him off. 'Yes, yes. Go . . .' He sounded tired and looked tireder. An old man out late in the cold, wishing he was somewhere else.

'Major,' Svetlana hissed.

'On my way,' Tom said.

They were halfway there, using trees for cover, when three shots rang from the turret and out on the lake someone screamed.

'Don't,' Svetlana said. 'Just don't.'

She swore at the sound of a whistle, slapping her head with her hand when a dozen mounds stood simultaneously. Movement in the gardens at the sides of the house showed other Spetsnaz were doing the same. Frantic shots cracked from the turret, and one white ghost fell, rolled once and spasmed.

'Svetlana . . .'

'They'll take care,' she promised.

She didn't believe it any more than he did.

Tom watched helplessly as white ghosts closed on the house in a wave. A stun grenade tumbled through a broken window, its blast blowing glass from the next window along. A man ran to the lopsided door, threw in another stun grenade and followed with tear gas. A crouching ghost slapped a charge to the side of the building, twisting away as it blew and smoke billowed around him. Their response to the sniper was swift and brutal and in no way sophisticated.

But it was effective.

Ghost after ghost rolled in through blown-out windows or slammed through shattered doors. Three Spetsnaz stood on a balcony, white ropes hanging from grappling irons behind them. They kicked in the window and entered, AK-47s levelled. Tom heard automatic fire.

One burst, then another.

Smoke billowed from a dozen windows.

All the doors were off their hinges. Shouts burst from inside as men moved from room to room reporting them clear. It was frighteningly familiar and eerily strange. These men were police, not soldiers. But they moved and reacted like a trained troop because that's what they were. Police acting as soldiers. While the British forces in Ulster were soldiers acting as police. Tom shook his head.

'She'll be all right,' Svetlana insisted.

'She'd better be,' replied Tom, meaning it.

'You want to go in?'

'If the building's clear.'

'Wait here . . .'

When Svetlana returned, it was with a flashlight. 'There are no fires and the tear gas is clearing. We're good to go.'

'Anyone seen Alex?'

'Not so far. Keep silent if possible.' She shrugged. 'They train them hard. They train them well. Let's keep things simple.'

'I'm their enemy?'

'Mine too,' she said. 'I'm just a little bit more sophisticated about it. I don't mind having a drink before killing you.'

Men holding dynamo lights looked up as Svetlana brought

Tom through the front door. Their facemasks hung loose and they had their goggles hooked over their helmets. They watched Tom warily. A man in leather jacket and jeans among men in uniform. A stranger with a uniformed major at his side. The air in the hall was still sharp from tear gas. He could smell cordite and smoke from the flashbangs.

When Tom made for the stairs, Svetlana followed.

The ruined house had been grand once, filled with servants, portraits, good china . . . the things revolution is supposed to sweep away. Horsehair poked from a leaking sofa behind them, paint flaked from a portrait they passed on the stairs, the landing wallpaper peeling back to bare wood.

'Problem?' Svetlana asked, when a man moved to stop them climbing the next flight of stairs.

'The sniper's up there, Comrade Major.'

'Dead?'

'As a rat.'

'Was he alone?' Svetlana asked.

'Yes, Comrade Major.'

'Good.'

Tom followed her up a spiral so rotten it sank like turf under his heel.

The sniper was on the floor of a little landing at the top. His rifle had been propped against the wall. It was small bore, bolt action. The kind of thing Caro's father might buy Charlie for Christmas. One of the ghosts had torn down a curtain and tossed it over his face. A courtesy Tom hadn't expected.

Svetlana didn't protest when he lifted back the cloth.

'Oh Christ,' said Tom.

Thirteen, fourteen? Tom doubted he was older.

He crossed himself, shut the child's eyes from instinct and began a prayer. It was short and to the point. He doubted the dead boy had any sins that really mattered. He refused to accept that the boy should be held responsible for those of his father. He expected God to reserve vengeance for who-ever was really responsible.

The boy was dressed in a camouflage uniform better suited to the desert and outmoded enough to have come from an army surplus store. It was at least two sizes too big for him, and an extra hole had been punched through his belt to make it small enough to fit round his waist. His face was perfect, his fair hair long for Russia, his eyes blue and already dimming before Tom's fingers smoothed his eyelids.

A row of machine-gun bullets had opened his chest.

Blood welled from wounds that looked neat enough from the front but would, Tom knew, be a matted mess from behind. The best you could say was that the child had died quickly, quite possibly in the first moment if one of the bul-lets had opened his heart.

'Fuck this,' Tom said. 'Really. Fuck this.'

'You recognize him?' Svetlana asked.

'Beziki's other son.'

'You're sure?'

Tom nodded mutely, remembering the photograph the fat man had produced at supper. How would he feel if he lost Charlie as well? How could the fat man possibly cope? Tom wanted cold anger. He wanted his numbness back. All he had was a hot flame for a heart.

'Why would Beziki's boy do this?' he demanded.

And Svetlana's answer came as easily as if it was obvious.

'Because he had no choice. Because he was protecting his father or someone else. Because the consequences of not doing it were worse.'

'Ah,' said a voice. 'They said I'd find you here.'

Vedenin's words made Svetlana stiffen. The minister came

to stand behind her. He barely glanced at the sniper. The old man's face was drawn, his thoughts turned inwards. 'We've found children.'

'Children, sir?' Svetlana said.

'A dozen or so. In the cellar. Behind locked doors.'

'Are they all right?'

'You'd better come with me.'

Trying not to think about what he might find, Tom followed him down the spiral staircase, past a dozen men he barely noticed. If he'd had the adrenaline rush of battle, it might have been different. If you could call killing a child holding a rabbit rifle battle. But all he felt was a growing dread as Vedenin led the way to where steps descended to vaulted cellars below.

At the bottom, five children sprawled on a rug.

Three boys, two girls, all young.

They could have been sleeping, but they weren't. In the middle stood a two-litre bottle of Coke, the real thing, not some Soviet copy. It was a quarter gone. Paper cups lay nearby. A crime-scene photographer was already shooting the corpses, his flash bleaching out their faces and throwing shadows on the wall.

'Any more?' Tom demanded.

'In the next room.'

'How many?'

'Eleven so far.'

'Is Alex one of them?'

The old man looked shattered, on the verge of tears. All the bombast, all the pride in his elite troop had gone out of him. Whatever he'd been expecting, it wasn't this. 'I don't know,' he said. He gestured helplessly at the cellar beyond. 'You tell me.'

20

In the Cellar

Tom stepped unthinking over bodies, moving past the ghosts, who shuffled aside to let him through. An officer dipped to retrieve a half-empty Coke bottle and sniffed it, putting it down more or less where he found it. Only the camera flashes and photographers suggested that this was a crime scene.

The rest of them seemed to have forgotten that.

Five more bodies lay in the cellar beyond, one of them dark-haired and on her front with a denim jacket neatly folded under her head, as if she were sleeping. Her arms were pale, her jeans new, her plimsolls undone. The one shaken free said her death had not been as peaceful as her form made it seem.

Kneeling, Tom reached for her.

When he hesitated, fingers gripped his shoulder hard. He could smell Svetlana's scent and feel the heat of her on the back of his neck. 'Do it,' she said.

He rolled the girl over and saw a stranger.

Very beautiful and very young, but a stranger. Unbroken but for the fact she was no longer alive. The police hadn't let him see Becca. What the paramedics cut from the Mini the authorities put in a box after the autopsy, screwed down the lid and advised Tom not to look. Even now, even this many months later, he felt guilt that he hadn't made someone show him.

'Yours?' Vedenin asked.

Mine's already buried, Tom almost replied.

Taking Tom's silence as a negative, Vedenin followed Tom towards the door to the cellars and stopped to talk to the Spetsnaz officer who had briefed him earlier.

'Six boys, five girls,' he said on his return. 'That's the lot.'

'Eleven in total,' said Svetlana.

'Twelve,' Tom corrected her. 'With Beziki's boy upstairs.'

Comrade Vedenin stared at him. 'That's Gabashville's son?' His face, already pale, was unreadable as he reached into his pocket for a cigar, lighting it mechanically, his first puff a stronger imitation of their warm breath in the frozen air.

'Yes, sir, I think so.'

Vedenin peeled a strip of tobacco leaf from his lip and flicked it on to the crime scene floor. He looked round the room and when he turned back his face was hollow, almost haunted. Dropping his cigar, barely smoked, he ground it under his heel without really noticing, his movements mechanical.

'At least your girl isn't here. I suppose that's something.'

'I pity her mother,' Svetlana said.

Both men turned to stare at her.

'If Alex were here and dead, at least she'd know where her daughter was. As it is, she still won't know and we're no closer to finding her.' She shrugged at Vedenin's look. 'A hard truth is better than no truth. You ask her mother.'

'Svetlana . . .'

'I'll wait outside,' she told him.

'Her childhood was complicated,' Vedenin told Tom, lighting another cigar. 'Sometimes the ones with complicated backgrounds make the best officers.' He looked Tom up and down, as if seeking proof of this. 'I'm told yours was similarly messy?'

'Who told you that?'

'People,' he said heavily.

The way Vedenin kept staring round the cellar made Tom wonder whether he simply couldn't believe what he was seeing or hoped somehow that if he looked hard enough he might change it. Several times the minister opened his mouth to say something before changing his mind. Finally, he stubbed his cigar out on the wall, barely a quarter smoked and in total disregard of the need not to corrupt evidence.

For a second, his hand hovered over the pocket where he kept his cigar case and then he shrugged. 'We should go,' he said.

'What happens now?' Tom asked.

'Svetlana will drive you back to Moscow.'

'I mean here, sir. What happens here?'

'I imagine the case will go to the local *militsiya*. I can see no evidence of a cult. Can you? Simply local delinquents squatting in a ruined house and poisoning themselves with homemade alcohol. It happens daily. I shouldn't say that to a foreigner but you must have heard rumours. They'll try to match the dead to files on missing children. Well, someone will. I doubt they'll find much.'

'And Gabashville's child?'

'If this is him, then he obviously fell in with a bad crowd. Given his upbringing that's hardly surprising. The cult of individuality. First they want rock music, then . . .' The old man looked around him. 'You get this.'

A howl of sirens from the road prevented Tom from answering.

A few minutes later, panting paramedics hurtled in, too late to do anything but kneel by each body to confirm death and decide in which order to load the stretchers. A crumpled-looking man in a cheap suit came in after them, glowering at the sight of the Spetsnaz.

'If you'll excuse me . . .' Vedenin said to Tom.

He wandered over and within seconds the crumpled man was nodding seriously, and nodding some more to confirm that he was paying attention and agreed with everything the minister said. It was a surprisingly effective display of power on Vedenin's part. Vedenin clapped the man on the back one last time, nodded curtly to the Spetsnaz officer and headed for the door, glancing over his shoulder to say Tom should follow.

Outside, the first stretchers were being carried down the track.

Three ambulances were parked behind two VV trucks, the only ones left. Despite a paramedic's shout, Tom clambered into the first ambulance and began pulling back a sheet. A growled order from Svetlana stopped the paramedic from trying to drag him out of there. She watched Tom go from stretcher to stretcher with something close to pity in her eyes. By the time he'd checked the last of them, a tight knot of fury had taken root. He'd known Alex wasn't there.

The pain in his chest made him look anyway.

'Where's Vedenin?' he demanded.

'The minister's gone home.'

In what? Tom wanted to ask.

A forlorn man in a crumpled suit by the side of the road gave him his answer. Vedenin had taken the pathologist's car.

'We should leave,' Svetlana said, heading for the Zil.

To Tom's puzzlement, she opened the heavy rear door for him and he clambered in, feeling the cold leather like ice through his jeans. The huge car coughed into life and the paramedics and Spetsnaz stood back to let them edge out of the lay-by on to the empty road beyond. 'Better,' Svetlana said.

A mile later, she pulled off the road, hard ruts frozen to the sharpness of stone juddering under her wheels. She killed the lights, leaving the stars needle sharp now that the clouds had passed. Leprous moonlight lit the hills to one side.

Tom reached for his door handle, wondering if she'd already drawn her sidearm. When she didn't turn, he clambered out, slamming the door with a thud so loud it dislodged snow from a fir behind him.

Now was when she should drive away.

Then reverse fast and hard.

He'd seen a man killed that way.

That had to be what this was about. Vedenin leaving so he didn't have to be around when the rubbish was tidied. *I'm shivering,* Tom realized. Alcohol, or the lack of it. Cold perhaps. God knows, it was cold enough. He refused to accept that it might be fear. The car didn't move and Svetlana remained where she was.

Eventually, Tom realized that he was meant to take his place up front.

Shaking imaginary drops from the cock still safely in his jeans, as if he'd been pissing a bucketful against the Zil's back wheels, he slid himself on to its front seat. His heart racing, his nerves shot. One hand was shaking so fiercely it wouldn't go in his pocket. His certainty that she'd been about to kill him seemed suddenly pitiful.

'How long has it been like that?' she asked.

'The hand? Six months.'

'What does your doctor say?'

'Nerve damage from a bullet to the shoulder made worse by a badly repaired vertebra and a trapped nerve.'

'Do you believe him?'

'No.' Tom shook his head.

Svetlana smiled grimly and said she wouldn't either. If

they were good doctors, proper doctors, what were they doing in the army anyway? The local bars were shut, she added, but a military base on the way back had an officers' mess that was bound to be open. He'd be able to get vodka there. Without waiting for his reply, she put the Zil into the first of its two gears and the huge car moved away, steady and remorseless as a festival chariot dragged by an elephant.

Tom waited for her to mention what had happened at the ruined house.

He waited long enough for the road to widen and become dual carriageway and then single lane again. He waited while road signs counted off the miles to Moscow and villages became towns and then fields again.

Too much was wrong with what had happened.

How had the VV known Alex was there? If she'd ever been there. And what evidence was there for that? Tom waited, and he waited.

And she said nothing.

They slowed at the sign for a military base and Tom shook his head, the guards on the gate turning to watch them as they cruised by. The roads were long, Svetlana's driving uncharacteristically careful and the hour late, and Tom found his head nodding and jerked himself awake time and again. When sleep came it was welcome, until the dreams came too. He woke to find Svetlana watching him.

'What did I say?' he demanded.

'You said nothing.'

'Then why are you staring?'

Leaning across, she put her fingers briefly to Tom's face and her fingertips came away wet. 'You cry in your sleep,' she said. 'I didn't know people could do that. Perhaps they can't. Perhaps it's just you . . .'

The hand Tom lifted to his own face shook badly.

'Are you sure you don't want me to find you some vodka?'

'This isn't about alcohol.'

Svetlana sighed.

'It's not,' he insisted.

'Whatever you say.'

'Have you heard of *Macbeth*?'

'One of your generals?'

'A play by one of our great writers. Shakespeare.'

'I know Shakespeare. Tchaikovsky turned his *Romeo and Juliet* into a fantasia and Prokofiev wrote a ballet. I saw that traitor Nureyev dance it in London when I was a child.'

'Why go if he was a traitor?'

'Because he could dance. So, this play of yours . . .'

'A woman has someone killed and believes her hand is cursed.'

'Your hand is cursed?' She slowed the car and for a moment Tom thought she was going to pull over. Instead she kept the speed at a steady thirty and waited. When he didn't say anything, she asked, 'This curse is something you did?'

'Something I did. And something I didn't.'

'The didn't has to do with your daughter?'

'How do you know about that?'

'Sir Edward sent your file across. We insisted. We didn't expect it to be quite so comprehensive. What was the did? That bit was missing.'

'I doubt the ambassador knows. In fact, I doubt it's on file anywhere . . .' That was the truth of it. The only way it would ever find its way into his file was if the powers that be decided to hang him out to dry. And if they wanted that, he'd have been under oath in London preparing to face a select committee.

'I killed two people.'

'People you shouldn't have killed?'

'So I'm told.'

'Then why aren't you in trouble?'

'I'm here, aren't I?'

'I mean real trouble.'

'Because they can't prove it.'

'Or don't want to prove it,' Svetlana said.

Somehow Tom had known she'd understand.

'So,' Svetlana said, 'vodka no longer helps?'

'Vodka always helps. But tomorrow I'll have to tell Alex's mother about tonight. And Alex's stepfather will be on to Vedenin asking what happens next.'

'I'm not sure he's the right man to ask.'

'Who is?'

Svetlana dropped down into first to take a corner so tight the Zil only just fitted around it. She was negotiating tight bends on a country road that obviously hadn't seen a snow-plough in weeks, and Tom realized they were off any route he recognized. They were heading east of Moscow, which had to be that low glow in the distance, like a fire.

'I'm taking you to him,' she said.

'Where does he live?'

'At home.'

'Whose?' Tom asked.

Svetlana smiled. 'Mine.'

21

The Commissar

They pulled up outside a small wooden house with closed shutters. A vegetable garden could be seen to one side, carefully framed by picket fencing but buried under a thick layer of snow. Tom rocked in the wind that ripped across the open space in front of the house.

'You'd better stand back,' Svetlana said.

She knocked, knocked again and stood smiling in the bright beam of a torch, apparently undeterred by the double-barrelled shotgun that poked through beneath. It disappeared immediately.

'Who's he?'

'An Englishman.'

An old man peered at Tom from between a heavy moustache and even heavier brows. He looked as Stalin might have if he'd let his hair grow long and go white. He stepped closer and the gun came up again.

'Not German?'

'I'm English,' promised Tom. 'Honestly.'

'He speaks Russian. How do you know he's not a spy?'

'If he is,' Svetlana said, 'at least he's not a German spy.'

The man grunted and stepped back to let them in. He lit a hurricane lamp, which instantly filled his front room with the stink of paraffin, and pushed a half-burned log back into what was left of the embers of a fire. It glowed and caught along a splinter, and he smiled when Svetlana immediately dropped to her knees and fanned it into flames with a strip of cardboard she found by the wall. He was still smiling when she finally stopped feeding the flames with kindling and put a new log on top.

Climbing to her feet, she said, 'This is my grandfather.'

When Tom offered his hand, the man glanced at his grand-daughter.

'Really English?'

She nodded and bony fingers closed around Tom's, reminding him for a second of both the strength and feel of his mother's, which were also broken at the nails and cal-loused enough to catch on his skin when she took his hand as a child.

'You call my grandfather "commissar",' Svetlana said.

'So,' the commissar said, 'why are you here?'

'He needs vodka.'

'I didn't say that . . .'

'Only one,' she told her grandfather. 'Make it big.'

'And then you'll be off . . .?'

'Unless you'd like us to stay?'

The old man's expression was unreadable, to Tom at least. Perhaps Svetlana knew her grandfather's thoughts because she blushed a little, and knelt to push some of the kindling a little further into the flames and add another log.

'Stay, if you must,' he said.

'He can sleep there,' Svetlana said, nodding to an old sofa covered with a half-bald tapestry blanket of trees and flowers.

'If he must,' the old man agreed.

The house was old and small and made from stripped logs on the outside and roughly planed planks within. The room Tom was given obviously did for reading and writing and eat-ing and lazing, everything apart from cooking and sleeping from the look of it. It was comfortable in a way he liked.

Small and sparse, as if the shaggy-haired old man had pared his life down to essentials, refusing to let the detritus of a long life overfill the space around him as most old people did.

The vodka Svetlana brought him was huge.

Tom drank it down in one after she'd gone and settled himself on the sofa with the blanket and his thoughts.

Talk to me, Caro used to say.

In the early days, that was. At night, in the darkness.

She never had an answer when he asked, *About what?*

What could he have told her anyway? Even then, half of what was in his head wasn't safe for her to know. The other half he didn't know how to put into words. So they fucked, a lot. And for a while that did instead. He thought of the fucking and the darkness and the silence afterwards. Two people who didn't know what to say to each other when the *Oh God*s and the *Oh yes*es and the grunting were done.

What Tom didn't think about . . .

What he didn't let himself think about were eleven dead teenagers on a frozen cellar floor and a blue-eyed boy with his chest opened by bullets. Those would lead him straight to Becca, rigid with terror in her final seconds before her white Mini hit its tree. *Instant,* the police said. *Instant,* said the coroner.

Instant can be a long time.

It was so cold in the room that he curled into a ball like a hibernating animal and pulled the musty blanket around him and felt himself shiver against the cold, his thoughts and the horror of what he'd seen in that cellar.

He never used to be this weak.

Of course, he could put his jeans and jacket back on, but that would mean throwing off the blanket and losing what little warmth he'd collected. He might not have been anywhere colder but he'd sat out far worse, and was on the edge of despising his own self-pity when a door creaked and he wondered which of them needed the privy outside at the back.

'Move over,' Svetlana whispered.

'What are you doing?'

'Getting cold.' Lifting the blanket, she felt its thinness and sighed. When Svetlana returned, she had another blanket, equally old from the feel of it, although the darkness made it impossible to see. She climbed in beside Tom and he felt the warmth of her hip through a cotton gown as she barged him further over.

'What are you doing?'

'I want to see if you cry in your sleep at night too.'

She folded his arm across her as if it was the most natural thing in the world, shaped her body to his and curled in tight, her warmth warming him until he began producing warmth of his own She removed his hand when it found her breast and placed it firmly on her hip, which was hard and muscled and badly ridged just above the wing of her hipbone. 'Bullet?' Tom asked.

She nodded and he put her hand to his leg.

'Pistol?' she said.

'Rifle.'

Her finger traced the scar.

'Small calibre,' she said doubtfully.

A moment later she was so deeply asleep her breath sounded like waves stroking shingle. He woke once in the night and found her gone, rolling into her space, which was still warm. When Tom woke again, she was back and he found they'd shifted sides. A shutter was folded back to show streaks of red. He thought it early morning until he looked at his watch. It was morning right enough, just

157

not early. The ambassador would be wondering where he was. Looking around him, Tom wondered where he was too.

'You don't,' said Svetlana from behind him. 'Cry, that is. Well, not when I was watching. Now I must use the privy.'

'You're awake.' If the old man glanced towards the double blankets, that was all he did. Shuffling to the kitchen, he left the door open and Tom saw him tip two spoons of coffee into a saucepan, fill it with water from a jug and put it on to boil. He put out a mug, hesitated and found another two, and looked beyond Tom to where his granddaughter was coming in from the cold. Her nightdress was thick but her nipples still stood out and she crossed her arms reflexively.

'Just coffee,' she said, as if he'd asked.

The commissar cut bread, grilled it, added a slice from a slab of cheese and put it in front of her. 'Eat,' he said.

Dragging on his jeans, Tom found his jacket and took himself outside, deciding it was best to leave them to it. The old man was eating toast and Svetlana was pouring coffee when he returned. 'Sit down,' she said.

Tom glanced at her and she scowled.

'It's my country.'

Her grandfather grinned sympathetically as Tom took his place. Leaning forward, he said, 'She's never brought anyone back here before . . .'

Svetlana spun round.

'Well, have you?'

'It's a working relationship,' she said stiffly.

He glanced at the crumpled sofa. 'Of course it is. Now tell me why you're really here. You could have driven another hour and spared yourself this.'

'I like it here. I like seeing you.'

'The second of those is true,' he told Tom. 'The first is not.' Reaching for his coffee, he winced at its heat or maybe its taste, which was bitter as ground acorn. 'She doesn't lie,' he said. 'Not usually. Only about that. So, ask what you came here to ask. Or say what you came to say . . .'

Svetlana told him everything.

She began with Alex going missing, Tom's search beyond the ring road and his trip out to the university before that. Where, she told her grandfather, he'd talked to one foreign student and beaten up another. Things Tom didn't know she knew. She ended with the drive out to Vedenin's dacha and the storming of the ruined house. She was frank about the stupidity of the attack.

'Apparent stupidity,' the old man corrected.

He made her start again from the beginning and asked questions that Svetlana had Tom fill in when she didn't know the answer herself. Then he had Tom describe the attack and listened for discrepancies. He asked about internal politics at the embassy, the ambassador's popularity, his competence.

Tom told him about the note Alex was meant to have left, and the one Sir Edward received later, while stressing that he'd seen neither, only knew what he'd been told about the first, and had been informed by Sir Edward that he didn't have sufficient security clearance for the contents of the second.

'*Sir Edward*,' the old man said contemptuously. 'That's the English. Still clinging to their titles.'

Svetlana looked at him.

'Commissar is different,' he said. 'Commissar is a rank.'

'Which has been abolished.'

'Not while I'm alive it hasn't.' Her grandfather lifted toast crumbs from his plate to his mouth with his thumb and shuffled himself and his thoughts into some sort of order. 'You sure you want him to hear this?'

Tom was the *him*, obviously. The jerk of the old man's chin was dismissive enough to render him invisible.

'He was at the siege.'

'That would never have been allowed in the old days.'

'Things change.'

'Usually for the worst.'

'You know that's not true.' Svetlana's voice was sharp.

The old man's hand found hers for a second. 'Not always true,' he agreed. 'I'm old enough to remember Ilyich . . . Vladimir Ilyich Lenin,' he told Tom, who was apparently back in the conversation. 'And the early days of the Boss. Stalin wasn't bad then. It was only towards the end . . .'

Svetlana sucked her teeth.

'Sveta disagrees. But I was there.'

Pushing back his chair, he left and returned a few seconds later with a rack of medals that he tossed clatteringly on to the little table. 'The usual,' he said, 'plus some extra.' Putting a Communist Party card next to them, he added a KGB card and finally a fading NKVD card, from the days when the People's Commissariat enforced the Party's will.

The man pictured on the last of those was just about recognizable in the white-haired pensioner in front of Tom.

'My granddaughter comes to me for advice occasionally. Usually alone. Eventually I hope to understand what is different about this time.'

'The missing girl is English,' Svetlana said.

'That is not enough.'

'Did you know a man called Golubtsov?' Tom asked.

The old man looked at his granddaughter and his glance was sharp. 'You brought him here to ask that?'

'He was NKVD,' Tom said. 'His son died in Berlin.'

'I know who he was. Everyone knew who he was. Marshal Beria's deputy. As for his son . . .' The old man looked sour.

'Have you any idea how many young men died for Berlin? We lost a hundred thousand, three hundred thousand wounded or too sick to stand. Two thousand armoured vehicles destroyed. The enemy lost more.'

He sat back and Tom watched Svetlana make herself wait. She looked younger in her nightgown, with one of the blankets from his sofa thrown round her shoulders. When it became obvious the old man intended to say no more, she shrugged and turned to Tom. 'Who mentioned this man to you?'

'Someone I met.'

'It was Gabashville,' she told her grandfather.

When Tom looked at her, she added, 'We have every word you said to him in that steam room on tape.'

'Then why ask me if you already know?'

'To see how often you lie. Now,' she said, 'introduce yourself.'

Pulling his embassy pass from his jacket, Tom added his military ID, and then, because he still carried them, dipped into the back of his wallet to extract four or five tiny photographs, shuffling them to find the one he wanted.

Not Caro in a pair of Levi 501s, with his Honda 450cc in the background. Not Charlie in gumboots on a tractor. Not even the snapshot of Caro holding Becca the week she was born. The photo Tom wanted showed him in a cassock, in the days before he met Caro and changed denomination. He looked very young indeed to be training for the priesthood. Younger than he had remembered.

'Now I understand,' the old man said.

'I didn't know this,' Svetlana said. 'This was not in his file.'

The old man's smile was grim. 'Then it is a lucky coincidence. I too trained in a seminary. Outside Tsaritsyn, which became Stalingrad, then Volgograd. Now, I've reached an age when some days I wonder if it will become Tsaritsyn again.'

He smiled at his granddaughter's shock.

'Allow an old man his thoughts.' To Tom, the commissar said, 'Stalin trained in a seminary too. So that's three of us who found another faith. In the end, I suspect, faith fades, then perhaps comes back transmuted. Now, tell me about Minister Vedenin. How he behaved. How he reacted.'

The commissar shut his eyes to listen.

At one point Svetlana got up to boil another saucepan for coffee, but Tom could see her listening, matching her reactions to his.

'Now the actual attack.'

The more Tom told the commissar the less sense it made.

An elite force of VV shock troops, the Soviet Union's gendarmerie, perfectly able to take up position in the snow and lie motionless until darkness but shocked to discover a ruined house protected by one teenage boy with a rabbit gun.

They hadn't been expecting resistance.

It made Tom wonder what they had been expecting.

'See,' the commissar told his granddaughter. 'Your friend doesn't need me.'

She slammed a mug of coffee down in front of Tom, slopping it over the edges of the mug. She banged another down in front of her grandfather, and gripped her own mug so tightly Tom thought she'd crush it. Her glare when she looked at Tom said she regretted bringing him, that she wished he wasn't there. 'Vedenin believed she was there, didn't he?'

'Yes,' Tom said.

'Did he?' The commissar asked.

'I think so,' Tom replied.

'Then you should ask yourself two questions.'

Tom already knew what they were. What made Minister Vedenin think Alex was there? And why wasn't she?

More to the point . . . had she ever been there?

If so, and if she had been taken from the house before the attack could begin, Tom needed to ask himself who had her now.

Mary's Room

The rooms in the embassy became less grand the higher you climbed. That was the nature of mansions. Rooms to impress, rooms to live in, rooms for those who served those who lorded it below. If William Morris, the socialist scion of a famous banking family, could build his red-brick mansion to that pattern, why should a tsarist shipping magnate be more modest?

In Morris's case, the windows in his servants' quarters were above eye level to stop them looking down on what he and his pre-Raphaelite friends were doing in the gardens. Sleeping with each other's wives, mostly. The only reason Tom knew this was a school trip to Red House at fifteen. He'd tried and failed in the gardens to do to a girl called Jane what Rossetti undoubtedly managed with William Morris's wife, Jane's namesake: get his hand up her skirt.

'You're looking thoughtful,' Mary Batten said.

Tom's gaze was impassive.

'Do I want to know what you're thinking?'

'I doubt it,' he said.

Mary Batten's office was in the attic of the embassy. It was small and narrow-windowed, with little in the way of view. What interested Tom was not the things an estate agent would have to twist to make them sound palatable but the fact someone like Mary Batten, who could have an office next to the ambassador's if she wanted, would choose to exile herself here.

'It's quiet,' she said, before he could ask. Adding, 'Sir Edward thinks you're trouble. Is he right?'

'Trouble and me are first cousins at best.'

'Don't be flippant, Fox.'

'I'm not. You might want to read this . . .' Tom handed her a sheet of paper.

It was not the report he was meant to be writing on the place of religion in Soviet culture, and whether it could be leveraged to the West's advantage. To which the answer was yes, obviously. If Stalin could rip down a cathedral and replace it with a swimming pool, then, with the right leverage, the country could be persuaded to fill in the swimming pool and put up a cathedral. What he gave Mary now was a step-by-step walk-through of everything he remembered about the fuck-up that was the infiltration of the ruined house by the lake. With a postscript pointing out that Sir Edward had only Minister Vedenin's say-so that Alex had been there at all.

Mary skimmed it, stopping twice.

'You're saying they attacked early?'

'I'm saying they didn't need to attack at all.'

She grunted to herself, reached for a mug of coffee that was already empty, then nodded her thanks when Tom refilled it from a Cona machine on a side table. Wincing at its bitterness, she reread the final three paragraphs. The ones about elite VV Spetsnaz troops trampling a crime scene as if they were teenage delinquents kicking over sandcastles. Looking up, she said, 'I probably won't make copies of this.'

When Tom snorted, she smiled.

'Anything else?' she asked. That was his cue to leave, but there *was* something.

'Is there anywhere we can get decent coffee?'

'Why would I want to do that?'

'So you can report back to Sir Edward on my mental health?'

'Report,' she said. 'You don't need "back".'

'Have you ever met my wife?'

Her eyes narrowed. 'I knew her at school,' she said. 'It wasn't a close friendship. You don't strike me as Caro's type.'

'I'm not,' Tom said.

'If you'd wait outside . . .'

A couple of secretaries used the corridor as Mary made a call, put down the receiver, hesitated for a moment, then made another. She kept her voice too low for Tom to hear more than the occasional word.

'Right,' she said, appearing in her doorway.

Instead of leaving the embassy, she led the way down to a kitchen he hadn't known existed. Inside the little room was an espresso machine of the type Tom recognized from Bar Italia in Soho. It looked like an engine from a fifties' idea of a space rocket. 'The diplomatic pouch has its perks,' she said, seeing his surprise.

Less than a minute after they'd arrived, the tiny room cleared without Mary saying a word. It couldn't be easy being black, a woman and, if rumour could be believed, single.

'So,' she said, 'how are you?'

Tom looked puzzled.

'So I can report back to Sir Edward.'

'I found a cellar full of dead children. How do you think?'

'Fair enough. What do you really want to talk about?'

'Minister Vedenin. He was shocked. Properly shocked. The more I think about it the more certain I am that he expected to find Alex there. Instead he found no Alex and a dozen dead children. So perhaps someone took Alex before we arrived?'

'Assuming she was there at all.'

'Vedenin thought she was.'

'You think Vedenin thought she was.'

'I'm certain of it,' Tom said. He was too. Writing out his account of the attack on the house had helped him put his thoughts in order. Vedenin had been confident, almost smug in his belief that Alex was about to be saved. Tom was pretty sure that was the word he'd used. Vedenin's shock at finding a cellar full of dead children had deflated not only his confidence but his entire being.

The man had looked as if he'd been sucker-punched.

Perhaps he had been, politically at least. The question was by whom?

And Tom couldn't shake his feeling that Vedenin's son was involved somehow in Alex's original disappearance. He'd been so certain of it that he'd wondered for a moment, back in the burned-out warehouse, whether the boy he'd found with his wrists wired behind his back could be Vladimir Vedenin.

Instead of whoever 'Kotik' had really been.

Mary snorted when Tom said this.

'They're untouchable. The Vladimirs of this world. As long as their fathers are alive. Even after, if they're already on the ladder, they're probably well placed enough to protect themselves. How much do you know about the Mafia?'

'Beziki . . .?'

Mary Batten picked up the tiny cup of coffee she'd made and sniffed the espresso inside. 'The real Mafia,' she said.

'I've watched *The Godfather*.'

'That's probably good enough. Now imagine a whole state given over to Vito Corleone's children and grandchildren. Vedenin's no worse than the rest. Special schools, special shops, a different class of travel. He's young, spoilt, indulged. But so are rich kids everywhere. The difference is that here the law really can't touch them. He ran down his father's chauffeur; it was recorded as an accidental death. One girl-friend had a breakdown. Another needed an abortion . . .' Mary hesitated, sniffed at her espresso again. 'That last rumour might have been spread intentionally.'

'In God's name why?'

'To make his interest in girls seem stronger. Vladimir did a year in London at the LSE, during which he kept his nose clean. No drugs. No gambling. He was at a party in Chelsea where a rent boy drowned, but there was no suggestion he knew the boy. Being photographed with Marlene Dietrich is about the most exotic thing he's done. Oh, and hunting wild boar with a crossbow.'

'No unhealthy interest in young girls? No interest in cults?'

'That's all we have on file. You really think Vladimir's involved in Alex's disappearance?'

Tom nodded.

'But you have no proof?'

Beyond the way he'd touched Alex's wrist at the party? The arch, almost contemptuous way he spoke to his father? The way his gaze slid across people without really seeing them? Something about the young man made Tom's skin crawl.

And there was his mocking comment about the soldier who ran his father's security. *Dmitry left us.* The sharpness of Minister Vedenin's look.

Tom thought of the body found after the fire.

'How do I get to question Vladimir?'

'You don't, unless Sir Edward agrees. Even then it would need to be arranged through his father. I doubt Vedenin would allow it and if he did, I imagine he'd want to sit in on the meet-ing himself. More likely, he'd question the boy himself without us being present. That's if he allowed questions at all.'

'The minister's protective?'

'He's his father.' Finally sipping her espresso, Mary closed her eyes. When she opened them again it was to fix Tom with a steely gaze.

'The boy's handsome, charming and able to work a room. He probably touched the wrists of a dozen women, mine included. Find me another one who's disappeared and I'll put in a formal request to talk to Vedenin about his son. But if you go after the boy, you need to understand you're on your own.'

23

Wax Angel

Once upon a time there was a girl. Very young, very beautiful, very clever. She was not that girl. She'd never been any of those things. Not really. But she'd given birth to the girl who was . . .

Wax Angel had problems getting beyond that.

She didn't like the bit that came next, not when it had happened and not now. The girl, the beautiful girl, was on the list of things she tried not to remember.

Perhaps top of it.

Crossing the stream of traffic on Petrovka Street without looking – one of life's little thrills, and God knows there were few enough these days – she kept the Englishman and the rusty Moskvitch shadowing him in sight. The Englishman was walking slowly and in something of a daze, which was just as well given the state of her knees. She hoped his thoughts were happier than hers but, judging by the bleakness in his face, she doubted it.

Once upon a time there was a girl. Very young, very beautiful, very clever. She was not that girl. She'd never been any of those things. Not really. But she'd given birth to the girl who was and an ambitious little fool had turned her daughter's head with flattery and presents and later denied the child she carried was his.

They were bad days in the shadow of worse ones. The state was poor and food scarce but the USSR had Sputnik and the Americans didn't, and there was supposed to be consolation in that . . .

From the back of a maroon-and-cream Volga, the model with the ivory steering wheel and chrome grill with a five-pointed star, she'd watched people queue for hours for food and wondered if the old men behind the Kremlin Wall really thought being able to watch a satellite launch on the newsreel made up for that.

No one asked her to queue, obviously.

They simply asked her to dance and dance she did.

All of the great roles in all of the great theatres. Until London. Nureyev wasn't even meant to be on that tour. He was too temperamental, too unreliable. The little brat was only there because the Kirov's lead had injured himself. Anyone but a fool could see that Nureyev was self-obsessed enough to do something stupid, like defect.

Wax Angel's beautiful girl was gone by then.

She shouldn't have been surprised that the rest of her life followed.

The Englishman was speeding up now, head down and shoulders hunched in that heavy wax jacket of his. She let him go like a fish that snaps its line and surges on.

She knew where he was headed like a lamb to the slaughter.

Where he always went: to get drunk with the cripple and get fed by General Dennisov's pyromaniac daughter. Following him had been fun. Especially as he obviously considered himself too skilled to be followed. But she was Wax Angel . . . There'd been times she'd lain for hours in rubble to get the right shot, and left without declaring herself, if the target never materialized.

Besides, she was a beggar. Beggars didn't exist in the Soviet Union, so being invisible was easy.

She wondered if the Englishman knew their father was

dying, if he realized the general was holed up in Leningrad in a dark and gloomy flat, brooding on his legacy and the ingratitude of children. These days you could add cancer of the body to cancer of the soul.

In her experience, injured wolves were worst.

They were cursed, that family. The Englishman should ask not about the general but about the general's own father. Now there was a story to make nightmares look like nursery rhymes.

Dennisov was at his own bar, perching awkwardly on a chrome stool that hadn't been there the last time Tom visited. The flask of vodka in front of him was empty. The bowl of soup beside it was full. Yelena glared from behind the bar, swept through the curtain in the wall of records and let it flap heavily behind her. As if everything wrong in her life was Tom's fault.

Her brother had fewer customers than usual.

Those who were there clustered round the cracked screen, watching one of their own play Tetris with Zen-like intensity. The room was in near silence except for the slow thudding of a water pipe, the hammering of fingers on the keyboard and the growl of traffic from the street below. Just as suddenly as she had left, Dennisov's sister reappeared. It was obvious she was spoiling for a fight. So obvious that the Tetris-watchers switched their attention to Tom.

'What do you want now?' she demanded.

'Who said I wanted anything?'

'You always want something,' Yelena said. 'It always causes trouble. Why don't you just leave us alone?'

She was right and it was true, he did want something. He wanted the use of Dennisov's motorbike, the one the Russian was too crippled to ride any more.

'What's happened to everyone?' Tom asked.

'We're out of vodka.'

'This is a bar. How can you be out of vodka?'

'He drank it . . .' She put her hands on her hips and glared at Tom. She looked tired and pale, and readier than ever to speak her mind. 'It's your fault,' she said. 'It's always your fault.'

'Yelena,' Dennisov said.

She glared him into silence. 'If it wasn't for him, they wouldn't have come back. If they hadn't come back, you wouldn't be scared. If you weren't scared, you'd drink less. If you drank less, we might have some vodka left to sell.'

He nodded at each of her points.

'So,' she said, 'how is it not his fault?'

'I like him.'

'Because he drinks as much as you.'

Dennisov squinted at Tom and shook his head. 'He drinks like an Englishman. For a Russian, he's practically a monk. Look at him; he's been in here two minutes, possibly three and he hasn't even asked for alcohol.'

Yelena put her hands to her head.

No fight. Not even a real argument.

The Tetris-watchers went back to their game, just as the man playing stopped being able to key the blocks fast enough and swore as lines built up and filled the screen. He gave up his place reluctantly.

Dennisov said, 'My sister's not happy.'

'He should leave,' Yelena said.

'She thinks we shouldn't be friends. She doesn't trust you.'

'Why?' Tom asked.

'Why is none of your business,' Yelena said.

Dennisov ran his hand through his cropped hair, wiping his fingers on his trousers. 'They came back, okay? They came back . . .'

'Last night,' said Yelena. 'When the bar was shut. They

173

wanted to know if you'd been in. They wanted to know if we knew where you were. They said they had a photograph of my brother changing dollars. That's treason. They could send him to the gulag. My brother told them he wouldn't wipe his arse on dollars.'

Dennisov grinned. 'Things were a bit better after that.'

'Who are *they*?' Tom asked.

'You know who *they* are,' he said crossly. 'There's only one *they*. All those old men standing shoulder to shoulder on the podium, barely able to stand each other.' He shook his head sadly. 'Yelena's right. You don't belong here. Go home, see your kid, make peace with your wife, put flowers on the grave of your daughter. This isn't your fight.'

'I can't leave.'

'Try?' Dennisov suggested.

Have you? Tom wondered.

He knew the answer. For all Dennisov bristled at every mention of his wife, he'd probably never stopped trying. Dennisov drunk in his bar was the tip of the emotional iceberg. The bulk of the man's misery lay below water.

As for Tom, how could he explain that he'd pinned his entire hope of redemption on finding Alex? He needed redemption as much as she needed saving. If she was still alive to be saved. If there was enough of him left to be redeemed. He wouldn't allow himself to leave the Soviet Union until that was done. He couldn't . . .

Tom knew how absurd that was, how arrogant, how messianic.

He didn't care.

'They'll kill you,' Dennisov warned.

He didn't care about that either. When Tom shrugged, Yelena looked as if she wanted to slap him, so he turned to go. Dennisov grabbed him.

'We still have beer,' Dennisov said.

'Out of date? From your glorious neighbours?'

'Of course.'

Yelena sighed. 'Tell my brother what you want this time.'

The Ural was a rip-off of a 1940s BMW flat-twin, still turned out in the thousands by at least three factories in the Soviet Union. The plans were found when the Red Army took Berlin. The electrics were poor, the headlight weak and the drum brakes virtually useless over fifty. Not that that was a problem, since the bike hated going over fifty anyway. Dennisov kept it in a little courtyard at the back of the bar.

On first kick, the starter was soft.

The second built pressure and the flat-twin fired on Tom's third kick, ticking over with a satisfying if smoky thud. Before Dennisov had let him kick the bike into life he'd insisted that Tom build a small fire under the crankcase. When Yelena protested that it wasn't necessary, he told her that knowing how to warm oil was an essential skill for an honorary Russian to have.

'Bring the bloody thing back in one piece,' Yelena said. 'He likes it, all right? It doesn't matter that it cripples his stump to ride. It's his. From the old days.'

'When he still had a leg?'

'No,' said Dennisov. 'When I was with Sophia.'

'His wife.' Yelena spat.

'My sister doesn't like her,' Dennisov said, as if that wasn't obvious.

'No one likes her,' Yelena said.

24

Back to the House

Caro's family probably said the same about him, Tom decided. He was on the road out of Moscow and replaying Yelena's final comments in his head. Her certainty, her brother's hurt. She'd put her arms round Dennisov, hugging him. It was as close as she could get to an apology without taking her words back. Then she'd found a can of petrol, begged Tom for the use of his lighter and disappeared.

The next thing Tom knew, a pile of waste in the corner, which he would've thought too damp or cold to burn, went up in a whoosh of flame that reached the bare branches of a sad-looking tree, before falling back to a fierce roil of suddenly black smoke.

'I like flames,' she said, when Dennisov sighed.

Taking the Ural's toolkit from his hand, she extracted the screwdriver and trotted out to the main road, nodding politely to Tom's shadow before stabbing the front wheel of his rusting Moskvitch. When the man swore, she shrugged.

'Always the delinquent,' Dennisov said with pride.

The shadow was on his knees in the slush, fitting a jack under the car, with his spare tyre leant against the sill, when Tom thudded round the corner in goggles and helmet, wrapped in Dennisov's flying jacket, Alex's enamel badges pinned to its lapel. He doubted the kneeling man even knew the man on the Ural motorbike was him.

Tom was beyond the turn-off to Sveta's grandfather's and

way beyond the limit permitted to foreigners before his absurd and self-inflicted anger at what Caro's family might say subsided and he relaxed his shoulders and began riding more safely. If he was stopped out here by *militsiya*, he was on his own. Mary Batten's parting comments had made that clear.

Dennisov had made it clear too.

If Tom was stopped, he'd taken the bike without approval.

I get it, Tom thought. No one approves. He was pretty sure he didn't approve of himself either. The road was different in daylight, harder to recognize. He pulled in at the same petrol station, taking his turn in the queue and handing over a wad of roubles in silence. He bought a meat-filled potato at a truck stop a dozen miles later, pissed behind the canvas screen and shook his head apologetically at a very tired and very cold prostitute who offered him company.

An officer of the traffic police was examining the Ural when he got back.

Tom hesitated and his hesitation proved enough to catch the man's attention. Tom was way beyond the limit for foreigners and travelling without the right papers. Indeed, without any papers at all. The officer stared at Tom's goggles, his helmet, flying jacket and borrowed army boots, and only relaxed when Tom threw a lazy salute.

Slinging his leg over the saddle, and with his heart pounding, Tom kicked the engine into life and managed a tight turn without being stopped, asked for his papers or dropping Dennisov's bike on the gravel.

The Ural might look like a BMW but it accelerated like a tractor.

So Tom tucked himself into the slipstream of a lorry heading for Leningrad, used its drag to protect him from the side winds howling across the open fields and fell into a familiar reverie. Riding instinctively, his movements fluid and without thought, he let his mind spin off into memories of how he and Caro began and why they had married. Although that was obvious: Becca. She'd been conceived behind a hedge on the A31.

The Hogsback had become Tom's favourite run out of London the moment he bought his first bike. Caro liked the greasy spoon on the southbound side, with its bacon sandwiches and parked-up trucks and chipped mugs of hot sweet tea. She'd asked him to give her a lift down to her parents' place. He discovered later that the local station was less than two miles from her gate but she'd wanted to arrive wearing his biker jacket and riding on the back of his Honda 450cc Black Bomber.

To wind up her father most likely.

Her first real boyfriend, with all that entailed – and for a well-brought-up girl of eighteen, just out of boarding school, it entailed everything – was Japanese. He had a proverb: *Even a cracked pot has a lid that fits*.

Caro had changed boyfriends and kept the proverb. Tom never knew if she was the pot and he the lid or the other way round. It didn't much matter now.

He was still a diversion in those days.

At least that's what he'd thought he was.

They'd met outside the American Embassy during a protest march. He'd dragged her out of a riot seconds before some sergeant could split her head with his truncheon. Tom told her to go home, Caro told him to get lost and they went from there. *Friends only*, they agreed. The first time he kissed her she'd been surprised.

Not shocked; he was the one who'd been shocked.

'I thought you were queer.'

He'd looked at her, doubly shocked.

'That moustache. Those black leather jackets. Isn't that why most men go into the Church these days?'

'Not this one,' he said.

'What's the reason for this one?'

He should have had an answer. For weeks afterwards he'd worried about not having an answer. And then he'd worried that an easy answer would be wrong. But he should have had a ready answer. So he made one up. Well, worked one out.

In case anyone asked again.

Three months later, half hidden under his leather jacket, his vow of abstinence in shreds and his hand helping Caro with his flies, she lay on her side giving him a blowjob at the edge of a field beside the A31. It wasn't the first time they'd done that. It was the first time they went further.

She was already pregnant when she climbed from his bike, ostentatiously tucked her arm through his and led him up the biggest run of steps he'd seen outside a town hall. The first thing her father did, after pecking his daughter on the cheek and reluctantly shaking Tom's hand, was ask him to take his motorbike round the back and park it by the stables.

Three months after that they came down again, by train this time.

And the machine that was Caro's family kicked into gear as Tom and Caro's future was remade around them. The 450cc Honda was one of the first things to go, along with the tattered remains of his Catholic faith. Tom's bishop was surprisingly understanding. A quick word with a friend of Caro's father became an interview at the Officer Selection Board in Westbury, initial training at the Chaplaincy Centre in Bagshot, a few months in Belize with an infantry unit, followed by a short course at Mons, with the offer of military intelligence afterwards. At some point someone up the line decided he'd make a better intelligence officer than a chaplain. Since he made a crap chaplain, it was hard to disagree.

He should have been grateful, he supposed.

The other options had been Christie's or the production department at Jonathan Cape. His departure for a state-run boarding school in Kent, which was one up from a children's home and several down from a real boarding school, had split him from his sister. Getting Caro pregnant had upset his mother; Tom turning into a Protestant destroyed her.

She died too soon afterwards for peace to be made.

The Ural was tucked so tightly behind the lorry Tom almost missed his lay-by, skidding to a halt fifty paces beyond and walking the bike backwards because he was too cold and the road too icy for him to turn it round. Parking out of sight, he pulled the Ural on to its centre stand, draped Dennisov's helmet over its handlebars and set his collar against the wind.

Snow filled the previous night's tyre tracks, ageing them to memories.

The footprints of the paramedics were similarly faded; Tom's own were starkly obvious as he set off through the woods that screened the house from the road. The hide the Vnutrenniye Voiska had built for Vedenin was gone. There was blood out on the ice, pale, but darker when Tom kicked away new snow above.

He felt shamed by how badly he simply wanted to get back on Dennisov's bike and ride away. The house spoke of hollowness where there should have been activity. Where was the crime scene team? Why had no one come to challenge him?

Tom forced himself to the middle of the lake, staring at the derelict building. And then, when he could put it off no more, he crossed what remained of the ice, feeling every freezing inch of the water beneath his feet. Shattered windows glared like eye sockets in a skull. Casings for plastic bullets looked like dropped toys in the snow.

He could swear the house was watching him approach.

Its gaze was cold and flinty as he crossed the last few yards of ice and clambered on to the lawn where the paramedics had gathered. What could be darker than the deaths of twelve children? Whatever it was, he felt it watching him.

Unable to face the cellar, he headed first for the turret.

The body of Beziki's boy was gone, obviously. The curtain used to cover him was tossed to one side. Bullet holes in broken plaster showed where he'd been shot, bloodstains on rotting carpet where he'd fallen. The crime scene team hadn't even bothered to collect all the brass. Two small-calibre cases remained by the wall where they'd rolled after the boy ejected them.

He pocketed them both.

Someone would have told Beziki by now. Tom doubted they'd been gentle.

It was cold in the turret. Far colder inside than out. So cold that when Tom muttered a prayer for those who had died that day each word formed a wisping trail. His teeth were chattering by the time the prayer was done, his fingernails purple. He was cold enough in his bones to need a hot bath, cold enough in his soul to regret not bringing a hip flask to fill the emptiness.

Looking out of the window through which Beziki's boy had fired, Tom saw flitting shadows and looked again. He saw nothing. He felt his guts tighten and his resolve waver. Trauma. Post-trauma. Shock. You can put names to behaviour. If you're a psychiatrist, that's your job. His decision to come here alone hadn't been a conscious one. Not even consciously unconscious. If you could put it like that.

Nothing moved beyond the window that shouldn't.

The wind creaked branches and rattled shutters. Clouds scudded across a gunmetal sky, slab on slab, thick as sheet armour. The far edge of the narrow lake, where the hide had been, fell in and out of shadow. He thought he saw a figure where the hide had been but when he blinked, it was gone.

The wind was rising, no doubt about it.

A shutter on the floor below flung itself back, hit the wall and blew closed again, as if the house was self-harming. And Tom knew he couldn't put it off any longer. He had to go down to the cellar, because why else had he come? After one last look from the turret, he forced himself down the stairs and stopped, standing to the side of a different window. Nothing out there. Nothing to justify this fear.

Do it, he told himself.

The door was sealed, which was something.

Someone at least regarded the cellar as a crime scene.

Cutting the seal with his pocketknife, Tom pulled a torch he'd borrowed from Dennisov out of his jacket pocket and shone it into the darkness. Unable to do anything else, he followed after.

A scratching from below made him flick off the beam.

It came again, sharp and brittle. Tom waited and the sudden silence waited too, until he wondered if they were trying to wait each other out. When the noise came again, Tom held the torch out to his side to throw off whatever waited and flicked it on, pinning a glittering-eyed rat to the cellar floor in the beam.

'Fucker,' he hissed.

Rearing back, it showed yellow teeth.

For a second they glared at each other, and then the rat scuttled for darkness and Tom let it go. Other than the two of them, the cellar was empty. Everything in there had been collected up and spirited away. The rest of the house was a shambles but the cellar floor was so sterile you could have set up an operating theatre. Whatever Tom had hoped to find, he was too late. The scene had been professionally cleaned and he didn't believe for one second that the cellar contents had been boxed and bagged as evidence.

Leaving the rat to its depressingly pristine kingdom, Tom stamped back to ground level, shut the cellar door and turned the key. He was just replacing the lead seal he'd cut from the handle when the hair on the back of his neck prickled and his fingers froze on the handle. Behind him, someone coughed politely.

A man waited, back-lit in a doorway, his face in darkness.

'English,' Tom said. Which was true. 'Police.' Which wasn't.

The man's arm lifted and Tom saw a crossbow.

And then the shock was real and a quarrel pinned him to the cellar door, the feathers at its notched end jutting out from below his shoulder joint. The sight of them brought a wave of nausea; pain arrived a second later. The man took a step towards him, his fingers reaching for the Lenin badge pinned to Tom's jacket.

'Mine, I think.'

He'd removed it and was about to reload the bow when Tom's name was shouted loudly from outside, and the man swore, stepping back into the brightness behind him.

This was not how Tom had expected death to be.

25

The Ice Beckons

If I can make it to the road . . . The lights of a lorry are away to one side and if I can reach the road before it arrives . . . If the driver is a Prod or sick enough of the situation . . . There's something odd in relying on help from a Protestant.

I'm going to reach the road, though . . .

All I have to do is scramble down this slope and up the other bank and on to the tarmac. I look a mess. My donkey jacket is ripped and stinking of smoke and petrol. I've lost a boot somewhere, and three nails from my toes and one of the toes.

I wouldn't stop for me.

I can hobble and hope though. Hobble and crawl and even run if I ignore the pain. The sleet in my eyes saves me the effort of crying. My once-white T-shirt is stained with mud. The lights are closer now. The lorry is so close I can hear the growl of its engine as it drops gears to begin climbing the hill.

I'm not sure if it's two men behind me or three, how they're armed or who told them who I really was. They knew, though. Looking back, I should have known they knew. The whiskey, the hearty clap on the shoulder, the jokes and jibes about friends in common. By the end everyone in the room was faking.

I'm over the ditch and on the slope and the lorry's lights are dragon eyes getting closer when the punch comes. I lose my breath as I stumble, winded and suddenly cold. The ground is sodden, the lorry on the road so close I don't know why the driver doesn't stop. When the lorry accelerates, I have my answer. I try to stand to face the man behind me; but I can't stand and there's no man and my leg won't work. When the second punch comes, I know there's a bullet in my back.

Darkness edges in and the world is fading when the old man and two others come to stand over me. One of them nudges me with his foot.

'Nice shot.'

'Fucking brilliant.'

'And in this light, pal. In this fucking light.'

'Should have known.' It's the old man who speaks. The one who doesn't swear. He kicks my prostrate body hard. Stamps on the side of my head. They leave my body where it is. Leave time and blood loss to do the job.

For reasons known only to God, they don't.

'Tom . . . *Tom* . . .'

When the darkness cleared Tom found himself nailed to the cellar door by an arrow below his shoulder. The world he woke up to wasn't quite the one he'd left. It never was. The last time he surfaced from something like this, he'd found that colours had changed. Something felt different this time too, although it was too soon to say what. He thought he saw a flash of grey beyond the doorway and wondered if it mattered. When crows rose from trees outside, he wondered what they were trying to say.

The stub of arrow jutting from his shoulder was as long as a thumb; the rest of it was hidden inside him, except for the point, which was in the door, obviously. His knees were locked rigid, holding him up by accident.

Blood was dripping down the inside of the jacket to make a puddle on the floor. Tom looked at it numbly. Dennisov, he thought, as the darkness tried to sweep back in. Dennisov wouldn't get his bike back . . .

Then the light flared and Tom fell into unconsciousness.

He dreamed he saw Alex, hunched and naked, under a sky

so vast it belonged to a different world. She was sitting hip deep in snow, her fingers holding a wax angel.

'It's okay,' he said. 'It's okay.'

'No,' she said, 'it's not.'

She was struggling to mend its wing.

At his best in a crisis. That was what Tom's CO had said about him. This was certainly a crisis, so he should be good. But all he could do was stare numbly as his blood found a crack in the broken tiles and filled it. Last time he'd been shot, his body had been fired up by adrenaline. This time round . . . *You're in shock.*

You can't afford to be in shock.

Two parts of himself were having a conversation.

You were probably meant to think of yourself as 'I' when talking to yourself.

He'd have stepped forward and pulled himself free if it weren't for the memory of being warned never to pull out a knife blade in case it was the only thing stopping you bleeding out. He'd shout but . . . But what? He'd feel too stupid?

He'd rather die than be embarrassed?

Wasn't that a little too English? Maybe marrying into Caro's family had changed him more than he knew. How long had he been out cold? Long enough for blood to pool at his feet and colour to leach from the world beyond the door.

Not enough never to wake to see those colours again.

His fingers slipped on blood when he tried to worry the arrow free from the door, so Tom wiped them on his jeans and tried again, wondering if he was imagining feeling the arrow move. Its shaft was metal, thinner than a pencil. He worked it from side to side, moving himself at the same time and knowing that only fear stopped him giving up, that only stubbornness stopped him simply stepping away from the door.

The arrow moved a tiny bit more each time.

His breath was broken glass, his face so wet and his fingers so red he felt as if he were crying blood rather than tears. His chest was tight, his guts knotted, his world reduced to white pain. *This is how a butterfly feels*, he thought.

In the doorway stood a figure, light forming a halo around his head.

He isn't really there, Tom told himself. *You're hallucinating*. If he could split into different parts that talked to each other, perhaps one of them had gone to the door.

'Major Fox?' it enquired.

So polite, this hallucination.

Tom didn't want to greet it pinned like a butterfly.

Grabbing the already loosened bolt, he yanked it free and lurched towards the man, who stepped back hurriedly as Tom stumbled past and through the open door and found himself on his knees in the snow outside. Staring up at a grey sky.

'*Tom* . . .'

Sveta's shout boomed again across the ice.

She stood on the far side of the lake, hands up to shield her eyes from the sinking sun and her boots planted firmly in the snow. Boots, jeans, a red jersey, bright as a target. It was the first time he'd seen her out of uniform. She waved, and then stopped mid wave as someone stepped up behind him.

Hands lifted Tom from his knees and Vladimir Vedenin smiled at him. Realizing it was Vladimir did what the crossbow bolt hadn't. It jolted Tom awake, adrenaline sharpening the landscape around him.

'What are you doing here?' Tom demanded.

Vladimir smiled. 'I could ask the same . . . That must hurt,' he added.

Tom didn't trust himself to speak.

Turning away, Vladimir shouted, 'He's injured.'

'How badly?'

'Very. You should go and get an ambulance.'

'I'll do it now,' Sveta shouted.

'Don't . . .' Tom's yell was a crow's croak.

Sveta turned back.

'Don't leave me. I want you here.'

For a second she hesitated, then shrugged, her decision made. 'Okay, I'll wait.' To Vladimir she shouted, 'Take the track round the side and meet me here. All right?'

'If you insist.'

The Russian put his hand under Tom's elbow to hold him up as they turned towards a camouflage-patterned open-top 4x4 parked under nearby trees. Vladimir glanced once at Sveta, who stood watching. His face was thoughtful.

'UAZ-3151,' Tom muttered.

'You know your models.'

It was the only Soviet 4x4 Tom knew, and he only knew that because it was brand new, almost impossible to get in the civilian model, and someone at the embassy had been talking about it. He wasn't even sure why he'd said it.

'You're friends with Svetlana?' Vladimir asked.

Tom managed a nod.

'I heard she took you to meet her grandfather.'

'We needed somewhere to stop . . . His house was on the way.'

'On the way to where? No one gets to meet her grandfather. Even my father doesn't get to meet him. The man's in self-imposed exile. He has no visitors and rarely goes to Moscow. Why would he see you?'

'We talked about Alex.'

Vladimir's hand tightened on Tom's elbow and he increased

his speed towards the vehicle, only stopping when Tom twisted away. Sucking his teeth, Vedenin said, 'Now, this is a mess.' They were at the UAZ by then. Its seats were shiny, unscratched and unstained, smelling of new plastic.

'I thought you came alone.'

'I did,' Tom said.

'Yet your friend is here. You'd better get in.'

'Bleed on it,' Tom said. 'I'm going to . . .'

'My father will get me a new one.'

You'll need it, Tom thought as a burst of pain told him the arrowhead had ripped the seat back behind him. The other door slammed, the starter motor coughed.

'I saw Alex,' Tom said.

Vedenin turned off the engine.

'Here?' he asked.

'She was sitting in the snow.'

'That's ridiculous.' Biting the inside of his lip, Vladimir looked over to where Sveta was staring at the suddenly stalled 4x4. 'You can't possibly have . . .'

Tom's heart stuttered, held still for a semi-quaver and restarted, thudding like a fist inside his ribs. He'd been right. Vladimir was involved.

He smelled pine needles.

Vosene, that was the smell.

Becca's pine-scented shampoo when Caro washed her hair as a child.

Hand shaking, Tom found his lock knife. His fingers were cramping by the time he opened the blade. Vladimir had restarted his vehicle, forced into a five-point turn by the tightness of the trees. The Russian only realized Tom had a knife when it touched his groin.

'Where is she?' Tom demanded.

The UAZ shuddered to a halt.

'Major. I should call you Major, shouldn't I? I don't know what . . .'

The blade had been honed to cut cloth like paper. It probably helped that Tom's fingers were shaking so badly. Vladimir whimpered and tried to push himself deeper into his seat. Tom wouldn't have wanted to be where he was sitting either.

There was something Tom wanted to say.

It required finding the words.

'Artery. Sphincter,' he said carefully. He drew the blade lightly over Vladimir's thigh. 'Straight, you might have time to get help. Like this . . .' The blade sketched a diagonal. 'No chance. A minute at most. Where is she?'

'I don't know . . . *Enough!*' Vedenin begged.

Tom glanced down but there was no blood spraying.

'Tom?' Sveta's call echoed off the trees loud enough to send a crow in a ragged spiral, a flapping black rag against the grey sky. 'Everything all right?'

'Everything's fine,' Vedenin shouted.

'I was asking the major.'

'Drive,' Tom told Vedenin.

The Russian restarted his engine and put the 4x4 into gear, twisting his steering wheel to complete the final turn that would give them a track through the trees.

'That way.' Tom pointed at the frozen lake.

He had no intention of letting Vedenin use any route that took the 4x4, Vedenin or himself out of Sveta's sight. Her presence was, Tom had no doubt, the only thing keeping him alive.

'Major, that's not wise.'

Tom adjusted his grip on the knife.

With a clank of transmission, the UAZ abandoned the track and headed slowly down the bank on to the marbled ice, Sveta yelling in protest.

'He insists,' Vladimir shouted.

The mounds were just mounds. The reeds and rushes merely windbreaks that had collected drifting snow. Tom wondered how strong the ice was. If he even really cared . . . Except he had to. There was Alex, and Charlie. It wasn't Charlie's fault Becca died. It wasn't Alex's fault either.

'She crashed her car.'

'Who did?' Vladimir asked.

'You shot me.'

'I'll get you to a hospital.'

'Say what?'

'An accident. A hunting accident . . .'

'Faster,' Tom told him, adjusting the knife.

The crawling 4x4 was halfway over when the ice boomed and Vladimir braked. A crack appeared in front of them. Off to his right, Tom watched another forming.

'We need to get out,' Vladimir said.

Tom shook his head.

'Please . . .' When Vladimir looked across at Tom, he had the anguished eyes of an El Greco saint and the cheekbones of a rock star. Jim Morrison, if his dad had been a Soviet minister, not a US admiral. 'Alex came of her own free will.'

'To you?'

'No.' Vladimir shook his head furiously.

'Dmitry?'

'How do you –'

'Where is she now?'

'I thought he was going to give her back.'

Sveta was watching, frozen at the lake's edge.

'Vladimir. *Who has Alex?*'

Twisting the key, Vladimir floored the accelerator, changing up fast. '*You don't know him.*' The young man's final words were a strangled scream. He was headed straight for Sveta when the ice gave and the 4x4 pitched forward, its grill hitting the far bank head on. Rocketing forward, Vladimir slammed into the metal bar at the top of his windscreen. When he bounced back into Tom, he was already slack as a rag doll.

Darkness descended.

26

Sisters of Mercy

Becca was on the chair when Tom woke, knees drawn up the way she used to sit in front of the TV, an expression of fierce concentration on her face. Woe betide anyone who disturbed her as she lost herself in the adventures of a saggy old cloth cat. 'Mummy's leaving you,' she said.

'I know.'

'You're crying,' she said.

'I've been doing a lot of that,' he told her.

'I didn't know you could cry. But, you know, it wasn't like we saw much of each other when I was alive.'

'Becca . . .'

She looked at him, head twisted to one side. 'Did you ever see *Once Upon a Time in America*? You should. You'd like it, I think. Peter took me to a screening in Portsmouth. They shouldn't have let us in, but . . .' Becca shrugged. 'It was Portsmouth. Mummy was away. You were too. You were always away.'

Shimmering behind her were rolling hills and green glens. A cool breeze from a world beyond. Tom hoped it was heaven but he was worried because it looked like Crossmaglen. His daughter looked happy, though.

Happier than he remembered.

Then she didn't. 'I should tell them you're awake.'

'Am I awake?'

The nurse unfolded her legs and stood stiffly, like someone who'd spent far too long sitting in a badly designed chair. She padded across the room, backlit by a window bright enough to make him squint as she leaned slightly forward and stared at him. Her hair was the wrong colour and her face Slavic, but her eyes were almost the same. Only not quite. They belonged to someone alive.

The ceiling blurred and Tom's throat tightened and he couldn't stop hot tears running down both sides of his face. He felt so empty, human and helpless and he finally understood why dying boys called for their mothers on the battlefield. If there was a God, he wasn't here.

'It's the drugs,' she said. 'It's okay.'

'Alex . . .?' he asked.

Alex was on the chair when he woke again.

Knees up, the way his daughter used to sit in front of the TV, with an expression of fierce concentration on her face. Back in the days when Becca could still lose herself in the adventures of a saggy old cloth cat.

'You took my tape,' she said. 'Didn't you?'

'Which tape?'

'You know. The one he gave me.'

'How could you possibly know that?'

'I don't,' she said, as if it was obvious. 'You do.'

'Is that significant?'

'Doubt it. It's an out-take from a recording session. He got it from a man in a bar when his boss was in America. He didn't even know who the band was.'

'You did.'

'Of course. Their poster's on my wall.'

'Alex?' Tom squinted into the light. 'Are you really here?'

'Obviously not,' she said. 'You're hallucinating. Who did you think I was last time?'

'Someone I loved. Just not very well.'

194

'What happened?'

'I killed her.'

The girl in his dream looked shocked.

'Unless she killed herself,' Tom said hastily.

'I'd better tell them you're awake.'

'But I'm not,' Tom said.

'You were shot with the wrong kind of arrow. That's the truth of it. If you'd been shot with the right kind, you'd be dead. You'd have holes that couldn't be mended.'

'I've got those anyway.'

'Do you know what a field point is?'

Tom nodded.

'Me neither.'

'You're here, aren't you?'

Alex shook her head so fiercely that she disappeared and Tom found a nurse shaking him by the wrist. She was middle-aged and dumpy, slightly sour-faced, as if wondering what this man was doing in her hospital.

She looked nothing like Alex or Becca at all.

Next came a man who wanted answers. A doctor came first though.

He checked Tom's shoulder, which he unbandaged and bandaged again, then he looked at a machine with chrome-ringed dials too much like a Mini's dashboard for Tom's liking, and made a note of what the speedometer said.

Then, pushing up the sleeve of Tom's gown, he found a vein. In England the gown would be paper, with ties at the back.

This one was cotton and it had buttons.

'Where's Alex?' Tom asked.

'Who's Alex?'

'The girl.'

'There isn't a girl.'

'She talked to me about my daughter.'

'This isn't going to hurt,' the doctor said.

There was a light overhead, hanging from a flex, and sometimes it was too bright to bear and other times barely on at all. The room wouldn't stop spinning and it wasn't a room Tom recognized.

He was pretty sure he hadn't been this drunk since he turned twenty-one. He tried to find the pub but the room didn't seem to have one. There were no other customers either. The sky was wrong for Belfast, the temperature wrong for a Belize brothel. Tom had just decided he was on his back on the pub floor when someone dragged a chair across the floor and sat by his bed.

'What is your wife's name?'

'Caroline. I call her Caro.'

'Why?'

'Everyone calls her Caro.'

'Your daughter. What happened to her?'

'She died.'

'How did she die?'

'She crashed into a tree.'

'Did you cause her to crash into a tree?'

'Yes. No. I don't know.'

There was silence, then a chair creaked, paper rustled and the voice came closer. 'Now, more recent things. What happened with Vladimir?'

Tom could remember this one. 'His jeep went through the ice.'

'Did you force my son to drive across the lake?'

'He should have had skis on his plane.'

'Major . . . why did he drive across that lake?'

'Why do boys do anything?'

There was an exasperated sigh.

The next person Tom saw was Sveta, who arrived with a young man in wire spectacles. She came flanked by two men in uniform. When they made to follow her in, she barked at them to stay put. Hefting his case on to a chair, the young man opened its lid, flicked a switch on what looked like an oscilloscope and began turning dials, while listening through one side of a pair of oversized headphones.

He nodded to Sveta.

'Who were you expecting?' Tom asked.

Sveta waited until the young man had dragged his case out of there before answering. 'The Americans, obviously.'

That's when Tom realized his room was bugged. Although probably not by the Americans. 'Alex was here earlier.'

'You've had a fever,' she said.

'Sveta, I saw her.'

'Hallucinations. You just wish you had.'

'You were at the house, weren't you?'

Sveta nodded.

'Why?'

'I followed you. Obviously.'

'Did Vladimir follow me?'

'Vladimir's dead.'

Tom stared at her, shocked. 'Really?'

'Really,' she said. 'His jeep went through the ice. You were dying. An ambulance brought you here.'

'An accident,' Tom said.

'Vladimir? An accident,' Sveta agreed. Pulling a scrap of paper from her pocket, she dug around for a pencil. *We're going to get you out of here.*

Tom didn't want to leave.

He wanted to stay in case Alex came back.

Sometimes it was better to stay. Sometimes that got you answers.

The night a foot patrol in Belfast decided to kick the shit out of him he'd been ordered to pull out. He'd have left next day. Instead he made himself a cast-iron cover story. The best thing was the soldiers didn't even know they'd helped build it. He'd been in a white transit, with a ladder on top, heading up the Falls Road, and he'd put his headlights up the moment he spotted them.

Patrols hated that.

After bringing his van to a halt, they smashed his lights front and back with their rifle butts before starting on him. Two boys, barely older than fourteen, in denim jackets that stank of cigarettes, dragged him up to A&E. Tom told the triage nurse about the patrol and she wrote him down as a drunken fall.

One of the boys' dads was outside when she was done.

He shook Tom's hand, took him to the pub, poured a couple of pints down him, told him to keep up the good fight and introduced him to the boys. The pints mixed nicely with the painkillers the nurse had slipped into his pocket as he was leaving. They mixed so nicely he couldn't . . .

'Concentrate,' Sveta ordered.

'It's the injections.'

'Your records show orally administered analgesics.'

They were using truth drugs. He knew they were using truth drugs.

'I think it's sodium . . .'

She held up her hand before he could add *pentothal.*

When the light returned, she was gone and a serious-looking man in a white coat stood next to Tom's bed, a huge syringe in his hand. Tom's eyes widened and the man looked more serious still. When Tom tried to move, he discovered that his arms were fixed by his sides. A wide leather strap tightened his chest, and from the feel of it there was one across his stomach as well. At an order from the doctor, a nurse hurried forward and fixed a final strap across his ankles. The brass buckles that Tom could see were tarnished, the belt holes stretched.

Not like this, he thought.

His muscles strained as he tried to fight free.

'It's only a sedative,' the doctor said. 'This won't hurt.'

He lied. A bruise blossomed where he missed Tom's vein the first time, his fingers shaking as he stabbed at the crook of Tom's elbow, too frightened by those waiting outside to do his job properly.

The world spun so fast people thought it stood still.

It spun in orbit around the sun. The day didn't fade. Night didn't fall. The angel of death that had hovered so close to Tom's shoulder in recent years refused to come. Instead, the door opened and Comrade Vedenin entered. He glanced back once and the suited men behind him stayed where they were.

'How are you feeling?'

'Constrained.'

Looking at the straps, Vedenin sighed.

With an expression of quiet distaste, he began undoing the buckles and unpeeling the curling leather straps. 'How are we ever going to take our proper place in the world if we insist on behaving like this?' Having undone the strap across Tom's legs, he freed his right wrist before walking round to free his left. By now the room was spinning so fast the syringe might as well have contained neat vodka.

'You were right,' Vedenin said. 'Sodium pentothal. We borrowed the idea from you. More reliable than the old methods. So I'm told.'

He made himself sound ancient.

'What do you want?' Tom asked.

'The truth.'

'About what?'

'About anything would be good.' Pulling a chair from under a desk, he turned it round and sat splay-legged. 'Let's start with the obvious. Do *you* know where your ambassador's daughter is?'

'She was here. Earlier.'

'I doubt that very much.' Vedenin's gaze was steady.

'Do you know?' Tom asked.

'No,' Vedenin said, 'I don't.'

Tom believed him.

'Now. Did you kill my son?'

'He drove on to the ice.'

'So I'm told. Why did he drive on to the ice?'

'Why does anyone do anything?'

'Please answer the question. Did you kill my son?'

The room was hot. A strip light overhead rotated like a slowly turning 'copter blade. Tom could hear its thud coming across the hills as he clung to damp turf and hoped they'd find him without him needing to stand or wave.

Don't leave me here.

It was all the man beside him could say.

His pleas grew weaker as the flow of blood trickled through tufts of rough grass. He was a good man, the dying man, as wife-beating racist porridge lice went. He'd simply done one tour too many, been in the army too long. Been too close to retirement to think this would happen. *Fuck them all,* he said.

As last words went it beat *Mummy*.

'Shit,' Vedenin said. 'How much did that idiot give you?'

The bruise on his arm was yellow. The light above his bed was neither a single bulb on a twisted flex nor a fluorescent tube. It was hidden behind a flat recessed panel, sleek enough to belong in a New York hotel. The walls were pale green, the floor marbled. There was a long line of neatly made-up beds. Occupants: one.

'Where am I?'

'The KGB's new hospital,' Sveta said.

'Why am I here?'

'We don't trust other hospitals.'

The commissar arrived later that night.

Six soldiers walked behind him. Having confirmed that Tom was still alive, and still here, he told two to guard the door, two to guard the stairs and the last two to stand guard at the hospital's entrance.

'Let's see Vedenin move you now,' he said.

He kicked at a marble tile with his heel. Complained about the waste of state money. Felt the thickness of the curtains. Sneered at the flowers in a large vase. Criticized the effeteness of the mosaic on the far wall, and asked which idiot had signed off on a black glass desk that belonged in a science-fiction film.

'As for that . . .' he said, pointing at the luminous panel overhead.

'What about it?' Sveta demanded.

'Find out who designed it, so I can have him shot.'

When he saw Tom's shoulder, he smiled. 'Been upsetting people, I gather.'

'Not intentionally.'

The commissar snorted. 'How do you feel?'

'I've been better.'

'Believe me, you could be a lot worse.'

'Don't doubt it,' Tom said.

The fact that he could barely feel where the crossbow's bolt had skewered him meant he had to be on opiates of some sort. He wondered why Sir Edward was letting the Soviets look after him. Then wondered aloud if Sir Edward even knew what had happened.

'Of course he knows,' the commissar said. 'Sveta called the embassy. Said she knew they'd want to help and could they tell her where Sir Edward had been the afternoon you were shot.'

He shrugged. 'They didn't think it was funny.' Glancing at his granddaughter, he added, 'I'm not sure she meant it to be funny. Now . . . Let's get this over with.'

A doctor was summoned. In her hand was yet another syringe. She tapped the shaft to dislodge a bubble, squirted a thin jet of clear liquid to check the needle was full and reached for Tom's arm.

'This won't hurt,' she promised.

For once it wasn't a lie.

'Tell me your name,' Sveta's grandfather said.

'Tom Fox.'

'Your full name.'

'Thomas Alan Fox.'

'How old are you?'

'Thirty-nine.'

'Your file says thirty-eight.'

'It's probably right.'

The recessed light panel overhead was suddenly less elegant and altogether harder-edged, even blinding. If Sveta's grandfather had shone a lamp in Tom's face, he'd probably have confessed to being any age the old man liked.

'Why are you in Moscow, Major Fox?'

Tom told him about the select committee and his need to be kept out of sight.

'What are you likely to tell them?'

'The truth.'

The commissar laughed.

'Now. Did you kill the boy?'

'What was his name?'

The commissar said something and a door slammed.

Tom thought the old man had gone until he heard the scrape of chairs being pulled closer. He could smell soap and hair cream, damp wool and cigarettes. Sveta's scent was there too, lighter, younger.

'I'm talking about Vladimir,' the commissar said.

'He drove on to the ice.'

'Why did he drive on to the ice?'

'We took a short cut.'

'He's good,' her grandfather said.

'Told you,' Sveta replied.

The old man did the next injection himself.

Tom wanted darkness but all they gave him was sleep. When he woke, it was to daylight and the commissar asleep in the chair. He wanted it to be Alex. Every time he woke now he wanted it to be Alex. And Tom understood that he hadn't really been wanting darkness. If he had, he'd have found it months ago.

He was holding out for absolution.

The old man looked sour when Tom said that.

'You think I'm not? Let me tell you about darkness,' he said. 'It crept across our lives like a shadow. We brought it back with us from Berlin. It's never gone away . . .'

27

Vistula, Spring 1945

Knocking woke him from memories of the last days at Stalingrad, during which he had questioned a Waffen-SS officer beside the statue of the crocodile, with its ring of broken children holding hands. The Nazi was on his knees, and the commissar had a pistol to his head. 'Where are you from?'

The man repeated his name, rank and number.

'From the city? From the country? From a village? You look like someone who comes from a village.'

The officer glared. 'Berlin,' he said finally.

'Look around you,' the commissar told him.

Obediently, the man raised his head and stared at the ruined windows, which stared blankly back.

'See what you've done? This is nothing to what we will do.'

And so it proved. The Germans brought their panzers within range of the Red Army guns before the Soviet forces even crossed the Vistula. It was insane. The commissar had begun to wonder if Hitler wanted to lose. Maybe he knew he was going to die and wanted to take his Reich with him, like some barbarian king buried with his chariots, horses and slaves.

Twenty-six months later he still didn't regret pulling the trigger on the kneeling German. Why would he? Half a million Soviet soldiers had died to hold Stalingrad. At least that many more were wounded. Between them they killed three-quarters of a million fascists and took 91,000 prisoner. A handful of those were generals, who looked surprisingly well fed compared to the emaciated state of their troops. It wasn't as if one Waffen-SS officer was going to be missed either way.

The knocking continued.

'What is it?'

A girl put her head round his door and he reached for her warmth on the sheet next to him and felt foolish when she smiled in the light of the candle she was carrying. 'I'm working,' Maya said. Across her back was a sniper rifle, its telescopic sight firmly in place. 'So I'd better go. But the boy thinks there's something you should see. He didn't dare wake you himself.'

'Another suicide?'

But she was gone.

German women began hanging themselves before the Red Army even arrived. Those with families did it only after they'd cut the wrists of the small children, even babies. The commissar had told his men not to requisition buildings without first checking their attics, where such suicides could usually be found, in various states of decay. Things were bad enough without his men going down with fever.

When the men couldn't find German women to rape, they raped the Ukrainians, Poles and Byelorussians they freed from Nazi slave camps. Three days was the unofficial rule. Three days of raping and looting, drunkenness and murder. After that, the mayhem was meant to stop; but drunken *frontoviki* with submachine guns were difficult to control and sometimes it was simply safer to allow them extra days.

'In the stables,' Dennisov said.

The man with him nodded. 'We just heard, sir.'

Dennisov and Kyukov were waiting for him by the front door. They looked serious.

*

The stable was hot, for all that winter lingered outside.

It stank of straw and dung from a nag that the soldiers had slaughtered for food that morning, butchering the carcass and dividing the meat between the tank crews and their support troops. The animal had been stunned with a bullet to the brain and finished with a second bullet, both fired head on. The filleting of the horse had been crude, brutal and swift. The men were hungry.

The butchery inside the stable was altogether more elegant, if you could apply that word to the three family pets skinned and hung in size order by their back legs from a beam. The commissar wasn't sure you could.

Neat, perhaps.

The scene was mockingly neat.

The flat smell of fresh blood filled Major Milov's nostrils as he forced himself inside to examine the tableau. Whoever had butchered the family pets had trimmed their carcasses so well it was impossible to tell whether they'd been male or female without getting closer than he wanted. He'd seen his share of dead humans. Soldiers beheaded by grenades and gutted by shrapnel. Family pets, though . . . The commissar had considered himself inured to feelings of disgust. It seemed he was wrong.

'Get the others.'

Dennisov would know whom to fetch.

They were the ones who'd been with him from the start. The ones who'd made it this far. The ones, although no one really dared think this, who might just make it through to the end. A month now, two months . . .

Then they'd be in Berlin.

'Comrade Major?'

Turning, he found Beziki, scruff-haired, half the buttons of his stolen uniform undone, half a loaf of bread pushed inside his shirt. The kid was their mascot, picked up on whim and never put down in case he carried their luck away with him.

'Leave,' Major Milov said. 'This isn't for you.'

The boy stared at the skinned animals. 'I've seen worse.' His voice fought for bravado. 'Much worse.'

'Of course you have. Now leave.'

The kid saluted clumsily and didn't even bother to shrug or twist his mouth or protest. He simply slipped out of the barn as Kyukov and Dennisov came back with the others. 'Fuck,' Vedenin said.

'Take a good look.'

The commissar stepped aside so they could all see the three dogs stripped down to red maps of muscle and sinew, forelegs bound, twine threaded behind the tendons in the back legs of each.

'This one's alive. It's quivering.'

Kyukov, obviously. Fearless, almost permanently drunk, quite possibly insane . . . Major Milov should have known he'd be the one to go close enough to discover that for himself. 'Probably just post-death spasms,' he said.

'No, sir, come and look.'

Kyukov left him no choice but to go closer.

The commissar felt rather than saw Kyukov grin as he forced himself to swallow bile. Then Dennisov – too old to be a lieutenant, apparently incapable of being promoted – pushed in and Kyukov stepped back.

'There's something else,' Dennisov said. 'Fayzulin's been found in the pigsty shot through his head.'

'Anyone with him?'

'The pig woman.'

The commissar didn't have to ask what they'd been doing, well, what their dead corporal had been doing. Screams from the outbuildings behind told him others were still doing the same. 'She killed him?'

'She says not.'

'You think she's lying?'

'There was a Luger hidden under the straw.'

'Shoot her. Make an example. Shoot the old man too, burn the farmhouse.' Major Milov looked at the animals hanging from the rafters. 'Fetch flamethrowers. Burn this place to the ground while you're at it.'

They left an old woman, her five-year-old grandchild and a shivering aunt, knees to her chest, arms wrapped tightly around herself, alive but dead-eyed beside the smoking ruins of the farm in which they'd lived.

'You could have been kind,' Maya said.

He knew what she was saying.

'I don't kill women.'

'You shot the one in the pigsty.'

'That was different. She killed a soldier.'

'You think what will happen to them won't be worse?'

'It's not as if they didn't do it to us.'

Pulling on her leather cap, Maya buckled it tight and clambered up the tank's side, lowering herself into the cramped compartment below. This model took five and had a radio. It still stored its fuel tanks inside though, and they all understood that a direct hit meant death. It was better that way. You wouldn't want to live, if you were what crawled from the flames.

It was two weeks before she made peace, and then only because they'd been racing towards Breslau when the order came to wheel left, run back along the banks of the Oder and help flush out the German Seventeenth. She came to find him in the cottage he'd requisitioned, stripped herself naked despite the cold and slipped in beside him, her arms tightening around him as he reached for her.

'You wouldn't understand,' she said.

He guessed she was right.

It was the last major tank battle either of them fought.

Major Milov was pulled out of the line a few days later and taken back the way he'd come to the HQ of an NKVD general fifty miles behind the lines. The general handed him an order signed by Beria himself.

The commissar had been chosen for his loyalty, his bravery in battle, because he had been one of those who defended Stalingrad and because the combination of trained tank commander and political officer had caught the eyes of Stavka. Whether that meant the Chief of Staff of the Supreme Headquarters of the Armed Forces or Stalin himself the commissar didn't know, and didn't dare ask. From now on, though, he was outside the military chain of command and would report to those who reported direct to Beria or to the Boss himself.

As the commissar undoubtedly knew, the responsibilities of the NKVD went far beyond simple anti-partisan operations and the apprehension of turncoats, deserters, cowards and malingerers. They included the creation of *sharashkas*, secret defence establishments, and the future protection of the Soviet state.

'You understand?' the NKVD man said.

'Yes, Comrade General.'

'We will pick you a team.'

'Comrade General . . .' Major Milov hesitated, but only for a second. 'I'd like to keep my old team. I command good soldiers. We fight well, we work together and our luck has held.'

The general flipped open a file.

'Your particular friends being Maya Grossman? Vasily

Gusakovsky? Pyotr Dennisov? Ilyich Vedenin, Rustam Kyukov? And Erekle Gabashville, that wretched urchin who travels with you?'

'He's our luck.'

Sharp eyes examined him through tiny wire-framed glasses. 'You believe he contributes to your success?'

'Yes, sir.'

'Then you'd better look after him, hadn't you? Now, Dennisov. You know his father was a tsarist?'

'He doesn't talk about his family.'

'He doesn't have a family. His mother died, his father was shot.'

'How old was he?'

'Does it matter? Kyukov's the same. Same occasion.'

'Kyukov and Dennisov grew up together?'

The NKVD general sat back, looked at a file on his desk and fixed his gaze on the commissar. 'Did you bother reading their files?'

'It must have slipped my mind.'

'Indeed. Well, they've both been useful on occasion. You'll be able to tell me when this is over whether it's time the state gave them a little more trust.'

'May I ask what the job entails, Comrade General?'

'Reaching Berlin before the Americans for a start. Oh, don't worry. They're bogged down in . . .' He consulted a piece of paper. 'The Ardennes. A forest in Belgium. You'll be there long before they're even close. But that's what this is about. There's a man we want in Berlin. The Americans want him too. Your job is to make sure we get him.'

'A high-ranking Nazi?'

'One of their best scientists.'

He paused and after a second Major Milov realized the general was waiting to see if he would have something to say.

In staying silent he seemed to have passed some sort of test. The NKVD general smiled.

'Keep your team then. Although we're going to give you an extra man. He's there to look at the scientist's papers, check that they're the real thing. Only then will you make him an offer. Amnesty for all past crimes. Safety for his family. Free travel to the Soviet Union. His own lab. His choice of staff. A dacha.'

'May I ask . . .?'

'A bomb,' the general said, scratching at the side of his nose with his pen, 'to end all bombs. We can't let the Americans have it. Stalin himself has told Beria to make sure we get there first. Stalin . . .'

There was a baby-faced lieutenant waiting by a brand-new US lend-lease Jeep, looking deeply uncomfortable in a uniform so new Major Milov doubted it even had lice. His hair was too long and he looked too clean. When he saw the commissar, he shuffled to attention, looked as if he was wondering whether to salute, hesitated and did so anyway. Badly.

'You must be . . .' The commissar consulted his orders. 'Golubtsov?'

'Yes. I mean, yes, Comrade Colonel.'

'I'm a major.'

'I was told you were a colonel.'

Colonel Milov skim-read the rest of his orders and it turned out the boy was right. 'Stand straight,' he said. 'Let me look at you.'

Thin face, high cheekbones, slightly sallow skin and Asiatic eyes behind thick lenses held in place by wire frames. He was slight enough to be a child and visibly trembling under the older man's gaze.

'How old are you?'

'Twenty-three, Comrade Colonel.'

The commissar would have put him at seventeen at the most. 'And how long have you been in uniform?'

The boy flushed. 'They gave me this an hour ago.'

'What did you wear on the march?'

Golubtsov looked apologetic. 'They sent me by train.'

'From Moscow?'

The boy nodded.

'All right. You drive.'

Golubtsov was more embarrassed than ever. 'I can't, sir. That is, no one's ever taught me the practicalities. I understand the theory of course.'

'Of course. What can you do?'

'I'm good at sums in my head. I can see shapes too.'

'In your head?'

'The shapes the sums make.'

'Get in,' the commissar said. 'And shut up. You give me a headache.'

Back at base, Dennisov, Kyukov and Maya came out to look at the Jeep and quickly switched their attention to the baby-faced lieutenant. The commissar could tell that Maya was taken with him. In a sisterly fashion, which had her hacking at his hair with a knife until he looked as unkempt as the rest of them, and stamping his cap into the slush, slapping it against a nearby wall to make it scruffy. After which, she slashed the top button from his jacket and told him to get some dirt under his nails.

She laughed when he dropped to a crouch and took her order literally.

'Someone's son?' she asked as soon as they were alone.

'Undoubtedly . . .' Colonel Milov slid the orders over and watched her read them twice, the first time quickly, second time slowly, going back over the last few lines as if puzzling something out.

'No more fighting? We're leaving the front line?'

'For the moment. Do you mind?'

'I thought *you* might.'

He pushed across the glass of brandy he'd poured himself and looked around the farmhouse kitchen. Germany was a strange mix of the untouched and the utterly ruined. There'd been more food in the last few weeks than he could have imagined, in the countryside at least, where people could grow their own crops, kill their own animals and store grain. He'd been through towns where the inhabitants' faces were skull-like with starvation, and the only males over seventy or under twelve.

Would he mind being out of the war?

Not really. It was already won.

He didn't doubt they'd reach Berlin first.

There would be brutal battles on the outskirts, worse ones in the centre. But it wouldn't be Stalingrad, where all the USSR had had in its favour was boys to sacrifice.

'If they want us to capture this Nazi scientist of theirs, then he must be important.'

'And the order comes from Stalin?'

'Beria, at least. And I doubt he'd do anything without Stalin's say-so. So yes, the order to hunt down this Schultz comes from the Boss. You'd rather be in the sniper division?'

Maya hesitated.

'I could say you're too good at the job to be wasted like this, that we'll need marksmen of your calibre to take the city.'

'It would break up the group.'

'Giving us Golubtsov changes things anyway.'

'You won't mind?'

'Of course I'll mind. I'll miss you.'

The look she gave him was so shocked the commissar realized he'd never admitted anything even close to that before.

28

Burying Vladimir

Who knew so many dead men would turn up to watch Vladimir Vedenin be buried? Now, if they were burying his father, that would be different. Wax Angel could imagine the dead turning up to watch that. Although she doubted they'd be that keen to have his company.

Not that some of the living were that keen either.

Wax Angel pretended not to see the dead in their ragged uniforms flitting between the trees. She'd been pretending for so long she sometimes wondered why they didn't simply give up and go home. There'd be gaps in the ground waiting for them, mounds in fields and forests that were missing their centres. A lot of her friends and enemies, lovers and family had gone into unmarked graves. You couldn't really bury that many properly; you'd never have time for anything else.

Be practical, give a coffin this Christmas.

That had been a German joke in the winter of '44. Before the Red Army arrived to abolish Christmas for ever. She wondered how many of the old men pretending not to notice her remembered it. The commissar would.

Men like him never forgot.

Snow had fallen in flurries but the paths in the cemetery had been cleared overnight. Dead birds had been collected from beneath their trees and tossed into a bin near the entrance. It was always the small birds that died. Their faster metabolism meant they burned more energy, and they had shorter lives anyway. In summer she was happy to feed the birds on the rare occasions she had food to spare. In winter, never . . . She moved too often and starved too regularly to allow winter birds to come to depend on her. They might come back to where she'd been, find her missing and lack the strength to fly elsewhere. She had enough on her conscience already without that.

Comrade Vedenin, Commissar Milov, Erekle Gabashville. Even General Dennisov, squat and hobbling like some poisonous gnome. At least the general's best friend wasn't here. With any luck Kyukov was dead. She hoped he hadn't expected hell to welcome him.

Even Satan had standards . . .

Wax Angel watched the old men make their way to the graveside. Judging by the folds in their faces and the swept-back hair that had long since stopped being silver, she was still the youngest of them all. Most of them had been born before the century changed and were alive when Gisbert von Romberg, the Kaiser's ambassador in Switzerland, had arranged for Lenin to be shipped through Germany to Russia in a sealed one-carriage train. One of the dumber decisions of history.

These were the canny ones.

Brave, wily or timid enough to survive the Stalin years.

The son's coffin arrived on the shoulders of six officers from the Vnutrenniye Voiska. Dressing up wild dogs didn't make them any less wild or less canine; but she was prepared to admit they stood straight and looked smart enough to carry a box containing a dead idiot. Minister Vedenin took his place behind.

As worthless a piece of shit as ever lived.

Mind you, you could say that about most of them.

The state paid for funerals and by tradition all were open

to the public. Although the earliness of the hour and the
suited young men with hard eyes by the cemetery entrance
had been sufficient to put off the simply curious.

General Dennisov's drunken, one-legged son was there.
As was the boy's bastard half-sister, looking as simple as ever.
Her brother was in full uniform with a rack of medals. The
effect was ruined by the fact that he obviously hadn't shaved
in days. The drunk and his father exchanged glances only
once, a cold wintery glare that both held and then broke in
the same moment.

The half-sister barely raised her eyes from the ground.

It was the girl beside General Dennisov who interested
Wax Angel. Blonde, stiff-faced and beautifully dressed. Western clothes by the look of them.

It took Wax Angel a moment to recognize her.

General Dennisov's other daughter. The dutiful one. The
one who'd been . . . Wax Angel looked at Vladimir's coffin,
now static on the shoulders of soldiers who stood rigidly to
attention, in awe of those who watched them. Vladimir and
the girl had been due to marry, Wax Angel was sure she'd
heard something about that.

The girl didn't look broken-hearted.

If anything, she looked relieved. Her father, however,
looked furious.

Behind Dennisov's drunken brat, watching with much the
same fury as the son watched his father, was the gangster.
That was what the old men labelled Erekle Gabashville, for
all that Beziki was more honest than most. He watched them
all, and there was something taunting about his gaze. He was
stood back, in the shelter of a leaf-stripped tree. The rich-
ness of his sable coat was an insult to the uniforms around
him, just as his cigar was an insult to their solemnity.

The old woman was impressed.

She didn't trust him. She wasn't even sure she liked him. But she was impressed all the same. It took balls for him to come to this.

The fool in the coffin would get a red star on his grave-stone to mark his service. Just as the state provided a grave plot and paid for the funeral, so it provided the gravestone. With an inlaid motif if one merited it.

A musician might get staves of music, an artist a brush and palate, a poet a quill or a pen. In one case, a famous nov-elist got a neatly carved typewriter. When they buried her, Wax Angel doubted they'd even know what name to put, never mind inlay her stone with ballet shoes.

At a nod from Vedenin, the soldiers began to lower the long box.

The man's eyes were unreadable and Tom could barely imagine the feat of will to keep his face impassive. Tom had been so drunk, so numbed by alcohol at his own child's funeral, that he'd almost passed for sober.

Vedenin, however, *was* sober.

His cheeks were dry.

His oration, when it came, was measured. The man spoke as slowly and as precisely as the honour guard had marched and the coffin been lowered . . . His son was a young man taken early. A good Party member. A faithful servant to a state that would miss him. His military service had been exemplary, his loyalty to Soviet ideals fierce. He was too young to be taken from the world by so pointless an acci-dent. But, as the boy's father, Vedenin was proud of what he had achieved. As proud as he was sad at the thought of the gifts his son would never have a chance to use in the service of the state.

Men, powerful men, for all they were old and shuffling

and hunched inside their damp coats, listened intently and nodded at the appropriate places. It was hard to tell whether they agreed, disagreed wildly or were simply thinking of something else entirely.

Their own families, their own deaths?

Their breakfasts?

When the words had been said and handfuls of earth thrown on the coffin, the old men turned to go, and Tom watched Vedenin absent-mindedly wipe his fingers on his trousers. On Vedenin's lapel was a tiny gold badge with Lenin picked out in red enamel. He saw Tom looking at it and bristled, then caught his anger and swung away.

'That badge . . .' Tom began.

'The Order of Lenin,' Sveta said.

Her grandfather had one too. His was also gold, not the platinum from which Dennisov said newer badges were made. If Vladimir had taken his father's Order to give to someone else, Tom doubted it was Alex.

So who had Vladimir given it to?

And had that person been the one to give it to Alex?

A token of love, probably. What else would it be at that age?

Tom thought of the young man burned alive in the warehouse with his wrists wired behind his back, the jade ring he'd been wearing. Another token of love, if ever there was one. *Military. Kept to himself.* That was what the crop-haired boy outside the Khrushchevka said when Tom and Dennisov went looking. To get close to someone military, they had to trust you. Certainly to get close enough to kill.

Vladimir had thought himself untouchable.

Spoilt, indulged, motherless. He struck Tom as the jealous kind.

Jealous and murderous even. What was it Mary Batten had

said? That he'd accidentally reversed over his father's chauffeur, killing him.

An accident, obviously.

A dead rent boy in a pool in Chelsea, when Vladimir was doing his year in London at the LSE. No suggestion that they'd known each other, equally obviously.

Tom was beginning to think it went like this . . .

Someone Vladimir liked, someone young enough not to frighten a fifteen-year-old English girl, falls in love with Alex. Alex decides to run away, being too unhappy and too swept up in her first love to be less stupid.

Vladimir takes it badly. He takes it very badly indeed.

Alex's boyfriend dies. And Alex . . .?

Why was a way not found to return her?

Except that it had been found, hadn't it? The deserted house, the overblown muster of crack troops, Vladimir's father's shock when she wasn't there. Something hadn't simply gone wrong between the planning and execution.

It had been sabotaged.

The more Tom thought about it the more certain he was that he'd got that right.

Examining the mourners, who looked as if they should be smoking cigars in their clubs, or chain-smoking in dark pubs and complaining about the state of the world, he wondered whether the man who sabotaged Alex's return was here, whether the others knew who he was or if he was quietly gleeful at remaining hidden.

A double bluff from Vedenin?

That had been Tom's first thought, once he'd got over thinking Vladimir Vedenin had been behind Alex's abduction, which wasn't an abduction anyway. But Vladimir's father was destroyed. A big beast and dangerous, but hollowed out by the loss of his son.

Beziki?

The way he was watching the others told Tom that his being here had nothing to do with respect. Dennisov's father? Sour-faced and eaten up by cancer, if the commissar was to be believed. Or the commissar himself, who moved serenely among the mourners as if unaware that every single other person in the graveyard was watching him, his grand-daughter included?

One of these, or someone else entirely?

It was Beziki's gaze Tom felt most.

It wasn't hard-eyed like Vedenin's, who still couldn't bring himself to believe that Tom had had nothing to do with his son's death. Nor mistrustful like Sir Edward's, who'd been staring at him on and off since he realized Tom was here.

It was watchful.

The gangster seemed to be wondering whether he could manage a word with Tom without having to talk to anyone else, whether he could still trust Tom if they did talk. The Georgian was heading for Tom and Sveta when he suddenly stopped and Tom realized that the commissar had appeared behind them.

'So . . . how's the sling working?' the commissar asked.

'Well enough.'

Looking over to where Sir Edward stood, Sveta's grand-father smiled.

The commissar had been looking amused since the ambas-sador arrived. As amused as you can be at a funeral without being openly offensive. 'I'm told that at Sad Sam you're the subject of rumours. It would seem Sir Edward's heard them too.'

'About Vladimir's death?'

'Oh, nothing like that. Poor boy. Such a tragic accident. No, these are far more scandalous. Apparently you've defected.'

'You know that's not true.'

'Rumours don't have to be.'

'So tell him that.'

'Why don't you tell him?' the commissar said.

Office workers were streaming from a nearby metro station, heading for grey concrete blocks. An orange snowplough rattled its way along the road, followed by impatient cars. As the first of the black sharks parked there growled to life, it simply pulled out ahead of everything else, claiming the lane reserved for it and it alone. Tom turned from watching it depart and saw Anna glaring.

It seemed rude not to go across.

'How could you?' Anna demanded.

'How could I what?' Tom asked, then couldn't be bothered to make an argument of it. 'I haven't. All right? You're being played. Well, Sir Edward is.' He jerked his chin towards her husband.

'Why would the Soviets do that?'

'I don't know,' said Tom. 'Why don't you ask them? Alternatively, Sir Edward could ask them. Or Mary could do it for him, if he's too gutless.'

'It's the drugs,' Sveta said, appearing at Tom's elbow.

She shook Anna's hand, saluted a scurrying Sir Edward with a briskness bordering on contempt and prepared to steer Tom back to where her grandfather was talking to an old man who stood so stiffly Tom decided he must be a general.

'He's not defecting,' Anna told Sir Edward.

'Is he under arrest?'

Sveta stopped. 'Why would he be under arrest?' She sounded genuinely puzzled. For a moment Tom suspected she was wondering whether he should be.

'If he's not,' said Sir Edward, 'why are you taking him?'

'He needs to go back to hospital.'

'We have hospitals of our own.'

'Our doctors don't believe he'd survive the flight.'

Sir Edward gave her a disbelieving glare.

Tom thought the ambassador might address him directly, perhaps ask if what Sveta said about him not being a prisoner was true. A question he wasn't sure he knew how to answer. But Sir Edward simply turned on his heel and took his wife's elbow, urging her forward when she didn't move. Tom watched Anna shake free and imagined it would be a long drive home.

'This missing girl looks like your daughter?' Sveta asked.

'No. Bec was blonde, pretty, fine-boned.'

'You liked her?'

'I barely knew her.'

'Do you think your daughter realized that?'

Tom thought of Becca, so neat and private.

So terrifyingly self-contained.

It was six months since Becca had died. Did her mother have equal quantities of despair or fury raging beneath the surface? Did Caro fall asleep at night wondering if tomorrow would be the day she'd drive her Mercedes into a tree?

'Yes,' Tom told Sveta, 'I think she might have done . . .'

29

House of Lions

Cancer of the spirit takes you two ways. Those who do terrible things barely notice it eating away at them. Those to whom terrible things are done never forget and rarely get over it. Sometimes, rarely, perhaps not so rarely, you don't even know which kind you've got, which kind you are . . . It was an army psychologist who told Tom that.

The man was mostly full of shit but he got that right.

At least, as Tom told Sveta, he got it right enough for it to stick in Tom's head like chewed gum to the bottom of his shoe. If he was going to be this depressing when drunk, she replied, he might as well be Russian. In case he hadn't noticed, she had her pick of Russians, or would have if her grandfather didn't scare them all off. Tom might want to try being more English. How were the English when drunk?

Sentimental or violent, Tom told her. If she was really unlucky, both.

They were in the House of Lions, the mansion block Stalin had Zholtovsky design for his marshals. It was essentially retirement quarters for the most senior military figures in the Soviet Union, an overpowering yellow building facing Patriarch's Ponds. Sveta's grandfather not only had an apartment there, he had the biggest. The old man was asleep, after the funeral.

'Going to change,' Tom said.

After waiting fifteen minutes for him to return, she went

searching and found him still fully dressed and asleep on a narrow bed she'd used when staying there as a child. So now they sat, by themselves, in the old man's study, a room so completely panelled with dark wood it was like squatting in a cigar box.

Lighting a papirosa, Tom looked around for an ashtray and nodded his thanks when Sveta pushed across a heavy alabaster monstrosity.

'I thought you were taking me back to hospital?'

She shrugged. 'This is close enough.'

'You want a cigarette?'

'No,' she said, 'I don't. Smoking is bad for you.'

'So is getting shot.'

'With smoking there is a choice.'

They sat in silence for a while after that.

The demi-god in a large oil painting, staring across a rolling plain of T-34 tanks towards the fires of hell, had to be her grandfather, Tom realized. He'd already worked out it must be her grandfather's sword on the wall. Overhead, a little chandelier hung heavy with tears. There was a feeling of emptiness, old memories and ghosts too tired to leave about the musty room.

'Venetian glass,' Sveta said, following Tom's gaze. 'A present from one of his mistresses. She had the sense to leave him.'

'I heard that.' Shouldering the door open as if it had personally insulted him, the commissar came in and slumped into a leather chair so ruined that flakes came off on his elbows.

'Doesn't make it untrue . . .' Sveta hesitated, which was unlike her. 'Where did you find that?' she asked, indicating a tiny wax angel that was standing on the mantle. She looked at her grandfather, who stared back impassively. Neither given nor denied permission, Sveta picked it up anyway, turning it over.

She looked troubled.

'Granny . . .'

'Would have loved it. Yes, I know.'

The wax angel's face was blank-eyed but beautiful.

'You'd better put it down,' the commissar said. 'It's evidence.'

'*Really?* In what?' Standing up, Tom held out his hand and instantly regretted removing his sling as pain lanced his shoulder.

'Careful,' Sveta said crossly.

She handed him the figurine and Tom turned it over in his fingers, as he turned his memory of the ragged woman selling those figures over in his head. It was possible that beggars selling wax angels were commonplace in Moscow.

Then again, possibly not.

Before Tom could decide whether or not to say that he'd seen something like it, the old man growled, 'That dead boy's part of this.'

'Beziki's son. From the cult house?'

'Gabashville's other boy. The one found in Red Square. He was frozen, you know. That's where this began.' The old man scowled. 'And don't call him Beziki. He's a bad man. Only his friends call him Beziki.'

'Sometimes bad men are the only friends to have.'

The commissar's laugh was sharp as a fox's bark. Nodding at the sideboard, he ordered his granddaughter to pour him a brandy. Adding please only when the sudden set of her jaw suggested she was going to refuse.

'His eyes were frozen,' the old man said suddenly.

Tom waited. The first Beziki had seen of his boy was in the mortuary. Until now, Tom hadn't even known the com-

226

missar had been at the original crime scene. A dark thought curled like smoke. How many people had as much power as the commissar . . .?

'I like him,' the old man said. 'Believe it or not.'

Sveta looked shocked.

'I know, I know. He personifies the worst of our antisocial elements. But once upon a time we'd have found an outlet for that.'

'The eyes?' Tom prompted.

'Frozen white. Unseeing.'

Sveta snorted. 'The dead see nothing.'

'They see everything,' her grandfather corrected. 'It's their mouths that disappoint. They never reveal what the eyes see.' He held out his glass. Sveta didn't protest but she scowled. 'I ordered an autopsy,' he said.

'On the frozen boy?'

'On the children from the deserted house.'

'I thought they'd been buried?'

'I had them dug up.'

'Chlorine?' asked Tom, remembering a sourness to the air.

Prising himself out of the rotting chair, the old man headed for the kitchen and rooted in an under-sink cupboard, handing Tom a cereal-sized packet with a rat's face behind heavy cross hairs. 'This is usually the people's choice.'

'They used strychnine?'

'They used nothing,' he said flatly.

'Your pathologists couldn't identify the poison?'

The commissar's eyes flared. 'There was no poison. No poison, no stab wounds, no bullets to the back of the head, no bruises around the neck, no water in the lungs, no reddening to the skin where their mouths had been held shut. Nothing.'

'So . . . something your people haven't met before?'

Tom watched the commissar consider this. It didn't make him any happier.

What were the options, though? Short of magic – and Tom was discounting magic – you had something so new or subtle that the pathologist couldn't identify it, or else a pathologist's report based entirely on lies. And who'd dare lie to the commissar?

This was a question demanding further thought.

'Something military,' Tom said. 'Something new. That's the most obvious answer.'

'Vladimir doesn't have that kind of reach,' Sveta protested.

'I doubt it was him,' her grandfather said.

'Who then?'

'My guess is his father.'

'But why? Why would the minister do something like that?'

'Major Fox?' the old man said to Tom.

Because they were both staring at him, he thought about it, remembering the party at Vedenin's dacha on the night of the attack, the boy's childishness, the way the minister fussed. If he'd decided Vladimir was guilty, the answer was obvious.

'He was protecting his son.'

'I'd probably say,' the old man said, 'he *thought* or *believed* he was protecting his son. Vladimir's always been his weakness. Now, let's get this out of the way. Did you make Vladimir drive across the ice or not?'

Sveta froze at her grandfather's question.

'Yes,' Tom said.

'Why?' The old man's question was bald, his tone neutral.

'He kidnapped Alex.'

'You think.'

'I know.'

'How do you know?'

228

'In the same way Vedenin knows I killed his son.'

'He doesn't know,' the commissar said. 'He believes.'

'When has belief ever been less dangerous than knowledge?'

The commissar looked at his granddaughter and smiled. 'He's not a fool, your friend. That's something.'

'When have I ever brought a fool home?'

'You're comparing him to Nicolai?'

She bit her lip and looked away. When Sveta looked back, the commissar was smiling and there was pride, exasperation, perhaps worry in his gaze. Her cheeks reddened until he laughed and she got up to take his brandy glass and pour him another, but really to touch her grandfather's hand as she gave it back. There was a closeness Tom wouldn't have thought either capable of showing, a fondness he wouldn't know how to display himself.

How do you judge your father if his father was more monstrous still?

Tom didn't slam his son's head into a wall, tell him his ma was stupid and he shouldn't have been born. He didn't make his own father's mistakes. But he knew he'd made more than enough of his own.

Tom drank too heavily that evening, washing down codeine with tumblers of the old man's brandy, and spent a dark and painful night in a single bed in a cold box room that overlooked a road rather than the snow-covered pond. He counted off the hours until morning while dodging the worst of his thoughts and wondering where Alex was being held now. In the few moments he did manage to sleep, he dreamed of Alex, buried in a box and running out of air. She wanted to know why he wasn't digging faster. It didn't seem right to say, *I'm digging as fast as I can . . .*

*

'You look terrible.'

'Dreams.'

The old man nodded as if he understood.

Sveta and her grandfather were up and breakfasted when Tom joined them. The commissar pointed at a plate of pastries. 'Take a couple of those if you're hungry.' He looked sympathetic when Tom shook his head.

On the street, a familiar but different crop-haired boy waited by a Zil. Familiar, in the sense that crop-haired drivers are largely interchangeable. Different, in that he wasn't the one Sveta's grandfather wanted.

The old man saw no irony in announcing he was going to fire his usual driver for calling in sick. Even when Sveta pointed out that if he was prepared to fire him he could hardly claim he wasn't willing to be driven by anyone else.

'Open the bloody door then.'

The commissar clambered painfully into the back, glared at the young man shutting his door for him and waited for Sveta to climb in the other side. Tom took a seat in the front and opened his own door, earning a glare from the driver.

The Zil kept to the central lane, even when the roads were clear, and ran red lights as if they weren't there. They stopped only once, beyond Moscow's edge, having suddenly turned off the main road at the commissar's orders on to a snowy track that delivered them, twenty sick-making minutes later, to what announced itself as a Health Spa for Heroes of the Soviet Union.

It looked like a Swiss hunting lodge, with the skull of a huge ram fixed over the door, and the single black Volga parked out front suggested that the clientele was limited. A path from the car park to the front door had been salted and all that remained of last night's snow were patches of slush, surrounded by red mud or puddles.

Sveta sighed. 'Should have known you'd want to stop here.'

'Come on then . . .'

The maître d' blinked at the sight of Sveta's grandfather and escorted him past a dozen empty tables to one in the far corner, pulling back his chair.

'It's been too long, commissar. Too long.'

'You know what I want.'

Bowls of peppery soup, platters of fresh white bread, saucers of creamy butter and coffee as good as any Tom had ever tried arrived in sequence. From the taste of it, the coffee was heavily laced with brandy.

'Good for hangovers,' the commissar told him. 'Have another.'

Yellow-tusked boars glared down at the nearly empty room from either side of a stone fireplace filled with a raging fire. A spread of antlers so huge they looked almost prehistoric hung above the mantel. The only other diner finished his meal, glanced at their table and came across, stopping a few feet away.

'Fyodorov,' he said, introducing himself. 'Leonid Nikolayevich . . .'

'I remember who you are,' Sveta's grandfather said without looking up.

'So sad, Vladimir Vedenin's funeral.'

'What do you want?'

The man swallowed, obviously wondering if he should simply go. The commissar's shoulders were stiff with anger, Fyodorov's face almost pleading. Tom wondered what the story between them was and how far back the enmity went.

'Well?' the commissar demanded.

'Is it true that Gorbachev's calling a small summit?'

'Who knows?' the commissar said. He made it sound like *Who cares.*

'It's just . . . I heard he telephoned you recently.'

The commissar froze, the spoon halfway to his mouth. 'Can I ask who told you that?'

'Word gets around. Is it true?'

'I'm nobody these days,' the commissar said coldly. 'The oldest of the old guard.' He raised his head and for the first time looked at the man who'd interrupted his lunch. It was a bleak and unforgiving glare. 'Still, I'm sure I can arrange for someone to talk to you about it if you'd like?'

'I'm sorry. I didn't mean . . .' The man retreated, walking backwards as if taking his leave from royalty. Sveta's grandfather sighed.

'Preserve me from Chernenko's fools.'

Returning to his soup, the commissar kept at it until his third bowl was empty and he'd scraped the inside clean with the last of the bread. A waiter with a greying moustache removed the bowl and nodded when the old man demanded yet another coffee. When Tom reached into his jacket for his papirosa, the waiter glanced at the old man. 'You'll have to go outside.' Sveta's grandfather said.

The waiter began to say he knew how unreasonable the rules were, that he regretted they applied even to a guest of someone so important, only hushing when the commissar waved him into silence.

'This is a health spa,' he said. 'Clear mountain air for hardworking Party members. You can hardly expect to smoke over your food.'

When Sveta began to push back her chair, her grandfather put his hand on hers.

'I'm sure the boy will be fine.'

'I'm sure I will,' Tom said.

Having stopped off at the urinals, he took himself through a door marked *Gardens* into the sharp smell of pine needles, heading up a snowy path towards a circular bench built round a bare oak at the top of a small hill.

His shoes were sodden before he reached halfway.

At the top, he stopped and lit a papirosa, stared down at the spa below and wondered the obvious. How the fuck did he come to find himself here? In Russia, in the middle of winter, alone on a bench, miles outside Moscow, jagged up on painkillers, staring down at what seemed to be a clinic in name only.

There was no obvious answer.

Not even when he lit a second cigarette.

Money, sex, violence . . . Call them love, banking and politics if you must. Most crimes were birthed by one of the three. Most revenge, if revenge was what Alex was, began with them. High overhead a hawk circled in the cold air, spiralling higher and higher, with its gaze fixed on a particular spot. The sun was already low and the bird's underside glowed as if coals filled its belly.

Follow the money.

Few currencies came softer than the rouble. What did you follow in a state where money was printed to order by the people who ruled, and it bought nothing in non-Soviet states anyway? If he couldn't follow the money, he should follow the power.

Tom was wondering whether he should be getting back when he saw the commissar's driver start up the hill towards him, hands deep in his pockets, shoulders hunched and head down. He guessed that meant the answer was yes. Taking a last drag at his papirosa, Tom ground it into the snow and stood up from his bench.

As he did so, the young man's hand left his pocket and gunmetal glinted in the winter light. Only instinct threw Tom sideways. Pain from his wounded shoulder drove a scream from his body as he rolled, knowing his stitches had burst. The first shot passed overhead. The second hit the snow beside him and Tom rolled again, waiting for a third shot that didn't come. The boy's automatic had jammed.

When the waves of pain receded, the Russian was almost on him.

The young man's boot kicked out and Tom rolled away, managing to avoid a blow that would have smashed his collarbone. He rolled again, saved by slush his attacker slipped slightly on the mud beneath the snow. Then the boy steadied himself and headed straight for Tom. He was younger, stronger, uninjured.

It was, Tom realized bleakly, going to be an uneven fight.

Down below, Sveta yelled and his attacker hesitated. Her shout came again and Tom saw Sveta and then her grandfather, the maître d' and a fat man in white who had to be the cook. The cook had a frying pan in his hand.

Sveta ordered the boy to drop his weapon.

When Tom's attacker went back to wrestling with the gun's slide, she asked if he was mad. Did he know who her grandfather was? He would be executed. His family would be arrested, sent to the gulags. Still the boy struggled with his weapon, swearing as Tom climbed unsteadily to his feet.

'Shit,' he said. 'Shit . . .'

'Give me the gun,' Tom ordered.

The boy yanked at the Makarov. 'You can't have her.'

And the round jammed in the chamber was ejected, the hammer cocked as the slide jacked back, and another round rose in the magazine and slid itself into place. For a second, when the boy spun away, Tom thought he intended to shoot Sveta. Instead he raised the automatic in one fluid gesture, opened his mouth and swallowed the barrel, firing without giving himself time to think.

Bone, blood and brains rose in a fountain from the back of his head, splattering themselves over Tom. The boy's body crumpled and lay shuddering in the snow as nerves twitched and life left him. The commissar looked horrified, but Sveta was already racing uphill towards them. A pistol in her hand that Tom hadn't known she'd been carrying.

30

Back at the Dacha

You can't have her...

The things Tom was to remember about that night were not those he felt he should remember. He should have been worrying at the boy's last words, running through all their possible meanings.

He, Tom, couldn't have her?

Nobody could have her?

What if the boy hadn't been talking about Alex? His accent had been strange. Definitely not Muscovite, perhaps Baltic. He might have been speaking colloquially and talking about his weapon.

Give me the gun.

You can't have her.

It was the second time in days Tom had stared death in the face.

He should be more frightened. At the very least he should feel grateful that he'd been granted more time to find out what had happened to Alex.

Actually, he did feel that. He simply didn't feel anything for himself.

What he was to remember were the little things, the fragile and illusive threads that held the fabric of those hours together. The sound of an unexpectedly loud clock striking after midnight, the little dacha falling back into what he'd thought was silence until he noticed the creak of its walls and the tap of a branch against the window of a different room. The scuttle of a mouse, so different to the skittering of the rat in the cellar before he was shot. The pad of an elderly tomcat checking all was right with the world. All these. And a slowly growing sense that those words *had* to refer to Alex.

She was still alive. What else could *You can't have her* mean?

Against that, he was no closer to finding her.

Sveta's grandfather had settled back into his little dacha as if it was a second skin, drinking brandy from a heavy goblet, fussing over his mog, telling Sveta to take Tom outside and see to his shoulder, while he made a telephone call.

'I've no idea,' Sveta said, when Tom asked who he was calling.

'Can you find out?'

'It's not my business,' she said. 'It's not your business either.'

'Then why am I here?'

In answer, Sveta tipped neat vodka on to a rag and began wiping dried blood from Tom's shoulder. When he yelped, she raised her eyebrows and Tom kept his jaw clamped after that while she tacked his wound shut with a stitch of ordinary thread.

'Where did you learn that?'

She glanced towards the dacha. 'Where do you think?'

That evening, after her grandfather had retired to bed, she showed Tom the stars. They seemed colder and clearer in a sky that was darker and wider than any he remembered. There was no moon and no cloud cover. The nearest town was too small to cast any light and the capital far enough away to be a haze on the horizon.

On nights like this, she told him, she expected Mongols to ride out of the darkness on their shaggy ponies, with their bows over their shoulders. At least with enemies like that you knew where you stood. She smiled when she said that. Then told him it was time he went to bed, because tomorrow her grandfather would want to talk again about what happened when the house was stormed.

'He thinks Alex is alive?'

'Probably. Until she's more useful dead.'

Tom didn't find that reassuring.

Shutting the front door behind them, he shot the bolts at the top and the bottom while Sveta looked on amused. She checked the windows herself and pointed up the narrow stairs, telling him to turn right. No sofa this time. He had a box room at the end. Her bedroom was at the other end. Even from downstairs they could hear her grandfather in the room between, his snore as slow and regular as a blunt saw across dry wood.

You can't have her.

Should he tell Sveta what the boy had said?

To turn it round, why hadn't he told Sveta already? Why hadn't he told her grandfather? Because he didn't trust a man who'd send Sveta and him outside while he made a telephone call? But if he couldn't trust the commissar, who among the Soviets could he trust? That thought brought its own questions. And then he remembered Dennisov.

He trusted Dennisov.

'That boy who tried to shoot me . . .'

Sveta hushed Tom into silence. They'd left the boy on the hill in the snow and kept going, with Sveta in the driving seat. The spa would take care of it, Tom had been told. It hadn't happened. It was not to be discussed.

He would be wise to remember that.

She indicated that he should climb the stairs ahead of her and they went up together, pausing for Tom to get his breath at the top.

'Your shoulder hurts?'

He nodded.

'If Vedenin sent him, my grandfather will find out.'

Sveta shut her door without looking back and Tom went to the box room he'd been assigned and halted, looking for the bed. It was in a cupboard. Rather, it was the cupboard. A set of drawers beneath supported a coffin-like frame on which sat a rolled-up mattress. Unrolled, it fitted exactly.

Painted roses curled inside the doors, which were pierced by heart-shaped air holes.

The wooden wall at his feet showed a naïf painting of the forest behind the hut. The cupboard roof above had the stars he'd seen outside. The only wall unpainted was behind Tom's head. This was lined with copies of *Pravda* so old they showed pictures of Khrushchev. Curiosity made him peel back a corner. Behind Khrushchev he found Stalin and behind Stalin the edge of a saint's halo. In pain or not, Tom was grinning as he turned out the light.

The dreams came in hard and fast and he found himself in a valley, a house on fire behind him and a bastard with a sniper rifle coming after. They hunted him through dark drizzle across a sodden hill under a moonless sky and only the lack of a moon saved him. He dreamed of a white Mini crashing into an oak tree on a dry road under a bright moon, and wept because he could do nothing to stop it.

He knew the man being hunted was himself and didn't care enough to want him to escape. He knew the girl in tears inside the Mini was his daughter and no matter how much he cared her car still carved a brutal scar into the trunk of the oak tree.

He could describe the scar it had carved precisely.

When the Mongols on their ponies appeared, burning

villages, nailing priests to doors and filling the mouths of princes with molten silver, he was grateful for their kindness. They were riding away as they rode in, to the sound of waves on shingle, or a blunt saw across dry wood, when Tom woke with a jolt.

The lights were off, the dacha quiet and the doors to his cupboard shut. But someone else was definitely there. Silent and still. Not touching but crouched above him. They were good. They had to be. It must hurt like hell to hold yourself up by digging your knees into the sharp edges of the bed's box frame.

Clenching his fist, Tom readied to strike.

'Don't,' Sveta said.

A hand found his face, wiping away tears he hadn't known were there.

'Always so sad,' she said.

With her knees still on the frame, she pulled the blanket from his chest and dipped forward to kiss him almost quizzically. Her breasts were heavy against his ribs and Tom realized she was naked; then she reached under the blanket and found him.

'*Sveta* . . .'

'Good Marxists . . .'

Tom felt her fingers tighten.

'Always seize the means of production. That was a joke,' she added, in case he hadn't realized. 'From my school.'

Very slowly, very precisely, she stroked him.

And then, with her knees still on the cot's sharp edges, she lowered herself on to him, lifted herself off and lowered herself again. Her movements carried a precision he'd never imagined anyone could bring to sex.

Only the fact she suddenly gripped his shoulders while her insides quivered told him she'd come. Then she lifted herself away and moved her knees from the cot's edge to crouch by his feet. 'Did that hurt?' she asked.

'Everything hurts.'

'Welcome to Russia.'

When Tom went downstairs the next morning, Sveta's grand-father was sitting at a tiny table in the hall, which had been laid for breakfast with a patched white tablecloth and mis-matched china. An *Oxford Book of English Verse* lay open on the table, a dictionary beside it.

'Know this one?' the old man asked. '"My name is Ozy-mandias, king of kings . . ."'

'"Look on my works, ye Mighty, and despair"?'

'Indeed. My colleagues would say the Soviet Union is the rock on which history has broken, perhaps even ended.'

'Rocks can be worn away.'

'They can split, they can crack, they can sink beneath the waves. Seas can dry, however. Seabeds rise to become moun-tains in their turn.'

'That could be poetry.'

The old man looked at him, the sharpness of his gaze soft-ening as he glanced towards the kitchen. 'I've come to believe history scans,' he said. 'It very definitely flows.' Nodding towards the kitchen, he added, 'I should have you killed. My granddaughter would never know. Vedenin would hardly object. I doubt even your ambassador would make much of a fuss. Sudden fever. Blood poisoning. A fatal reaction to poor-quality Soviet antibiotics.'

'Why would you do that?'

His gaze returned to where Sveta banged pans, clattered crockery and occasionally paused, looking exasperated as she opened cupboards and drawers she'd never bothered with before. 'Why do you think?'

'Frying pan?' Sveta shouted.

'Isn't one,' the old man shouted back. 'Use the coffee pan.'

The splash of water in a bowl and grumbling told them she was washing up the saucepan she'd only just finished using.

'Then why don't you?' Tom said.

'Two reasons,' the commissar replied. 'One, she's not serious. She'd never have let you bed her that quickly if she was.'

'The second?' Tom asked, feeling deflated.

'She's playing.'

'At what?'

'Being happy.' They watched from the little hall as Sveta broke eggs into the saucepan, accidentally smashing the yolk of one and deciding to turn fried eggs into scrambled while there was still time. 'You did bed her, didn't you?'

'It was the other way round.'

'You're the first since her husband died.'

'I didn't know she'd been married.'

'She'll tell you if she wants to.'

'It was unhappy?'

'She adored him. He was a cosmonaut, a good man. The first stage didn't separate from the second. His rocket exploded shortly after take-off.'

'I didn't know.'

'If he'd succeeded, we'd have had our moon landing.'

'He went alone?'

'Three others. You know how ground control signed off? "May nothing be left of you, neither down nor feather . . ." Nothing was, just back to the atoms where everything began.'

'I'm sorry,' Tom said, not knowing what else to say.

'Me too. Now, what was it you wanted to ask?'

'Were you behind the gunman at the spa?'

The commissar smiled. 'It's taken you this long to ask?' He

242

picked up his coffee, looked at it and put it down again. 'Would I tell you if I was?'

'Quite probably.'

The old man grinned. 'You don't think it's Vedenin?'

'What if that's too obvious?'

'Hurt Sveta and I'll have you killed. Probably do it myself. Other than that, what reason do I have to want you dead? Well, what reason would I have had then?'

31

Ural 650

The bike grinding its way up the darkened track was a 1970s Ural 650, with its famously awful K301 carburettor swapped out and the original 6-volt dynamo replaced by a 12-volt model. Other than that, the machine was original. A bit rusted in places, particularly on the chrome. The black plastic band sealing the seam around the two-part petrol tank had rotted but it didn't leak, at least not enough to be dangerous. The gearbox leaked though. There hadn't been a Ural built where the gearbox didn't leak, and that included the model built by workers wearing white gloves and delivered to Stalin.

The man riding the bike regretted not buying the sidecar model.

It would have given him better balance. On the other hand, what with only 40 horsepower to the flat-twin, the sidecar's weight would have made the track in front of him impassable. It wasn't the ice that made the going hard, it was the frayed edges to the road and the sharpness of the bends that had the engine thumping and forced him to change down and down again.

Between a drop in revs and the unhealthy thud of gears meshing, he heard a shot from the woods and flinched, bringing his motorbike to a slithering halt, even as he wondered if he should have accelerated for all he was worth, which obviously enough wasn't much. At best, he'd give the shooter a slowly moving target.

244

The woman who stepped from between trees trained her rifle on him almost casually as she crossed the track, twisting slightly to keep it sighted while she lifted a snow rabbit from the ditch where it had tumbled. It kicked twice and then she had it by its back legs, and swung it so the back of its skull caught the edge of her raised heel. She glanced down to check it was properly dead and then she shifted her attention to the Ural, jerking her rifle to indicate that the rider should climb off.

He shook his head.

Working the bolt, she slotted another round into the rabbit rifle, raising its muzzle enough to aim at his knee, which still hugged the petrol tank. The leg out of sight kept the motorbike balanced on the slippery ground.

'Get off,' she ordered.

He looked at her and they both knew he'd refuse.

But then the early sun came up from behind the trees and brightness filled a patch of forest that had been dark and Dennisov looked at the young woman holding the rifle and felt his heart lurch as she stared back at him.

She had a serious face.

A face that belonged, it seemed to him, to someone who'd never stopped to wonder if she was plain or attractive, and was all the more attractive for that. It wasn't that he hadn't been shot before. It wasn't that there hadn't been days he'd have happily shot himself. It was simply that it would be a pity to be shot, even only in the leg, by the girl from his childhood poster, because that was obviously who she was.

So he shrugged to show that sunlight on her braids had changed his mind, considered which leg to swing over the tank, what he should do with the bike afterwards and whether the track was too slippery to let him pull the bike on to its centre stand.

The answer to the last was probably.

As to which leg, he should probably use the one that worked. So, twisting, more clumsily than he would have liked, he stepped back from the bike, decided he definitely wouldn't manage to get it on to its centre stand, and lowered it as far as he could, before letting it drop.

Stepping away, he watched her eyes widen and saw not only the moment she noticed his metal leg but also the moment she jacked the unspent round into her hand without even noticing. Pushing up his goggles, he said, 'Dennisov, captain, retired.'

'Major Milova.'

The man sketched an unorthodox salute. 'You're going to have to help me right the bike, I'm afraid.'

They looked at the Ural together. The machine was heavy and hot enough to melt snow on the track beneath. 'Did you have it adapted?'

Dennisov shook his head.

'Then isn't it hard to ride?'

He grinned. 'Damn near impossible.'

Coming closer, she wrinkled her nose. 'You're drunk.'

'For me, this is sober.' He was shivering with cold as he took his hip flask from inside his flying jacket and watched her realize he was wearing only a stained singlet beneath. It made him wish he'd found a clean one.

'Army issue?' she asked.

'How did you guess?'

It wasn't a serious question, although the question her eyes asked when she glanced down at his leg was serious enough.

'We crashed,' he said.

'I know.'

He looked at her slightly oddly, as if wondering how she knew, and she stared back, perhaps balancing what she'd read in the files with the cripple in front of her. If she'd read the files, then he knew what she'd be thinking: he was less handsome than his official photograph. He hoped she'd think him more real. She could probably see him killing his own CO for incompetence. Regretting it afterwards maybe. Suffering sleepless nights.

But she could see him do it. That was fine. He had.

He could see her not minding that much. That was fine too.

'Crash?' she asked, nodding at a scar beneath his stubble.

'It's nothing.'

'This one too?' She touched a star-shaped pucker at the edge of his eye.

'Shrapnel,' he told her.

'You could have been blinded.'

He shrugged, and smiled as her mouth twisted. He wondered what else was in his file. Whatever it was, he'd found the right place. Looking at Marshal Milov's granddaughter, Dennisov decided that simply seeing her walk out of the trees into sunlight had been worth the ride.

'You've been shot?' she asked him.

'Oh, yes. And crashed, obviously.'

'Heavy calibre?'

'Of course.'

'How many times?'

'A real man never tells.'

He liked her laughter. He liked the way she walked round to the other side of his Ural without being asked and gripped her end of the handlebars, bending at the knees to lift the machine properly.

They came up the track towards the dacha together, with Dennisov's bike between them, Sveta with her rifle now slung across her back, and Dennisov limping on the side with his prosthetic leg. He wore leather jeans, cut off on that side at the knee and bound with twine to make them windproof. In the dawn light, they looked as if they'd wandered in from another era.

'Thought you couldn't ride that thing any more?'

Dennisov looked at Tom and grinned, his smile wide and his eyes crinkling at the edges. There was a sense of achievement, of pride in the way he patted the tank as if the Ural was alive. He glanced sideways at Sveta before he answered.

'Wasn't sure I could.'

His eyes flicked beyond Tom and he straightened up, coming almost to attention before Tom even had time to turn. Tom knew who was there. The commissar stood in his doorway, wrapped in a patched dressing gown, white hair almost to his shoulders, and the gap between door and frame narrow as possible to keep in the warmth.

'From Moscow?'

'Yes, sir.'

'For me, for her, for him?' He glanced between them and waited for Dennisov's answer.

'You, sir.'

'Any idea why they didn't telephone?'

'I believe it's off the hook, sir.'

The commissar smiled. 'Any trouble getting through?'

'The guards at the bottom stopped me. My papers convinced them. Comrade Vedenin's signature probably helped.'

'Vedenin? Nothing good then. In you come.' Looking at Tom, he said. 'If you could put that thing round the back . . .'

By the time Tom returned, the others were gone. The churned-up snow in front of the dacha was silent and deserted. Two rabbits hung on a hook by the door. A second later, a shot from the woods told him where Sveta was.

He imagined Dennisov was inside the house.

Not wanting to disturb the commissar or interrupt Sveta's hunting, Tom stayed where he was, settling himself on the front steps and digging in his pocket for a papirosa. He had three cardboard filters at his feet and a fourth about to go that way when he heard the front door open.

'The old man wants you.'

'You okay?'

'Sure.'

'Do I ask why you're here?'

'He'll tell you.' Dennisov clapped him on the arm as he edged past, made unsteady by the ice below the steps rather than alcohol. In the forest beyond, wood pigeons rose from frosty trees at the sound of a shot and one fell fluttering.

'That is his granddaughter, right?'

'It is.'

'Guess I'd better fetch her back.'

The old man's desk looked like an old man's desk: a letter opener in the shape of a sabre, an enamel mug with pens in it. A telephone, with the receiver now back on its cradle. Untidy piles of memos probably forgotten even by those who had written them. A fountain pen left open and dried.

Tom doubted that even the commissar knew what half the papers were.

Perhaps it didn't matter. Or perhaps hydroelectric dams went unbuilt, regiments undispatched and prisoners unreleased, unquestioned or unexecuted, awaiting his approval. The commissar was examining what looked like a shopping list, occasionally crossing an ingredient out, when Tom came in.

Leaning closer, Tom saw names.

Under the list, flapping loose, a second sheet, filled with

so many overlapping circles it looked like a travesty of the Olympic logo. The commissioner sighed. 'I miss the days when we fought enemies we could see.'

He nodded towards a photograph of a girl holding a rifle.

She was blonde, with a country girl's shoulders. She looked so like Sveta that for a moment Tom thought it was her. Only the girl's uniform was older, her sniper rifle had a fat scope and looked far heavier.

'Seventeen,' the commissar said. 'Seven kills. Hadn't even kissed a boy, never mind anything else.' He smiled fondly. 'So fierce. So determined.'

'Sveta's grandmother?'

'Yes. She was young. Too young, really. Although not as young as her daughter, poor child. They were bad times. In a way I'm glad she's not alive to see what we've become.'

He answered the question without Tom asking it. 'Weak, corrupt, soft . . .'

'That was taken at Stalingrad?'

'We fought because we believed. We really believed. And because we were outnumbered and because we'd be shot if we didn't. But we believed.' He turned one piece of paper over on top of the other, hiding both.

'Stalingrad or Berlin. Blood and iron. The Motherland destroying their Fatherland. Everything comes back to that. For better or worse, that clash was where this world was made. We became monsters. Our only defence is that they were worse. Now they're gone and we remain and you're ashamed to admit we were allies. Without us, you'd be speaking German. Without us, you'd have a swastika on your flag. Do you doubt that?'

'I'm a soldier,' Tom said. 'I've had men die. I looked at your casualty rates. I've no idea how a country could take that level of damage and survive.'

'Ask your friend Dennisov.'

'He says you're a bunch of alcoholics.'

'He's right. But there are worse things to be. Hypocrites, for a start. We fought. We died. What did Erekle Gabashville tell you about us?'

'Nothing,' Tom said.

The old man's gaze was hard, as if trying to find the lie inside that word. He glanced beyond Tom to the window and Tom turned to watch his friend and Sveta walking from the trees. Another rabbit hung from Sveta's hand and Dennisov was carrying her hunting rifle. The old man sucked his teeth. 'I'm sorry,' he said. 'I hoped it wouldn't come to this. They've found Alex's body. Your friend brought the message.'

'Found her where?' Tom managed finally.

'Opposite my apartment. At Patriarch's Ponds.'

32

Return to Moscow

Tom's shoulder hurt so brutally he pulled the Ural off the road at a food stall and let the Zil disappear into the distance. Wolfing down half of what in England would be called a vegetable pasty, he tossed the rest into a bin, wiped his fingers on its paper wrapper and washed down four codeine with sour coffee.

About ten miles down the road a pain in his gut joined the one in his shoulder and neither came even close to the ache in his heart. Catching up with the Zil, he tucked himself into its slipstream and went back to mourning Alex. He was trying to remember the party.

What she looked like.

Exactly what she'd said.

He could remember the bloody ballroom, its absurdly ornate chandelier hanging from a duck-egg-blue ceiling like a crystal-wrapped chrysalis. The heavy moulding of the cornices. The plaster panels, some bare, others filled with gilt stucco or dark paintings. All hideous.

He could remember those well enough.

He was doing his best not to cry.

He could remember the balcony door creaking, Alex taking her place beside him, leaning on the stone balustrade and staring at the frozen river.

Got a cigarette? she'd asked.

So young. How in God's name had he not realized she was

that young? The harshness she'd put on the G of *Got*. The studied insouciance with which she'd taken her place beside him and stared where he stared.

He'd passed her a cigarette without comment.

I'll need a lighter.

He'd put his Bic on the balustrade and watched it wobble in the wind until she closed her fingers around it. Black nails, he remembered. That jade ring.

These are foul.

She had that right.

With its stub of tobacco only half gone, she'd flicked the papirosa over the edge and they'd watched it plummet to the snow below.

You don't say much, do you?

Too much and not enough. Always was his problem.

What had brought her out there in the first place? Had she known the balcony was occupied? Had it been as simple as seeing him slip away for a fag break and wanting to cadge a cigarette for herself? Had she expected him to refuse? Had she expected to find herself alone? Or was it all part of winding up her mother and stepfather?

Tom hadn't asked if they knew, if they'd been told about the body.

In the back of his head, like a video loop, Vladimir Vedenin endlessly smiled and touched her arm. That was what Tom remembered. That was what he remembered most clearly.

Vladimir Vedenin touching her arm.

Not the wind on the balcony and the discarded cigarette. Not her comment about his swearing, which had been made only to force a confrontation.

Vladimir touching her arm.

And the strange, strange expression on his face before she turned to see who it was, when he thought she wasn't looking.

Had she already made her plans to run away?

Had Vladimir already made his plans to kill the boy she ran to?

For mile after mile, wind whipped tears from Tom's face and the grey road unravelled in a flat ribbon leading him back to Moscow and the horror waiting for them all at Patriarch's Ponds. As the very outskirts became simply outskirts, and their little convoy crossed the motorway used almost as a character in Tarkovsky's *Solaris*, Tom kept trying to remember Alex.

Dark hair and a wide face, high cheekbones and slightly pointed chin.

How much of the remembering was he making up? How much came from simply having seen photographs of her afterwards? And that conversation? Why would Alex force a confrontation about nothing in a room full of ballgowns and uniforms, people there out of politeness, duty or because it was their job.

Why him? Why then?

Tom struggled to remember who'd been watching.

Mary Batten, certainly. She'd started moving across the moment he grabbed Alex's arm, then made herself simply watch how the confrontation played out. And below Alex's cuffs, barely visible in the dim light, raw welts marking both wrists, made by a metal comb, the edge of a steel ruler or the back of a knife.

He'd told her how to do it properly if she was serious.

You didn't need to persuade your parents to buy you a Mini.

You didn't need to find a moonlit night and a long straight road. You didn't need to tell your college friends you had gastric flu and you were going home. There were simpler ways. Kinder ways. Ways to make your intentions obvious.

'Wrist to elbow, if you're serious.'

That conversation was no accident.

If it hadn't been for his benefit, then whose? Unless it was sleight of hand. In which case, what had she been so busy hiding in plain sight? That she was already packed and ready to run? Tom knew he was missing something. Not that it mattered much now, not really. But he'd been missing something.

They all had.

The Zil was already parked when Tom turned in under an arch, narrowly missing an old woman sheltering in its shadow. A *militsiya* guard stepped in front of the Ural, then stepped back at a shout from behind. A sergeant hurried over, hissed something at him and the guard took the bike as Tom climbed off, and was pulling it on to its centre stand before Tom even had time to remove Dennisov's gauntlets.

They were behind the House of Lions, which the locals gave other, less kind names. The Zil emptied and Tom watched Sveta and her grandfather make for a narrow set of steps, while Dennisov strode over to meet him. Jerking his chin at the Ural, Dennisov said, 'Okay?'

'Crap engine. Hideous shocks. Steers like a dead cow.'

'Soviet engineering at its finest.'

They smiled sadly at the lameness of the joke.

'I'm sorry about Alex, okay? Really sorry.'

Tom shrugged, and Dennisov thanked him for riding the bike back, saying he'd have done it himself had his leg been up to it. Tom wasn't sure the commissar would have let him. From what he could see looking in through the Zil's rear window, the old man had been questioning Dennisov most of the way.

Questioning him intently.

Sveta's grandfather growled something from the steps.

'Be careful,' Dennisov said. 'He's furious.'

'With me?'

'With everyone. He's taking the girl's death as a direct challenge.'

Storerooms and small offices, tired linoleum and institutional green paint – it was obvious this part of the House of Lions wasn't meant to be seen by anyone important. Its corridors were rank with ghosts and memories. Every room they passed through had that mustiness found in houses where no one lived. Heavy radiators warmed only damp air. When they reached the bottom of a set of concrete stairs, Tom looked at his friend. 'I'll manage,' Dennisov said shortly.

Hand to the rail, the Russian dragged himself up, the steel tip of his leg scraping each step in turn. Ahead of him, Sveta and her grandfather kept going for another two flights before halting on a landing.

'Shouldn't have ridden that bloody bike,' Dennisov muttered.

'Stump hurts?'

'Bastard's bleeding.'

'Codeine,' Tom said, dragging a packet from his pocket.

Dennisov swallowed a couple dry, shrugged and swallowed a couple more. When they came up behind Sveta, the commissar was saying, 'We'll get the best view from here.' The window he'd chosen was tall and wide, and so badly fitted Tom could feel the cold wind before he was close enough to see the chaos below. The *militsiya* had cordoned off Ermolaevsky Lane, the road on the north-western edge of Patriarch's Ponds, and the only vehicles inside were military. Beyond the wrought-iron railings, the snow-covered grass was thick with uniforms.

What looked like a tent turned out to be lacking a roof.

They'd used a windbreak to cordon off the crime scene. Sveta's grandfather was glaring down and as his gaze slipped sideways, he swore. It was fluent and brutal.

A British embassy Jaguar was trying to enter Ermolaevsky Lane.

As they watched, the driver climbed from his seat and began to remonstrate with the officer barring his way. A thin strip of police tape was all that divided their worlds. The *militsiya* man was shaking his head when Anna Masterton pushed open her door. *It would be Anna,* Tom thought. Turning back, she said something to someone inside the car and slammed her door hard.

The commissar said, 'Fox. Deal with it.'

'I'll go with him,' Dennisov said.

'Take the lift then.'

At the lift doors, Dennisov stopped, looking back to check he was out of the commissar's earshot. 'You and Sveta . . .?'

'*Dennisov.*'

'Just wondering.' The man's face was unshaven, his eyes bloodshot, his hair cropped so badly it looked like tufts on a peat bog. His vest was the one he'd arrived in and it had needed a wash then. He was almost sober, though. A sheen glazed his skin and one eye was twitching. By anybody else's standards, he looked terrible.

For Dennisov, he looked good.

'You can tell me,' Dennisov said.

'This isn't the time.'

'When is?' he demanded crossly. 'For people like us?'

'Like us?'

'Broken,' Dennisov said. 'Buggered. Running on the wrong voltage. In need of new parts.' He was reaching for the button when Tom stopped him.

'You like Sveta?'

Dennisov nodded, something close to anguish in his eyes. Something that made Dennisov glance down and away so that Tom couldn't see anything more. 'Yes,' he said, sounding sad. 'I like her. But if you and Sveta . . .'

The truth came easily.

'There is no me and Sveta.'

They made a strange enough pair coming out of the House of Lions for the *militsiya* guard by the tape to turn to see what had made the Englishwoman stare. When Sir Edward and Mary Batten climbed from the Jaguar it was to try to intercept Tom before he could reach Anna. They'd left it too late.

Dennisov straightened his jacket and Tom found himself rearranging the collar of the coat he'd borrowed. When the guard put up his hand, Dennisov produced a Party card from his pocket and flicked it open. The man's salute was an instinctive, unthinking reaction.

'Is it Alex?' Anna demanded.

'Anna. How do you know about the body?'

'Is it Alex, damn you?'

'We had a call,' said Mary Batten, coming up behind her, 'from a Welsh girl at the university. She was given a message for you. We're trying to find out who asked her to pass it on. Now, unless you're being intentionally cruel, is it Alex?'

Tom took a deep breath. 'So I'm told. I'm really sorry.'

'I don't believe you. It can't be. They wouldn't . . .' Sir Edward stepped around him, scowling as the guard blocked his way. The guard looked to Dennisov for instructions.

'One only,' Dennisov said. 'It's a crime scene.'

'I'll do it,' Anna said.

'Anna . . .'

'I said I'll do it.' She didn't look at her husband again.

Leaving Dennisov to handle Sir Edward, Tom led her into the park.

KGB officers watched them approach, their gazes suddenly flicking to the House of Lions as one of the heavy doors creaked open and Sveta's grandfather appeared on the steps. He nodded abruptly to a thin man in a sable coat just outside the entrance to the windbreak and the man nodded back.

'Is that Marshal Milov?' Anna asked.

'Yes,' Tom said.

Anna's eyes were ringed, her face hollow. She'd lost weight and new lines had etched themselves into her face. All hope had gone out of her. 'Edward says we can't trust you any longer. There's no proof you haven't gone rogue.'

When he put his hand on her arm, she jerked away.

'Let's get this done,' Tom said.

This time, when he offered his arm, she took it, gripping his flesh so hard it hurt. Together they walked towards the windbreak hiding the scene from the skaters still laughing and shouting on the ice beyond. A loudspeaker bolted to a nearby tree deafened them with a waltz, soon replaced by something softer.

'She looked forward to coming here,' Anna said.

'Moscow?' Tom said, surprised.

'To skate. Alex was good at skating. We used to do it back home.'

Did she realize that she'd already begun talking about her daughter in the past tense?

'Major Fox,' Tom told the man in the sable coat. 'This is Anna Masterton, the British ambassador's wife. We're here with . . .'

'I know,' he said. He nodded to Anna. 'Lady Masterton.'

His English was barely inflected, his suit immaculate. It

wasn't Soviet, unless those at the top of the Party had special tailors to go with their special shops.

'I was in our embassy in London. A long time ago.'

'A military attaché?' Anna asked.

He smiled. 'How did you guess? I am a general, these days, for my sins.'

She must have known what he was a general of . . .

'If you're ready?'

She'd been ready the entire time they were talking. She would never be ready. She made no answer. The man held back the canvas and Anna walked through, Tom following close behind. She stumbled, caught herself and Tom and the general hastily stepped back, both watching her fight for control.

A marbled body lay in the middle of trampled snow.

'My God,' Anna whispered. 'What have they done?'

'Frozen her,' the general replied. 'Probably bled her first.'

The killers or killer had also shaved her head and eyebrows and body hair before freezing her. She looked as perfect as a statue, her face turned slightly to one side, her upper lip slightly raised, revealing the tiniest sliver of teeth. She looked so young, so innocent, so unbearably naked.

Dropping to his knees, Tom touched her shoulder. Her skin was hard as glass and white as marble. Not caring that a Soviet general was watching him, he made the sign of the cross over her body. The action was too instinctive to be denied.

When he stepped back, Anna took his place, putting out her hand to touch the girl's cheek. Tears streamed down her face.

'Why would anyone do this?'

'Anna . . .'

Holding up her hand to still him, she climbed to her feet

without Tom's help and turned to the general, casting one last look at the frozen girl.

'That's not my daughter.' Seeing him glance at her tear-streaked face, Anna added, 'I mean it. But she's still somebody's child.'

'It looks like her?'

'She,' Anna said crossly. '*She* looks like her.'

'You're sure it's not your daughter?'

'*Of course I'm sure.*'

But you weren't, Tom thought.

For a moment, right at the beginning, you weren't sure at all.

And for all he'd worked at remembering Alex on his ride down, he hadn't known it wasn't her. 'How alike are they?' Tom asked. Alex's mother took a moment to compose herself, and even then her bottom lip trembled and she rocked backwards and forwards, apparently unable to answer.

'Anna?'

'The mouth is right. The cheekbones. The nose too.' She looked at the girl and shrugged sadly. 'The body type, obviously enough. I don't know about the eyes.'

Ice white, they stared blindly at the hard, grey sky.

The general said, 'I would imagine those match too.'

'But she has an old cut on her ankle and Alex doesn't. And her wrists . . .' Anna fell silent and Tom knew what she wasn't saying. There were no scars on this girl's wrists.

'Why shave her head?' Anna demanded.

The general answered before Tom could.

'Because that way you had to look harder. It took you longer to be certain. Even then, perhaps for a second, you weren't entirely sure. Her nakedness is to shock. The shaved head is to disquiet you.' When he looked up and stepped back, Tom realized the commissar had come to join them.

'To disquiet us all,' the commissar said.

There was a fury in his eyes, a darkness that had been there when Tom described finding the dead children in the derelict house.

Tom trusted the commissar as much as he trusted any of the Soviets. But he wondered what wasn't being said, and whether he trusted the commissar too much.

Whether he should trust him at all.

33

Autopsy

The Central Forensic Laboratory was a modern masterpiece of chrome, concrete and glass designed by one of the Soviet Union's most impressive architects. So Tom was told. Since the post-mortem was scheduled to take place at a red-brick morgue just south of the river, he'd have to take that on trust. From the look of the place, Tom imagined it must have been there since tsarist days. The marble slabs with gutters for body fluids in the autopsy room suggested he was right.

'You're here to observe,' the woman who led him there said severely.

'The marshal has already explained that.'

He was to use 'marshal' in public. The old man had already explained that 'commissar' was fine for family use and between friends, but to avoid upsetting strangers Tom should use his official title. 'Marshal' would do. They'd know who Tom was talking about. There weren't that many of them left.

The young woman with the spectacles, stern face and pristine white coat looked at Tom, her face unreadable.

'The marshal?' she asked finally.

He nodded.

'If you would just excuse me . . .'

She vanished, leaving Tom in a poorly lit room with two empty marble slabs and a third with a body covered by a sheet, under a vaulted ceiling supporting a bank of strip lights that had yet to be turned on. Saws and chisels, pliers and small hammers arranged on a metal rack looked as if they belonged in a carpenter's workshop. When the young woman returned, she looked flustered.

'You're not a doctor?'

'No,' Tom admitted, 'I'm not.'

'But it was your embassy who wanted you here?'

'The embassy approved the plan. It was the marshal who suggested that the embassy might like someone to attend.'

This wasn't even close to true. Sveta's grandfather wanted him there. He wanted a report on everything Tom heard or observed. He'd be getting his own report later. He was interested in how they'd compare. Also, Tom imagined, his attendance was punishment for having doubted the competence of Soviet pathologists. The commissar had said that it might be a good idea if he saw one in action for himself. Unfortunately, presumably for very different reasons, Sir Edward had agreed.

'I was scheduled to perform the autopsy.'

'There's a problem?'

'I'm a qualified forensic pathologist.' She glanced away, slightly embarrassed. 'Newly qualified. My chief is lecturing at the university this morning. He won't be here until noon. I'm afraid we'll have to reschedule.'

'I'm sure you'll be fine.' When the young woman looked doubtful, Tom repeated it. 'Really,' he added. 'I think we need to start.' He could hardly tell her that if she delayed he might not turn up at all next time. He'd almost stopped at Dennisov's for a vodka on his way, only changing his mind when he realized that if he had one drink he'd want another and be even less likely to go.

Shrugging, the woman removed the lid of a reel-to-reel tape recorder, plugged it in at the wall and slotted a microphone's jack into place, pressing record and giving the date. She stopped the machine, rewound the tape, hit play and they both listened to her say, '1986, January ...' And then that day's date.

She gave them that way round.

Then she checked a large clock on the wall, hit record again and gave the time, their location and her name. She asked Tom to give his, and he did. Her manner, which had been uncertain, firmed as she turned on the overhead lights and lifted the sheet covering the body. Tom couldn't help it; he leaned forward and touched the girl's face.

The young pathologist frowned.

'I'm sorry. She was hard as marble last time I saw her.'

'You were at the crime scene?'

'With the marshal.'

The woman nodded, as if his being here was perhaps beginning to make sense. 'It would be best if you didn't touch her again.'

Becca's body had been broken when she went on the table, Tom reminded himself. She hadn't looked like this. So perfect. So unbroken she could be a statue or simply asleep. Frozen for ever between adulthood and childhood.

Lovers, ambition, marriage, children. A whole life unlived.

'Are you sure you want to watch this?'

He was shaking. His whole body was trembling.

'Unfortunately, I have no choice.'

'In that case ... Adolescent female. Height: 5, 4. Weight: 110 pounds. Age: 14 to 16, older if malnourished, younger if well fed ...' The pathologist's sour expression said she thought that unlikely. 'No birthmarks, scars or tattoos. That's unusual,' she told Tom. 'Girls found dead like this usually have one of the last two, often both.'

'What does that suggest?'

'She wasn't a delinquent.'

'Has she been identified?'

'The Soviet Union is huge. Children go missing. Sometimes they go missing in one republic and their bodies are found in another. Communication between police departments can be slow and sometimes complicated.'

Tom guessed that meant no, and the pathologist didn't expect her to be.

Turning her attention to the body, she said, 'Her head has been shaved, her pubis and underarms also. There will be no hairs from the body for testing.' Picking up an inkpad, she took prints from each finger in turn, sliding the filled cardboard slip into an envelope.

'They'll be checked against the files,' she said.

Then she picked up an old-fashioned magnifying glass and crouching close, slowly examined every inch of the girl's face, neck and shoulders and arms, breasts, stomach and abdomen, her thighs and lower legs, and finally her feet.

When that was done, she examined her legs, buttocks, back and shoulders, her neck and skull, before turning her on to her front again. 'No gunshot wounds, no stab wounds, no bruising, no fibres, nothing under her fingernails, virtually no signs of decomposition, one puncture wound consistent with a thick-gauge needle in the crook of her left arm . . .'

Tom remembered at the last minute not to touch.

'She's been bled,' said the pathologist, while Tom examined the area. 'You can see from her colour she's been bled. Also, no lividity.' She indicated an area along her bottom, torso and shoulders. 'Blood would be settling here.'

Bending the dead girl's knees and separating her legs, she examined her genital area, scowling as she straightened up.

'She was a virgin.'

'Are you sure?'

'Do you want to check for yourself?'

Tom stepped back and dipped his head in apology.

'Nothing in the vagina.' With a resigned look, the young pathologist turned the dead girl over. 'Nothing in the anus either. Sphincter presents no evidence of stretching. Muscle tone normal. I'll do the swabs later. Commencing X-rays . . .'

Sliding on a body-length lead-lined apron, she suggested Tom might want to leave while she did this. When she let him back in, she was holding a Practika 35mm with a flash-gun mounted on top. 'I've taken the photographs as well. I can have a spare set printed if you like?'

'The marshal has seen the body. I doubt he wants to see it again.'

'What about your ambassador?'

I don't believe you. It can't be. They wouldn't . . .

Who wouldn't, Sir Edward?

'He has a stepdaughter of this age. I doubt he wants to see them either.'

'Let me know if either of them changes their mind. Usually, at this point, I'd take blood samples to check for alcohol or drugs.' She shrugged. 'I'm not sure that'll be possible. My instinct is she was bled almost dry. So we'll need to take our sample directly from the heart . . . Are you sure you want to watch this?'

Tom wasn't, but he would all the same.

'Your choice.' Picking up a scalpel, the pathologist sliced from one shoulder round the underside of the dead girl's breasts to her chest bone, repeating the manoeuvre on the other side, before cutting down to her pubis.

'Now we fold this back to see if her ribs are broken.'

They weren't. She talked to the tape recorder as she worked, telling it what she was doing and what she could see.

'Removing the ribcage.'

Taking what looked like secateurs, she snipped each rib in turn, grunting with exertion by the last of them. The front of the ribcage lifted away.

'The lungs show no damage. I'm going to try to extract blood directly from the heart.' Fitting a long needle to a syringe, she did so, smiling slightly as the glass cylinder filled. 'Blood sample taken. Heart looks healthy.'

What had looked to Tom like a sleeping girl when the sheet was first pulled back – too young to be there, too beautiful to have anything bad happen to her, as if either of those things made any difference – slowly became less and less human as the pathologist methodically removed the trachea, cut out the heart, did the same to the lungs, then removed and weighed her large and small intestines, liver, kidneys and spleen. Each was inspected for damage, each had a sample taken, each was weighed, each was described as healthy.

The pathologist took urine from the bladder before removing it. She checked the girl's ovaries, fallopian tubes and uterus before removing those in turn. She cut the bladder's connection to the urethra, as she'd cut the rectum's connection to the anus. The contents of the girl's stomach were safely in one container, the contents of her intestines in another. There was, the pathologist told the recorder, no indication of internal bleeding, no obvious signs of poisoning. The only unusual thing about the subject was her lack of blood.

'I'm going to check for deep damage.'

Tom looked over and she sighed.

'Evidence that she was tied up, held down, generally restrained. If she fought against her ropes or someone's grip, it will show. If we're lucky . . .'

Cutting into the dead girl's wrists and ankles, the pathologist found nothing. She did the same with the buttocks and along the length of the back. Then she cut into the shoulders, elbows, hips and knees looking for ligament damage.

'It had to be done,' she said.

To Tom, it sounded like *worth a try*.

The room felt hot, although it was close to zero and the young pathologist kept shivering, despite a bar heater in one corner. Tom had been breathing through his mouth since the pathologist emptied the contents of the upper bowel into an open container. You can get used to anything. He knew you could get used to anything. But he wasn't sure how you got used to this.

'Are you all right?'

'I'm fine,' he said. They both knew he was lying.

'In that case . . . that just leaves the head.' She checked inside the mouth for damage, signs of a gag, signs of injection. 'No biting of the tongue, no biting of the lips. I'm taking swabs from the tooth-gum junction.' She glanced at Tom, her face impassive. 'That's the best place to test for spermatozoa.'

She checked the girl's eyes for any tiny broken blood vessels that could indicate strangulation or choking but found none. There was damage from freezing, even Tom could see that, but the KGB general at the crime scene was right. Whoever chose the girl knew the eye colour they wanted.

'No signs of trauma to the outer skull, no obvious fractures or bruising . . . We'll open it anyway.' For once she was talking to Tom rather than her tape recorder. Having cut round the dead girl's head, just above eye level, the pathologist forced back the scalp and took a handsaw to the skull beneath.

It was brutally hard work.

After that, she used a small chisel to separate the top of the skull, turning it round to use a small hook on its handle to prise off the skull cap. She weighed the girl's brain matter-of-factly, took a tissue sample, as she had from every other organ, recorded that it looked entirely healthy and stepped back, peeling off her rubber gloves. The procedure had taken an entire morning.

'How did she die?'

She looked at him blankly, no longer impressed that a member of the Politburo had sent him, no longer worried that he came from a foreign embassy. Her eyes were shadowed and her face drawn; she looked somehow older than when he'd met her only hours earlier. Tom wondered how many autopsies she'd done and whether this had been the worst. If it was, it was worse than she knew. The girl hadn't died because someone wanted to kill her. She'd died because she looked like someone else.

'Pending test results, I would say exsanguination.'

'Bled out?'

The pathologist's nod was abrupt.

'Is there anything useful you can tell me?'

'She was fifteen or sixteen. A virgin. Adequately fed. Probably not a delinquent. Physically slightly underdeveloped for her age. Her death was not violent in the usual sense. She had no bruising, no signs of having been held down. No signs of having been chained or starved. No signs of sexual abuse.

'My guess, and I'm not meant to guess, is she gave blood. Perhaps someone volunteered her. Instead of taking 500ml, they took the lot. No one cared enough about her to stop them. She was frozen very shortly after, probably commercially, since the ice damage is evenly spread.

'I have no idea why she was frozen. Your ambassador or the marshal might know more than me about that.'

'Will you tell me if they discover her name?'

'If anyone bothers to tell me.'

Tom gave her his card, just in case.

34

Forgiveness

'You look like you've just seen a ghost . . .'

'Worse,' Tom said.

Yelena looked worried. 'What's worse than a ghost?'

'What's left after the ghost is gone.'

She brought him a flask of vodka without being asked and poured the first glass for him. And then, because there was nowhere for that conversation to go, he asked about the three men getting savagely drunk in the corner.

Yelena sighed. 'The fat one's getting married.'

'When?'

'Tomorrow. If he can still stand up. Those are his best men.' She glanced over to where Dennisov glowered from behind his bar. There was no food tonight, apparently. Dennisov had announced that he was sick of the smell of his sister's cooking. 'He's already threatened to throw them out twice.'

'Dennisov objects to them getting drunk?'

'He objects to them getting married.' Without her kitchen and pots and clattering to hide behind, Yelena looked unhappier and jumpier than usual, watching her brother when she hoped he wouldn't notice, glaring back if he did.

Stamping across, Dennisov said, 'What are you talking about?'

'Weddings . . .'

Her brother spat.

For a second Tom thought Yelena would slap him.

'My sister thinks I should sober up. She thinks I should ask my father to use his influence to find me a suitable job. Something appropriate.'

'Not him,' she said sharply. 'There are others.'

'I like this bar,' Dennisov said. 'I intend to stay.'

'My brother married young.'

'Yelena . . .'

'It's a poor excuse. But it's the only one he's got.'

Head down, she started for the kitchen and Dennisov put his head in his hands for a second, shook it bitterly and started after her.

'Let me,' Tom said.

The kitchen felt wrong with the stove unlit and no steam from the saucepans. In one corner, the fridge still chugged noisily. So Tom slipped past Yelena to thump it, as he'd seen her do. For a moment the coils were silent, and then it started again.

Yelena scowled. 'You're going to get my brother into trouble.'

'They've been back?'

'He's being watched.'

'I'll leave . . .'

When Yelena's shoulders slumped, Tom knew that only the chance of a quarrel had been keeping her together. He almost regretted not giving her the fight she needed. But he'd seen families who needed fighting to hold them together. Families held together with belts. Marriages held together with fists.

He shook his head.

When he looked back, Yelena was staring at him. Her voice when she spoke was carefully neutral. 'My brother said you're a priest?'

'Technically.'

'Are priests allowed to see ghosts?'

'Yelena . . .'

She wasn't much older than the girl in the mortuary, Bec's age at most. She had a life to live, as the others had. Tom had a sudden vision of her laid out on a slab, another life ended. He closed his eyes against the thought and opened them to find her still staring at him. Looking into her eyes was like looking into a cave and seeing the embers of a fire right at the back.

He wondered how far inside herself she was hiding.

As far back as he'd been hiding at her age? The trouble with coming from where he and Yelena came from was that you couldn't help recognizing each other.

'Tell me,' he said.

'What should I tell you?'

'Whatever it is you need to tell me.'

He put his hand to her face without thinking, feeling the warmth of her skin, the blood beneath and the heat of a life yet unlived. Her eyes widened and behind them something changed. The emptiness in her face vanished and Tom felt the air quiver as if someone had drawn a note by brushing past a bell.

The light in the kitchen felt more liquid than he remembered, reminding him of dusk in the tropics. But the only light came from a lamp outside, and that cast a familiar sodium glare. He knew before she asked what she wanted. What everyone like them wanted: absolution. Tom wondered if Dennisov believed too.

It would help explain the man's despair.

'Should I kneel?'

'I'm not sure God cares about stuff like that.'

He thought she was going to kneel anyway, but she simply grabbed a chair, turned it round and sat, with her arms folded across the back.

'Are you really a priest?'

'For my sins,' Tom said.

She looked shocked and he reminded himself to be kinder. She was a kid. How heavy could the sins she carried be? 'Say those that you remember,' Tom told her. 'Start with the one that is most difficult to say . . .'

'I killed someone.'

He blinked, and said the first thing that occurred him, which wasn't at all how it was meant to go. 'Did they deserve it?'

Yelena nodded.

'Would someone have died if you hadn't?'

Her eyes became distant.

'Yelena?'

'Yes,' she said.

'You?'

She nodded again.

'Say it.'

'Me.'

To save yourself was no sin. Tom considered saying that but he knew it wouldn't be enough for her. She was waiting for his reaction.

'Are you planning to kill again?'

Yelena shook her head.

'Good,' Tom said. 'You're forgiven.'

'You can't . . .'

'I just did. You took a life to save a life. It makes no difference to God that the life you saved was yours.'

'You're sure?'

There were words to be said, ritual to be observed. A whole series of responses he doubted she'd ever been taught. This was enough. This would do. 'Yes,' he said, kissing her forehead, 'I'm certain.'

If God existed, he wouldn't mind, and if he didn't, it wouldn't matter.

In Tom's experience, the hardest part of forgiveness was learning how to forgive yourself. He knew that wasn't theologically sound, but he didn't actually give a shit at this point. She'd needed absolution. God knows, he could recognize that.

He told Yelena her penance was to live well.

Not piously, not meekly. Well.

Before she could open her mouth to object, he told her she had no idea how hard it would be. She stood, words unborn in her mouth. Then her face crumpled and her shoulders shook. And Tom dragged her to him, wrapping his arms tightly around her. Her hair smelled sour and felt oily under his fingers when he stroked it, as he would for a sobbing child. 'It's all right,' he promised. 'You're going to be all right.'

They were like that when Dennisov found them.

'What the fuck?'

He would have said more if all talk in the bar hadn't abruptly stilled, leaving only Moya Brennan's ethereal voice. His customers might as well have vanished, so suddenly did all conversation stop. Although if they had, a solitary ghost would be clicking skeletal fingers against the keyboard.

'Fuck it,' he said. 'What now?'

Straightening his shoulders, he pushed his way back through the curtains and Tom expected to hear him bark a question. Instead, he became part of the silence.

'All right if I . . .?'

Yelena wiped her eyes crossly. 'I'm coming too,' she said.

Instead of the KGB they found Dennisov frozen behind his bar, looking uncertainly at Sveta, who'd come in full uniform and was staring around as if wondering who to arrest. Everyone she stared at looked away except Dennisov. Her gaze locked on his and he turned bright red.

'You should have taken the job my grandfather offered you,' she said.

275

'I've already had this argument tonight.'

'Not with me. Not about this job you haven't.'

'No,' Dennisov said. 'With her.' He nodded at his sister.

Yelena stared at her brother. 'You were offered a job?'

He ran a hand across his skull.

'A desk job. Nothing I wanted.'

Sveta glared at him and he looked away.

In his filthy T-shirt and cut-down trousers, his stubble almost long enough to be a beard, his prosthetic leg as rusty as the ruined jeep from which it had been cut, he shuffled his feet like an adolescent, the metal one squeaking on the floor. 'I was talking about the job,' he said suddenly. 'All right? I was talking about the job.'

'Introduce me,' Yelena ordered.

When her brother just stood there, she marched across and introduced herself. Sveta and Yelena's handshake was wary, their body language stuttering awkwardness. But something clicked, because Sveta nodded and went to stand at the zinc counter while Dennisov's sister filled a flask with vodka, found a glass, rejected it as being too dirty, found a cleaner one and put it in front of her visitor. Then, and this was something Tom had never seen, she found a glass for herself and filled that too.

'He's a fool,' she said.

Sveta nodded.

The two women clinked glasses in silence.

Killing hers, Sveta shook her head when Yelena offered her a refill, and stamped across to where the Tetris screen was filling faster than the player's frenzied fingers could clear. He stepped back as the blocks overwhelmed him.

'You shouldn't give up,' Sveta said sternly.

The man turned, the only person in the bar not to know she was there.

'Not until you're dead. Not even then.'

She pushed him aside, snorting at the filthy screen. Ignoring the line of roubles marking people's places, she stepped up to the keyboard and when a customer opened his mouth to object, Tom shook his head. Before the man could decide whether Tom had that right, Dennisov was beside him, Sveta's vodka flask in hand. He put it down on the zinc and stayed to watch.

Yelena glanced between the three of them.

The look she gave her brother was a surprisingly cool appraisal. If she were a soldier, you'd know she was wondering whether she could trust her companion. As it was . . . perhaps it was the same. Although the slightly protective way she came to stand beside Dennisov told him it was more complicated. Tom was beginning to realize how fiercely they looked out for each other.

'You have to . . .' Dennisov started to say.

'I can work it out.' There was no malice in Sveta's voice. She was simply stating a fact. She wasn't the type who needed instructions.

Yelena grinned.

The newcomer let the blocks fall, concentrating on speeding them up, slowing them down, shifting them from one side of the screen to the other.

There was no attempt to play.

If anything, Sveta seemed to be memorizing shapes and movements while seeing how fast she could lose. When the screen backed up, she dug into her pocket, slapped down another rouble, planted her feet firmly, twisted her head to release the tension in her neck and nodded to herself.

Having reset the game, Sveta waited for the first block, spun it through 180 degrees, slammed it across to one side of the screen and sped it down, already repositioning the next piece in her head. She was good. Tom realized how good when the regulars fell silent. It was a new silence, which had nothing to do with her uniform or the strangeness of there being a woman in Dennisov's bar.

His customers drank as heavily as ever, chain-smoked and coughed and occasionally vanished through a cracked door into the urinal, but mostly they watched blocks building in lines until the lines vanished, two, three, four at a time.

The blocks fell faster and faster and still they vanished.

At one point they built so high it seemed inevitable that she would die. Men shifted and muttered but Sveta simply continued her war of attrition, holding out for another ten minutes. And, all the while, the number in the corner climbed and climbed until it was way above any score anyone else in that bar had known possible.

'Don't go to war with this woman,' Yelena told her brother, when Sveta finally mistimed a move, the screen filled and her game came to an end. 'You'll lose.'

Sveta smiled at her.

'Could you give me a hand?' Yelena asked.

She was talking to Tom, who followed her through the curtain into the kitchen behind Dennisov's wall of records. Flicking on the gas, she poured cloudy and overused oil into a frying pan as black as any Tom had ever seen and began slicing sausage directly into the oil, shaking the pan occasionally to stop it sticking.

'How can I help?' Tom asked.

'Answer a question honestly.' She glanced towards the curtain to check that neither of the others was coming through. 'You've slept with her, haven't you?'

'Yelena . . .'

'You have. Haven't you?'

'Maybe. Perhaps. She slept with me.'

'There's a difference?'

'In my experience.'

'In mine too. What do you think of her?'

'Smart, determined, damaged, a little strange.'

Yelena nodded. 'You think they'd be good together?'

'You'd try to stop him if not?'

She gave Tom's question serious thought, and in the silence she scooped slightly charred sausage from the pan and dumped it into a glass bowl, which she held over the flame by its edge with her bare fingers to warm. 'Maybe. Then again, maybe not. Anything's got to be better than the bitch.'

'His wife?'

'Ex. She got her divorce.'

'He signed?'

'Must have done. The decree came through today.'

'No wonder he's a mess.' Digging into his pockets for his flat key, Tom stamped out to where Dennisov was standing next to Sveta and slapped his key on the zinc between them. 'My place is yours if you want it.'

Dennisov looked at him. Sveta looked at the key.

'You'll need to talk your way past the guard.'

Dennisov waved at Sveta's uniform as if to say that wouldn't be any trouble and Tom shrugged and told him that *militsiya* major or not, her comings and goings would still be noticed and noted.

'And you?' Dennisov asked.

'He means,' Yelena said, 'where will you be sleeping?'

'I'll use his bed here.'

Yelena blushed, Dennisov looked torn and Sveta sighed. 'It's not you sleeping in *his* bed that bothers him,' she said.

Tom said it was fine. He had something he needed to do.

35

Spinning the Wheel

The house he'd been taken to the time they bundled him into Beziki's car was in darkness. No one answered when Tom leaned on the bell push and listened to an old-fashioned bell ringing deep inside. If Beziki was there, Tom had no sense of him stirring. A light came on in the house next door, and then in a house opposite, and Tom turned up his collar, pulled down the fur hat he'd bought when he'd first arrived in the city and slipped back into the shadows.

He wasn't entirely sure why he'd lent Dennisov his flat.

Instinct, probably. The same instinct that took him down Gorky Street.

The scaffolding was still up around the restaurant. The sign had been replaced though. It now said that the project would be finished in three months – instead of being late, which was what the previous sign had said. The lights were out behind the glass and the place looked deserted. He knocked on the door anyway and when that failed to produce a response, he walked round to the side and hammered on a window.

A couple on their way home, long coat for the woman and tan leather jacket for the man, looked in from the main street, almost said something, changed their minds and shrugged at each other. It was maybe half ten, maybe just before. Moscow shut earlier than any city Tom knew.

'Drunk,' he heard the man say.

They continued on their way and Tom went back to hammering on the side window, wondering how long it would be before the *militsiya* arrived.

Beziki beat them to it.

A door was thrown open inside and his bulk filled the unlit space. Stamping towards the side window, he peered through the glass, his eyes hooded and his mouth set. When he realized it was Tom, he nodded. Tom waited while he threw back the bolts and dug into his pocket for a key.

'This is a bad time,' Beziki said.

A revolver hung from his fingers. He had the fierce sobriety of the God-fearingly sober or the absolutely and unremittingly drunk. He held himself under such tight control that Tom had no idea which it was until Beziki breathed brandy on him.

'You have company?' Tom asked, looking at the revolver.

'Not any longer.' The fat man hesitated for a second, then shrugged. 'Strangely enough, I've just finished writing to you.' His eyes were so haunted that Tom was surprised he couldn't simply see the ghosts behind.

'I'm sorry,' Tom said. 'About your sons.'

'I always knew. No matter how hard I hoped, I always knew I wouldn't get the second one back. It was my decision. My stupidity.'

'You should have given them what they wanted?'

'What they wanted shouldn't have existed.'

Stepping back, Beziki gestured him in.

The restaurant floor was filthy, the tables pushed to one side and the chairs stacked against the wall. The room smelled dusty and unused. It looked so desolate in the light coming in through the front windows it was possible to believe Tom had imagined the waiters and endless dishes of his last meal here. They walked through to the back, avoiding a trestle with roller trays full of congealing white emulsion.

'I sent everyone away,' Beziki said.

He led Tom to a small, dark and empty room with what looked like a cupboard door at the far end. He tried the handle, swore and dug into his pocket for the Soviet equivalent of a Yale key. The room beyond was in darkness too. A lavishly furnished darkness with the silhouette of a chandelier overhead and the shadows of ornate chairs and the outline of a chaise longue against the far wall.

'My office,' Beziki said.

His hand hovered over a light switch and then he decided to do without. Instead he pulled back one heavy curtain to let in the yellow haze from a side street beyond. A truck growled its way along Gorky Street, coughing as it changed gears. 'Sit,' he said.

Tom pulled up a chair and waited for Beziki to take his place behind the heavy desk. The man put the revolver down as casually as if it had been a paperweight. Then he opened a folder, slipped out a photograph and pushed it across. It took Tom a moment to work out what he was seeing.

Six Russian soldiers stood round a seventh. Most of them were barely more than boys. The seventh was tied to a chair and clearly terrified. They were in the ruins of a cellar, with half the ceiling fallen in behind them. With a shock, Tom recognized Sveta's grandfather as the oldest. 'Berlin?' he said.

'Of course. Where else?'

Two of the group stared at the camera.

One looked solemn. The other was grinning.

'General Dennisov,' Beziki said. 'And Kyukov, his attack dog. They grew up together. These days, Kyukov's in a camp. With luck he'll die there.'

'Grew up together where?' Tom asked.

'Beyond Volgograd, Stalingrad as was. You heard of the Tsaritsyn Monastery? It was the scene of a massacre. Became an orphanage after that. I bribed the Oblast for the records. They arrived by truck. Boxes of mouldering cards. Kyukov's were what you'd expect. No mention of Dennisov at all. These days he claims his father was a Cheka officer. I couldn't even discover when he had the records cleaned.'

'There are other photographs?'

'Take them with you when you go. I was going to drop them at Sadovaya Samotechnaya. Do what you want with them.'

'Who's in the chair?'

'Now there's a question.'

'Beziki . . .'

'He was a junior political.'

'You had political officers on the ground?'

'Of course. The colonels told us how to fight, political officers how to think. I was too young. They wouldn't let me in. I had to wait outside.'

'Why did they do it?'

'Ask them. Better still, don't. Burn the file. Go home, mourn your daughter, comfort your wife, reassure your son. Let the dead bury their own bloody dead . . .'

'I have to find Alex.'

'Ask yourself why she matters more than doing any of that. Now, tell me about yourself. Tell me who Tom Fox really is.'

'There's not much to tell.'

'That's a lie.'

Tom ended up filling in the gaps.

The brief campaign in Belize where Tom, as a very young lieutenant, found himself drinking in a shack with a machine-gun-toting bishop. His years of walking across Hungerford Bridge from Waterloo to the MOD, mostly in a suit, occasionally in uniform. How far his work for military intelligence took him from what he'd once thought of as God's business.

'You know the motto of the chaplaincy?'

Beziki shook his head, stubbed out his cigar with half still to burn and selected another, rolling it between his fingers and listening to it crackle, before biting off the end and reaching for his desk lighter.

'In this Sign we Conquer.'

'Justinian.'

Tom looked at him and Beziki shrugged.

'I believe,' he said. 'That's one of my problems. Get to my age and you begin to wonder what's waiting. I can justify every dead Nazi. I don't regret a single one. They invaded and we chased them back to their nest and destroyed it. There are things after that . . . I'm going to find those harder.'

Tom nodded to show he understood.

'Do British priests believe in God?'

'Some of them, perhaps.'

'I'm not sure ours do. They're state-appointed. Mind you, it probably beats being a ticket inspector if you're a smart boy who can keep his nose clean. We have freedom of religion, you know. It's in our constitution. It's just that most citizens have the sense not to exercise it. Was that you? A smart boy who didn't want to inspect tickets?'

'I need a drink,' Tom said.

'I heard you were cutting down.'

'They lied.'

'Not from what I hear.' Pulling open a drawer, Beziki took a fresh bottle of *chacha* and broke the seal, filling its long metal top until the viscous liquid threatened to overspill the thin metal edge. Pushing it across the desk, he said, 'Here.'

Tom downed the makeshift shot glass in one.

'Need another?'

Tom shook his head. 'I watched a dead girl being disembowelled this morning,' he said. 'It was very methodical. Very precise. She began as human and ended up as cuts of meat. And nowhere could I see space for a soul.'

'You just tell yourself you don't believe. Now, this vocation of yours . . .'

'It wasn't much of a vocation. Not really.'

And memory took Tom back to a small church on the edge of an army camp where his dad was based, somewhere hot and nasty, where the local gods were darker and stronger and had taken the trappings of the new religion. He'd come, aged seven, looking for answers to the only question that really bothered him.

'How do you get God to give you something?'

'You don't.' The padre, tired and sweating and ready for retirement, had looked at Tom's stricken face and softened his words. 'It doesn't work like that.'

'What if I offered him something?'

The man had smiled. 'You have a very Old Testament view of the world. I know people kill cockerels round here, but my advice is pray.'

'But I could make an offering as well?'

'Nothing living.'

'What then?'

'A promise, if you must.'

'That would help?'

'Well,' said the sweating man, conceding defeat or perhaps humouring the small boy with a swollen lip and bruises on his face, 'it might.'

Silently, Tom made his promise on the spot.

If God would get rid of his dad, he'd serve him.

A priest was what his mother wanted him to become. He'd always known.

Tom had meant God to kill his dad. Instead, He'd had him arrested. Awaiting court martial for rape and theft wasn't as good as being dead but it would do. When Tom told his ma he was going to become a priest, she smiled for the first time in a year. It was she who told Social Services when she and Tom got home, and it was Social Services who found a Catholic school in Kent that took boys from difficult backgrounds for boarding.

36

Finding Schultz, Berlin, April 1945

How could you find one German in a city full of dead men when most of the living lied about who they were, what jobs they had held and where they lived? After three false leads, and sorting through the bodies of the old men who had been forced into Volkssturm battalions to defend Berlin to the last and killed before they could even really start fighting, Colonel Milov was in a foul mood.

Beziki decided to stay silent.

He still trotted at the commissar's side, drawing amused glances, sometimes disgusted ones. He didn't see what the problem was. Other battalions had pets. Some had cats, one had a goat. His had him, Beziki.

The air around him stank of sulphur from artillery fire, while dust filled the ruined canyons of the streets like fog. Most of the government buildings were roofless, with dark holes where their windows had been. Later he would discover that a quarter of a million had died during these last few weeks of war. The only dead in sight were a dozen bodies slumped below the U-Bahn sign towards which the commissar was striding.

They were boys Beziki's age, none in uniform. Their hands were tied behind their backs and a line of bullet holes in a wall showed how they died.

'Recent,' the commissar said.

He was talking to himself.

Beziki knew that the Germans killed their own people for showing insufficient enthusiasm. So did his side. It was just that recently the Germans had become much less enthusiastic about this war.

Glancing at the bodies, Beziki shrugged and examined the U-Bahn's steps. Dr Schultz, the scientist Colonel Milov wanted, was somewhere down there in the darkness, forced into a Volkssturm battalion by some idiot with a death wish. That was what the commissar said, anyway. He also said there were 200,000 German soldiers supposedly protecting two million Berliners. If you could call a force cobbled from children, old men, released prisoners, the sick and the insane soldiers. There were fewer now.

Behind the commissar and Beziki, ministerial office blocks burned in hissing fury. Artillery fire, the thud of mortars and the crash of walls collapsing, roofs caving in and the clatter of tank tracks formed a backdrop to an incessant crackle of small-arms fire. There were fewer bombing raids now the fighting was street by street, building by building and hand to hand.

It would be over in days, the commissar said.

Howitzer fire from the Zoo gardens fell on Soviet troops trying to take the Reichstag. The building had been empty since it was damaged by fire in the 1930s but that just meant German soldiers had been able to dig themselves into the rubble. Beziki was grateful he wasn't in there trying to get them out.

'Wait,' Colonel Milov told Beziki.

He removed the NKVD tabs from his own collar.

The boy understood. The man was a tank commander, and a commissar before and after that. 'Right,' he said. 'Let's retrieve our man.'

The major he approached swung round crossly, realized he

was talking to a senior officer and bit back whatever he'd been about to say. It seemed that two hundred, perhaps three hundred Volkssturm were holed up in the underground station.

'I'm delighted that you haven't attacked. But do you want to tell me *why* you haven't attacked?'

The major pointed to a girl in the entrance holding a soiled pillowcase tied to a broom. 'I thought, Comrade Colonel, I thought . . .'

'You thought right.'

The commissar stopped in front of the girl, who stared at him wide-eyed and gripped her makeshift white flag more firmly than ever. She was thinner than any girl Beziki had seen. Poor, dark-haired, possibly foreign. Her eyes were dark and sunken, her cheekbones painfully sharp and she was chewing her lips, which were chapped. Beziki adored her on sight.

She had been sent to say there were women and children inside.

'And?' the commissar demanded.

The girl blinked. After a moment, she repeated her words. 'What do these women and children have to do with me?'

Obviously panicked, the girl glanced towards the dark steps down to the metro station below, hesitated and turned back, words spilling over so fast that the corporal sent to act as the commissar's interpreter had trouble doing her job.

'You're meant to let them go.'

'Who says?'

'A Major Kraus. He said she was to tell the Russians there are civilians. Then the civilians would be allowed to go and the soldiers remain.'

'Are the soldiers Volkssturm?'

It seemed they were. Lots of them. What was lots to a frightened girl? A dozen? A hundred?

'Ask her if they're in the tunnels.'

The tunnels had fallen in. Bomb damage. They were on the platforms. Apparently he had to let the civilians go, or they'd be killed in the fighting. There were sick people down there too, old women, babies.

Beziki watched, wondering what the commissar would do.

It seemed that the commissar was wondering the same thing himself. Catching Beziki watching him, he smiled sourly. 'It seems,' he told the boy, 'that this major wants them out of his way.'

'Makes sense,' Beziki said.

'For him, perhaps. Not for me.' To the interpreter he said, 'Tell the girl to tell the major I want to talk to him.'

'He said she was to talk to you.'

'Why her?'

'She's Romanian. It doesn't matter if she gets shot. What should I reply?'

'He must talk to me himself. Ask how many staff he has.'

The girl looked puzzled at the question.

'When he walks, how many walk with him? One, two, five?'

Two, apparently.

'And soldiers of his own?'

A few. Very few, it seemed. Most were Volkssturm, old men or boys her age. The real soldiers were dead. Or they'd run away.

'If her major wants to negotiate free passage for civilians, he's to talk to me. And tell her to leave her bloody broomstick by the wall.'

'Comrade Colonel . . .'

In a street behind them, an M-34 fired and the Soviet major who'd had his men facing the U-Bahn steps twitched. Beziki waited for the ringing in his ears to stop, and watched the commissar nod to say the major should continue.

'Sir . . . we should shoot them all.'

'There's a man down there I want. As for the rest . . . Three months ago, I'd have agreed. Now, we're going to need them.'

'To do what, Comrade Colonel?'

'Rebuild this, repair that. Berlin's ours. I imagine we'll be keeping it.'

The major smiled as if that hadn't occurred to him, and it probably hadn't. It wasn't his job to have thoughts like that. It wasn't really Colonel Milov's job either, but that didn't stop him.

'Sir,' Beziki said.

'Seen them.'

A tall Waffen-SS major was climbing into the daylight, flanked by two lieutenants, the girl trailing behind them like an unwilling shadow. The major was the commissar's age, which made him almost twice as old as his lieutenants. The major picked out his adversary without difficulty.

'This won't take long,' the commissar said. Then, to the German: 'Major Kraus?'

The two officers stared at each other.

'You wish to surrender?'

The German smiled thinly. 'There is no question of surrender. Orders have been issued. We will fight to the last man.'

'Whose orders?'

'The Führer himself.'

'Your Führer is dead.'

'I do not believe it. Even if it were true, all the more reason to obey.'

The commissar looked at him thoughtfully. 'How many civilians do you have sheltering in there?'

'Two hundred.'

'And troops?'

'Three hundred crack troops.'

So, no more than a hundred Volkssturm at most. 'The girl said your army was made up of old men and children.'

The major's face tightened. 'They will do their duty.'

'I do hope not.' Drawing his Tokarev, the commissar shot him through the head. Beziki gasped as blood and brains splattered the German aide-de-camp standing slightly behind the major, gasping again when the commissar killed that man before he even had time to finish wiping his face. The junior lieutenant had his Luger levelled when a sniper's rifle cracked from a building high behind and the German boy went down with a bullet between the eyes.

Beziki managed a grin.

Lieutenant Maya; it had to be.

She wouldn't let the commissar forget that shot in a hurry.

'Go down there,' Colonel Milov told the interpreter. 'Tell them Berlin has fallen. The major has surrendered. Tell them I'm looking for Dr Schultz. He is to make himself known to you. He is not in trouble. He will be well looked after. Say we have his family in protective custody already.'

'We've done it?' Beziki asked.

The commissar looked down at him. 'Yes,' he said, clapping the boy on the shoulder, 'we've done it. Now, stand still . . .'

Digging into the backpack Beziki carried, the commissar found the loaf of black bread and chunk of cheese the boy had stolen that morning when he thought no one was looking. Nodding at the Romanian girl, he said, 'Take your little friend somewhere and share this. I'm sure she'll be grateful.'

When Beziki got back, the commissar was questioning a nondescript German in an ill-fitting uniform. The man was carrying a rabbit rifle.

*

A woman came down the steps of the house crying, wrapped her arms round Dr Schultz and held him so tightly he might as well have been straitjacketed. After a moment, his hand came up to stroke his wife's hair and she buried her face in his neck and began wailing. Behind her, a blond boy of about fifteen and a girl a few years younger looked on, embarrassed. They'd had a day or two to adjust to being safe and to turn back into children. Although the manicured lawns of the strange concrete house, the blossom on the neatly pruned cherry trees and the neat rows of peas in the vegetable garden suggested that the war had never come that close.

The only person who didn't look happy was a hard-faced woman in her sixties dressed entirely in black, who didn't bother to hide her contempt either for the returning man or for his new Russian friends. Eventually, Dr Schultz peeled his wife's arms from around his neck, took her hand and led her inside. When they reappeared an hour later, he was freshly shaved, his mismatched uniform had gone and he was wearing a dark suit, white shirt and red tie. She was smiling.

'My turn,' Lieutenant Golubtsov said. He dug into his pocket for a notebook with a pencil pushed into the gap between the sewn pages and the spine. When he flipped it open, the commissar was surprised to see the pages were empty.

'You've memorized the questions?'

The boy looked embarrassed, as if the commissar had just said something stupid. 'There aren't questions, as such, Comrade Colonel. I simply need to make sure our German understands his physics, that the answers he gives me make sense.'

'And you're qualified to judge that?'

'Oh yes, sir. I mean . . . I hope so.'

Having misplaced them, the commissar found Golubtsov and Dr Schultz two hours later in the garden, drinking tea from china cups and eating pepper biscuits, with their heads bent together as if they were old friends. The notebook that had been empty was now full and Golubtsov was grinning.

'He's the real thing?'

'Oh yes, sir. Very definitely. He's absolutely brilliant. I've just been telling him how much he'll enjoy life at Moscow University.'

'You've explained the travel arrangements?'

'Yes, Comrade Colonel . . .'

The German would leave on a flight from Tempelhof to Moscow first thing next morning. The rest of his family would follow by train within the week. That would allow them to take their prized possessions.

'And the poodles?' the lieutenant asked. 'He really can't take the poodles?'

'They'll be well looked after,' the commissar replied, knowing he'd shoot the animals the moment the family was gone. When the lieutenant asked something, Dr Schultz nodded firmly, patting his pockets.

'What did you just ask?'

'If he had all his working notes. Those are to go with him on the plane. My father was quite firm about that.'

'Your father?'

The boy named a high-ranking member of the NKVD, a man whose position gave him direct access to Beria, possibly to Stalin himself.

'Who else knows of this?'

'That my father's Beria's right-hand man?'

The commissar winced.

'Kyukov asked. Then Dennisov. I thought they were being *funny*. I thought you knew. People always know.'

'Well,' the commissar said, 'we didn't. You can travel on

294

the same plane. Dr Schultz will need someone to babysit him. I'm sure you'll do fine.'

An hour later, the general who had given the commissar the job of retrieving Dr Schultz called. Having praised Colonel Milov's success, and saying that he'd never doubted for a minute the colonel's competence, loyalty or ability, he added that he'd be happier if Lieutenant Golubtsov remained in place. His father would also regard it favourably. The boy spent too much time wrapped up in his books. It wouldn't hurt him to get a little experience of the real world . . .

What he meant, the commissar realized, was that it wouldn't hurt for the boy's father to be able to say his son had been in Berlin. After the battles were done, of course. But why mention that? The boy could go back to his university with a handful of medals and a couple of photographs of himself in uniform.

Glittering careers had been built on less.

'Comrade General . . .'

'You do know who his father is, don't you?'

'I do now,' the commissar said.

There was silence on the line.

'I mean,' said the commissar, 'I can think of nothing better than the chance to fly home, to be safe with my family.'

'Your wife is dead. Your father is dead. I was under the impression that your lover was with you . . .'

'Russia is my family. I was speaking figuratively.'

'Of course you were.'

The line went dead.

The next time the commissar saw Golubtsov he was with Dennisov and Kyukov and they were heading out in the lend-lease Jeep. The lieutenant had a borrowed helmet pulled low over his face, a hunting rifle jutting from between his knees and a bottle of champagne in his hand.

Kyukov was grinning.

'Sir . . . Sir . . .'

The commissar came awake without even realizing he'd pulled the Tokarev from under his pillow until Beziki twisted away and threw up his hands as if to ward off a bullet. Dropping out the magazine, the commissar worked the slide to eject the round he'd jacked into the chamber on instinct.

'We're under attack?'

'No, sir.'

'The war's ended?'

The boy shook his head.

'Stalin himself is on the phone?'

'No, sir.'

'Then why the fuck are you waking me at whatever time of night this is and who the fuck said you could enter my room without knocking?'

'Sir. I think you'd better come.'

'What is it?'

'You'd better see for yourself.'

At the front door, the commissar found Dr Schultz, his wife and son being prevented from leaving by Maya and a sergeant he only vaguely recognized.

'What are you doing here?'

'I came to see you,' Maya said. 'Unfortunately for me.'

Telling the sergeant to keep the family inside, she led the commissar down the steps. For all its brutalist concrete and glass, Dr Schultz's house looked so peaceful at night in its tended gardens the commissar wondered if Allied pilots had been told not to bomb it. The Red Army had certainly had.

'Golubtsov's missing,' she said. 'Kyukov and Dennisov

have taken the jeep. They've gone to find him. They sent Beziki to Golubtsov's room to see why he'd gone to bed early and Beziki found . . . He found a blood-covered dagger. One of those swastika ones. You're not going to like this.'

She led the commissar between the cherry trees towards a stable block beyond them. Beziki stood by the stable door, looking green in the light of the hurricane lamp he held in his shaking hands. There was vomit at his feet.

'Who's in there?'

'No one, sir.'

'No one?'

'Except . . .' Turning aside, the boy spewed what was left of his supper on to the cobbles of the stable yard. He was still apologizing when the commissar said: 'Give that to me.'

Taking Beziki's lamp, he pushed open the door.

Inside was hotter than hell. Bales of straw piled against the walls generated their own heat. It took him a moment to notice anything wrong. For a split second after that, his mind simply refused to accept what he was seeing.

Hanging by her heels from a rafter, Dr Schultz's younger child was a flayed mockery of everything that had once been human. It was only when he got closer that he realized she was still alive. Raw flesh glistened with lymph from where her body had fought to protect itself.

Her eyes watched him get closer, her shoulders hunching at the sight of his uniform.

Black blood at her mouth made him realize her tongue had been cut out. Stepping back, he lifted the lamp to force himself to look at her and managed only a moment. Then he flicked open his lock knife, put his hand to her back, wincing as she arched away with a silent scream. As his blade slid between her ribs, she stiffened and then her body went slack.

37

Questions and Answers

'The boy tied to the chair is Golubtsov?'

'It destroyed his father. Destroyed us too. We simply didn't realize it at the time. For a month or two we thought we'd got away with it. No one else knew the truth. There was no reason why they should. Then things got complicated . . . *We have no choice*. That was what the commissar said.' Beziki sounded sick. 'You know Milov's daughter killed herself? I lost my sons. Vedenin's boy is dead. Your friend Dennisov refuses to have anything to do with his father. We brought this on ourselves.'

There was such despair in Gabashville's eyes that Tom wondered what he was missing. The man in front of him was thinner than Tom remembered, his face almost hollowed out with misery. Skin and flesh folded over nothing inside.

'You gave him a clean death?'

'You know we didn't. You don't tie people to chairs if you intend to give them a clean death. You put them against a wall.'

'It was war,' Tom said. 'Bad things happen.'

'You don't understand . . .'

What didn't he understand? Tom thought of Beziki at Vladimir Vedenin's funeral, on the edge of things, and wrapped in his sable coat, like the ghost of Hamlet's father. Vedenin's tight politeness to the other old men. The bitterness with which General Dennisov watched the proceedings. The way the commissar ignored the general entirely. What should that tell him? Apart from the fact that they seemed more like a family trapped by old hatreds than the rulers of one of the most powerful states in the world.

Trapped . . .

That was the answer.

What could trap men like these?

'It wasn't really him?' Tom said. 'Golubtsov wasn't the killer?'

Beziki looked more haunted than ever. 'We thought it was,' he said. 'For God's sake, I found the knife in his room. What was I meant to think?'

'You were meant to think that.'

'Yeah. Only Golubtsov was untouchable. But then another flayed body turned up and the commissar decided he wasn't untouchable after all. So we did . . .' Beziki reached blindly for his glass, realized it was almost empty and drank the drops in the bottom. 'We did what the commissar said we had to do.'

'And another flayed body turned up?'

Beziki gazed at Tom, owl-like.

It wasn't that hard to work out though. If the murders had ended with Golubtsov's death, all this would be a grim memory, walled off and consigned to wherever grim memories go to be ignored if they can't be forgotten. The answer could only be that they'd killed the son of Marshal Beria's deputy and the murders had kept happening.

'They decided it was me,' Beziki said.

'But it wasn't?'

'The commissar thought it was. He thought I'd tricked him by blaming Golubtsov. I couldn't believe it. I was their mascot. I thought we were friends.'

'Who was it?'

'Not me,' Beziki said fiercely. 'That's the only thing I know for certain. Dennisov maybe. Vedenin. For a long time I thought it was the commissar. I figured that had to be his reason for trying to blame me.'

'What happened to the Schultz family?'

'Dr Schultz flew out the next morning, shaking and distraught that his daughter had been raped and strangled. That was what the commissar said had happened. His wife and son left the day after. Only his mother-in-law refused to go, said she wasn't going to live among rapists and murderers. It didn't matter that we told her renegade Nazis had done it. She was a Nazi. She didn't believe us.

'When the British took over our sector, the bitch went to them and reported her granddaughter's death as a crime. For reasons I don't understand, a young lieutenant decided to investigate. I'm told the commissar recently indicated that, purely for historic reasons, he'd like a copy of that report. London refused.'

'Why are you telling me this?'

'Work it out.' Pouring Tom another *chacha*, Beziki took another for himself and pushed across the silver desk lighter when Tom reached for his papirosa.

'Want one?' Tom asked.

'I prefer these.' Beziki extracted a robusto from his burr walnut humidor, lighting the cigar slowly. 'They were good boys, my sons. Better than me at that age anyway. I know you were there when Misha died. My contacts are good. I knew within half a day. So, tell me what happened.'

Looking at the revolver on the desk, Tom wondered if that would be wise.

'Please,' Beziki said.

'Your boy was in a turret with a rabbit rifle. Single shot, lever action, small calibre.'

'A tenth birthday present. I'd have given him mine, the one I first used to shoot Germans, but it was lost in the war.'

'He was good,' Tom said, knowing that was important.

'I taught him myself. We shot pumpkins, then melons, then apples.'

'It was dark when we arrived. Spetsnaz had been watching the house since the afternoon. It was surrounded on all sides and they'd been told, at least I was told that they'd been told, it was occupied by a cult.' Tom hesitated. 'I'm sure Vedenin thought Alex Masterton was there.'

Beziki had been in enough battles to know it stank before Tom was halfway through his story. Tom stressed how good a shot Beziki's son was, how one boy with a rabbit rifle pinned down Internal Troops.

'Briefly,' Beziki said.

'Yes,' Tom said. 'Briefly.'

He told the man how his son had kept fighting to the end, how an officer had closed the boy's eyes in death and covered him with a curtain as a mark of respect. Beziki listened and Tom had no idea what he thought, because his eyes were shadowed and his face hidden behind cigar smoke the light from the alley wasn't bright enough to cut through. When Tom reached the part about the locked door to the cellar, Beziki leaned forward, listening intently.

'They were told they were having a day out,' Beziki said.

That was when Tom knew Beziki's contacts really were good.

There'd been no mention of the siege in the press. No mention of children missing from any orphanage or children's home. Nothing about a cult, a deserted house, an attack by Internal Troops or a dead delinquent found on a landing below an octagonal wooden turret. From what Tom had heard, Beziki had been summoned to the central morgue and invited to identify the multiply-shot boy on the slab as his son.

It was an intentional cruelty.

The state killed the boy and the state buried the boy and his father's involvement simply extended to being invited to identify a corpse and being notified of the time of his son's funeral. 'He was given a choice,' Beziki said. 'My life or his.'

Picking up the revolver, he looked down its barrel, shrugged and spun the cylinder, which clattered like a rattle. 'There are people you should kill the first time you meet them. People you do kill but shouldn't have. Both of those will come back to haunt you.' He looked at Tom and smiled sadly. 'You know this. Of course you know this. Some people kill from hate, some from duty. Some love the thrill. Others do it to keep boredom at bay . . .

'I couldn't give up my comrades. Not even for my sons. My sons wouldn't give me up. I don't know what they told my first boy. Perhaps nothing. Perhaps they simply killed him and dumped him in front of the Kremlin. But I know they told Misha that if he fought they'd let me live. If he didn't, they'd kill him and kill me anyway.'

'How do you know this?'

'Someone told me.'

'Beziki. Which someone?'

'He's in a cellar, tied to a chair.'

Erekle Gabashville – gangster and father, veteran and renegade – thumbed back the hammer on his revolver and flipped the cylinder.

'They?' Tom said.

'Is that your question?'

Beziki lifted the revolver, the heavy desk a barrier between them. His thumb found the hammer and his finger threaded through the trigger guard. His gaze was clear and his hand surprisingly steady. 'Let's assume that's your question.'

He pointed his revolver at Tom.

Its hammer fell in a dry click.

'*Beziki* . . .'

Into the silence that followed, Beziki said, 'There's only ever been one "they". You should understand that.' He tossed a newish Party card on to the desk between them. It flipped open on a youthful face Tom didn't recognize.

'He's nobody,' Beziki warned. 'Ask who and waste a turn.'

'Do you know where Alex is?'

Spinning the cylinder, Beziki lifted the revolver to his head and, without giving himself time to hesitate, pulled the trigger.

'Yes,' he said, 'I do.'

'Where?'

'That's a different question. My turn. Did you kill Vladimir Vedenin?'

'Beziki, for God's sake . . .'

'Do you want to find this girl or not?'

What glued him to this chair, Tom wondered. A certainty that it would end like this? As if he had ever imagined it would end like this. The fact he didn't want to appear a coward? The fact he was getting too drunk to stand? Or was it that he wanted to find Alex? He wanted that more than anything in the world. Beziki pulled the trigger while Tom was still wondering.

He was coming to hate that dry click.

'Yeah,' Tom said, 'I killed the little shit. Now, Alex . . .'

'Here we go.' Spinning the cylinder like a roulette wheel, Beziki stopped it suddenly with his thumb and placed the muzzle to his temple. The hammer fell on an empty chamber.

'Where is she? Three Sisters. My turn. Why kill Vladimir?'

Tom flinched as the hammer fell.

'He took Alex.'

'Alex took herself. Into the arms of Dmitry, the boy found

burned in that warehouse. Vladimir took her from him. They'd been lovers.'

'Alex and Vladimir?'

'Vladimir and Dmitry.'

Christ, he really should have followed up on that.

'So who took her from Vladimir?'

'Now there's a question.' Spinning the cylinder, savagely this time, as if aware that the joke had gone on too long, Beziki put the revolver to his head. As his finger tightened on the trigger, he smiled at Tom and mouthed: *I did.*

38

Phoning Home

The revolver was thrown in one direction, Beziki's head in the other.

The flash inside the small room was so bright its edges were etched on the inside of Tom's eyes. There would be muzzle burn. A star-shaped wound where flaming gases peeled away Beziki's scalp. Tom was too blind from the brightness to see Beziki slump sideways and then slip from his chair.

Tom was out of his seat without knowing it, hunched below the edge of the window as if the shot had come from there. He knew the smell of death and cordite, because it was a smell you never forgot. It was the hammering of his heart that was unexpected.

He didn't turn on the desk light.

That shot had to have been heard and a sudden light in the window would attract attention. And what was there in that room that Tom needed to see more clearly than it could already be seen? If hell had a colour, it was the sickly glow of cheap sodium.

He pushed the *chacha* bottle into the pocket of his Belstaff.

'Damn you,' he muttered.

Then again, that wasn't his job these days.

Making do with a prayer short enough to be indecent, Tom suggested that God give Beziki a pass on the bits of his life he'd been worried wouldn't pass muster. Then he shut the man's eyes from habit, picked up the bottle cap he'd used

305

for a shot glass and slipped it into his other pocket. He wiped the ashtray just in case.

Beziki's file went into the front of his jacket.

As yet, no one was hammering at the window. No sirens were racing towards him down the street outside. *He killed himself. Yes, I know my fingerprints are all over the room. We were playing Russian roulette. A very one-sided version.*

No, I don't really know why.

Tom had no idea whether offices occupied the building opposite. He just didn't want to still be here if anyone came to investigate. Nor did he want anyone to see a light go on after the shot, think it was odd and remember to tell the police when they started going door to door. He let Beziki's little office stay in darkness, and retreated through empty spaces tinged not with blood, emptied bowels or cordite but sawdust and the flat smell of emulsion, until the cold freshness of night welcomed him.

'Don't fall,' a voice said.

He spun round, already prepared to fight.

'I mean, alone, at night, in the middle of winter . . .'

Slowly, very slowly, he turned to find bright eyes watching from the darkness of a church doorway. Wax Angel unfolded herself, layer after layer of rags, her frayed clothes fluttering in the night wind.

'Those are the kind of conditions in which a man can fall.'

Tom gaped at her.

'Believe me,' she smiled encouragingly, 'I know . . . Your friend in there was a good man, for a bad man. I've known good men who were much worse.'

Tom glanced in both directions.

'It'll take them ten minutes,' Wax Angel said. 'Possibly longer. Do you need my help?'

Tom shook his head mutely, found his voice and thanked

her for her offer. Sharp eyes glanced at the door behind him and she looked thoughtful.

'Better get going then. Let me know when you do.'

Tom understood. He really did. Two children dead . . . How could Beziki go on living having let that happen? But what had he meant, *I did*?

If he took Alex from Vladimir, where was she now?

Or had he lost her, and if so to whom? It seemed to Tom that an increasingly brutal game was being played and he only hoped the commissar was right.

That Alex was still more useful alive.

In his first befuddled steps, before the bitter wind sweeping Gorky Street sobered him up, he knew he had to dump the bottle, find a telephone and check on his own son; everything else came second to that. Only, calls from Moscow went through a central exchange that noted who wanted to make the call, to whom and the number dialled.

He couldn't simply check into a hotel and use their telephone because foreigners couldn't simply check into hotels. Hotels had to be booked in advance through Intourist, and just turning up and demanding a room would probably get him arrested.

Tom's only choice was the embassy.

A place he'd been trying to avoid.

Putting his head down, and trying to look as anonymous as possible, he stamped his way south, listening for sirens and finally hearing them break the night far behind him. They rose and fell and stopped, and he breathed a huge sigh of relief when they remained stopped and didn't come closer or start up again.

He was just another drunk in a country full of drunks, as careful to avoid walking into lamp posts and slipping off an icy pavement as the next man. That probably helped, he realized. No one looking at him would have taken a second glance.

The walk from Red Square to Maurice Thorez Embankment took Tom over the bridge but, of course, the river was frozen, which he'd have remembered if his brain had been engaged. Denied an easy option for disposing of the *chacha* bottle, he drank what was left of it, prised up the grill of a storm drain, wiped the bottle and dropped it in, kicking snow over the top and settling the grill. That was when he realized he probably should have pocketed the Party card from Beziki's desk.

Tom looked round to check whether he'd been seen.

No one in sight, not even his shadow. If he even had a shadow these days, which the commissar had assured him he hadn't.

He'd never have dared take the risk if he'd been sober, but there wasn't much chance of that these days. Slipping out of the alley, he turned the corner and saw the embassy lit up ahead.

'Cold,' he sympathized.

The Soviet guard grinned. 'As a fish's tit.'

He took the papirosa Tom offered and they stared up at the building's ornate facade. 'Which sergeant's wife did you screw to get stuck with this?'

Drawing deeply on his papirosa, the *militsiya* man coughed as he hit cardboard and tossed the charred filter to the snow. It was a cushy job and they both knew it. On the other side of the wrought-iron gate his British counterpart was dead on his feet, kept upright by the wall of his hut.

'You could probably get in without waking him.'

'That would be unkind . . .'

The Brit peered at Tom's pass blearily.

'Long night?' Tom asked.

'So cold.'

'You're newly out?'

'How did you know?'

'Haven't seen you before.'

In reception, Tom asked a young woman who came out from a side room to get him an outside line and gave her the number. She reached for a pad, scrawled it down and read it back. 'I'll be in the library,' Tom said.

'Is this number a direct line, sir?'

'Probably not.'

'Should I ask for anyone in particular?'

'Ask for Charlie Fox.'

There was nothing Tom needed from the library except silence and access to the telephone in the far corner next to the microfiche reader. For want of anything better to do, he pulled down the Foreign Office list for 1961, which was the most recent there. There was a 1949, a 1946 and a 1938, all bound in fading red leather. He found what he wanted exactly halfway through.

Under M, obviously enough.

Edward James Stought Masterton, b. 15 December 1925. Educated Eton College and Balliol. Married 1945 Nicola Montefiore. Commissioned into the Life Guards February 1944. Military Cross, Juno Beach, Normandy, June 1944. Attaché to the Commandant British Sector, Berlin, July 1945. Granted a certificate as Third Secretary in the Foreign Office 11 October 1946 . . .

That MC was unexpected.

Tom thought of the slightly fussy, fiercely reserved diplomat and imagined him under fire. He could see Masterton controlling himself, controlling his men, refusing to retreat under withering fire. He could see him in the shattered ruins of Berlin too, ordering work details, helping set up hospitals, reporting on the state of refugees. Tom knew he'd never look at the man in the same way again.

He'd never like him.

He might respect him from now on, maybe.

The rest of the entry gave the predictable rise of a diplomat who'd found his spiritual home. *Transferred to Paris. Second Secretary in 1950. Transferred to Moscow. Acting First Secretary in 1955, substantive 1959. Transferred to Washington . . .*

His first ambassadorship was Buenos Aires, in the mid 1960s.

Was that a good posting and was Nicola Montefiore still around? Alex would have been born around 1970. A death, a divorce? What had happened to his first wife? Come to that, what about Anna Masterton's first husband? Tom assumed Anna had been married to Alex's father.

She struck him as the marrying kind.

Taking down a *Who's Who* from 1977, he found Sir Edward newly married to Anna Elizabeth Sophie, née Wilde, previously Powell. An earlier edition had a list of Powells and Tom ran down them, looking for someone whose world might have crossed with Sir Edward's. Although he suspected bitterly that everyone in the damn book crossed with everyone else's at some point.

Brigadiers, diplomats, industrialists . . .

Dozens with the right name but none looking more likely than the others. Until right at the end he found an RA, exhibitor at the Summer Exhibition, professor of Art at the Slade. Married to an Anna Elizabeth Sophie, née Wilde. No children. It was 1968; they wouldn't have done yet.

What was it Anna had said that day on the embassy steps? *Cancer, prostate. Alex took it badly . . .*

And later, *Alex was six. We were divorcing anyway . . .*

How long had Professor Powell had cancer? More to the

point, when was it diagnosed and when did he start chemo? Tom ran through what he remembered of his own father's death. A long slow war of attrition, with the cancer winning in the end. First infertility, then impotence, then a loss of strength and temper.

Although the last might just have been his old man.

What if Sir Edward was Alex's real father? What if Professor Powell wasn't her father after all? What would that change?

Tom was returning the *Who's Who* to its place on the bookcase, rather unsteadily, when another thought hit him, delayed by alcohol, tiredness and his shock at Beziki's death. So he stopped, took down the gazette and found Sir Edward's entry again, tumblers falling into place.

Sir Edward had been in Berlin at the same time as Beziki, the commissar, General Dennisov and the others. *When the British took over our sector, the bitch went to them and reported her granddaughter's death as a crime* . . . That was what Beziki had said.

Reported her granddaughter's death as a crime.

On a hunch, he found a tatty *Who's Who in the Politburo*.

The copyright page dated it to the late fifties and it was printed on rice paper. Individual entries were solid little blocks of black in tiny text. Ivan Golubtsov, the NKVD official mentioned by Beziki, had been alive. His boss, Lavrentiy Pavlovich Beria, Marshal of the Soviet Union, head of the NKVD, had not . . . Golubtsov's entry was brief: *b. Odessa, 1897. Joined the Party in 1919. A deputy to Beria, he survived his master's fall in 1953, retiring shortly afterwards to live quietly in the Crimea. Married, later divorced . . .*

There it was.

One son, killed in Berlin, 1945.

The city had fallen in May. The British occupied their sector in July.

By the end of that month Golubtsov's son was dead.

Things got complicated . . . Beziki had said that too. Was Sir Edward on the edges of that complication? Was he in fact part of the complication? Tom was nagging at *things got complicated* when the telephone rang, dragging him back to now.

Tom had his line.

'Charlie . . .'

'This is Mr Marcher.'

What kind of people introduced themselves as Mr anything?

Schoolmasters, apparently. In this case, Charlie's housemaster. 'It's Charlie's father,' Tom said. 'Major Fox. Calling from the Moscow embassy.'

Tom could almost hear the hesitation on the line.

'Forgive me. Is it urgent?'

Beziki slumped at his desk . . . Beziki's son dead on the rotting floor of a ruined house . . . His other son, the one Tom had never seen, dumped at the Kremlin Wall . . . The girl who was not Alex, white as marble on trampled snow. Gutted and dead on a mortuary slab . . . A fading photograph of a terrified boy tied to a chair.

He needed to know his own son was safe.

'It is to me.'

'Is it something I can deal with?'

'No,' Tom said firmly. 'I need to talk to Charlie.'

'He's in bed,' Mr Marcher said. 'The smalls have lights out at eight. I'll ask Matron to wake him.'

'Thank you.'

Charlie came to the phone and Tom heard him shuffle himself on to a seat, and a creak from the chair as he pulled his legs up under him, which was how he always sat at home. 'Daddy?'

His voice was strange and Tom realized that the master was still there. He should have asked for Charlie to be left alone.

'Is everything all right?'

'Of course,' said Tom, knowing he should be the one asking that. 'All good. I just wanted to say hello.'

'Only, it's after lights out.'

'I know. Mr Marcher told me. He was kind enough to have Matron wake you.'

'I was awake anyway. Are you sure you're all right?'

Charlie's voice was clipped and polite and more distant than could be blamed on an international line. He was holding himself tight, waiting for his father to come to the point, wondering what he was about to say.

'It's okay. Nothing's wrong. I simply wanted to talk to you.'

'It's after lights out.'

'Charlie, I know that.'

'I should go back to bed if there's nothing wrong.'

An adult voice at the other end said something and Tom lost Charlie for a few seconds to a conversation he couldn't hear because his son put his hand over the receiver. When Charlie came back on the line, he sounded uncertain. 'Are you sure nothing's wrong? Mummy's all right, isn't she?'

'I'm sure Mummy's fine.'

'She . . .' Whatever Charlie was about to say died on his lips.

This had been a bad idea, Tom realized. A guilt and alcohol and shock bad idea. A being in the wrong city and alone late at night and the only person he could still say he truly loved being a small boy a quarter of the world away bad idea. He should have known it was stupid. Maybe he had. But he'd still asked for a line and picked up the phone when it rang. 'Charlie, I'm sorry . . .'

'What about? Why are you sorry?'

His son's voice was so polite, so proper. Tom hardly recognized it.

Becca and all the things she hadn't said weighed on him. All the things he should have known. All the things it was his job to know. She'd been polite too. Polite and distant, unnaturally so. His hand shook so badly he had to lift the receiver away from his ear. He steadied himself to end the call.

'I love you. That's what I telephoned to say. All right? You look after yourself and I'll see you soon. That's a promise. All right?'

'Daddy . . .'

'I have to go now.'

Charlie began crying, really crying.

The telephone was taken from him and Charlie's housemaster came back on the line. 'This is Mr Marcher. Is there anything the school should know? We prefer to know if something has happened. So we can take proper care of the boys.'

'It's nothing.'

'Nothing?'

'I just wanted to talk to my son.'

The man took a deep breath and bit back what he wanted to say, asking instead, 'You're sure there's nothing we should know? Your son's been unsettled recently. We really do prefer to know, you know.'

'Nothing beyond his sister having killed herself, and his parents' marriage being in meltdown, and being sent to a school he hates because living at home is . . .' *Fuck.* Tom knew he'd screwed up before the words were out of his mouth. 'Worse,' he finished.

'I see. I think we'd better get Charlie back to bed.'

The telephone was put down almost gently and the line crackled and cleared, until only the sound of a familiar dialling tone accompanied the raggedness of Tom's breathing and the hammering of his heart.

39

Caro Calls

He should have known Caro would call. The school would telephone her and she would telephone him. It was as inevitable as tomorrow's hangover. If he'd bothered to think things through, he'd have expected it. He just might not have expected it in the time it took him to find a *Times Atlas*, discover it didn't have Three Sisters listed in the index and decide he needed coffee before anything else.

In the embassy's upstairs kitchen, Tom took a cracked Royal wedding mug from the dish rack, tossed in a spoonful of someone's Maxwell House and filled the mug from the communal kettle. Ripping the top off a UHT milk carton, he added two sugars and stirred thoroughly. The three digestives he stole from someone's packet were an afterthought, as was the glass of water he drank before carrying his haul back to the library. He'd put the biscuits on a plate rather than in his pocket, so his hands were full when he pushed his way through the door to the sound of the telephone ringing. It kept ringing until he found somewhere to put his plate down.

'Tom Fox,' he said eventually.

It was the young woman on the desk. She had a call for him.

'She's very insistent that she speak to you.'

'She?' He was sounding drunk even to himself.

'Yes, sir. She says she's your wife.'

The woman dropped out of the call and Tom suddenly had silence and distance and the sound of expensive shoes shuffling and fury held tightly in check. A clock was ticking in the background and he knew instantly where Caro was. In the drawing room of their house, using the telephone on the Victorian card table. There was a comfortable chair nearby but he could tell that she was standing up.

'Caro?'

'How could you? How could you be that stupid? How could you be that cruel?'

'What am I meant to have done?'

'What am I meant to have done?' Her mimicry was brutal. She did anger well, Caro. It was rare for her to show more than irritation, but when she did she meant it. Tom stopped halfway into the chair and stood instead. This was plainly going to be a standing kind of conversation.

'You know perfectly well what you've done.'

'Charlie?'

'Yes, Charlie. What possessed you?'

'You said I should call him more. You said I should make an effort.'

'Don't you dare make this about me. You called him. You had him dragged out of bed for no reason. He's in floods, damn you. Matron's put him in the sanatorium for the night and she's going to keep an eye on him herself . . .'

You had to be really sick to be sent to the sanatorium. Mumps, measles, misery. The infectious diseases. The ones that could spread.

'You've always been useless.'

'Caro . . .'

'Bloody useless.' She was shouting so loud she could probably be heard next door, and the house was detached. 'Fatherhood's not that hard, Tom. Other men manage it. At

316

its most basic, all you have to do is provide and protect. No one's asking you to do more. No one's ever asked you to do more.'

They both knew Caro's money did the providing.

His salary was good enough. But it was nothing like good enough for the house and schools and life that Caro had wanted for herself and her children. She'd probably have forgiven him if he'd made general. She'd have liked that. Her grandfather had been a general. 'Are you listening to me?'

'I drifted . . .'

'You drifted?'

'Caro, I wanted to talk to him.'

'Why? Why did you want to talk to him on a week night, an hour after lights out? What was so important you called him from Moscow to make him cry? In God's name, what did you actually say to him?'

'I told him I loved him.'

For a moment there was silence.

'You did what?' Her voice was different, almost soft. She stopped shouting and he heard the chair creak as she sat down. He did the same.

'Why?' she asked finally.

Flipping open Beziki's file, Tom looked at one of the photographs and shut it again. His heart was in his mouth and his chest was tight; his shoulder hurt like hell, but that wasn't why he had to set his jaw to stop the tears falling. There were conversations you had when you got together, others you should have along the way, some you never manage. But apparently there were also conversations you had to have when things were ending.

It was too late to save his marriage. Even if he'd wanted to, and he wasn't sure he did, he was pretty sure Caro didn't.

317

He'd lost the war, probably before they'd even fought the first battle. But some truces were better than others.

'Tom . . . Are you still there?'

'Still here,' he said.

'Talk to me.'

'I never told Becca I loved her. Not once.'

'She knew.'

'I never said it, Caro. I never said "I love you".'

'I'm not sure parents do. Not like that. Children know though.'

Did they? Tom wasn't so sure.

'But it wasn't enough,' he said. 'Was it?'

The air chilled and before she could snap back, he said, 'I'm not talking about you, I'm talking about me. I should have said it and it wasn't enough. I didn't want Charlie . . . In case anything happens . . . I don't want Charlie . . .'

'What do you mean, if anything happens?'

'It's messy. At this end. It's really messy. I've got myself into something.'

'Into what?'

'That's the point. I don't know.'

'I thought you were just writing a paper. Isn't that what you do for the MOD? Research things and write papers? Recognize patterns before others can see them. That's why you're over there, isn't it?'

'My job sometimes gets more complicated.'

There was silence at the other end, not cross or irritated, just watchful. He wondered about all the things she wasn't saying.

'Those long research trips . . .'

'Weren't always to the places I said they were.'

'Tom.' Caro sighed.

'I'm sorry.'

'What's different this time?'

'The Soviets have borrowed me to help with something.'

'I didn't know that was even possible.'

'Things are changing.'

Maybe too fast. Certainly faster than some people on both sides like.

Beziki had talked too much about Stalingrad for it to be simply the alcohol. Stalingrad had been playing on Beziki's mind. So had Berlin. The man had been about to kill himself. Tom didn't doubt that this was what he'd interrupted by hammering on the window of the restaurant. On the verge of suicide, surely you thought about the things that had brought you there? Stalingrad . . . and Berlin.

The link was there and it mattered.

Tom twisted the bezel of the signet ring Caro had bought him when they married round to the side. A reminder to ask her for a favour if the time seemed right. He'd been wondering who could help him with an answer. It was obvious.

Caro's father.

The old bastard knew everyone.

Although Tom couldn't imagine why her father would help him.

'Tom . . . Are you still there?'

'Yeah,' he said. 'Look, an English girl's gone missing in Moscow. They're keeping this out of the papers but it makes sense for both sides to talk.'

'That's where you come in?'

'Yes, that's me.'

Caro's voice was wary. 'You think she's dead?'

'I hope not. But I'm scared she might be.'

'This is about Becca, isn't it?'

'That's how it started,' he agreed. 'Now, if she is still alive, I just want to stop this one dying. There was a girl yesterday

319

morning, a different girl. They shaved her head and left her naked and frozen in a park. I was at her autopsy.'

'Jesus. How old?'

'About Becca's age.'

'Tom . . .'

'I know, I know. I should step back.'

'You're not ready for this.' Her voice softened. 'It's been hard for all of us. I should have realized it's been hard for you too.'

'A man I really liked killed himself tonight.'

'Dear God . . . Are you allowed to talk about it?'

'Best not. You're in the drawing room.'

'How do you know?' She sounded surprised, not suspicious.

'The Georgian carriage clock. I can hear it ticking.'

'It is distinctive, isn't it?'

'Yeah . . . Can you do me a favour?'

'What?' She went from relaxed to on edge.

'Look, your father's on the Intelligence Committee. Ask him if there's anything I should know about Edward Masterton's time in Berlin. He was there after the war in the sector we inherited. Can he check what the lord chancellor has on file to do with those days. Your father won't want to do it. Largely because it's for me, and I don't blame him. But say it matters . . . Well, it may.'

'Tom. Berlin was forty years ago.'

'I know it's . . .' Another set of tumblers fell into place and Tom sucked his teeth. *Christ, he could be such a fool.* 'Oh fuck,' he said.

'Tom!'

'Sorry. I'm sorry. It's just . . . Of course it is.'

'What's Berlin got to do with this girl?'

'Everything. Nothing. I'm not sure any more. But I know

there's a forty-year block on releasing some intelligence documents.'

'1945 to 1985. They'll be released already.'

'Caro, it's forty years, plus one for safety. Otherwise, release December in January and it's still only thirty-nine . . .'

Tom might not be making sense to her, but he was making sense to himself, which made a change. What did Sir Edward have on one of the Soviets? More to the point, what did that man have on him?

'Can you mention the forty years to your father too?'

'Anything else?'

'Yeah . . .' Tom hesitated.

'Say it.'

'We're over. Aren't we?'

'I could be cruel,' she said. 'I could say we've been over for years. But I don't think I want to. Not now. I would have said that before we talked. Now I'm not sure it's even true. But yes, I think we're done.'

'Thought so. Look, I'm sorry for calling Charlie. You'd better be the one to tell him we're divorcing. I probably shouldn't call the school for a while. And I'll sign the papers. You get them ready and I'll sign them. All right?'

'Send me the name of your solicitor.'

'One solicitor is fine. I'll sign whatever you put in front of me.'

'Tom, come on . . .'

'I don't want the house. I'm not interested in your money.'

'I know,' she said with a sigh. 'That's always been one of the problems. You're sure about us only having one solicitor?'

'Of course. I trust you.'

'You bastard.' Her voice was amused. 'Now I can't possibly shaft you.'

'There's always that.'

They muttered their way through kind goodbyes, kinder than their goodbyes had been for years. Both sad. Both of them knowing, Tom imagined, that the putting down of the receiver ended one stage of their lives and began another more thoroughly than signing papers ever could.

40

The Oak Tree

The bed was a mess. One of them, probably Sveta, had had the decency to strip the bottom sheet and put it on the cotton cycle in the Candy in the kitchen. It had been spun but was still damp when Tom got back to his flat around noon. So he looped it between two chairs like a makeshift tent, and that made him think of Charlie, which didn't help.

The rest of the flat was suspiciously clean.

Everything in the kitchen had been washed and put away. The bath had been wiped down and was free of suds. That said, both Tom's towels and his bathmat were sodden, most of the loo roll was gone, his champagne had been drunk and the bottle was missing. So they'd either taken it as a souvenir or dumped it with the rubbish outside.

Talking to Caro had thrown him.

Much of his protective anger was gone and without it he felt unshelled, rolled by events through the grit of his misery. In part through desperation, in part because he couldn't put it off any longer, he made himself a jug of coffee using the real Colombian he'd brought from London, ripped open a fresh packet of papirosa and borrowed the cracked saucer from under the cactus for an ashtray. Then he put Beziki's file on his living-room table, laid the photographs out like cards, with their backs to him, and began with the bank statements.

Beziki had kept money in the Bahamas.

The idea that a Soviet gangster would have a Western bank

account stunned Tom but it was the truth. The man had also had accounts in Prague, Budapest and West Berlin. The money he had with the Royal Bahaman was several times Tom's salary. He checked the figure again to be sure. And having made sure, he slid that bank book and that one only into his pocket, leaving the others where they were.

It was slow going sorting through the rest.

Beziki's handwriting was atrocious and he'd kept all the accounts himself. *You would, wouldn't you?* Tom thought. This wasn't simply extortion and money laundering. This was extortion and money laundering in a country where both were punishable by death.

From a land deed on file it looked as if he'd owned a farm in Latvia and a vineyard in Georgia. Tom hadn't even known private citizens could own land in the USSR. Account books for the farm and vineyard came next. Money in and money out, money loaned to neighbours and money repaid, rates of interest, new loans opened, old loans closed. A list of restaurants and companies in Moscow, Leningrad and Tbilisi came after that. Money loaned and money repaid. Sometimes, increasingly often, simply money paid in. Money went in monthly, the same sums every time. Occasional red dashes indicated a sum not paid. An occasional line through a name indicated an account closed. It was dark by the time Tom finished with the bank statements, land deeds and the flimsy little account books with their spidery notation, obviously written by someone who came to literacy late.

A brown envelope held pages torn from notebooks, mixed in with badly typed forms and reports, some so old they related to the secret police in the days, immediately after the Revolution, when it was still known as the Cheka. Most were later, though.

They all related to the Tsaritsyn Monastery.

It took Tom an entire packet of papirosa to translate the comments about traitors, kulaks, recidivists and duty done, and work out what was actually being said. In the late twenties and early thirties, in the aftermath of a failed kulak rebellion, the monastery had been a clearing house for those involved, the families of those involved, those who might have known those involved.

The net widened.

The numbers killed ran into hundreds, then thousands, then tens of thousands. Brothers were forced to kill brothers, sons their fathers, daughters their mothers. Those who refused died with those they refused to kill. The descriptions were cold, almost clinical. The state was diseased.

Stalin's purges were at their height.

They had a duty to reduce the contagion.

Two supposedly trustworthy locals carried out the work of organizing the slaughter. An ex-officer of the Imperial Veterinary Service, Pavel Nikolayevich Dennisov, and his ex-sergeant, Aslam Arkanovitch Kyukov. In time they had proved themselves untrustworthy and had been dispatched in their turn.

Tom read the two names again.

To find a Dennisov or a Kyukov might mean nothing.

To find both, linked like this . . . He needed to see what else, if anything, he could discover about the place. The last piece of paper was a newspaper clipping, yellow with age, ripped in two and glued together. The monastery was to be bulldozed and an orphanage built on its ruins.

Tom almost left it there, but then he made himself start on the photographs.

The first showed Gabashville's boy dead in the ruined

house. The curtain covering him had been yanked back and camera flash bleached his features.

The next showed him post autopsy, the Y-shaped incision across his chest sewn clumsily shut, the bullet wounds clearly visible. The photograph was official, or copied from an official one. Autopsy notes were glued to the back.

I should have realized it's been hard for you too.

For you *too*. He'd given no thought to how grim it was for Caro.

Other, older photographs followed. An old man with a young boy. Two serious and thickset women on a fur rug in front of a fire with a wall of books behind. A girl, with ribs like a rack of lamb, with a girl younger still. A poster above the bed showed the older girl in *Giselle*.

Tom went back to the first and looked more closely.

Not at what was being shown, an old man in a leather chair, smoking a cigar, while a naked boy knelt in front of him. He looked at the background: high ceiling and tall windows, paintings of windblown steppes and photographs of men in uniform. The commissar's generation or the one below.

And if it wasn't taken in the House of Lions, then it had been somewhere similar. There were a handful of others like this, some old, some new. One showed a young, smiling Vladimir Vedenin. There was a photograph of his father too, smiling across a cafe table at a young blonde girl Tom found unsettlingly familiar.

If the photograph hadn't been old, he would have said he'd seen her recently.

Trying to work out where gave Tom such a headache he washed down a handful of codeine with bad East German beer, and topped the painkillers off with a couple of sleeping pills. Then he made himself drink a pint of water against tomorrow's hangover and went to bed early, betting against sleep. He lost.

When the phone rang at dawn, Tom ignored it. He ignored it again when he was down to the dregs of his morning coffee and Beziki's photographs were spread untidily across the table in a fan in front of him. The same boys, the same old men, the same girl across a cafe table. If he stopped now, he'd find excuses to avoid looking at the last few.

The photographs in this envelope were older than the rest, smaller in format and taken with a 35mm fixed-lens camera, a good one. There were twenty-four shots, with the negatives included. The two yellowing strips of celluloid were so friable their perforated edges had begun to break away.

The first photograph showed the Reichstag, the streets around it bombed back to ruins, seven very young soldiers and a boy clutching a sniper's rifle in the foreground. The men had forage caps, the boy a cloth *budenovka* with the flaps tied up. It wasn't hard to recognize Beziki in the skinny urchin grinning for the camera.

In the second, a smiling officer pointed at a newspaper. It showed a blonde girl with complicated plaits proudly clutching a sniper rifle. The four or five photographs after that had the same snapshot feel. Young men pointing at Berlin street signs, or drinking from beer steins. Young men astride captured BMWs, grinning from the seats of an open-topped Mercedes, sitting fully clothed in a row of enamel baths holding champagne bottles. There was one of Kyukov, with his arm round a German girl, whose eyes were flat and smile tight. Another of the same girl naked in a tub, with suds too thin to hide her breasts. A photograph taken at her family flat, showing an old man, a small boy, the girl from the tub and a hollow-faced woman who might be her mother. They sat at a table laden with rations. Kyukov stood behind the girl, grinning from under his forage cap. The photographs changed after that.

Everything changed. The buildings were different, the skies less grey.

Tom couldn't work out if it was a different city a few months later or simply a different part of Berlin. The smiles were gone, replaced by sullen anger. The baby-faced boy looked haunted. The jackets of the other officers no longer hung open. There were no girls, no motorbikes, no champagne bottles. Their senior officer – who Tom knew was Sveta's grandfather – looked thoughtful, more than thoughtful, brooding.

The last eight photographs told a dark story.

The baby-faced lieutenant was bare-chested and tied to a chair. He had a gash across his upper chest and a forage cap stuffed in his mouth. His lips were broken, his face bruised and one of his ears bleeding. In the next photograph, he had a second gash. His eyes were wide, he was straining against his ropes, flesh bulging between twists of hemp as he struggled to break free. A sliver of Russian uniform stepped out of the photograph as another stepped in. In the photograph that came next, those entering and leaving the picture were gone but there was a third cut, deep enough for flesh to gape. Butchery, pure and simple.

So it went on, photograph by photograph, cut by cut. In the second to last, the man was dead, or as good as. The blood on the floor had already started to congeal. He'd long since pissed himself. On the back of each photograph was a smudged thumbprint. It took Tom a while to realize each one was different.

The last photograph . . .

Tom looked at it. He looked at it for a long time.

328

When the entryphone buzzed, he ignored it, as he'd ignored the house phone earlier. By the time there was an actual knock at his door he'd translated the splashes of semi-literate Russian on the plank held by Dennisov and his rather long-haired, disconcertingly beautiful Tartar friend.

The Tsaritsyn Boys.

Four German teenagers hung from the tree that formed the last photograph's centrepiece. A second plank, nailed to its trunk, stated that they'd been executed for the horrific murder of a Soviet officer.

Dennisov looked pious. Kyukov was grinning.

41

Another Knock at the Door

'All right, all right . . . I'm coming.'

Flipping Beziki's file shut, Tom headed for the hallway.

The Tsaritsyn Boys. Beziki had talked of the orphanage there. Built, it seemed, on the ruins of a monastery where a massacre had happened.

Tom expected it to be one of the other Sad Sam residents at the door; they were all expats with not enough scope to do their jobs and too much time on their hands. Unless, of course, it was whoever lived directly below wanting to complain about whatever noise Sveta and Dennisov had made. Tom imagined they'd probably made some. Instead, he opened the door to Mary Batten from the embassy, looking furious.

'Fox . . .'

'What are you doing here?'

'Is your telephone broken?'

'No, definitely not. It's been ringing.'

'Then why the bloody hell didn't you answer it?' Pushing her way in without being invited, she glanced through to his bedroom before tossing her satchel on to the only decent chair in the living room.

'Alex's?' she asked, looking at the Amstrad.

Tom nodded.

'We'll be wanting it back.' She wrinkled her nose at the papirosa filters overflowing from a saucer on the table and opened the window without asking. Ice-cold air cut into the smoky room.

She tossed a package on to the table. 'This came for you.'

'What is it?'

'Look at the docket.'

Only Caro's father would use the diplomatic mail to transport 'Divorce Papers' and mark them 'Deliver Immediately'. Ripping the package open, Tom extracted a folded compliment slip with the House of Lords oval at the top. *Apparently this is your price for divorcing my daughter in a civilized fashion.*

'Deal with that later,' Mary said. 'I'm here about something else.'

Extracting from her satchel something that looked like an oscilloscope, she unfolded a four-way antenna, connected a battery, flicked a switch and glared at Tom.

'Just what the *fuck* did you think you were doing?' She jabbed her finger at him. 'You were *seen* leaving Gabashville's offices. Understand? I mean, Christ, have you completely lost your senses?'

'What do you mean I was –'

'You were followed.'

'By an old woman?'

'I doubt it. You were seen leaving Gabashville's offices. He's dead, you know. Of course you fucking know. Christ, Fox . . . I gather you came straight to the embassy, had two telephone conversations and left again. Which is about as stupid as you can get.'

'I left you a note,' he said.

'What note?'

'Alex's boyfriend worked for Vedenin.'

'Oh shit . . .' She stared at Tom. '*Worked?*'

'He's dead. I think Vladimir killed him, then took Alex.'

Mary looked so appalled Tom imagined she must be working out how to tell the ambassador. 'Go on,' she said.

'When Vladimir's father realized, he panicked. The cult house was set dressing. The soldiers were meant to go in, find Alex and return her. Only someone took Alex and left Beziki's son in her place. That's why Vedenin was so shocked. He wasn't expecting bodies.'

'You think that someone was Vladimir?'

You don't know him! Tom remembered Vladimir's anguished shout at the lake. 'Yes. But he was working for someone else. Not Beziki. My guess is Beziki took her after Vladimir died. Now, of course, he's dead too.'

'How much of this can you prove?'

'None of it.'

'Why would Vladimir kill Alex's boyfriend?'

'They'd been lovers.'

Mary put her head in her hands. When she looked up, took a deep breath and fixed her gaze on Tom, he knew it wasn't good. In fact, he knew what Mary intended to say before she said it.

'You're out of this. Now more than ever. Moscow can keep this out of their papers until hell freezes over. We don't have that luxury.'

Reaching into her pocket, she put a buff envelope on his table.

'Official,' she said. 'Immediate effect. You're on sick leave. Sir Edward doesn't expect to see you at the embassy. You have no authority to talk to anyone about Alex on his behalf. I need to think about what you've just said. In the meantime, the Soviets will deal direct with me.

'One final point. This isn't Northern Ireland. You can't just go around killing people. You're damned lucky Gabash-ville was a recidivist. They're going to chalk his death up to suicide. In return? God knows what they'll want . . .'

'Mary. It was suicide.'

'So you say.'

'Tell them to check the revolver. My fingerprints aren't on it.'

She stared at him.

'Could you do something for me?' Tom asked.

'Why the hell would I do that?'

'There's an old guide to Imperial Russia in the embassy library. I'm hoping there's a reference to a monastery in Tsaritsyn. Since I'm banned from Maurice Thorez Embankment, could someone deliver it?'

'This is to do with your report?'

'That's why I'm here.'

'It's a pity you didn't remember that earlier.'

Tom thought of pointing out that it had been Sir Edward who had dragged him into the hunt for Alex. He thought of saying it and decided not to bother. Four boys, Alex's age, hanging from an oak tree. He knew that photograph was going to haunt him. When Mary glanced at Beziki's file under its saucer of papirosa butts and said, 'What's in there?' Tom shrugged and stood, edging her towards the door.

'Nothing to concern you,' he said.

Neither of them bothered with goodbyes.

The enclosed are due for release next Jan under rules covering confidential papers relating to the British takeover of what became our sector in Berlin. They are to be returned to me and only to me. Understand that I am doing this only because my daughter has asked me to, and in hope that you will give her a civilized divorce . . .

Without bothering to read them, Tom put the forms face down in a drawer in the bedroom, under an airline blanket left by the previous occupant. Then he boiled some pasta, drained it over the sink, tipped a small jar of Heinz Italian Sauce on top and shovelled the food into his mouth without tasting it, or even noticing that he hadn't, and went back to what else was in the envelope.

Accompanying the forms for his divorce was a large white envelope that had the seal of the House of Lords embossed on the flap. Its glue strips were shiny and unused. A second envelope, inside the first, was the familiar buff of official envelopes everywhere. A torn stamp glued across its flap as a security seal showed George VI looking like a slightly nervous accounts clerk.

Attached was a compliment slip from Century House, 100 Westminster Bridge Road. A note, typed on a manual typewriter and unsigned, reminded Caro's father that the enclosed were originals and should be returned to Kew rather than Chancery Lane, and were not to leave his possession under any circumstances. Also, the director would be interested to know what had brought papers as obscure as these to his lordship's attention . . .

Inside were several sheets of paper, the first typed on flimsy, using a manual typewriter that needed its ribbon changing. The paper was headed *Office of the Administrator, British Sector, Berlin.* It suggested the Soviets be reassured that the accompanying files would not be acted upon.

There were, inevitably, no accompanying files.

It was the *Parteiadler*, the Nazi eagle above the swastika, perching over the words *Polizeistation* on the sheet below that made Tom blink. The page was filled with tiny, impossibly neat script. Someone had crossed the eagle through. Not scrubbed it out, simply crossed it through. The sheet below that looked to be a translation of the German.

On 24 July 1945, Frau Elsa von Wiesen arrived at the station and asked me to speak to the English on her behalf, as she didn't know their language and the soldiers who guarded the doors to their HQ were, in her words, fools. She had a note-book belonging to her traitorous son-in-law Dr Schultz. She insisted that the English would want it. I was to tell them that. (Frau von Wiesen was the wife of a high-ranking Party member and has not adjusted well to the change in her situation.)

I gave her son-in-law's name to the English lieutenant to whom I have been making my daily report. An hour later he appeared at the police station with a translator, told me to get into his Jeep and ordered me to guide them to Dr Schultz's house immediately.

Frau von Wiesen's actual statement was missing, destroyed perhaps, or simply not included. Its translation was typed on flimsy using the same machine as before; its ink ribbon still needed changing.

She opened by saying she'd hidden the biggest of her son-in-law's notebooks because she didn't want the Bolsheviks to get it. He hadn't dared confront her, as he didn't want the Bolsheviks to know it was missing. She would give it to the English if they promised to investigate her granddaughter's murder.

I knew something was wrong. I knew they were lying. They'd hung her from her heels like a slab of meat and . . . Having read the first line of the next paragraph, Tom made do with skimming the rest and felt his guts tighten.

Hadn't even cut her down . . .

Yes, I'm certain . . .

One stab . . .

According to Frau von Wiesen, her granddaughter had not been raped and strangled by Nazis or newly freed foreign workers as Colonel Milov insisted. She'd been skinned alive and hung by her heels by one of his staff. Either he or one of the others had then stabbed her, a single thrust to the heart.

Her neck was unbroken. Far from being raped, she had died a virgin.

Tom hardly dared think about how the old woman might have discovered that.

Her daughter and grandson had gone to live in Moscow with her traitorous son-in-law, who was meant to be a brilliant scientist. But if he was so brilliant, why hadn't he saved the Fatherland? She'd refused to go with them, even though her daughter had begged. She'd noticed that her son-in-law didn't beg. He didn't even try to change her mind. She'd always suspected he was a Bolshevik really. She wouldn't have been surprised to discover he was a Jew.

Lots of people were, you know.

The lieutenant had asked what made her think it was Soviet soldiers and not any one of the thousands of newly released foreign workers, most of them intent on revenge, who had done this? The simplicity of her answer made Tom lurch in his chair. She had watched her granddaughter being taken to the stables by one of the Russians. It was too dark to say which. He'd been thin, looked young. They all looked young to her. Why hadn't she gone to help?

Dear God, what was he? An idiot?

Had he no idea what had been happening?

Did he think for a minute Colonel Milov's man wouldn't simply shoot her and then outrage the little fool anyway? Better to go with one Russian and pretend it was willingly and hope he'd protect her from the others. How was she to know he'd torture her granddaughter like that? There'd been no noise, no sound.

She was certain. She'd left her window open.

No one screamed. No one came running. When the Russian came out later, he'd joked with one of the others who was sitting on a deckchair in the garden, getting drunk. That one had set off towards the stables, changed his mind and returned to his chair and his bottle.

No, she couldn't describe him either.

Small, thin, young. They all looked like starved rats. Except their colonel – he was built like a manual labourer, squat and ugly. Spoke like one too. No, of course she didn't speak Russian.

His voice. His accent. His manner.

A letter on crisp white paper from the Cavendish Laboratory in Cambridge thanked the British Administrator for the diary and asked if there was any chance of talking to Dr Schultz direct. An apologetic note in reply regretted that would be impossible. The last note was on half-size official flimsy.

Whoever had typed it hadn't bothered with an HQ address or a date more specific than Sept 1945. *There it was.* Tom felt a thrill of excitement as he skimmed the page. The officer had examined the evidence and talked extensively to his Soviet counterpart, in the eyes of his CO perhaps too extensively. There was no merit in Frau von Wiesen's story. It was a crude attempt to smear Britain's allies and the Soviets' original conclusion that Dr Schultz's daughter had been raped and murdered by newly released forced workers was a sound one and should stand.

He would inform Frau von Wiesen of this decision.

Tom understood why the decision to take the notebook and sweep everything else under the carpet had been made. He might not agree with it but he understood.

The Soviets were our allies, the Germans our enemies.

The war with Japan was not yet over. Half of Europe was a morally bankrupt wilderness hovering on the edge of anarchy; the UK and America's alliance with Soviet Russia was already fraying and what action could the Administrator have taken anyway? Moscow was unlikely to offer up a handful of its victorious troops on the say-so of an elderly card-carrying Nazi who happened to be the mother-in-law of a nuclear scientist they'd kidnapped, offered refuge to, protected . . .

But was that the sole reason for the decision?

The only person who could answer that was the man who'd written and initialled the note, *EJSM. Edward James Stought Masterton* . . . How many other British officers had there been in Berlin in 1945 with those initials?

Maybe Sir Edward wasn't stunned into inactivity by the disappearance of his stepdaughter. Maybe fear was behind his icy control. Maybe Tom had things entirely back to front.

Sir Edward knew exactly what he was facing.

42

Handing Over the Notebooks

Dennisov met Tom at the door to his bar. Given the speed with which he moved from behind the zinc, he must have been watching from the window. Behind him, the room was hot and fuggy and crowded with a lunchtime crew only half as drunk as those who'd be there that evening. 'We're shut.'

'Beziki took Alex.'

'I don't care. I don't believe you. As I said, we're shut . . .'

'He told me before he died.'

'We're shut,' Dennisov repeated loudly.

'The bar is full of people.'

'To foreigners,' Dennisov said. 'We're shut to foreigners.'

Behind the counter, Yelena glanced up and looked away. Sveta didn't even do that. She finished a bowl of something, knocked back a beer and took her turn at the computer. That pretty much guaranteed everyone in the bar stopped looking towards the door and began watching falling Tetris blocks instead.

Stepping out on to the walkway, Dennisov shut the door behind him.

'What's Sveta's score now?' Tom asked.

'You don't call her Sveta,' Dennisov said with a scowl. 'Only her friends call her Sveta. You can call her *Major*. Svetlana, if you must.'

'This is about Gabashville?'

'Fuck Gabashville.'

'Dennisov, what's going on?'

'She told me. She told me how you took advantage of her.' He glanced at the concrete wall behind Tom and the steps down to the street. That was where Tom had come in, watching Dennisov throw someone down those steps.

'Sveta says I took advantage of her?'

The Russian glared. 'She doesn't have to.'

'It was once, for God's sake.'

'So you admit it?'

'Dennisov.'

'You told me nothing happened. *I asked you*.'

'You asked what was between us. I said nothing. It was once. Someone had just tried to kill me. I was . . .' Tom didn't have to say more. The sour twist of Dennisov's mouth said he understood. Sex could be complicated or simple. Sometimes it wasn't about sex at all. Sometimes it was about convincing yourself you were alive.

'Once?' Dennisov said.

'She was being kind.'

'You took advantage of her.'

'Dennisov. She was being kind.'

He looked at Tom, then glanced through to where Sveta was lost in her game, manipulating blocks at impossible speed, oblivious to the crowd pushing in on her, or the lover and ex-fuck at the door edging back from a fight. Would she mind if they fought over her, Tom wondered. Would she be pleased? Appalled? He imagined all she'd display would be contempt.

'Anyway,' Tom said, 'she didn't know you then.'

Dennisov's face cleared and Tom cursed himself for not coming up with that sooner. 'You're right,' Dennisov said. 'She didn't know me then. When I saw her . . . with that rifle and a rabbit hanging from her hand . . . The light was on her hair. And the trees were dark and sharp behind her. You've seen that poster in my room. I felt . . .'

A *coup de foudre*.

Tom could honestly say he'd never had one, had never felt his entire happiness depended on someone returning a smile. Not even in his teens, when that kind of insanity was just about acceptable.

'You like her?'

Dennisov smiled. 'It's been a long time.'

Not sex, Tom doubted it had been a long time for that. There were a lot of prostitutes in Moscow for a place where official statistics proved the selling of sex had been abolished. Perhaps Dennisov meant it had been a long time since he'd been with a woman he loved.

If Dennisov wanted to think of Sveta as a simple country girl of the forest, content to bring back food for her grandfather, then let him. Tom was fine with that. He hoped they would be happy. He suspected that they both deserved some happiness.

'Dennisov, what's the penalty for killing a political officer?'

The Russian's eyes went flat. 'I didn't,' he said.

'I know. You killed your CO. Sveta told me. Before the two of you met. All right? Before the two of you met. Now, what would it be?'

'How long ago?'

'Berlin.'

Dennisov froze. He looked at Tom from under lashes far too long for a man's and if he'd seemed drunk or nearly drunk the moment before, he was sober now, the alcohol burned from his veins by whatever darkness was in his heart.

'You have the photographs?'

'How do you know about them?'

'I found my father's set as a child. As you can see . . .' He lifted his scarred hand, the one Tom thought had been damaged in a helicopter crash. 'We burned them together. He had me hold each one over an open fire until it caught.'

'How old were you?'

'Six.' Dennisov looked away so Tom couldn't see his eyes.

Tom followed Dennisov to the walkway's edge and they stood side by side, passing a papirosa between them while Tom looked for his shadow, half intending to offer the man a drink, but his usual doorway was empty, and the couple who stumbled down the street a minute later and fell into the doorway, their hands already reaching into each other's clothes, were too preoccupied to notice those watching from above.

'We should go in,' Dennisov said.

Tom agreed.

'Oh, so he's talking to you now . . .'

Yelena nodded to Tom and scowled at her brother, making it clear that he wasn't included in her politeness. Having dumped a bowl of soup in front of Tom unasked, she produced a large chunk of dark bread and a cold can of East German beer, only reluctantly relinquishing vodka duties to her brother.

'I should probably ask what you did for her,' Dennisov said, once Yelena had retreated to her kitchen. 'But I'm not sure I want to know.'

'She's a good kid.'

'That's not the general view.'

'This stuff with your father . . .'

'He always treated my sister entirely properly.'

Tom waited as his friend vanished inside himself for a moment. When he reappeared, it was to say, 'His friends weren't always that careful.'

Behind them, the bar erupted into cheers and Dennisov looked relieved at the distraction. Sveta had beaten her best, which was Moscow's best. She'd gone from stranger to regular in an impressively short time; her uniform and gender no longer a hindrance. When she spotted the two men behind the bar – Tom still in one piece, Dennisov missing no more bits than usual – she looked relieved. It lasted less than a second and her face was impassive again by the time she joined Tom.

'He made the leg himself,' she said.

'From the leaf spring of a jeep?'

Her look said she considered Tom to be simple.

'What then?'

'From the landing gear of his helicopter, obviously.'

Tom thought of the organization needed to ship a pointless strip of twisted metal from Afghanistan to Moscow just so that some crippled, barely sane ex-pilot could machine it into something useful. He could see Dennisov's friends doing it. 'I'm impressed.'

'You should be ... First Vladimir Vedenin, now Erekle Gabashville. My grandfather wants to know if he should be worried.'

'I didn't kill Beziki.'

'That's what you said about Vladimir.'

'When are you going to talk to your grandfather next?'

Sveta's face closed down as she waited to see what Tom wanted. What he wanted was any information the commissar might have on Kyukov.

'He's in prison,' Sveta said.

'You know who he is?'

'I've heard the name.'

'Everything okay?' asked Dennisov, reappearing from behind the bar. He had a flask of vodka in one hand and two

343

shot glasses in the other. Unusually, the flask looked full and both glasses were empty.

'All good,' Sveta said. 'We were talking about your leg.'

'She likes it,' Dennisov said. He sounded slightly disbelieving. Smiling at Sveta, he said, 'We're going through to the back.'

'Want me to join you?' she asked.

'Best not,' he said.

He blushed slightly when she stared at him.

'Trust me on this,' he begged.

Unexpectedly, she smiled in turn. 'On everything.'

He flushed bright red. He blushed so fiercely he looked like a twelve-year-old ready to pull her pigtails. Then he swivelled, pushed past his sister, cast a glance back at Sveta and vanished through the curtains, leaving Tom to follow.

Yelena rolled her eyes.

In the kitchen, Dennisov was already pouring Tom a vodka. He looked put out when Tom asked for coffee instead, and only slightly happier when Tom pulled what was left of his Colombian from the pocket of his Belstaff and began making coffee with that.

When Dennisov tried to clear a space at the little fold-up table, only just avoiding tipping plates to the floor, Tom stopped him. 'Let me,' he said.

By the time Tom had filled the sink, Dennisov had the file open and was flicking in disbelief through one of the account books. 'You know what this is?'

'I've a pretty good idea.'

'You stole these?'

'Beziki gave them to me.'

The chair creaked as Dennisov sat back, his hand reaching for his glass. With it halfway to his mouth, he changed his mind and put it down. A moment later he asked if there was enough coffee in the saucepan for two. 'Shit,' he said.

344

Several minutes later he said it again.

By then he'd skimmed the account books, totted up half a dozen columns using a calculator the size of a brick, checked something in an atlas he scooped from under his bed and sat in silence for several seconds, looking longingly at his vodka.

'Yelena!' His shout was so loud it made Tom jump.

His sister came through scowling, stopped when she saw her brother's face and put her hand on his shoulder, a gesture somewhere between a question and reassurance.

'All good in the bar?'

'Food's done. Everyone has a drink.'

'Sveta all right?'

'She's playing her machine. You want me to fetch her?'

'No,' Dennisov said. 'Maybe best not. Not yet. You look at these and I'll make more coffee.'

'I can do that.'

'I'd rather you read these.'

So Yelena did, her eyes flicking from column to column as she skimmed the pages, occasionally turning back to double-check a figure. Only once did she reach for the calculator, and then, like her brother with his vodka, her hand stilled halfway and she did the sum in her head. Finally, she flicked to the last page of the last account book to check the date. It was two days earlier.

'What are you going to do with these?' she asked Tom.

'Give them to your brother.'

Dennisov choked on hot coffee.

'You can't,' Yelena said. 'I mean . . .'

'I'm not Russian,' Tom told her. 'I don't have the contacts. I can't make the deals. I can't make the old contracts stick. I can't bring the old lieutenants to heel. You need muscle for something like that.'

'I have friends,' Dennisov said.

'I'm sure you do. All those men coming back from Afghanistan looking for something more than they had when they left. All with new skills and weapons training. All used to obeying orders.'

Yelena looked thoughtful.

'As for things like the farm,' Tom said, 'I'm not even sure Russians can pass property on to foreigners.'

'They can't,' she said.

'There you go. It has to be your brother. I've taken one of the bank books and left you the rest. And I might be able to access the West Berlin one for you.'

'I should turn you in,' said Dennisov. 'You've just offered to help with money laundering. You've confessed to being there when Beziki died. You've . . .' He shrugged. 'Proof of criminal conspiracy. Illegal accounts. Extortion. Corruption. You're trying to compromise an ex-officer. This is probably a Western plot.'

'You know where the telephone is.'

'There will be money,' he said. 'For you. Regularly. There will be money. We can work something out later. What can I do for you now?'

Answer a question, Tom thought. But he wasn't sure if he should ask it. And if he did, who they might tell.

'Give me a vodka,' he said instead, wondering how long it would take Sveta to get him his other answer and how badly he was going to dislike it when it arrived. 'And then I need to get home.'

'You mean the flat?' Yelena asked.

Yes, he supposed he did.

43

Yelena's Offer

Sveta turned up next morning in full uniform, her blouse ironed, creases sharp on her trousers, her boots so highly polished they looked made from patent leather. She carried her cap, with its wide red band, double strands of gold braid and oppressively large badge, under her arm. Since the last time Tom had seen her she'd been wearing a fur *ushanka*, dyed blue and with a badge half that size, he wondered what point she was making. 'Official business,' she said.

Tom looked at her.

'That's what I told the KGB man on the gate. He knew I was coming anyway. My grandfather may have telephoned ahead.' Pushing past Tom, she glanced round his flat and maybe he imagined that her gaze stopped for a moment on the bed. Memories of her first night with Dennisov, perhaps. When he'd got back, the entire flat had been so sterile it might have been a steam-cleaned crime scene.

'Coffee?' Tom asked.

'English?'

'Colombian . . .'

She was still frowning when he vanished into the kitchen, and by the time he returned, she'd picked up everything on the floor, arranged the books on the windowsill alphabetically and by size, collected together dirty cups, saucers and plates, and was sitting at the table cutting a dead branch from

347

the cactus using a silver penknife she folded away and returned to her pocket when he appeared in the doorway.

'How can you live like this?'

'Looks tidy to me,' Tom said.

The envelope with the Berlin photographs and the papers from Caro's father was the only thing untouched, still safe under its overflowing and untidied ashtray. Tom wondered whether he should find that suspicious.

'Soviet coffee is better,' Sveta said.

'As Dennisov would say . . . You have coffee?'

Standing up, she walked over to the Sony cassette recorder, flipped out the blank tape, looked at it and returned it to the slot, pressing play and turning the volume up when the familiar guitar intro of Alex's tape filled the room.

'Dennisov has this,' Sveta said.

'It's mine. Well, Alex's. I borrowed it back.'

Something occurred to him. Heading for the windowsill, Tom found the coloured-in cassette box with its *For Alex* on the back.

'Recognize the writing?'

'No,' Sveta said.

Her response was too instinctive, too fast.

'It's not yours,' Tom said. 'Not Dennisov's either.'

'You've checked?'

'In passing,' Tom said, watching her remember being asked to write out an address in English. She seemed almost impressed.

'My grandfather told me to tell you to be careful. There are questions that shouldn't be asked. And questions that should. A problem arises when those questions are the same . . .' Leaning down for a leather satchel that looked older than she was, Sveta unbuckled its flap and dug around inside. She half pushed the file across the table with a scowl. 'This is breaking the law.'

348

'That worries you?' Tom asked.

'What's the point of having laws if people don't keep them?'

Looking at Sveta, Tom realized she meant it.

'Kyukov was arrested in 1953 when Beria fell, and General Golubtsov, Kyukov's old patron, was forced to retire . . . Crimes against the state. He was a colonel by then. Kyukov couldn't prove my grandfather was behind the arrest but . . .' Sveta considered the matter carefully, her head tipped to one side, her eyes looking up and away, as if seeking guidance. 'I was going to say he suspected . . . but he knew, I think.'

'Where was he sent?'

'Stalingrad first, for old times' sake. Then a work camp on the Irtysh. Finally the gulag, beyond Lake Baikal but further north, between Yakutsk and Tiksi, according to the files.'

'Why so many moves?'

She turned the file so that it was the right way up for Tom and opened it at the first page. It was a bad week for nasty photographs. This one didn't show a boy tied to a chair. The victim was older, gang-tattooed and naked. One eye had been cut out, the other stared glassily at the ceiling. His guts were piled neatly on his chest like a circle of sausages. 'Kyukov's first day,' Sveta said.

'New camp. The old boss?'

She nodded.

Reaching for the file, Tom opened it from the back, sparing himself the other photographs and finding instead pages of harrowed notes from those least likely to be harrowed: prison officers, prison doctors, commanders of the local *militsiya* or the KGB. One camp commander asked simply for permission to kill the man.

This was refused, with a reminder that Khrushchev himself had ordered Kyukov to be kept alive. The NKVD general to whom this request had been sent was surprised that the camp commander would even suggest such a thing. The commander tried again after Khrushchev's death. When he was refused again, he asked that Kyukov be sent elsewhere.

This was granted.

Brief and brutal autopsy notes on Kyukov's victims told of flesh hacked from bones, informers found blinded, tongueless or both. Of a younger rival found flayed, whose skin never reappeared.

A younger rival found flayed, whose skin never reappeared.

A dead cat was hardly in the same league. But all the same, Tom thought of Black Sammy, strung from his back legs over the sink. And that memory brought others: that discarded copy of *Pravda* the night he first went into Dennisov's bar; a month-old issue of *Krokodil* left on a table in the canteen the day he went to find Davie, back when he thought this was all going to be a hell of a lot simpler and Davie was going to turn out to be Alex's boyfriend.

Both *Krokodil* and *Pravda* had mentioned flayings. A teenager found mutilated outside a river settlement in Siberia. Another discovered days later somewhere along the same river. Complaints about police inefficiency from the Russian version of *Private Eye*, counterbalanced by *Pravda*'s promises of imminent arrest.

'He's escaped?' Tom said.

He saw the shock on Sveta's face.

'It's either that,' said Tom, 'or he's been released.'

'Who told you?' she demanded. 'Even my grandfather's only just discovered that. How could you possibly know?'

Tom explained about the articles.

'He'll be working his way towards Moscow.'

'He's here already. Or he's been and gone.' Tom told her

about the dead cat, about dismembering its body and disposing of the pieces, pretending to himself and to whoever did it that it had never happened.

'He won't have liked that,' Sveta said.

'Believe me, I didn't like it either.'

Tom asked himself whether Kyukov had been behind the murder of the girl in the park and dismissed the thought. That murder had been too clean, too sterile. It wouldn't have satisfied Kyukov at all.

'I imagine General Dennisov will be pleased.'

'Why?' Sveta said. 'Would you want someone bat-shit insane as your self-professed best friend? I imagine he's terrified of the man.'

'He wasn't behind Kyukov's release?'

'Gorbachev declared an amnesty for politicals. Kyukov qualified. By the time anyone realized he'd be on the list he was gone.'

Tom considered that.

'Should you find him . . .' Sveta said.

'Your grandfather would like to know?'

'My grandfather would like him dead.' Sweeping up Kyukov's file, Sveta thrust it almost angrily into her satchel, pushed back her chair and glanced instinctively at her reflection in the window before straightening her collar.

Tom was too early for the bar to be open for lunch, and the blind was down over the door and the windows so steamy their glass looked frosted. He hammered on the door anyway. Yelena allowed herself almost a smile when she realized who it was.

Glancing both ways along the concrete walkway, she hurried him inside and shut the door firmly behind her. 'My brother's out,' she said. 'He'll be back soon.'

Tom had to fight the urge to ask where he'd been.

Dumplings boiled in a steel pan in the kitchen, the steam turning to condensation and running down the wall Tom leaned against, trying to stay out of Yelena's way as she chopped onions and piled them into a bowl. 'What are you making?' he asked.

'I'll decide later.' Having finished chopping, she glanced across at him. 'Need vodka?'

Tom shook his head. 'I've got a question.'

'For me?' she said. 'Or for my brother?'

'Three Sisters.'

'Chekov? The play?'

'It's where Alex is being held.'

Yelena's face was unreadable. 'Beziki told you this?' she asked finally.

'Before he shot himself.'

'Why didn't you tell us this before?'

Because I was trying to work out if I could really trust you didn't seem the right answer. Any more than *I'm still not entirely sure* was an acceptable rider to that thought. The problem was that he had to trust someone. The alternative was to reach a point where he wasn't even sure that he trusted himself.

Outside, Dennisov rattled his key in the lock and the sound of a woman shouting and a child crying on the walkway entered with him, fragments of misery that ended the moment he shut the door and headed for the kitchen.

'You okay?' Dennisov asked.

'He's asking about Three Sisters.'

Coming to stand beside his sister, Dennisov wrapped his arm round her and hugged her tight until she leaned her head into his shoulder.

'They're rocks,' he said.

Yelena nodded. 'There's a boathouse.'

'With steps down from the Cormorant's Nest.'

'There are two sets of rocks,' Yelena said. 'The Big Sisters and the Little Sisters. The Little Sisters are below the Cormorant's Nest . . . That's a castle in the Crimea,' she added. 'A little castle.'

Dennisov nodded. 'It used to be ours.'

'What happened?' Tom asked.

'It became someone else's.'

'Beziki's?'

'Yes,' Dennisov said. 'Gabashville's.'

Letting go of his sister, he retrieved a tatty school atlas from the box room and found a double-page spread of the Crimea, peering at it closely. When he couldn't find what he wanted, he turned to the index and then back to the spread, trying to find the coordinates.

'Give it to me,' Yelena demanded.

Tom wasn't even sure she looked at the page properly. But she jabbed her finger with such certainty that he went to stand by her side and peered at the jagged shoreline she indicated. There were few roads and no big ones. The colouring of the map and the tightness of the contour lines said she was pointing at cliffs.

'How do I get there?' Tom asked.

'You don't,' Dennisov said. 'Sebastopol's a closed city. You'd have no chance of getting travel papers. Even if you got to Sebastopol, you'd have no way of reaching the house. Tell your embassy. Let them tell the police.'

'The embassy aren't taking my calls.'

'You know . . .' Yelena said.

'No,' said Dennisov. 'Absolutely not.'

'They won't let him into the Crimea alone.'

'They won't let him in at all,' Dennisov said firmly.

'So he'll need a guide.'

'Yelena . . .'

'We'll take the train.'

'You really think anyone will sell him a ticket?'

'No,' she said. 'We'll take *the train*.'

Yelena looked stubborn, Dennisov close to tears. Something unspoken passed between them and then it was her turn to put her arms round her brother, hugging him fiercely. 'You said you'd never go back,' he said forlornly.

'I said I didn't think I'd ever be able to. That's different.' She looked him. 'You know it's different. If I don't go back now, I'll know it was because I was afraid and that will be worse. Tom will pretend to be you.'

'Yelena . . .'

'I'm sad. So very sad I have to see places where I was *happier*. Places from when I was young. Who could deny me that?'

Her mouth twisted at the thought.

44

The Train

'He goes, I go . . . We catch the train.'

Dennisov had lost his nerve about letting his sister take Tom to the Crimea but was losing his battle to stop her. This was a Yelena that Tom hadn't seen before, stubborn to the point of planting her feet firmly and sticking her fists on her hips. In anyone else it would look childish.

He doubted she'd even care.

She'd furiously brushed aside the matter of Tom having two legs to her brother's one, just as she'd rejected Dennisov's insistence that he go instead of her. His final offer was that they should both go and leave Tom behind. Her counter-suggestion that Sveta go with Tom he rejected with such force that Yelena laughed.

'I'm an only child,' Tom said in the taxi heading for the station.

'What makes you tell me that?'

'Watching you argue with your brother.'

'In my family, we're all only children,' Yelena said. The taxi driver glanced up at that and Tom realized he was a regular from the bar. Seeing Tom notice, the man concentrated on the road ahead.

'Don't hurt my brother,' Yelena said.

'What makes you think I'd hurt him?'

'I don't think you'd mean to.' She shrugged. 'I'm like that too. I don't mean to. Well, mostly not.' They went back to watching the traffic and Tom was grateful when the station came into view. 'Wait here,' she said.

She bought two tickets for a local line, and they changed at the next station. Disappearing into the women's lavatories, she reappeared five minutes later beautifully made-up and dressed as someone else. Her eyes when she saw him examining her were distant. Her face immobile.

As a child she must have been beautiful.

The stationmaster, a nervous-looking man in grey uniform, had gone inside, shut the door to his office and dropped the blinds. It seemed quite possible that he'd locked the door. The one time he'd glanced at Yelena, when they came up the steps from the underpass after changing platforms, he apologized.

'Here it is,' Yelena said.

The train approaching the platform belonged to another age.

It had a rocket-like nose that would have looked radical in the thirties and comfortably familiar by the fifties. A red star blazed in the middle. The green of the engine was so deep it could have been enamel. Its power unit was electric but the space behind its nose deserved a funnel. Behind it stretched carriages so dull they might have been cattle trucks. It took Tom a second to realize they were armoured. At least, the first five were. The sixth was varnished wood, with an observation platform, and could have been lifted from a Hollywood film about railroad tycoons. A shiny brass rail edged its observation platform. On the platform stood two snow-speckled bay trees in terracotta pots. 'They're replaced,' Yelena said, 'whenever they die.'

'How often is that?'

'In this weather? Every run I imagine.'

She flipped up the brass rail, indicating that Tom should

unfold steps for her. And a thin man in a dark suit, who carried a walking stick, pushed open the door of the observation
car and came to block her way.

'Yelena,' he said.

Her hand went to her mouth. 'I just wanted to . . .'

'Go somewhere you were *happier*. I know. You always were
a little whore. Did you really think I wouldn't find out what's
going on? I should have never let your mother have you.'

Yelena's chin came up. 'Well, she did. After you had her.'

'I believe your friend has some photographs that interest
me,' General Dennisov said. 'I'll deal with you later.'

Yelena wet herself.

The blond-haired boy had been waiting since morning, por-
ing over a Kremlin guidebook and examining plaques
dedicated to dead Soviet heroes with a fervour unlikely in
anyone that young. For those to matter, you had to be old
enough to remember the men they named. And he wasn't.

He was a thin little thing in a cheap jacket. Still, cheap
leather was better than no leather and his jacket looked thick
enough to keep out the cold.

Wax Angel would have swapped, happily.

It was his shoes that gave him away. It was always the
shoes.

They were too good for his face and his jacket, too well
made and too waterproof. You had to be issued with shoes
like that. The man watching him stood on the opposite edge
of Red Square, too distant to do more than register the other
was there. Occasionally they glanced at each other, then
looked away, but neither moved. She'd shambled across to
examine each. Drab clothes, good shoes.

You'd think the KGB would have learned by now.

She liked Red Square. It was here when the war was ended

that they brought the flags of the German Wehrmacht and burned them in front of the Lenin Mausoleum. She and the man she loved watched it happen, wearing their uniforms and holding hands. People around them had smiled . . .

After a while, a *militsiya* man moved her on from the doorway of St Basil's, oblivious to the little drama building up around him. So now she squatted by a wall, with a neatly trimmed little silver fir to act as her windbreak. She had her wax figures laid out on a scarf in front of her.

You weren't allowed to sell things in Red Square.

But then you weren't allowed to beg either.

The commissar had come in from his dacha again, delivered to that hideous monstrosity of a flat. He'd come in a week ago, stayed a night and gone. Now he was here again. An old fool he might be, but less so than the other old fools, and she was interested in what would keep bringing a man like him back to a city he hated, a city from which he'd exiled himself so many years before.

It had begun with the ice boy.

The moment she'd seen him in the snow she'd known it was a bad omen.

So beautiful, so cold, so very dead. She could remember boys like that. Ice white. Ice white or deep red. The deep-red ones were bad. The ice-white ones were worse. There had been too many of both.

The old fool knew soon enough that he'd been played and it was too dangerous to do anything about it. Things in the group had soured pretty quickly after that. She wondered what the drunken Englishman had on General Dennisov that he let the man live.

Mostly she wondered whether the foreigner would tell her if she asked, whether the old fool in the stupid apartment would if she asked him instead. Perhaps he didn't know. That would upset him, not knowing something he was afraid she already knew and was simply testing him. He'd been so upset as he knelt beside that body in Red Square she'd almost felt sorry for him.

Who was she fooling?

She did feel sorry for him. Old age was brutal enough without watching those you once called friends try to unravel everything you held dear. What use was power when your body grew too weak to obey orders, when those younger than you couldn't even discern the difference between what you asked for and what you intended?

It was different for her.

Her body had been twisted and turned and massaged and pummelled and finally broken. She had no illusions about how fragile it was. It was the spirit that was tough, the spirit that remained when everything else was gone. She'd carved the dead boy's face on to the angel to see him on his way.

Tried to wrap the boy's frozen fingers round it.

In a world increasingly held together by fraying promises and broken memories and the glue of old glories, someone had to do their job properly. It wasn't her fault the boy's little finger had broken.

As for the commissar finding her offering . . .

She should have known that would complicate things.

He'd known what the wax angel was, of course. They'd all known, the moment it appeared in the sky above Stalingrad. It was an angel. Only angels were forbidden, along with belief in anything but the state. So it became the Spirit of Russia, well, of the Soviet Union. Same thing really.

They put up a bloody great statue, gave her a sword, took away her wings and stuck her on a hill overlooking the city they'd renamed Volgograd. Two hundred steps to reach her, to represent the two hundred days in which people died defending Stalingrad. If they were that impressed by the sacrifice, they should have kept the city's name.

The statue was massive, far bigger than America's Statue of Liberty.

Wax Angel had seen photographs. They'd made her as ugly as you'd expect.

A tourist drifting past stopped and dropped to a crouch. He said something he couldn't possibly expect her to understand, then shrugged and pulled a five-rouble note from his pocket, gesturing at the largest of the angels.

He smiled when she nodded.

The *militsiya* man who'd moved her on started towards them, then suddenly decided not to bother. And all the while, the two men with the good shoes watched each other and waited. When a shiny foreign car finally drew up where Resurrection Gate once stood and a soldier bundled the Englishman out of a door in the Kremlin Wall and hurried him across to a grey-haired woman, Wax Angel was grateful. She was cold, the *militsiya* man was staring at her again and she'd decided there was something she needed to do. Something she should have done years ago. With luck, the commissar would appreciate her gesture. Although, if he didn't, it would hardly matter.

She wasn't doing it for him, not really.

Sir Edward's office was exactly as Tom remembered.

The desk was still impressively huge and largely empty. The same obligatory portrait of the Queen as a young woman hung on the wall behind, and a smug little photograph of Sir Edward and Margaret Thatcher smiling for the cameras. Tom was so tired he could barely find the energy to hate it.

He was no closer to finding Alex, no closer to bringing her home.

What was it Sveta had said?

The commissar thought Alex would be kept alive until she was more use dead. In his heart, Tom had begun to wonder if they'd reached that point, if she'd joined the line of children laid out on marble slabs or lost to unmarked graves.

'Are you listening?'

'Yes,' Tom said. Although he no longer knew to what.

'You should know,' Sir Edward said. 'that I've had to make a formal apology for your behaviour to the Kremlin, and assure the Soviets you tried to leave Moscow without authority and in complete disregard for standing orders.'

'You can imagine how much Sir Edward enjoyed that.'

The ambassador glanced at Mary sharply.

'I hope,' he said, 'that your stupidity had nothing to do with trying to find my stepdaughter. When you had direct orders not to interfere further?'

'Of course not, sir.'

'I was asked,' Mary said, 'if I knew what might make you act like this. I told them I had no idea. Quite possibly, you were simply drunk. You'd have to be to take a Russian girl with you.'

'You didn't say he took a woman with him.'

'Russian girls will do anything, sir, if they think there's a chance of a foreigner marrying them.' Mary stared at Tom, her eyes unforgiving. 'Did you consider her safety? Did you think what trouble she'd be in?'

'Dare I ask her age?' Sir Edward enquired acidly.

'It wasn't like that.'

'I imagine it was.' The ambassador sat back in his chair. There was something dangerous in his gaze, something so contained that Tom remembered his thought about Sir Edward knowing exactly what he was facing. This was a man holding his fury in check with a degree of self-control that was almost brutal.

There were new lines around the ambassador's eyes.

He'd shaved badly that morning, missing a patch of slightly greying bristles under his jaw. The fingernails of one hand looked almost dirty. Sir Edward's clothes were as beautifully made as ever, but he wore them with less assurance.

Mary, on the other hand, looked immaculate. Her turnout, as always, was the smartest in the embassy. Her voice, when she spoke, was as clipped as Sir Edward's and sounded borrowed from the 1940s. Tom wondered again how hard it must be to be black, a woman and senior in an embassy where everybody of any rank was automatically white and male.

Very, from the flat look of contempt he was earning.

He'd expected to be shouted at.

God knows, he deserved their rage.

Instead he'd been marched in by Mary Batten, who'd sat in a chair to one side and said little until Alex was mentioned. Lady Masterton was nowhere to be seen. This meeting was entirely official. Rather than shouting, Sir Edward was icily polite. That's how furious he was. Tom could hardly blame him.

'You shouldn't believe him, sir.' Mary said. The ambassador glanced at her. 'That this wasn't about Alex, sir.'

The ambassador sat back and rocked forward, patting his pocket as if searching for something – a sure sign of an ex-smoker. Tom knew the feeling. He wanted a cigarette too. And a drink. It was two days since he'd had either.

'I just wanted her found,' Tom said.

The ambassador was out of his chair before Mary could move.

Then she was moving too and came to stand very close beside Sir Edward, but not quite touching. She'd fallen into a fighting stance without even thinking about it and her gaze was on Tom. It said: *Don't move*. And Tom did what he was told.

'You know nothing about me,' Sir Edward said. 'Nothing about my marriage. Nothing about Anna's life before we met. Nothing about how we started. You have *no idea* how much Alex means to me . . .'

'*Sir,*' Mary said.

Sir Edward sat with as much gravity as he could manage.

'Get this idiot out of here,' he said. 'Arrange with London to send him back early. Meanwhile, he's to keep to his flat and write that damn report. At the end of which, he goes home and good riddance. Take back his embassy pass. Have his post delivered to the foreigners' block. Make sure I don't see him here again.'

'You won't,' Mary promised.

45

Talking to Owls

Sometimes you lose a piece of yourself. Sometimes someone steals it. She couldn't take back what was taken. But she could still take what had taken it. Wax Angel's logic wasn't the world's. The world's logic was safe and cowering and servile. She couldn't expect everybody to be as clear-eyed as she was.

The bus driver was reluctant to let her on board. Even more so when he realized she didn't have the money for a ticket. So she told him she'd fought in the Great Patriotic War so that little brats like him would have a future and if she'd known she would be treated like this, she wouldn't have bothered. He asked – very rudely, she thought – what she'd done in the war. Cooked, cleaned, encouraged the troops from the safety of a mattress?

She told him she'd been a sniper in Stalingrad.

She'd shot five German officers in four days, one of them a colonel.

While his own father or grandfather had probably been thieving from the shops or complaining that he couldn't march because his feet hurt, she'd been eating rats in ruined factories, wrapped in sacks for camouflage and to keep warm, and she'd been happy to do it, grateful for the opportunity.

The little shit would still have made her get off, but by now everyone over sixty was nodding and looking serious; some were watery-eyed and the driver had more sense than to push it. He'd let her travel to the next town and when she

364

shambled down the aisle to disembark at the concrete block that passed for its coach station, an old man in a nice coat who was going further stood up and stopped her.

'Here,' he said.

He tried to push fifty roubles into her hand.

When she shook her head, he insisted.

She'd looked at him.

'I was there.'

He was too. She could see it in his eyes.

He didn't seem surprised when she kissed his cheek. Simply put his hand up to touch the spot. It was fine, kissing his cheek like that. Quite possibly they'd known each other at some time.

The next bus driver had looked at her doubtfully but she'd told him she was on her way to see her grandchildren and waved the fifty-rouble note at him. He couldn't change it but he let her get on the bus anyway. You were hardly going to refuse someone travelling with a fifty-rouble note, were you?

It took her longer than she had thought it would to travel the distance.

All of it she did by bus, except for the last stretch where she begged a ride with a lorry delivering fridges. They were large and smart and white. Odd, really. In her memory, fridges were tallow yellow.

The driver assured her that these ones even worked. Mostly.

The last few miles were the most complicated. She was tired and hungry and felt as if she'd been travelling for days. It didn't help that she got lost, which forced her to retrace her steps back to a wretched small-town bus station. She got the right coach this time though, one that delivered her to the village where she got the lift with the lorry. The driver gave her coffee and shared his packed lunch, and though he opened the windows when she began to sweat a little under her rags, he did it casually, as if he simply needed air. She liked him.

Even if he did lie about his fridges.

She liked the crows by the roadside too. She'd always liked crows. They were so uncomplicated. They never minded what colour uniform anyone wore. Sometimes, they'd start trying to eat people before they were dead, but they were always apologetic when that happened. And they'd flap away like sharp black knives and wait until their meals were ready.

In the end, Wax Angel decided that it would be a good idea to rest so she curled up in the hollow of some tree roots a mile from where she needed to be, wrapped her rags around her so tightly they looked like leaves or feathers and fell asleep. A bear shuffled out of the trees in the hours that followed, stopped to sniff her, nudged her once or twice and went on his way.

A squirrel settled in the oak above without really noticing she was there. An owl came later and Wax Angel's sleep was filled with dreams of her husband and memories of childhood walks in the woods behind the dacha at sunset.

At dawn, she woke to thin sunshine through the firs and the huge-eyed, half-blind gaze of an owl up past its bedtime. It blinked once as it looked at her and flew away, quickly lost in the trees. Sighing, the old woman dipped into her pocket for a tiny angel, which she gave owl's eyes and placed where she'd slept. When it came to collecting debts, it was always best to have paid your own.

Then, with her back against a different tree, she reached again into her pocket, for a sharpening stone and a knife, spat once on the blade and again on the stone and began to get the best edge she could. There was something she needed to do. It was so long overdue she'd stopped imagining she'd ever do it. But there were circles to square and ends to tie, and all the other things her husband used to say, when he was still her husband and she was still somebody's wife.

They'd had a daughter. She'd died young.

Very young. But not before having a daughter of her own.

Her husband had brought up the grandchild and done a good job of it.

And even if he'd lost his own wife to the camps, and taken so long to find her she could no longer bear to be with him, or anyone really, girls needed mothers and Sveta should have had a mother of her own, instead of fading photographs of a beautiful blonde girl who killed herself before she was out of her teens.

It was noon before the sun rose high enough above the firs to glint off the blade Wax Angel had sharpened until it could cut cold air. The sun's position reminded her to eat, although she had to scrape a lot of snow away from a lot of tree trunks before she found anything worth eating. When that was done, she pushed herself to her feet, looked for signs of life and saw only the tracks of a bear. There would be men later, close to where she needed to go. There were always men. They always overestimated their abilities.

They always underestimated hers.

She was right about that. There were men, and they did overestimate their abilities. She slipped between the trees, silent and fluttering, and not one of them saw her coming. Not one of them lived to tell the tale after she'd gone.

46

At the Hotel National

'*Tom!*'

He was outside the arrival doors at Sheremetyevo T2 and looking, in vain, for a familiar face in a crowd of tourists just disembarked from Aeroflot flight 298 from London when he heard Caro calling his name.

Turning, he saw her lugging her huge pigskin case, which he took from her without thinking. They kissed each other's cheeks, briefly, perfunctorily. The way strangers kiss.

'What are you doing here?' Caro asked.

More to the point, Tom thought, *what are you doing here?* All he said, though, was, 'Meeting your flight, obviously.'

'You didn't call to say you got my message.'

'That's because I've only just found the bloody thing . . .' Holding up his hand in apology, Tom said, 'I got back to my flat late last night and only noticed the message in my pigeon-hole this morning. I came straight out.'

'I called your concierge.'

'My concierge?'

'Whoever answers your central telephone.'

'She spoke English?'

'Perfect English.'

'Still using this, I see.' He nodded at the suitcase Caro had owned long before they ever met. It was battered, built round a wooden frame and wilfully old-fashioned. *It was my great aunt's,* she'd said crossly, the one time he had suggested replacing it.

'I like it.'

Tom smiled despite himself. 'I know.'

'The taxi sign says that way.'

'I have a car waiting,' Tom said.

His wife looked as she always did: elegant and polished and beautiful. Tourists on their way out of Sheremetyevo glanced across instinctively, the women to examine her Jaeger coat, the men the figure it covered. Her expression as she clocked Tom's unshaven state was unreadable.

'Caro, what are you doing in Moscow?'

She hesitated, only for a second. 'I've brought the forms.'

'Your father already sent me a set.'

'He said you'd probably torn them up. He arranged my flight. The Foreign Office expedited my visa.' Of course they did. Papa had contacts. His son-in-law's lack of them was one of the things he'd always disliked about Tom. That and getting his daughter pregnant. 'Also, I thought you might show me round.'

'You thought I might . . .?'

'Moscow's one of the few places I've never been. It was Mummy's suggestion. She thought we could talk about Charlie, sort out who has him for holidays and half-terms, who pays what. She thought we should try to be civilized about it. You want to know why I'm here? That's why I'm here. I'm trying to be civilized.'

'Caro . . .'

'I know you don't like them. Okay? I know. But we could. You know. Be civilized about it.'

'I have to leave Moscow first thing tomorrow.'

'That's rotten.'

'I'm not being horrid. What hotel did Intourist assign you?'

'The National.'

Of course . . . What else?

'The car's out here.'

A huge car park sprawled in front of Sheremetyevo's concrete and glass building. Flagpoles fat enough to be missiles jutted from the tarmac, and grass beds marked the edges of the parking area. This being Moscow, there were more spaces than cars and the gaps made the car park look bigger than it was.

'Over there,' Tom said.

The stallholder from the market by the flyover who'd taken Tom to the embassy was already climbing from his vehicle. Only instead of his filthy Niva half-truck, this time he drove a black Volga with chrome bumpers and fins so exaggerated they belonged in a fifties film. Grinning at the sight of Caro, the man snapped out a ragged salute. 'Nice,' he said. Luckily, he said it in Russian.

'The National,' Tom told him.

The back seat was so worn its leatherette had cracked to reveal canvas beneath, and someone had patched the footwell with squares of office carpet. An acrylic vase glued to the dashboard held a faded plastic rose.

'It's not the Merc, I'm afraid.'

'Sold it,' said Caro. 'I drive a Mini these days.'

Tom was too shocked to reply.

'Solidarity,' Caro said, a word he'd never thought to hear from her lips. Catching his look, she hesitated on the edge of saying more, then said it anyway, her eyes misting. 'I bought a white one first. The garage were kind. They let me change it.'

'Caro . . .'

She flapped her hands in front of her face in a way that was quite unlike her, dismissing the tears that threatened to fall, dismissing the sentiment, dismissing everything except a need to stare straight ahead without blinking.

Dear God, how hard must that have been? Tom thought of her coming down in the morning and seeing a white Mini where Becca used to park. Because he'd bet she'd parked there too. How long did Caro last before she begged the garage to take it back?

He wouldn't have lasted a day.

'I'm sorry,' she said, a minute later when the threat of tears was behind her and they were on one of those twisting and chaotic under-signposted and over-complicated new routes out of Sheremetyevo and back to the city.

'Caro, it doesn't matter.'

Her silence said it did.

He thought of the two-seater 300SL, her family home outside Winchester and the softly rolling hills beyond, the roads that were so familiar she drove them from instinct, taking corners faster than was safe for anyone not born knowing the bends. She'd grown up there. Well, in the holidays. The rest of the year she'd boarded.

She rode her pony through the woods. Kissed her first boy against the witch tree. Went up Chalk Hunt a virgin and came down something else, something very else according to her mother when she found out.

'What are you thinking about?' Caro asked.

'The witch tree.'

She smiled sadly.

'Turn of the century,' he told her, as they approached the hotel. 'Shelled during the Revolution. Lenin ran his government out of here briefly. Very briefly. It was derelict by the thirties, renovated in the forties. Most of its furniture was stolen from pre-Revolutionary mansions. Some of it belonged to the Tsar.'

'You should have been a history master.'

371

'Might have been happier.'

She looked at him.

'Sorry,' Tom said.

'Don't be. That's probably the truth of it.'

He went in with Caro to explain, in Russian, that he was her husband and worked at the embassy, but she lived in England where their son was . . . This was enough for the girl at the desk to let them through. Getting past the *deshurnaya* by the lift on Caro's floor was harder.

'Your pass books?'

This one was younger than most of the women who kept the keys for the doors of the hotel floors they guarded, but no less hard-eyed. She took the pass book Caro had been given in reception and satisfied herself that Caro was a legitimate guest.

'And yours?'

Lacking his embassy pass, Tom offered his military pass instead, adding his passport when the woman scowled.

'*Propusk,*' she demanded.

Tom shook his head, switching to Russian to repeat what he'd said downstairs. Caro was his wife. Their boy was back home.

When the woman waved her finger, Tom produced his wallet, dug into one of its side pockets and pulled out a snapshot taken when they had just begun. He wore a black biker's jacket over a white T-shirt, Caro a pair of 501s and his blue jersey.

'That's us,' he said.

Taking it by the edges, the woman peered at it suspiciously.

'This is our son.' Tom offered her a photograph of Charlie taken when he was four. He sat, small and serious, in the bucket seat of a rusting Massey Ferguson, red gumboots dangling. He looked uncannily like a Soviet poster of a young pioneer.

When Tom looked across at her, Caro was biting her lip.

'You work at your embassy?' the woman asked.

'For my sins,' Tom said.

'Your wife?'

'Lives at home.'

The *deshurnaya* watched impassively as Tom returned the tiny photographs to his wallet. She didn't say he could go to Caro's room but she didn't stop him either . . .

'Where are the forms?' Tom asked the moment they were through the door.

Her body stiffened. 'In my case.'

'Would you mind if I signed them now?'

She did a double take, and Tom shrugged apologetically. He wasn't sure why, they were her forms after all. 'I'd like to get it over with.'

'You've changed,' she said at last.

The petition for divorce was handwritten in all the right boxes, signed by Caro but not yet dated. They had one child according to this.

Name: Charles William Augustus.

Age: 7.

DOB: 18.11.78.

Their wedding certificate was attached to the form. They'd married in the village church – Caro's choice. They'd had a bishop do it. That choice – her mother's.

Tom had the Mont Blanc she'd given him one Christmas in his jacket, in the little leather case she'd bought at the same time; she said nothing as he unscrewed its lid, tapped the barrel and ran the nib over a scrap of hotel paper. Having checked his pen had ink, Tom signed, before adding the date.

When he looked up, Caro was crying, silent tears dripping from her chin.

'Caro . . .'

It was the wrong thing to say.

She left her own room, abandoning Tom to silence and the newly signed forms. His signature on the wedding certificate was much the same. Hers was smaller and neater and more childish than he remembered.

Caro's teacup was empty and Tom's still upside down on its saucer when he found her in the tea rooms. She'd chosen a table in a corner, behind a pillar and almost out of sight. 'I'll order another pot.'

'This is fine.'

She ordered a fresh pot anyway.

'I thought . . .' She stopped. 'I thought, if you didn't mind, you could write to Charlie at school and say Mummy came to see me. We had tea and went for a walk. That sort of thing. It might help,' she added quickly, 'if he knows we're friends.'

'He's having trouble?'

'Unsettled. That's what Matron said.'

She sat back and sipped her tea, thoughts playing across her face like notes of an unheard piece of music.

'You remember Liz Sheridan?' she said suddenly.

'Vaguely.'

'She said she thought I should know . . .' The tightness in Caro's voice suggested she didn't believe her motives were that simple. 'She'd overheard his housemaster say . . .' Caro's mouth collapsed in misery. 'That there was nothing wrong with Charlie that having different parents couldn't cure.'

'God. I'm sorry, Caro.'

'For what?'

'Everything.'

Pushing herself out of her chair, she took the seat next to him.

Instinctively, Tom's arm went round her, her head came to rest on his shoulder and he stroked her hair as she cried. Silently at first, then swallowed sobs that shook her body and soaked his shirt. She sniffled and snuffled and gulped her way out of the tears. And Tom's hand, which had been stroking her hair, held her tight until a waitress came to clear their table and Caro retook her original seat as if nothing had happened.

'I miss her,' Caro said, once the waitress was gone.

'I know.'

'Do you?'

'Yes,' Tom said, his certainty surprising both of them.

Her hand reached across to grip his wrist. 'You don't mind me asking you to write to Charlie? I was worried you'd be cross.'

'You think it will help?'

'It would show him we're not enemies. It would show the school.'

'I'll do it tonight.'

She half stood, leaning across the table to kiss his cheek and seal his promise. She smelled, as she'd always done, of Dior and sandalwood soap and hairspray. But though she smelled like the woman he remembered, Tom knew she was already somebody else.

Later, in the bar, they talked about supper without actually eating any, and drank a bottle of Soviet Riesling and decided it wasn't worth ordering another and left it at that. At the lift, Caro reached out and put her hand on Tom's wrist.

He could nod goodnight, extract his arm and peck her on the cheek, pretend her fingers had never reached for him.

Instead, he looked at her and the gloom had softened the lines on her face, as it undoubtedly had his, and he realized that the strangeness of the day had sanded the brittle edges between them, for the moment anyway.

Tom had no real desire to go back to Sad Sam, and there were things he needed to say. Things it was important for Caro to hear.

'This means nothing,' she said.

He nodded.

Undressing, Caro hesitated only once, when she saw the two plasters crisscrossing Tom's shoulder. 'What happened?' she asked.

'Someone shot me. With a crossbow.'

She sighed, looked at him and moved in for a proper kiss.

The sex was slow and quiet. They stood in the window with the curtains drawn back, the room lights off, snow falling in fat flakes past their window and Manezhka Square spread out below them. Her body was as perfect as ever. She let him raise her foot on to a stool and slide into her, her breasts lifting in time with his thrusts. She had cried the very first time they made love, and she cried this time. Tom had no more idea why she'd cried then than now and knew that was his failure, not hers.

Before they slept, when all Tom really wanted was sleep, when his happiness was losing out to loneliness and he'd decided he didn't need to say the things he'd thought he needed to say, she asked about Alex. He couldn't even remember mentioning Alex. But apparently he had, the night she telephoned after he'd called Charlie.

'Tell me,' Caro ordered.

So Tom did.

From Alex cadging a cigarette on the balcony at the party,

and what he'd said about cutting her wrists, through to his being arrested as he tried to board Yelena's train and Sir Edward's fury afterwards. Then, because he'd started being honest and didn't know how to stop, he told her about Northern Ireland, about what he really did for military intelligence, about the people he pretended to be.

He touched her fingers to bullet scars in his leg and back, and they both understood what her not knowing said about when they'd last seen each other naked. And she lay, very still and very quiet, as he told her about being hunted across the hills above Crossmaglen and why he really hated multi-storey car parks. What she said when he was finished was not what he expected her to say.

'Did it ever occur to you that Becca's death might have been accidental? That she might genuinely have dozed off and hit a tree? That her being pregnant could have had nothing to do with it, that she simply hadn't told us yet?'

'Caro. How do you –'

'How do you think I know? I demanded a copy of the report. Tom, I don't need protecting. Rebecca was mine too. She could have been waiting for the right time to tell us. She might have had a clinic fixed. Ten weeks is early days.'

'It wasn't her boyfriend.'

'I know, I asked him.'

'I bet you didn't kick the living shit out of him first.'

'Charlie says Becca talks to him. He wakes up and she's on the end of his bed. They have to keep their voices down so as not to wake the other boys.'

'Dreams,' Tom said.

'You don't think . . .'

'That it's somehow true? No,' he said, 'I don't.'

'He says he thinks about her all the time.'

'I know.'

'How can you possibly –'

'Because I do too. And if I do, you two must.' Tom thought about it a little more. 'You know,' he said, 'I like the idea of Becca talking to Charlie. If you talk to him, and it seems appropriate, please tell him to send my love.'

'You've changed.'

'After something like that, how can anyone stay the same?'

'Becca told me once that she didn't believe in time. Days were dams that failed, hours sticks thrown into the water to measure its speed. Minutes little better than seconds, dust on life's surface, swept away before we could notice.'

'Caro, what happened?'

'To Becca? I don't know.' She buried her head in Tom's shoulder while he pretended not to feel her tears. 'Who knows? A stupid argument with . . . A party he didn't go to. It could have been a one-night stand.'

'She didn't drink.'

'You can have them without drinking.'

'It helps,' Tom said, feeling her withdraw slightly, and then her hand reached for his and gripped it tight.

He said, 'I worry that . . .'

'I have to believe she'd have told us if that had happened.'

'Told you . . .'

'Told one of us,' Caro said, smoothing the creases from Tom's face and kissing his neck as if the bad years had never been. Tom wanted to ask – so badly that he framed the words in three different ways, and held them all back because none were right – if the tenderness behind her kiss meant I remember you or goodbye.

'Go back to Alex,' Caro said.

So he described searching her room, his voice breaking as he told Caro about taking Alex's *Smash Hits*, *Jackie*s and *NME*s from her bedside cupboard, then carefully replacing

378

them. How he'd found the postcard, D and five kisses. How Davie Wong turned out to be a dead end, in not being her boyfriend, but how he'd given Tom an address for the party. How Alex had been long gone, but what remained of the boyfriend was there, tied with wire and quite possibly burned alive . . .

'Tom,' Caro sounded scared. 'Who are these people?'

'Monsters,' Tom told her.

She hugged him tighter. 'Don't be so blasé about it.'

'I'm not. But monsters are what I do.'

Sighing, Caro said, 'I think I preferred it when I thought you were wasting your time with computers, microfiche and old books . . .'

He told her about being shot by Vladimir Vedenin with a crossbow. How he'd been moved from hospital to hospital, until the commissar had extracted him and had him put, under guard, in a hospital for senior KGB officers. Tom even told her about making Vladimir Vedenin drive across the ice. That surprised him.

He hadn't intended to tell her that.

'He died?'

'He drowned.'

'Do you regret it?'

She listened in silence as Tom told her why not. His points weren't always in order. He doubted that many of them were very clear. He ended with what he'd been trying not to remember, what he'd originally thought the ultimate dead end, the reason he'd gone back to the supposed cult house.

The dead children in the cellar.

Then it was his turn to cry.

She held his head against her breasts, and when he was done, she asked if there was anything else. So he told her about Beziki's suicide. The way Beziki had spun the revolver's cylinder before he fired, the photographs of a boy being tortured to death in Berlin, and the sins of the fathers being visited on their children.

About the dead girl dumped in front of the House of Lions. How badly that had shaken the commissar. How badly that had shaken him.

About attending her autopsy.

'This is about Becca, isn't it?'

'Of course it's about Becca.' Tom reached down to find her hand, holding it tight. 'Well, it started out being about her. Now . . .'

Caro nodded. He didn't need to say it.

Now it was about Alex.

'You know what you haven't told me?' Caro said first thing next morning, when they woke to daylight streaming through curtains they'd left undrawn. 'Why it is that you can't spend the next few days with me in Moscow.'

So he told her what he'd told no one else.

About the deal he'd made with General Dennisov on the observation platform of the train. What the general had promised to let Kyukov do to Alex if Tom didn't give him the photographs.

'He has her then? Definitely?'

'So he says. He brought me a photograph of his own . . .'

Slipping from her bed, Tom took his jacket from the back of the chair and dug into a side pocket, finding what he wanted.

'It's not pretty,' he said.

Alex knelt naked on a recent issue of *Pravda*, her wrists tied behind her back, her head bowed and her hair fallen forward, but not enough to hide her tears.

'She looks like me,' Caro said.

'No, she doesn't . . .'

'Yes, she does. At the beginning. Before I lost weight, before I started having my hair dyed.' Leaning forward, she kissed Tom gently. 'My poor boy. Who else knows about this deal?'

'No one else,' Tom said. 'Only you.'

47

Bearding the Lion

It was cold but she'd been colder. Inside and outside, she'd been colder and she could stand Moscow's icy winds and wait, if that's what it took. The facade of the building she'd been watching was absurd. It had been absurd when it was built and it was absurd now, pharaonic architecture at its worst. Stalin always did have appalling taste. Yellow stone pillars rose like Egyptian obelisks, with windows between that belonged to a Parisian department store. The House of Lions was a mansion block by a set designer for a third-rate provincial opera, and a bad one at that.

Wax Angel knew she was being bad-tempered.

At her age she was allowed to be bad-tempered. The wind and the cold and the idiot *militsiya* man who had tried to move her on earlier were enough to make anyone lose their temper. He'd told her to move and she'd refused. They'd gone through this several times, as if it were a refrain, or responses to prayers, or the chorus to a musical spectacular or question-and-answer from some absurdist play.

Louder and louder, until everyone was looking.

That had embarrassed the young man. If he couldn't move on an old tramp – and a female one at that – how could he ever hope to impose order on the city? In from Azerbaijan, from the sound of him. He'd have done better if he was from Georgia. The crowd gathering might have given him more encouragement, or they might still have just watched in amused contempt, which was what they did.

'Why don't you just leave her alone?' a smartly dressed woman in a brown coat had finally shouted.

The young man had disappeared, promising to be back shortly.

'Shortly' had come and gone, and they were well into 'later' and there was still no sign of him. The crowd thinned too, as crowds always did, after the curtain had come down and the encores were done and the lights went up.

Pulling her rags more tightly around her, Wax Angel dug into her pocket for a stub of candle, found her pearl-handled knife and began to carve.

Over the years she'd simplified the outlines, stripped away their detail and individuality, the way the sculptors had done in the thirties, during that brief period when the Soviet Cubist Movement met Monumental Propaganda. The way the KGB did when they wanted to remind you that you were no one really, even if your picture had been on posters for the Bolshoi ballet company.

Recently she'd started to put the detail back.

A cheekbone where once she'd have put a flat plane, a wing where she'd have left a curve, eyes where blind indentations might have been.

She was, she suspected, becoming kinder to herself.

That or she was running out of time. That was possible. She'd had more of that than she'd ever expected. They all had. The war had withered life expectancies to months and days and sometimes hours. In the cellars of the Lubyanka, even hours had felt like years. That was where she'd learned to fracture herself – to do complicated multiplications of prime numbers, and something called the Fibonacci sequence which an old woman who had briefly shared her cell had taught her – while they did the things they had to do to your body.

She'd been young then, relatively.

That old woman in the cell, who had seemed so old, had probably been far younger than she was now. Everything after the war, after those dark days, Wax Angel should have seen as a bonus. Sometimes, though, she wondered if life wouldn't be easier if it simply matched her fears.

She'd been watching the House of Lions for a week now. Such a stupid building. Such a stupid name. Most of them hadn't been lions when they were young and the ones left were rank and mangy with their fur coming out.

He was in there, though.

She'd seen him arrive in that car of his.

The old cars had been properly beautiful. The ZiS 110B, now that was a real car. Great curves that flowed like riverbanks and the weight and strength of a tank. Black as a Steinway piano too, and when polished properly its bodywork glowed like Japanese lacquer. People used to look and point and smile. No one looking at his new car would smile.

They'd just think, *Big, powerful, ugly . . .*

So many things in the country now fitted that label. It wasn't meant to be like this. She knew that, and he knew that, and everyone who'd fought through those days knew it too, for all no one was allowed to say it.

He'd come with the girl.

She was a solid little thing now, tough as a weightlifter without the bulk and strong as a ballerina without the need to show off. Sometimes when you mixed grape varieties the vintage improved. Other times the wine soured. Occasionally, the results were startling. It was a long time since Wax Angel had drunk wine but she could remember that much.

It was time.

If anything, it was long past time.

At the door of the block, a guard moved towards her.

She waited until he was close and then locked her gaze on his.

He was young and pretty and blond in that slightly Baltic sort of way. There'd been a lot of blond and blue-eyed boys in Moscow once, prisoners of war all of them. She wasn't sure if this monstrosity had been built by prisoners but the university and the block for foreigners out by the flyover had.

'Tell the commissar I want to talk to him.'

The boy blinked at her. He gripped his rifle like it was his girlfriend's hand.

'Go on then. Make the call.'

'We have no commissars here.'

'You have one. I watched him arrive with Sveta and that crippled brat of Dennisov's. Go on, tell Marshal Milov his wife is here.'

48

Into the Den

The hall had been repainted. Of course it had. So many years had passed.

There was new carpet on the main stairs and Stalin was gone, Khrushchev too. He'd been replaced by a huge painting of the steppe, empty as rhetoric. You knew things were bad when they had to replace heroes with oversized picture postcards. There was not even a sturdy boy or pretty peasant girl to stare at the horizon.

So much had been hollowed out. So many pillars of the state turned out to be trompe l'oeil or cardboard. Only Lenin survived. God knows how. He'd be the last to go, she imagined.

This building had three of him.

A marble bust in the hallway on a porphyry plinth.

A bronze monstrosity on the half-landing, which had stood in the hallway until it was judged too ugly or vulgar to remain. Iliych's beard jutted fiercely at the future. His brows were heavy, his eyes all-seeing.

The final bust was right outside her husband's apartment.

Made of spelter, cheap and nasty, mass-produced for school foyers, Party offices and factory canteens. In this case a factory in Stalingrad that had produced tractors until it was converted to making armaments and later bombed flat.

A crack split Ilyich from shoulder to ear.

Wax Angel grinned.

She could remember the grenade that did that.

'Smug bastard,' she said, patting Lenin's head.

The guard from the front door who'd accompanied her this far looked terrified. She could tell the boy a few things about terror. They weren't born these days. Half of them would die without even realizing they'd been alive.

'Remember me?' she said to the bust.

'How could he forget?'

The commissar stood in his doorway, wearing a tatty yellow smoking jacket given to him by the Chinese premier back when Moscow and Peking were still friends. There was a strange look in his eyes.

If Wax Angel hadn't known better, she'd have said it was relief.

'Hello, Maya,' he said.

'Hello Comrade Commissar.'

Stepping forward, he swept her up in an embrace that seemed fierce for his age. He smelled as he'd always smelled, of sweat and soap and cigarettes. The dressing gown smelled as she remembered too, of mothballs that had done too little to keep the moths at bay if the state of his collar was anything to go by.

'You look like you,' he said.

'About time,' she said.

Behind him stood her granddaughter, wide-eyed and fully grown, Dennisov's drunken brat at her side. When Sveta put her hand to her mouth, the young man wrapped his arm tightly round her shoulders.

'Remember me?' Wax Angel asked.

Sveta burst into tears.

Wax Angel sighed. She should have realized the girl might be shocked.

'The commissar picked Lenin up and dumped him on a

grenade. Your grandfather's first and last romantic gesture. The blast cracked most of his ribs, put a hole through a rotten floor too. Just as well. If the floor had been concrete, he'd be dead. Daft bastard.' Turning to the guard, Wax Angel said, 'You can go.'

The young man went without checking with the marshal first.

To Sveta, Wax Angel said, 'Come on then. Let's have a proper look at you.'

Sveta glanced at Dennisov, who nodded her forward.

'A major, eh? Better than I managed.' The ragged woman walked slowly round Sveta and nodded approvingly. 'Good profile. Good posture. Good boots.'

'As for him . . .' She took a long hard look at Dennisov, in particular his rusting leg. 'Stands straight for a cripple, meets your eye. He'll do, if you must. Your grandfather was a slouch too. Except on parade. On parade no one's a slouch.'

'Maya, what are you doing here?'

'I could ask the same.'

'I live here.'

The ragged woman glanced at his waterfall of greying hair and snorted. 'Call this living? Some day you'll have to tell me if the House of Lions is a mausoleum or a zoo. Aren't you going to invite me in?'

'I'm on my way to the Hotel National.'

'Planning to set up a provisional government?'

For a moment she thought he was going to say that her remark was in bad taste. She was glad he didn't; that would have made her cross. She imagined that setting up governments, provisional or otherwise, had been on his mind a lot lately.

Instead he said, 'An Englishwoman wants to see me.'

'So do I. And I've brought you a present.'

She tossed what looked like a lump of rancid jerky at his feet. From the shock on the commissar's face, you'd think he'd never seen anyone castrated.

'Vedenin?' he said.

'Should have done it years ago.'

It was surprising how much better one could feel after killing the bastard who bedded your underage daughter. Sveta's mother had been beautiful and fragile and too innocent not to trust the man who ruined her. Too fragile not to take her own life.

'Maya . . .'

'You know I should have done it years ago.'

He wasn't bad for his age, the commissar. Slightly too impressed with himself, but men always were. At least he wasn't fat like Vedenin. Fat people bleed so badly. Vedenin had bled like a pig as she peeled the fat from his body.

Squealed like one, too.

'We talked a little about the old days,' Wax Angel said. 'About his habits. About who might have been leaving bodies around Moscow. And then I asked him what was really going on. We got to the English girl eventually. You know who has her now?'

She looked her husband in the eye, smiled grudgingly.

'Yes, I thought you might.'

49

An Ordinary Train

Tom watched the KGB officer's gaze slide over him, barely taking in his turned-up collar and pulled-down cap. Half the passengers were dressed in similar fashion. The choice was suffer the cold in this carriage or swelter in the one behind, which had heating enough for the entire train. The young man who'd followed Tom from the Hotel National opened his mouth to object, shut it again and let the officer lead him from the Moscow–Volgograd express at the first station outside the city.

'Black market,' someone muttered.

'Roubles for dollars.'

They looked out at Tom's shadow protesting loudly on the platform that he needed to be let back on to the train and watched him grow flustered when the doors were slammed and the diesel growled back into life.

As the train pulled away, Tom looked around, wondering who was watching him now. Someone would be. Unless General Dennisov was simply relying on Tom to deliver himself. That was always possible. As before, he was travelling without proper papers. Once again, he was headed for a city about which he knew almost nothing. There the similarity ended.

This train couldn't be more different. Yelena's had been luxurious, a gilded relic of an imperial mindset. This one couldn't have been more utilitarian. It rattled and stank, and the windows let in the cold and squeaked so badly that Tom wanted to find a screwdriver and tighten the screws himself because he wasn't sure he could stand another twenty hours of this.

After a while, he pulled a sheet of paper from his pocket and kept it angled to the window in case the fat woman next to him woke and wondered why her neighbour was reading something foreign.

No mention was made of the Tsaritsyn Monastery in any of the guidebooks for sale in the foyer of Caro's hotel. But Tom had a photocopy of an entry from the old *Guide to the Russian Empire* that Mary Batten had lifted for him from the embassy library.

Published three months before the Great War began, it said little about the monastery except that it was remote, rarely visited by tourists, and while a boat trip on the Volga was well worth the effort, Tsaritsyn Monastery itself had little architectural merit, certainly not enough to balance the inconvenience of two days' travel along rough cart tracks through unkempt forest.

A note in the margin, handwritten by someone taught letters in the old fashion, by endless repetition between ruled lines, agreed and disagreed.

The monastery itself was nothing, crude even by provincial standards.

But its medieval rood screen, originally from Kiev and presented by the local governor fifty years before, was a work of art, if not by Andrei Rublev, at the very least by a direct disciple.

When Tom next looked at his watch, four hours had gone by and most of the others had joined the woman next to him in dozing. Only an old woman and a whining child seemed resolutely awake. Tom noticed that though she gave the boy regular cups of tea from a tatty Komsomol thermos, and slices of bread and sausage, she drank and ate almost nothing herself and looked anxious when she saw Tom notice. He nodded, and after a moment, as if afraid of being rude, she nodded back.

Stations came and went.

A few people got off. A few got on.

At one station, the young woman Tom had decided was shadowing him clambered stiff-legged from her seat, dragged a cheap cardboard case from the rack overhead and left without looking back. No one replaced her. At least, if they did, they didn't sit in that carriage. He was left to memories and thoughts and found neither welcome.

Caro had cried when he said goodbye.

That was unexpected. He'd have said she'd grown to dislike him too much to be anything but grateful to have him out of her life. But he'd never been good with that stuff. And he was, he imagined, out of her life now, one way or another.

'Take care,' she'd said.

She'd gripped his shoulders in the foyer hard enough to make the desk staff stare and kissed him fiercely. 'Russia suits you.'

He'd looked at her, wondering.

'Here,' the boy opposite suddenly said.

Several people glanced round to see him offer to share his vodka. A handful of those looked hopeful, perhaps believing the Stolichnaya might come their way. It didn't. Tom took a hefty swig and let most run back, returning the bottle with a nod.

'Going or returning?' Tom asked.

The conscript's grin was an answer in itself.

Five minutes later, the boy was deep in a long and one-way

conversation about a bar brawl in Minsk. A minute after that, he was showing Tom a scar, which was still raw and curved, a hand's breadth above his hip from his belly to his back. As night drew in, the passengers settled, the main lights went down and half-lights came on, and the carriage might have been brighter, if most of those hadn't been broken, stolen or simply never replaced. Like birds roosting, people dropped off to sleep until only Tom, the kid with the scar and a girl who'd moved next to him after he told the story about the knife fight were awake.

In the end, Tom took pity on them and shut his eyes too.

The kids were discreet. You had to give them that.

Of all the things Tom might have felt, sadness was the most unexpected. Not at what they did but at the youth and innocence that let them do it. You needed both to be them. Tom knew, even before the diesel made an unscheduled stop just outside Volgograd, and the old woman and small boy went to the door to wave to *militsiya* officers who came aboard to usher Tom off, that if he could buy Alex the chance to be young and behave as badly, he would.

A Tartar in a tatty flying jacket, with its collar up, was waiting by the entrance. The man was grinning and Tom understood he was the joke. The man's eyes were black and unblinking, so flat it felt like looking into a void.

When he nodded to the *militsiya*, they let go of Tom's upper arms and stepped back, turning for the exit without saying a word. The man watched them go for a moment, his expression unreadable, then he gestured for Tom to step closer.

Without losing the grin, he said, 'You do what I say or we kill the girl. Understand?'

'Of course. I understand.'

'Now. You have the photographs?'

'I have the photographs.'

'Show me.'

'When I've seen Alex.'

'One photograph. To prove you have them.'

'You really think I'd come all this way without them?'

'You'd be unwise to.' The Tartar turned away and an old woman brushing snow off the opposite platform with a twig broom glanced over, hunched her shoulders and hurriedly went back to work. Some things it was safer not to see.

'You liked my present?'

Tom stared back impassively.

'That cat. I particularly enjoyed my share of the skin. Fiddly, removing all that hair, of course. But worth the effort.' His grin widened as they headed out of the station.

'Your transport awaits.'

Tom stared in disbelief at the open-top Jeep the Tartar indicated. It had snow tyres and metal front seats, no seats at all at the back, and its side windows at the front were wound down. There was nothing to protect him from the cold.

A short drive brought them to an apartment block at the river's edge.

'Alex is here?'

'You think we're fools?'

Broken bricks had been built into a wall that hugged the building's edge like ivy. Cut into them were the words *Not One Step Back*.

'You know where we are?'

Tom shook his head.

'You should. You know why the French surrendered? Because they were weak. You know why the Germans surrendered? Because they were weak. Sergeant Pavlov wasn't weak. He became what he had to become. We all did. Pavlov held this building against Nazi tanks, bombers and infantry for a month.

'All his food,' said the Tartar, 'all his drinking water, ammunition . . .' He turned to look at the frozen river. 'All of it came across that under attack from enemy planes. The Nazis lost more men trying to take this building than taking Paris . . . *Volgograd.*' He spat, phlegm sliding on ice at his feet. 'What sort of fools rename Stalingrad?'

'You were there?'

'In this house?' The Tartar shook his head.

'But you *were* at Stalingrad?'

There was something hard, entirely inhuman in the man's stare. He looked again over the frozen waters of the Volga and Tom knew that what he saw himself wasn't what this man saw. 'We learned to kill. We learned to like killing. After the war, they wanted us to go back to being who we'd been before.'

'You couldn't?'

'No one could. You really didn't recognize me?'

'Not until you mentioned the cat.'

'You're sure you have the photographs?'

He was the one grinning at the camera when Golubtsov was tied to a chair. The one holding the board in front of an oak tree from which four German teenagers hung, a board that read *The Tsaritsyn Boys.* In an earlier, more innocent picture he'd been peering at the engine of a captured Panzer, his hands streaked with oil, while the others simply posed.

'Kyukov,' Tom said. 'You were their engineer.'

'Mechanic. I was their mechanic.'

'General Dennisov's friend.'

Again that half-look into the distance as if sifting memories or consulting with ghosts. 'His oldest,' Kyukov said. 'His best.'

Tom shivered.

50

To the Island

Beyond Pavlov's House, beyond the city, beyond the reach
of pylons and factories and other signs of civilization, the
river's edge made the landscape timeless as a faded photograph. Tom was grateful when the forest began. Until the
darkness and tightness of the trees started to press in, and he
wished they were by the river again, for all the wind blowing
across it had been vicious.

Colonel Kyukov was dressed for the drive: pale leather
jacket with sheepskin lining, dark leather jeans and heavy-
heeled boots. He could have stepped from the turret of a
T-34 or ridden out from between the trees on a pony with ice
clinging to its mane. His flying jacket was good against the
wind, and its leather tough enough to turn a blade. Tom's
own jacket was Soviet, chosen to blend in on the train, and
next to useless.

The snowfall began shortly after they left the city, just a
few flakes at first, softening the air in front of them. They
built up on the windscreen until Kyukov swore and flicked
on the wipers, sending clumps of snow into their faces as the
screen cleared and he increased speed again.

'Where are we heading?'

'You'll see.'

The Volga came back into sight where it began a huge
turn, the river's far edge vanishing as it widened. Without
signalling, without saying anything, Kyukov turned down a

track to a ruined checkpoint, its bar pointed skyward like an accusing finger, its barrel weight buried in fallen snow.

A sign said go no further.

Falling snow was meant to make weather warmer. But when Tom began to feel warm, he knew it was the blood retreating from his limbs as his veins narrowed and his body began to shut down to protect its core. When he found himself fighting sleep and a desire to curl into a ball, he realized hypothermia was close.

'Tiring journey?' Kyukov's glance was knowing.

'I'm fine,' Tom said.

'For now.'

The Tartar returned his attention to the track.

Beyond the checkpoint, razor wire fenced a landing stage off from the firs. Scrub poking from the snow filled the fifty paces between the woodland's edge and the fence. Rusting searchlights on sentry towers told Tom guards had once policed that gap. *Absolutely No Entry* announced a sign.

Beyond the landing stage, far enough away to look like the opposite bank, was the tip of what Tom realized was an island. The real edge of the river was lost in falling snow. The Volga was wider than most lakes he'd seen.

Tom could just make out a matching landing stage on the island, with a slight fuzz to its edges that might be razor wire.

'A prison camp?'

'A school,' the colonel said. 'My school.'

'How many boys?'

'Hundreds. Thousands.'

Ramming the Jeep into gear, Kyukov headed for the ice and grinned as Tom suddenly sat upright.

'Ah, yes,' Kyukov said. 'Poor Vladimir Vedenin.'

The Jeep bounced heavily on ruts in the ice and then raced across the river at breakneck speed. Kyukov was grinning.

But then Tom was coming to realize that Kyukov was usually grinning, except when he was staring.

The staring somehow felt less dangerous.

The Jeep raced up an icy bank and through a stand of firs that opened on to a field, with a huge, two-storey building just visible through the falling snow. The building had all the elegance of a nuclear bunker.

Beyond it were rows of huts, dozens of them.

The door to the orphanage was missing and a white wolf stood in the gap, the fierceness of its gaze making clear that it regarded the approaching Jeep as the interloper. As Tom watched, it turned and vanished into the darkness inside.

Kyukov shrugged, as if he expected nothing less.

'They used to pay ten roubles for every one killed,' he said. 'No longer. There's no cattle now for them to kill and no one wears their fur these days.'

Thin light bled through broken windows into a foyer where a mosaic of blond boys, stripped to the waist and clutching axes, filled the wall behind a rotting reception desk better suited to a hospital.

Because of the missing front door, frost made the vinyl tiles of the reception area slippery underfoot. Those at the edges curled to meet the walls.

Tom shivered.

His school had had hose-down floors too.

Who knew when the building had last been used? Five years, ten years? It could have been more recently. It was impossible to tell how long it had been empty, how many generations had passed through here for indoctrination or lessons, whether they had hated this building more than the crude dormitory huts outside. There was a sourness to the foyer, a stink as if something monstrous had been left to rot rather than shriven, blessed and decently buried. It coated the inside of his nostrils the way the frost coated the tiles.

It pulled with smoky fingers at his mind.

Without warning, Tom vomited.

'Can't you smell it?'

'No smell,' Kyukov said. 'It's too cold for things to smell. That only happens when the ice begins to thaw. Believe me, I know . . .'

'Where's Dennisov?'

'You call him "general".'

'Where's the general?'

'He'll be along later. I'm to show you the girl and check you have the photographs. Although, as you've agreed, you'd have to be stupid to come here without them. The general will do the swap later.'

I have to be stupid to be here at all, Tom thought.

'How much further?'

'Save your breath for walking.'

The corridor Kyukov strode down was patched with damp and dirt and decades of misery that had leached into its walls. At the far end, a single door on to a yard was so blocked by falling snow that they had to kick it away to get through. A single set of half-filled-in footprints led to a gymnasium beyond.

The Tartar yanked back a new-looking bolt.

'You don't touch anything. All right?'

Tom looked at him.

'The general will be very unhappy if you touch anything.'

Kyukov stepped back and gestured Tom through. Tom went, his shoulders tensed, half expecting to be clubbed from behind. Instead he heard a bang as the heavy door slammed behind him and its bolt thudded into place.

'I'm going to get the general now,' Kyukov called. 'I'll be an hour or so. Say hello to the girl for me.' He went off laughing, leaving Tom on the wrong side of a reinforced glass door.

The left wall of the changing room had toilet cubicles with no doors. Open showers and a long urinal shared the right. A rack for clothes running down the middle of the room had benches either side.

What little light entered came through snow on a skylight above.

The general will be very unhappy if you touch anything.

It was only when Tom stepped into the gymnasium that he understood what Kyukov had been talking about. And when he did, he felt the room lurch and a hot anger rise inside him. He bit down on it, and felt cold fury take its place.

Alex hung by her ankles in the middle of the room.

She was naked, her head shaved and her flesh marble, her hands dangling a foot above the floor. Her hipbones were sharp, her ribs rabbit-like.

Dog tags hung from her neck.

Alex didn't react when Tom crouched beside her.

Her throat was cold beneath his fingers. She had a pulse, just about. Although her breathing was so shallow that her ribs barely moved. He checked the dog tags without thinking. Her stepfather's: *Edward J. S. Masterton.* An army number followed.

Dear God, could it get any messier? He filed that with all the other questions for which he'd only ever found half answers, and dug into his pocket for the lock knife he always carried.

'I'll get you down,' he promised.

She was way beyond hearing, at the very edges of this world.

Sawing savagely at the rope, Tom wrapped his other arm

tight around her hips. Even braced, he staggered as the rope fibres parted, only just catching her before she hit the floor. Laid out, with her body shaved and stark naked, eyes closed and barely breathing, she looked terrifyingly like the girl found frozen at Patriarch's Ponds.

The one he'd watched being cut open.

He couldn't bear for there to be another laid out on a slab.

Blood pressure. Heart beat. Lung function . . . Tom tried to remember the dangers of being hung upside down.

Blood had trouble leaving the brain. He knew that much. He was pretty certain being cold was a good thing. Unless she was too cold.

'Alex. Wake up.'

He slapped her cheek.

Nothing, not even when he did it harder.

Scooping her up, he headed for the changing room and found himself facing the bolted door. The door was sound, the glass reinforced with steel mesh; nothing he could see looked sharp enough or heavy enough to break it.

How long had he been here? Ten minutes, fifteen?

'Alex. Please.'

He watched one eyelid flutter.

'That's it. Come on, wake up.'

Her colour was slightly better, her ribs visibly rising and falling.

He felt for the pulse in her wrist and instinctively closed his fingers around hers, making a promise that he'd do whatever was needed, whatever he could. The promise so instinctive he barely realized that he'd made it.

'Alex. Please. It's me.'

She opened one eye, the first time she'd done so.

'I need you to wake up.'

Her eye closed, her eyelids fluttered and then she opened

both eyes at once. Her pupils were huge in the gloom of the changing room. Like a fool, Tom tried to stand her upright and grabbed her as she crumpled.

He needed Alex safe.

He needed her out of there.

Awake was what he needed most of all, but both her eyes were now firmly shut and her head lolled from side to side as he tapped first one cheek and then the other. Alex's breathing was definitely steadier, her ribs rising and falling almost normally, her heartbeat steadying.

She still looked starved, though. A ghost of the girl she'd been. It would take time to cure that.

Stripping off his shirt and jacket, Tom threaded her arms through the jacket's sleeves, tucked the dog tags inside and zipped it shut. The best that could be said was that it covered her to the thighs and would be warmer than nothing. His shirt he used as a makeshift skirt, tying it round her waist under the jacket.

It felt like he was dressing a small child.

Tom tucked the photographs under his belt, folded his lock knife and slipped it into his jeans pocket. When he looked back, Alex was staring up at him.

'Who?' she asked.

'Tom,' he said. 'We met at your stepfather's party.'

The girl's eyes focused on the changing room behind him and widened in shock, her question forgotten, his answer unheard. Tears rolled down her face. 'You're not meant to move me. He's going to be so cross.'

'We'll be gone before he's back.'

She tried to shake her head, then she shut her eyes and her head slumped as she slipped to the edge of sleep or unconsciousness.

'Don't,' Tom said. 'Stay with me.'

A moment later, Alex whispered, 'He'll catch us.' Her chin trembled. 'You could say you didn't understand his orders. He might believe that. You made a mistake. You're sorry . . .'

'Alex, I'm going to get you out of here.'

Her mouth twisted in misery. 'You don't know him,' she said.

His father had been a tsarist officer.

Not Kyukov, General Dennisov.

Tom had been told that or read it somewhere.

Criminals, recidivists, tsarists, Jews, separatists, the gulags were at their height in the thirties, filled according to Stalin's whim or paranoia. Kyukov and Dennisov had made it out of here as children.

This was a man who had survived Stalin by feeding his superiors to the machine.

To do that you had to know where the machine's hungers lay, what its weaknesses were . . . The commissar's entire cadre were compromised in one go by the photographs of the baby-faced officer lashed to a chair. All those threads tying the USSR's future leaders into one sticky web . . .

Careful planning or lucky accident?

Either way, the man was unstable, unstable as sweating gelignite with a faulty fuse.

Tom should have felt right at home.

Stepping up on to the double-sided bench running down the middle of the changing room, he clambered on to the bar from which clothes had once hung, balanced there precariously and grabbed for the skylight before he could fall. The window frame was so rotten its lock simply ripped away.

Now he just had to get Alex up there.

'I can't,' she said.

'You can,' Tom promised her.

'You're just making things worse.'

She was cross. Cross was good. Cross showed Alex was still in there.

When cajoling and encouragement failed, Tom fell back on cruelty.

Threatened with being hauled up by a rope, the girl let herself be balanced on the bench, boosted up to the rail and held upright until she found the edge of the skylight. 'Up you go,' Tom said.

He gripped her ankles, intending to lift her, but let go when he heard her whimper and felt blood on his hands from where Kyukov's rope had lacerated her. He thought for an instant that she was going to crumple, and he knew he wouldn't be able to catch her properly if she fell.

'Hold on,' he said.

'I'm trying,' Alex said.

'I'll make a stirrup with my hands.'

Shakily she raised one foot for the stirrup and Tom boosted her up, watching her foreshorten and vanish.

'Alex?'

He needed an answer.

All he got was silence. And then she was staring down, her eyes wide. The wind had roused her and she was hugging herself with one hand, holding the edge of the skylight with the other, and shivering.

'There's a Jeep.' She sounded scared.

'I'm on my way . . .'

51

Not One Step Back, Stalingrad, Winter 1942

'I volunteer, Comrade Commissar. Let me prove my loyalty.'

The haggard major stared at the boy who'd stepped forward. Before he could speak, the boy grabbed the wrist of a grinning Tartar a few years older.

'He volunteers too.'

His friend looked so surprised that the first boy gripped his shoulders, hugging him tightly and whispering what the major imagined was encouragement. Had Major Milov known the truth, he'd have been less moved.

'We can always desert.'

When the school's commander stepped forward, the major cut him off with a glare, staring out over the assembled boys. They stank of dirt and shit and too few showers, but no worse than those he'd left behind him.

'How old are you?'

'Eighteen,' said the boy. It was an obvious lie.

The Tartar might be eighteen. Just. The major found Asiatic faces difficult to judge, and the loyalty of their owners. But the smaller boy, the sharp-faced one – he was younger.

'Their crimes?'

'This one, thieving, delinquency, slander, rape. That one . . .' The school's commander nodded at Pyotr Dennisov. 'From a family of traitors.'

'Kulaks?'

'Worse. White Army officers.'

'Parents dead?'

'Father executed. No idea about his mother.'

The camp where Pyotr Dennisov had spent most of his short life was a *maloletki*, reserved for the children of traitors, renegades and recidivists. A few miles further into the forest was a *ChSIR*, which held wives of traitors to the Motherland. Part of a grouping outside Stalingrad, both supplied labour for the logging industry.

If his mother was still alive, Pyotr hadn't heard from her.

The prisons in the city had already been emptied, their inhabitants thrown into the front line. The Soviet Army in Stalingrad was out-machined and outnumbered by experienced enemy officers and professional soldiers. But what the USSR did have was a near-bottomless well from which to draw conscripts.

'What are you volunteering for?'

'To fight. To die.'

The commissar was surprised that the penal school hadn't been emptied before this. He'd have taken the lot of them by now. He was, however, puzzled by a boy who would volunteer rather than plead youth, or keep his head down and hope like the rest of his school. 'Your name?'

'Dennisov, Comrade Major. Pyotr Dennisov. This is Kyukov.'

'He doesn't speak for himself?'

'His Russian is not good.'

'You speak Turkic?'

'A little, Comrade Major.'

You didn't have to speak Russian to die. You didn't have to speak at all. You simply had to charge the guns, probably unarmed, wait until the man in front fell, pick up his rifle if he had one and keep going.

'Over there,' he told them.

The two boys went to stand behind the major as he turned to address the rest. He imagined by now that they had guessed what he intended to say.

Later, the words became so famous they were used in a poem by Yevtushenko, unless it was by Voznesensky. Back then, it was just a standing order: *When the man in front dies, the man behind takes his place . . .*

It was shouted so loudly and so often that by the time Pyotr reached the front of the queue he'd heard it a hundred times.

'Here . . .'

A corporal thrust a loaded rifle at him and gave a clip containing another five bullets to Kyukov behind. Kyukov's mouth twisted in displeasure at not getting his own gun.

'You'll get one soon enough,' Pyotr promised, as another corporal shoved them away from the head of the line. 'Not mine, though . . .'

'Thought we were going to desert?'

'See anywhere to run to? Anywhere to hide?'

The weight of the other conscripts, shoves from corporals and brave words from red-capped political officers — shouted through megaphones — carried the lot of them to the ruined edge of a railway siding. Falling snow made it impossible to see the far side and a whining wind howled through what remained of an engine shed.

'Over there,' Kyukov indicated a concrete signal box with a shell hole and half its roof blown away.

'When the whistle goes,' Pyotr agreed.

It went, and all but two of the first hundred poorly armed conscripts raced up a slippery bank and on to the twisted tracks, with only 'Not one step back' shouted from behind to disturb them until the machine guns opened up ahead and they started falling, their rifles unfired and grenades unthrown. Those behind snatched up weapons, as ordered, and died in turn, cut down like screaming wheat.

'Fuck. Fuck. Fuck . . .' Kyukov scrambled up the steps and collapsed on the floor. Pyotr crawled over him and peered out through a crack. Behind him the Tartar was still swearing. Kyukov had never been in a fight he couldn't win. Pyotr knew this. It was one of the reasons they were friends.

This was different.

'We're going to die here.'

Pyotr shook his head. 'No, we're not. We're going to become heroes.'

Enough blood had been spilt for patches of snow, ice and churned-up earth to smoke, steam rising from puddles in ever diminishing wisps until the blood cooled.

Snow fell. An hour later, with darkness also falling, an artillery barrage lit the sky to one side of them, and they could see that the bodies in the more exposed areas had become mounds, indistinguishable from the earlier snow.

'Heroes?' Kyukov said.

Pyotr smiled. He'd been waiting for the question.

'They keep heroes alive. That's why we're going to become heroes, so we can stay alive.' He could tell, looking into his friend's wide face and dark eyes, that he didn't get it, didn't understand how it would work.

'I'm hungry,' Kyukov said.

'We had breakfast,' Pyotr reminded him.

Kyukov grumbled, and Pyotr went back to examining the rows of metal levers that had once changed points on the track, trying to imagine this place as part of a normal station with unbroken rails and trains to take him elsewhere. A man might have to live a long time before that happened.

His way was better.

The enemy's side of the tracks was in darkness, but the glow of a fire showed from inside a machine shop with sandbags piled high at the front. A loudspeaker in a broken window above blared bad Russian across the gap, suggesting that they surrender and promising Red Army soldiers shelter, warm clothing and food.

Swiftly, a loudspeaker fired up on the Soviet side.

Soviet citizens did not surrender. There was no man here who wouldn't willingly give up his life for the Boss. It was the Germans who'd die here, forgotten by their wives, who were being fucked by filthy foreigners as their husbands froze or lost their balls to Russian bombs.

'You think that's true?'

'Wouldn't you worry about what was going on back home?'

'You think the Germans would really give us food if we surrendered?'

'I think they'd put us up against a wall. Our side certainly would if they caught us going over to the enemy.'

'Pyotr,' Kyukov said, 'look . . .'

'At what?' he said crossly.

'To the left. Wait for the next flare.'

Below them, in the lee of a broken wall that kept him free from drifting snow, a Russian sergeant lay, his face shrunken back to the skull. It was his watch Kyukov had spotted, gold by the look of it, looted from a German most likely. It wouldn't buy their way out but it had the makings of a bribe. 'Go and get it,' Pyotr ordered.

Kyukov shook his head.

'I'll whistle if anything moves.'

'It's too risky,' Kyokov said.

'Oh well, if you're scared . . .'

Slithering down the steps, feet first, keeping his body tight to the cold concrete, Pyotr Dennisov prayed that his movements were invisible.

A day in battle and he already feared the enemy's snipers. He was also furious at having trapped himself into doing this. At ground level, he edged around the base of the signal box, knowing that he was now exposed, with only his resemblance to one corpse among hundreds to keep him safe.

Cold had reduced the sergeant's corruption to a slow crawl. His eyes were gone, liquefied or taken by crows, his nostrils leprous and his teeth bared. He smelled of sour milk and frost had glued him so tightly to the ice that bits of his face came away when Pyotr rolled him over. Inside his jacket were photographs, folded letters and a silver cigarette case. Pyotr left the photographs and letters.

The leather of his watch strap was so frozen that it cracked slightly when Pyotr unbuckled it. He was turning to go when he hit his kneecap hard, the shock sending black waves through him. A rifle, bigger than any he'd seen.

The Russian corporal clutching it didn't want to give it up. Resting flat to the ground, Pyotr tugged again and kept tugging until the rifle slid out from under its previous owner. Pyotr's breath rose like steam.

How could they miss seeing him?

A flare went up and he hugged the ground, pushing in against the corporal, with the rotting sourness of the sergeant on his other side. He shut his eyes tight against a bullet that never came. After a minute's brightness, he sensed darkness return and night shuffle in from the shadows.

'What's that then?'

Pyotr rested the rifle casually in the corner.

'What do you think?' He weighed the watch and the cigarette case in his hands, changing his mind about using the watch as a bribe. This left the question: which did he want? The watch was gold, with a dial that was white and shiny, but the silver cigarette case held cigarettes, black ones with a gold band above each filter.

'Here,' Pyotr Dennisov said, throwing Kyukov the watch.

His friend flashed him a grateful grin.

Later that night, after Kyukov had set his watch to what Pyotr thought was roughly the right time, they sat with their backs to the wall, smoking a German cigarette between them, and Kyukov suggested a way out of there.

'Across the river,' he said.

'You'll be shot by our side.'

'Then let's go by land.'

'And be shot by Germans? No, stick with me. I'll get us out of here.'

Kyukov would stick with him, they both knew that.

They were just talking.

A cigarette against the darkness, and talk to fill silences that were almost more unnerving than the shelling and the crack of sniper fire.

First thing next day the Germans launched an attack on the siding and were beaten back. Their bombers came that afternoon, a long line of grey planes with black crosses on the wings. They started dropping their load half a mile back and the line of explosions ran straight towards the hut.

'We stay,' Pyotr said.

The older boy looked at him, his eyes uncharacteristically mutinous.

'We stay together. We stay here.'

'Pyotr . . .'

'What do you think they'll do to us if they discover we've been hiding in here since yesterday?' They both knew he was talking about their own side.

'They might feed us first.'

Pyotr took that as surrender.

Kyukov sat with his back to the approaching bombers, his arms wrapped around himself as if that could provide protection. And then, when the planes were past, the last of the German bombs falling into the Volga, he vomited.

'I'm hungry,' he said.

'We're both hungry.'

'I bet they have food.' He jerked his head towards the Nazi side. 'They said they had food.'

'They were probably lying.'

No one attacked next day and no bombers flew over the sidings, and all that happened was that Pyotr and Kyukov smoked the last of the stolen cigarettes. The day after that, they watched a German sniper in the ruins of a factory opposite kill half a dozen Soviet soldiers in a communication trench.

'We need to move,' Kyukov said.

He said it so often Pyotr barely noticed.

It was three days since they'd eaten, almost as long since they'd felt close to warm and Pyotr was regretting sharing his cigarettes. Crawling to the shell hole, he peered out. 'Something's happening.'

NCOs were gathering, Soviet conscripts being manhandled into a line. Political officers tugged their collars and gripped their megaphones as they began to rehearse their words.

'Look at that,' Kyukov said.

Out of sight of the enemy, two Red Army soldiers lugged a machine gun. When one slipped, her cap fell away to reveal blonde hair. The other helped his comrade up, then picked up the gun again. They were young, obviously a couple.

Kyukov grinned. 'Let's go down there.'

'And get killed? We wait . . .'

The whistle went and the troops raced up the icy bank towards the tracks, the two with their machine gun at the rear. As a German gun opened up, and soldiers at the front stumbled, they fell too. It was a ruse. Dropping into a crater, they slotted a circular magazine on top of the gun and opened fire the moment the last of those in front fell, the black magazine spinning like a record.

Its burst was brief.

The boy lunged forward to remove the disk and replace it. The next magazine burned out as fast and was replaced as quickly. They were lucky or well trained or simply desperate, because the enemy machine gun suddenly stilled. Pyotr thought that a fresh wave would charge from his side but all that happened was that those screaming kept on screaming and the enemy gun remained silent.

'Oh shit,' Kyukov said.

A mortar arced high from the German side.

It exploded the moment it landed; the boy busy replacing the disk jerked sideways, half the skin and all of his uniform ripped from his shoulders. The girl simply shuddered, her cap coming away again.

'Fucking, fucking fuck!'

It was the angriest Pyotr had ever seen his friend.

Grabbing the big rifle from the corner, Kyukov jerked at its bolt, which jammed. He hammered at the weapon with such fury that its magazine dropped away. The round that fell from the clip was fatter than Pyotr's thumb.

'Wait,' Pyotr said.

'Why would I fucking wait?'

'A bullet bigger than your dick deserves better.'

The sky was dark that night; the moon hidden by cloud and no flares lit their brutal little section of the city. An owl hooted from the factory opposite. How it survived and why it didn't simply leave was a question asked by more than the two hiding in the signal hut. They were the only ones to hear the whimpering from no-man's-land though. Both machine gunners had survived. If not being dead yet could be called surviving.

Between the moans of the injured, Pyotr and Kyukov's hunger and the eerie hoots of the owl, it was their worst night in the signal box yet. They were out of cigarettes, they'd had no food to start with and the tiny room stank from where they'd shat in one corner until neither had anything left to shit.

Sometime after midnight Pyotr made his decision.

'I'm going out,' he said.

'I'm coming.'

'You stay here and keep guard.'

Kyukov shook his head fiercely. 'I know where you're going. I know what you're going to do. I'm starving. I'm near dead with cold. You don't leave me behind this time.'

A man had to eat . . .

That was how Pyotr Dennisov justified himself.

He wasn't to know until later that cannibalism was rife on both sides, with bodies being stripped of their entrails before being buried, and sometimes going missing altogether. You had to have been cold and desperate and on the edge of starvation to understand. He doubted if his friend had any such

414

qualms. But then Kyukov marched to the sound of his own invisible drum.

Pyotr sharpened the knife. Kyukov used it.

That was their friendship in a nutshell.

Neither spoke later of what they'd done out there, under the cover of darkness, in the hollow of a crater, in a wasteland that barely merited being called a siding.

'No bones,' Pyotr had said. Nothing was to be left at the end that might be used as evidence. So Kyukov had cut flesh from the boy's flank, and peeled skin from his shoulder, rolling it tightly so that it looked like a fancy document tube.

'I'm done,' Kyukov hissed.

'Give me a moment . . .'

'What if they send up another flare?'

Before dawn, Pyotr crawled out again.

The girl was as he'd left her, her uniform badly buttoned, recently dead and her eyes now turned to the sky. Her flesh, when he undid the buttons, was as white as he remembered, white as ice and already cold enough to make him shiver.

He'd removed her hair. All of it.

He was glad he'd left the rest of her uncut.

Kyukov's boy had been enough to feed his cruder hungers.

An hour later, furious at the loss of their machine gun, frustrated by their failure to take the siding, the Germans brought up a Panzer that announced itself by smashing down the wall that had concealed its approach. It was huge, frightening, with the *Balkenkreuz*, the iron cross of the Wehrmacht, stark on its side.

'Fuck,' Kyukov said.

'Fuck nothing.' The tank got off one shot before Pyotr

jacked an anti-tank bullet into his anti-tank rifle and emptied the entire magazine, all five rounds, straight through the turret's roof where it was thinnest.

Few soldiers who retreated from a battlefield in Stalingrad were allowed to live. Pyotr Dennisov and Rustam Kyukov were among that number. Buoyed up by the destruction of the Panzer, the Red Army attacked again, crossing the tracks and overrunning the factory. The battle to take the ruined building lasted thirty-six hours and was fought room by room and floor by floor.

When it was over, the Red Army set up machine guns on the far side of the factory, anti-aircraft posts on its roof and brought in sappers to repair the rails. By then, Dennisov and Kyukov were across the river and behind the lines, waiting to see a small man who'd recently arrived from Moscow to put some backbone into the Soviet forces.

'What if he asks how we survived without food?'

'We starved, we survived on patriotism, on love of the Motherland, on a desire to do our duty. Eat the damn soup and look grateful.'

The first thing the fat little man asked was why they'd been cowering in a signal box for days. Because they were traitors? Because they were spineless, gutless cowards? The major with him, the comrade commissar who'd come to their school, actually smiled when Pyotr said that they'd found the big rifle right at the beginning and kept themselves hidden, waiting for something worth shooting.

'What are you grinning at?' the man asked.

Kyukov grinned some more. 'I'm alive. They're not.'

At a nudge from his friend, the Tartar explained in atrocious Russian how the Comrade Major had come to the school, how inspiring he'd been, how he and Dennisov had simply wanted to do their duty. How they'd survived on patriotism, on love of the Motherland.

And the little man listened, his mouth twisting, and finally sighed as if to say as answers went theirs would do. They were to be promoted and given medals. The comrade major would assign them to their next posts. Before that, someone from the army newspaper wanted to talk to them. They were to stand up straight, speak clearly and be sure to say that any man here would have done the same.

The man from the paper had a camera with a flashgun.

He took photographs, asked them to spell their names, ordered them to stare heroically into the distance, then told them to look shyly at the camera, and took one final photograph of them with their arms around each other's shoulders.

After which, at Kyukov's suggestion, he gave them his packet of cigarettes and looked shocked when Pyotr produced a silver cigarette case.

'Took this off a Nazi officer.'

When Kyukov glanced across, his friend smiled. 'I took it. My friend took his watch. We killed the bastard between us. We're going to hand them in so they can be sold or melted down to help towards victory.'

Putting down his camera, the man dug into his pocket for a notebook, licked the stub of his pencil and made a note, nodding approvingly.

52

The White Wolf

'Are you all right?'

Alex stood half naked in falling snow, on the roof of a gymnasium, on an island in the middle of a river, in the middle of winter, swaying from hunger, and wincing at every step Tom made her take. He meant, beyond that . . .

Tom was impressed when she simply nodded.

'Tell me if you're not.'

Crouching low, he headed for the rear of the roof, keeping close to the edge of the parapet. When he sensed that Alex wasn't following, he looked back.

'Come on,' he said.

She shook her head.

When he gestured her closer, she refused again.

So he went back to get her and she still wouldn't move.

'There's a wolf watching us,' she said.

He looked where she pointed but the earth was white, drifts of falling snow putting the dark huts in and out of focus. Nothing out there looked like a wolf to him. He saw Kyukov's vehicle though, parked to one side.

'We need to get to the Jeep,' he said.

It represented their only real hope of escaping from Kyukov.

As Alex opened her mouth to say something, a yell came from below and she shrivelled inside herself, her shoulders hunching and her face closing down.

'They know we've gone,' she said.

There was the crash of something being thrown over, followed by the rapid shots of a pistol being emptied into a wall. Someone was taking Alex's disappearance badly. Wrapping his arm round her shoulders, Tom steered Alex towards the rear of the roof, half holding her up.

'There was a wolf,' she insisted angrily.

'Did they inject you with anything?'

'Why?'

'I wondered.'

'It was white,' she said.

'I'm sure it was.'

Her face set in a scowl and she became, just for a second, the girl Tom remembered from the embassy party; only now she was dressed in his coat, with its collar up and her shoulders hunched, her feet bare and her legs barely covered by the makeshift skirt. She needed clothes. She needed shoes.

'What size are your feet?'

Alex stumbled to a stop. She looked bemused.

'Alex?'

'Four,' she said. 'They're four.'

His were no use then, not that Tom had expected them to be.

'I'll find you shoes soon,' he promised.

She looked up, puzzled. 'Where?'

At the rear of the gym was a workshop. That was good. So was the fact that it had a flat roof. She'd be less likely to slip from a flat roof. Beyond that was a walled garden, with ruined greenhouses and rows of snow-covered trees. The garden looked as if it belonged to another building entirely, the demolished monastery perhaps.

Lowering himself from the parapet, Tom dropped as

419

lightly as he could on to the workshop roof, breathing out when it held. He caught Alex round the hips, felt her slip through his grip and land on her knees.

She was crying. 'I'm cold,' she said.

'I'll find you some proper clothes too.'

She nodded uncertainly.

'Keep to the middle,' Tom suggested.

They'd crossed the workshop roof and were staring down at the garden when the gym door banged open behind them, the noise sharp on the wind.

'If we go down there,' Alex whispered, 'they'll find us.'

'We have to get to the Jeep.'

Dropping to the ground, Tom held up his hands to catch her.

'I can do it,' she said crossly.

He let her try, furious with himself when she fell.

'I'm okay. I'm okay.'

Fresh tears gave the lie to her words, and her thin shoulders shook so fiercely that Tom grabbed her, holding her tight for a moment. Her feet were purple and her fingers blue. The ridiculous skirt he'd fashioned provided no warmth. He wasn't surprised that she looked terrified.

'I know,' she said. 'We should move.'

Tom smiled. She was right, they should.

Unbroken snow stretched between them and the garden, with only the scuffs they'd made on landing to show that they'd been here. But the first steps they took would betray them. Falling snow or not, the general and Kyukov would have no trouble following their trail.

'They must have been hungry.'

'What?' Tom said.

He followed her gaze to the walled garden, with its heavy wrought-iron gate rusted open. Broken glass topped the walls where snow had slipped away. Alex was right. If you needed glass to keep orphans out of a vegetable garden, they must have been hungry.

Mind you, in the 1930s the whole country had been hungry.

'See the arch?' Tom said. 'You go first.'

'Why me?'

'Going first is lucky.'

'You mean I have less chance of being shot?'

Tom sighed. 'Something like that.'

'What happened to your shoulder?'

Tom glanced down. He'd forgotten the scar was even there. Although to remember it was to realize it was hurting again. 'Someone shot me with a crossbow.'

'Who?' she asked.

'Vladimir Vedenin.'

Alex's face tightened.

'He's dead,' Tom told her.

'You promise? Really promise.'

'He's dead and buried. I went to his funeral.'

'Good,' Alex said. And in her fierceness Tom could see the spark that still burned inside her, the one he hoped would help carry her through this. 'Did you come to find me?' she asked.

'Yes,' Tom said, 'I came to find you.'

'I don't even know your name.'

'Fox,' Tom said. 'Major Tom Fox.'

He held out his hand, feeling foolish.

Alex shook it, her fingers purple with cold, her grip childishly weak and her whole body trembling. All the same, she looked him in the eyes. 'Alexandra Masterton,' she said. 'Well, Alexandra Powell, really. It's complicated. You're the man who was horrid to me at the party, aren't you?

'Do you think you can run to that arch?'

She shook her head.

'Please,' Tom said, 'try.'

She limped off, clearing the gap without shots or shouts.

Tom followed, halting just inside the arch and looking back. Falling snow would fill the tracks they'd made, just not fast enough to hide them. It would, however, help keep them both hidden.

'I need to . . .' Alex said.

He kept guard as she headed for a ruined greenhouse; its sloped roof an uneven board of white squares and black gaps where glass had fallen in. When she reappeared, she was smoothing her makeshift skirt back into place.

'He watched,' she said, scowling because Tom had noticed.

'He?' Tom asked.

'The weird one.'

Kyukov? 'Did he . . .?'

'No.' She shook her head. 'Just watched.'

And the general shaved your head and body, Tom thought.

Between them, they starved you, stripped you, hung you upside down so your piss ran down your belly and across your face . . . He was glad she was angry.

In time, he hoped she'd be furious.

Tom watched Alex steady herself against a plum tree stripped of leaves, laden with ice and apparently lifeless. He'd like to give her time to stop, time to recover. But time was the one thing they didn't have.

'See that door in the wall?' he said.

'I get to go first again?'

'You've got it.'

Keeping to the side where the snow was thinnest, the wind having banked most of it against the garden's other wall, Alex limped for the doorway, moving so unsteadily that Tom had to fight the urge to go after her to help.

He'd be the target though.

No point in drawing down fire.

She made it and he closed the gap between them in seconds, moving Alex and himself further into the arch to hide them from sight. Kyukov's Jeep stood a hundred paces away, alone on open ground and visible from all directions.

'I'll hotwire it,' Tom said.

Crouching low, he looped round to its far side, doing his best to stay hidden. His heart sank when he saw footprints. He wanted to drive Alex out of there and keep going. They were 500 miles from Moscow and without papers. The closer he could get to the capital, the greater his chance of getting a message to the commissar. But it wasn't going to happen. The bonnet of the Jeep was slightly open. He knew without checking that its rotor arm was gone. He checked anyway.

53

Crossing the River

'What do you mean it won't work?'

'They took the rotor arm.'

'I don't even know what that is.'

'It's part of the electrics. Cars won't work without them.'

Alex's bottom lip trembled. 'You're meant to be getting me out of here.'

In her voice, Tom could hear petulance, and Alex's sudden scowl said she knew he could hear it, but she was doing a good job of hiding the fear. He was proud of her for that. Her eyes were wrong, though, dilated. It would help if he knew what they'd given her, because Tom was certain they'd given her something. And if it was nasty, she was going to have trouble going cold turkey later. Assuming he could buy her a later.

'They were going to kill me.'

Tom froze, feeling suddenly sick.

Alex huddled in the safety of the arch, her expression unreadable as she stared at the Jeep that would now be taking them nowhere. 'It would have been cold anyway,' she said. 'It doesn't even have a roof.'

'Alex? They were going to kill you?'

'That's what the weird one said.'

'Kyukov?'

She shrugged. 'The other one said he'd return me. The weird one said they wouldn't. His friend was keeping me alive until you arrived. He kept talking about photographs. What photographs?'

'They're from the war.'

'What's that got to do with me?'

'I don't think your being here is about the photographs. You're their guarantee that Sir Edward will help prevent the release of official papers.'

'That's not going to work. He took Mummy from Daddy. Did you know that? He doesn't care about me. He pretends to. He doesn't really. . .'

Tom remembered Sir Edward's shock when Tom mentioned the dead cat, his restrained despair and quiet fury at being trapped and unable to say by what. 'Believe me,' Tom said, 'he does care.'

Alex turned away and Tom understood the conversation was over.

'I'm cold,' she said a few seconds later.

'I'm sorry.'

'You haven't got a top. You must be cold too.'

Tom took it as the apology it was and nodded towards the huts.

'They'll see us,' she protested.

'We keep close to the garden's outside wall. Find a spot roughly in the middle at the end, head to the huts from there. It's a blind spot.'

'And the falling snow will help,' Alex said.

'And the falling snow will help.'

They set off, Tom's arm tight around Alex's shoulders as he tried to keep her upright and moving. When she stumbled for the second time, he stopped, bit down on his frustration and set off again more slowly.

Patience, he told himself.

If necessary, he was capable of waiting for hours, utterly

silent and still. He had done it that night in a Belfast car park. He simply wasn't patient around children, his own or anyone else's. And look where that had got him.

They stopped midway along the end wall, looking in both directions to check no one was in sight and they'd reach the right place. The first row of huts was two hundred yards away. 'What if they do see us?' Alex demanded.

'Weave,' Tom said. 'And keep weaving.'

'You think they'll shoot?'

If what she'd just said was true, Kyukov might.

If Tom had been on his own, it might be different.

He'd be back in the orphanage, bringing the battle to them. He'd fix a trap, find himself a weapon, embrace the darkness and find somewhere to wait them out. Break General Dennisov's neck – or Kyukov's, it didn't matter which – take the gun or whatever he found and kill the other. Alex made that impossible.

Tom considered leaving her at the huts and doubling back.

But she was cold and scared and barely able to walk on her own.

As Tom watched her limp beside him, her bare feet cutting prints in virgin snow, he knew he had to stay with her and keep going. Alone, if he got himself killed, that was his problem. But he was here with Alex, and if he got himself killed, then Alex was on her own.

He couldn't take the fight to them with Alex in hand.

All he could hope for was to outrun them, find something to keep her warm in one of the huts and keep going. They'd crossed the widest point of the river getting to the island. The river on this side had to be narrower.

Once back on the mainland . . .

Once back on the mainland what? Find a road, flag down a car, hope there was someone official who'd be prepared to arrest them, get a message to the commissar, to Dennisov or the embassy? It came to something when their least forlorn hope was being arrested. A pop came from behind them and Alex stumbled.

'*Are you hurt?*' Tom asked.

She picked herself up, her face white.

'Are you hit?'

Alex shook her head.

'Then run,' Tom ordered.

'My feet hurt.' She sounded close to tears.

Wrapping his arm round her, Tom dragged Alex after him, trying to steer her left and right when her instinct was to head straight for the nearest hut. Another shot followed and when Tom glanced back he saw a shadow through the falling snow, and another coming up behind it.

They were maybe seventy-five yards away.

You could kill with an automatic at seventy-five yards but more by luck than anything else. Accuracy wasn't good at half that distance.

A revolver, on the other hand . . .

At least they had the falling snow on their side.

'Keep weaving,' Tom said.

He picked her up when she fell, took her down with him when he stumbled in turn, and ran, half-blinded by snow, towards the huts that got closer with every step. 'Keep going,' he insisted.

'But the huts —'

'The next row. No, the one after.'

He led Alex at a slant towards a hut near the end, hoping the rows behind would keep him shielded. Then he doubled back, dragging her with him, and stopped at one hut before going to another.

'What are we doing?'

'Muddling the footprints,' Tom said.

It wasn't perfect because there wasn't time for perfect but it would do. At least Tom hoped it would. Pushing open a rotting door, he bundled Alex inside. The wooden floor sank with every step, fallen shutters revealing jagged glass. The only things inside were frames for empty bunks. A shot came from outside.

'Hush,' Tom said.

Alex put her hand over her mouth.

'They're shooting at shadows,' he said.

The coast looked clear in both directions.

'We'll try that one,' Tom said. The door to a hut opposite was already open. Better still, they found the window on the far wall missing.

'Through you go.'

Tom helped Alex up and over the sill, hearing her grunt as she landed outside. Scrambling after her, he looked back. The general was rounding a corner in the row of huts behind. He held his automatic drawn and was stepping sideways, with the weapon raised and ready to fire.

'What did you see?' Alex asked.

'One of them.'

'You should leave me.'

'Alex . . .' Tom wasn't sure what to say other than *Don't be ridiculous.*

So he put his arm round her again and ran for the last of the rows, finding a door unlocked and barging it open. 'Quickly,' he said.

A pile of rags produced torn trousers, a kapok jacket with one toggle missing and a cap with half its peak ripped away. The jacket was stiff with ice and quite possibly dirt. The cap had been chewed by rats, judging from the droppings.

'Alex. Come on.'

Turning her back, she slipped off Tom's jacket, let him help her into his shirt and then the padded jacket they'd found. Buttoning the front, she turned to let Tom tie the missing toggle's tape to the loop it threaded through. And Tom had a flashback to helping Becca dress. She'd been young. Young enough to accept help.

'Are you okay?' Alex asked.

'I'm fine.' Tom grabbed his jacket and turned his back while she scrambled into the trousers.

'What's that?' Alex said. He thought she'd heard something but she was staring through the filthy window towards a long building between them and the river. It was older than the orphanage, but not by much, one of those strange pre-war buildings that must once have looked very modern.

'We'll go round it,' he said.

Crouching low and keeping huts between themselves and where Tom hoped Kyukov and the general were, they ran for the trees along the river, Tom dragging Alex after him. 'Almost there,' Tom promised.

They cut between the pine trees, grateful for their sudden cover, and came out on the edge of the Volga, stopping in shock. There was no ice. Dark water stretched from their feet right across to the far bank. There was no way over.

'Why isn't there ice?' Alex demanded.

'I don't know.'

There had been ice on the river's other side.

There was still snow at their feet, snow falling around them and snow smothering the bank they couldn't reach.

Dropping to a crouch, Tom tested the water.

It was close enough to freezing to make his fingers ache and numb his hand. The only clue to the absence of ice was that fat pipes, coming from the building they'd gone round, disappeared into the water and a low mist hung over them.

'Think you can swim across that?'

Alex shook her head miserably.

'I'll help you,' Tom said.

'It's too far,' Alex said. 'I'll drown.'

She must know she was trapping them on the island. But this was Alex. Swimming was one of the things she did well, probably better than him. If she said she was too cold, too weak, too shaken, or a mix of all three, to swim across, he had to believe her. No matter how fiercely he wanted to drag her into the water and make her try.

54

Slaughterhouse Now

The Stalingrad Oblast Abattoir.

The words were carved into limestone above the building's double doorway. The door itself was locked and Alex huddled in the recess while Tom rattled the handle, peering through a thick glass panel until he realized there was movement inside.

'Get back,' he said.

Grabbing Alex, he stepped away from the door.

An old woman came to the other side of the glass, peered through it and shook her head, vanishing the way she'd come. As an afterthought, she turned on the foyer lights at a switch by a door she shut behind her.

'It's still in use?' Alex asked.

Tom shrugged, nodded towards a path that had obviously been cleared recently, because it wore only a thin skim of snow, and together they headed round the side of the abattoir towards a loading bay at the rear. Empty vodka bottles colonized one corner. Empty cans of local beer sat beside them.

A concrete ramp led to half a dozen sliding doors.

A landing stage was so dilapidated that one end had sunk beneath the water. A sign warned that no more than one cattle barge was to be unloaded at a time. The sign was as rusted as the landing stage was ruined. 'Keep watch,' Tom said.

Alex shuffled to the corner and peered round it.

'See anyone?'

She shook her head.

Tom tried each sliding door in turn.

All of them were locked from inside, and he was about to give up when he saw a narrow door set into the side of the recess that held the doors he'd been trying. He'd already worked out that cows went through the separate doors, probably straight into individual killing pens on the far side. The narrow door was padlocked. Tom didn't have a pick or any wire to make one but that was fine.

'They're here,' Alex said suddenly.

'Coming towards us?' he asked.

'No. They glanced this way. They've gone to the front.'

How long would it take them to find and follow their footprints? A minute? Less? Grabbing an empty beer can, Tom flicked open his lock knife and hacked out a triangle of metal, bending it over the back of the blade.

'What are you doing?' Alex asked.

'Making a shim.'

He pushed the shim's point into the outside of the padlock's staple, and tore his frozen fingers turning it, but felt the staple pop free.

'Hurry,' he said.

Tom shut the door behind them, jammed it from inside and hoped that neither the general nor Kyukov knew there'd been a padlock or realized one was missing. When he looked round, Alex was staring in horror at the killing pens, which had floors that sloped and gutters for shit.

'You've never seen one?'

Of course she hadn't. Tom almost apologized, but she took it as a straight question and was shaking her head. Tom had. He'd worked for a month in Donegal, killing twenty cows a day. There were bigger abattoirs but his had been family-run, and their speciality was not looking too closely at the state of the meat.

Where you had an abattoir, you had . . .

Tom looked around him. The gates were old but well oiled, the blood drains were clear and the slopes swept. He had the feeling the building hadn't been used for killing cattle in years; it felt too sanitary. But somebody was looking after it, and it was so neat that cows could be shipped in tomorrow, slaughtermen found and work begin immediately.

There would be a locked cupboard.

Beyond the slaughter floor, with its drains, was the inedible-offal room with its row of stainless-steel paunch tables. The layout was so familiar that Tom recognized it instantly. A door led off to a store with a metal cupboard at the far end, leather aprons hanging from hooks both sides and rubber boots in pairs along the floor.

'Try those,' Tom said, pointing to the smallest.

He was wrong about the cupboard being locked, though.

A dozen penetrating captive-bolt guns were racked in a row, with the blank cartridges needed to load them on a shelf above. Tom pushed the blanks aside.

'What are you looking for?'

'A pithing rod.'

'What's a pithing rod?' Alex asked.

Tom decided not to explain. 'Take one of the stun guns,' he said.

Alex shook her head.

'I can teach you how to use it.'

She took the thing reluctantly, looking horrified at its weight.

'Too much?' He meant the weight but when she nodded and said yes the tremor in her voice told him she was talking about something else.

He took the gun back.

'Stay close then.'

She shot him a glance Tom recognized.

What really disconcerted him was that the overhead rails were running, hooks slowly circling through the empty rooms above head height. They moved almost silently, on a well-oiled track that had obviously been kept clean and free of rust. Looking through a glass porthole into a huge freezer room at the hooks disappearing into the distance, Tom remembered the girl at Patriarch's Ponds, and the photograph of Beziki's son, white as ice and naked on the snow. That door was locked.

All the same, he shivered.

'What now?' Alex said it like Tom would know, and he was reminded how young she was, relatively speaking. What now depended on General Dennisov and Kyukov, on Tom getting close enough to kill one or both, on him keeping Alex safe if she really meant it about Kyukov wanting to kill her.

He'd always known they'd kill him. Well, suspected it, maybe. But not her.

She was a kid, hungry, filthy and frightened. Why was Tom there if not to take her place on the altar? That was the deal. That was always the deal.

Build a world that fetishizes sacrifice and some will find themselves cast as victims, while others believe they have a right to wield the knife. Some days Tom found it hard to pretend the New Testament had won.

'What now is I get myself a weapon.'

'You have one.' She nodded at the heavy stun gun.

Tom shrugged. You could put it to someone's skull, or against someone's chest, and the four-and-a-half-inch steel bolt would punch through bone or tissue. But that wasn't really what he had in mind.

'You really heard them say they planned to kill you?'

'The weird one said that.'

It was meant to be the photographs for the girl.

That had been the general's offer. Tom couldn't work out what had changed. But if it had changed, then he needed a real weapon. Something that killed at a distance. Something to keep Alex safe.

'Stay here,' he said.

'I want to come with you.'

'Alex. I'm planning to kill someone.'

'I'll stay here.' She looked around, at the door to the plant office, the door back to the processing room, the heavily insulated door of the freezer behind her. 'Where do you want me to hide?'

In the end he walked her back to the storeroom, checking that each area on the way was empty before entering it, listening for noises ahead or behind. But all either of them could hear was the slight clatter of the moving rail and the low thud of the refrigeration plant.

Taking a second captive bolt gun from the cupboard, Tom opened its breech and loaded the heaviest blank he could find, snapping the hammer back. 'I know you don't really want to . . .'

She took it from him gingerly.

'You'll find front of the skull works best.'

Alex looked so sick he almost regretted saying it.

Tom took the key from outside the door and swapped it to the inside. 'Lock the door behind me,' he said. 'Don't open it unless you hear my voice.'

'Take care,' Alex said.

He listened for the click of the lock before heading for the processing room. The plant was huge, far larger than the one he'd worked in. Stopping outside a manager's cubbyhole, he listened for voices, opening its door quietly, keeping to the side. It was empty, the desk neatly dusted, with an in tray bare of papers and a microphone in the middle.

Tom checked the next corridor for cameras but couldn't see any.

That was something.

There were low-level lights on the walls and the whole factory had the feeling of an aeroplane at night. It was the steel, the low-level background noise and the taste of static. Static was better than the stench of blood and shit and urine that usually filled buildings of this kind. Tom needed to find Kyukov and the general. If he was lucky, he'd find them before they found him.

He wasn't lucky.

The shot came without warning.

The really dangerous ones usually did.

It clipped the side of his skull and he lurched sideways, feeling pain flare along his temple, then training kicked in and he was retreating along the corridor, a hand clutched to his hair, his fingers sticky with blood.

'Give up,' Kyukov shouted.

Plant office or processing room?

The office had a door that locked, the processing room doors off.

Tom stumbled into the room with multiple exits and took up position beside the door, feeling his heart thudding in his chest. Wincing, he traced the bullet's path along the edge of his temple. He was lucky. The bone felt fine beneath.

There was a prickling on the back of his neck and he turned, worried that General Dennisov had somehow got behind him. The room was empty though; the other doors were as he'd left them, almost shut.

He stood closer to the wall and readied the bolt gun. His one chance was to put it to Kyukov's head and pull the trigger before he got through the door.

Steps advanced along the corridor and stopped.

From beyond the door came the sound of a man waiting.

Tom suddenly realized that he could see Kyukov's reflection in the side of a steel boning table. And if he could see Kyukov, then Kyukov could see him. Not clearly, though. Not clearly enough to identify what weapon Tom carried, just enough to tell that he was armed.

Tom breathed in, steadied his heart rate.

He would be ready if Kyukov came through that door.

Only the man had begun to back away. His blurred reflection shrank as he retreated along the corridor, before vanishing altogether. Adrenaline almost drove Tom after him, but then he'd be walking into a one-sided firefight.

The crackle of static began a minute later.

Alex, a voice said. *Can you hear me?*

Looking up, Tom found the loudspeaker.

I know you can hear me.

General Dennisov's English was good, his accent impeccable. But there was a flatness to his voice not caused by the factory's primitive speaker system. Tom began to edge towards the storeroom, hugging the walls of the processing room and flicking his gaze between the other doors.

There was only stillness beyond.

The door into the hall leading to the storeroom had been locked. Very carefully, Tom let go of the handle. He needed to go round. But if that door was locked, then whoever locked it could be on the other side. Kyukov, most likely. General Dennisov had to be in an office or a control room, somewhere with a microphone.

Your friend's injured, General Dennisov said.

There was silence.

Badly injured. And he's cornered. You should give yourself up. We'll let him live if you give yourself up.

'I'm not,' Tom shouted.

Could you hear that? He's lying. He's been shot in the head. There's blood everywhere. We can still get him to a hospital though. Don't you want him to live, Alex? Alex . . .?

Bastards, bastards.

He should never have left her behind.

Only how could he have got close enough to kill the general or Kyukov if she was with him? How could he kill them in front of her?

'Don't unlock the fucking door,' Tom screamed.

He had no idea whether she could hear him.

If she could, she paid no attention. A minute later, the speakers crackled back to life. *We have her, Fox. You know what to do.* The wretched child had opened the door and given herself up.

For him . . .

55

Hearts of Ice

It turned on whether Alex was right. If they intended to kill her, then surrendering would hasten that. She was only good as a bargaining chip while Tom was free. If they didn't intend to kill her, then not surrendering might get her hurt.

In anger, or to put pressure on him.

So, did they intend to kill her or not? The question went round Tom's head as he slid from empty room to empty room, listening at doors, following the echo of footsteps, trying to work out where they'd taken her.

Maybe, Tom decided, General Dennisov intended to return her.

It was Kyukov who'd told Alex she was going to be killed. Maybe General Dennisov hadn't been part of that conversation. Maybe it was Kyukov who didn't intend to return her.

Tom thought of the Soviet boys in Berlin, bound by the murder of one of their own, their lives haunted by the ghost of a German child whose death had been worse than Becca's ever could have been. He wondered whether Beziki had been telling the truth about not being in the room when Golubtsov died.

I am a jealous God, visiting the sins of the fathers on the children to the third and fourth generation . . .

There were times Tom hated the heartless bastard.

Now was one of them.

As he headed for the slaughter floor to check they weren't

holding Alex there, he felt rather than saw a shadow at the edge of his vision. Swinging round, Tom stepped back, tight to the wall.

The corridor down which he glanced was empty.

Returning the way he'd come, he cut through the offal room, moving to where he'd just been from another direction, and heard breathing. As footsteps approached, he tightened his grip on the bolt gun, rammed it against the head of the person turning the corner and only just stopped himself pulling the trigger. The dark eyes of a terrified old woman looked up at him. Very slowly, Tom removed the gun.

'Go home,' he said. 'You're not safe here.'

She pointed at the ground.

Looking around him, Tom said, 'You live here?'

She nodded.

'You know all the rooms?'

She shrugged to say of course she did. She was the one who cleaned them and kept the machinery operating.

'I'm looking for a girl.'

He would have said more but she was already moving. When she looked back, Tom realized he was meant to follow.

The old woman stopped outside the freezer room and stood as tall as she could to peer through the glass porthole in its heavy door. Stepping back, she gestured for Tom to do the same, flicking a switch beside the door so that he could see better.

Alex was in there.

She scrambled up as the lights came on, heading for the door, her arms hugging her body, eyes suddenly full of hope. She'd been stripped to his shirt and put in there half naked. She shook so badly it looked like she had a fever.

He stepped back so she could see who it was.

'Tom . . .' Alex pointed at the handle and Tom reached for it, feeling it refuse to turn. He caught the exact moment hope fled her eyes.

There was no key.

Then he saw a flap beside the door, flicked it up and found a number pad underneath. 'What's the code?' he demanded.

The old woman shrugged.

'Tell me the number.'

She shrugged again, stepping back when Tom raised his bolt gun.

'How can you not know the number?'

She spread her hands. It was a very Russian gesture.

'Where can I find the general?'

Fear filled her eyes and she was backing away before Tom could stop her.

He let her go, almost following her in case she went to tell the general where he was. Only then she'd have to explain about leading Tom to the freezer-room door. Why, he wondered, had she done that?

If she'd taken pity on Alex, why not the others?

Tom put his face to the porthole. Alex waited on the far side, still hugging herself against the cold.

'I'll get you out,' he promised.

She mouthed something he couldn't hear.

Tom hoped it was *Good luck* and not *Please don't go*.

Striding away from where Alex was trapped, Tom turned out the lights as he went until he'd put half a dozen rooms into darkness and still found himself facing only emptiness. Should he kill one of them or surrender himself, as the general demanded? How could he do either if he couldn't find them and they wouldn't face him?

'Fuck this,' Tom said.

Beneath a boning table next to a bandsaw he found rags and a small drum of industrial alcohol. He already knew where to find bottles: outside in the loading bay. Tipping alcohol into five empty bottles in turn, Tom stuffed rags in their mouths and headed back inside.

The first Molotov cocktail was lit before he even made it through the storeroom door. He hurled it into the cupboard holding the stun guns, hearing glass break and seeing fire blossom. The second and third and the half-empty drum of alcohol followed. He shut the door behind him.

Tom made it to the next room before the blanks started exploding.

Behind him, box after box went up, the clatter of spent cases slamming into walls, the steel door of the storeroom and the cupboard itself, loud enough to drown out all the other noises in the factory. It sounded like a small war.

Sirens wailed as fire alarms triggered, the remaining lights went down and emergency bulkheads flickered on in every room. The moving rail that had run without ceasing since Tom had entered the factory abruptly stopped. In the sudden silence of the alarms being shut off, Tom heard the clang of a steel door being thrown open.

There'd been another room and he'd missed it.

A second clang told him the door was shut again.

Kyukov came into the gloom, pistol held up and ready, his gaze fixed on the doors to the slaughter floor and the offal room. Throwing over a steel packing table, Tom ducked down behind it just as the man saw him and fired.

The bullet put a dent in the steel the size of Tom's fist. A second bullet followed. The third tore the metal.

'Should have surrendered,' Kyukov shouted.

In answer, Tom lobbed a Molotov high over the table's

edge and heard it smash on concrete. He threw the last one after it, hearing Kyukov swear and drop his pistol to beat at his burning clothes.

Tom closed the gap in seconds.

Putting the stun gun to Kyukov's right shoulder, he pulled its trigger.

The steel bolt lanced from the muzzle, shattered the man's shoulder blade and instantly retracted.

Kyukov screamed.

By the time he stopped screaming, Tom had his pistol. Clicking the safety catch, Tom pushed the gun into his belt without even thinking. Then he kicked Kyukov's legs from under him and slotted another blank into the bolt gun. Putting the muzzle to Kyukov's head, he demanded the code for the freezer door.

For a second, Tom thought Kyukov would obey.

'You want the girl to live,' Kyukov said. 'You'll put that down and get me upstairs. That's where the general is. In case you've been looking.'

Tom punched him.

When Kyukov looked up, he was grinning. His bloody teeth were gritted, his shoulder shattered and there was murder in his eyes, but he was grinning.

'That's not going to work,' he said.

'What's the keypad code?'

'I don't know. Ask the general. He'd know.'

'Give me the number,' Tom demanded.

'Or what? You'll shoot me through the head? That won't give you the number. Come on. Help me to the general. You wouldn't want Alex to die.'

'This is your last chance,' Tom said.

It was the man's widening grin that made Tom drop to his knees, put the bolt gun to Kyukov's other shoulder and fire.

Four and a half inches of steel bolt did its work.

'The number?' Tom demanded.

He had to wait for Kyukov to stop screaming.

'I don't know it,' Kyukov said. 'Honestly. I don't.'

Putting the reloaded gun to Kyukov's kneecap, Tom pressed down and curled his finger round the trigger.

'One, nine, four, five,' Kyukov said. 'One, nine, four, five.'

Tom pulled the trigger anyway.

Kyukov's scream lasted for ever. A for ever during which the noise of the exploding blanks in the storeroom died away, and once Kyukov's screams had stopped too, the factory seemed almost quiet.

'I told you,' Kyukov gasped. 'I told you.'

'What's the number?' Tom demanded.

'That's the number,' Kyukov said. 'I promise.'

1945 . . . The fall of Berlin, the end of the war. Where all this came back to. *That's the number.* It probably was too.

Tom left Kyukov on the floor.

'For really good results,' Kyukov called after him, 'you need to score human skin before roasting. And always eat hot . . .' He caught Tom's shocked look and grinned.

His grin suddenly faded as Tom came back.

The final bolt took Kyukov an inch above an imaginary line between his eyes, which was what the manuals recommended for larger animals. When Tom turned, he found the old woman staring at him. She shrugged.

He didn't expect her to speak.

He'd already worked out that she was mute.

The lights were off in the freezer room. That should have told Tom something. But he turned them on from instinct, still expecting to see Alex. When he couldn't, he flipped up the keypad's flap and punched in its code.

The door opened instantly.

The huge space was empty; Alex was gone.

He didn't need to search the room because there were no hiding places. It even felt empty. Unless that was him.

56

Voices

He should have fucking known. First no Alex and now no bullets in Kyukov's pistol. Tom was slotting the magazine back into place when he heard the low chop of a copter and ducked from instinct, peering through a window at the darkening sky. Crows, high and circling. Low clouds, with even lower ones scudding beneath.

No bullets, no Alex, no idea where his enemy was.

When Tom listened again, the copter was gone.

No flashbacks, he told himself. *Not now.*

In the silence, he heard what sounded like fire catching wood. The thud of a helicopter . . . the crackle of flames: he was back where he didn't want to be. The tightness in his throat said his body didn't want to be there either.

Fox, I know you can hear me.

The voice came from a drab green speaker bolted to the ceiling above him.

Are you listening? I hope you're listening . . .

The static returned for a second and Tom wondered whether General Dennisov was taunting him or simply deciding what to say.

Your little friend would like a word.

Major Fox? Alex sounded terrified. The tightness in her voice matched the tightness in Tom's throat. *I'm sorry,* she said. *I'm really sorry.*

I've been telling her all about your daughter. Such a sad story. I have

446

daughters of my own, you know. And I'm a terrible father. So I'm told. But so far neither has felt the need to kill herself.

Trace the wire . . .

Are you paying attention?

No cameras. Tom had to remind himself of that.

There was no way the general could be watching him.

There was an evil to the factory that was bone cold and implacable. Tom brushed up against it every time he let his focus wander. Tightening his grip on Kyukov's pistol, he felt foolish. Even if it had had bullets, the Markov could only kill things he could see.

The static came back for a second or two.

Electricity trickling along old wires to metal speakers once used to order the death or disposal of cattle as casually as a maniac like General Dennisov ordered the slaughter of people. Tom imagined Alex, wherever she was, very quiet, very careful. Becca sitting in her Mini hurtling towards a tree. The shriek of metal louder than any feedback whine.

He would find Alex.

General Dennisov wanted him to find her.

How long had he been following the speaker wire?

He lost it for a moment and breathed out only when he realized it had passed through a wall and that what he'd thought a cupboard was a door. Leaving one room, he stepped into it again, finding himself in its ruined mirror.

The complex comprised two abattoirs, back to back. As Tom shut the steel door behind him, he realized that he'd moved between worlds.

I wouldn't leave it too long to find her . . .

A jagged intake of breath gave way to Alex crying.

Nothing serious, the general said. *A dislocated finger. Not even an important one.*

RUN! RUN AWAY!

The girl he'd met at the party would never have shouted that. The man he'd been then wouldn't have known how to be proud of her.

He won't run, you know. That's his problem. Rules limit action.

And rituals don't? Tom thought darkly.

The treads of the stairwell were stained, the stench of urine so strong that even the cold couldn't lessen it. A box room off a half-landing held a rotting mattress, a filthy sleeping bag and the embers of an old fire lit directly on the tiles. A military surplus bag stood in one corner, the kind a newly released prisoner might own.

Major Fox . . . General Dennisov's voice was hard. The game, or whatever the man imagined it to be, was suddenly suspended. *What have you done to my huts?*

Tom abandoned the box room for the stairs, reaching a window.

Flames billowed from the first hut he saw, then the next, a hard white burn of phosphorus that softened to a civilian orange as wood and tarpaper caught. Taking the next twist at a run, he stopped at another window. All the rows were in flames. The huts in the first row blazed so fiercely they must be visible for miles.

How long before the authorities arrived?

Above him, Tom heard a door slam, Alex's protests cut short and steps moving fast and hard along a landing. By the time Tom reached the landing only eddies and echoes remained, a sense of Alex passing through rather than Alex herself. Looking round, Tom saw steeply rising steps.

Instinct drove him up.

57

Hands in the Fire

The final run was concrete, metal strips along each edge, side walls stained by rain and possibly urine. The sour stink grew sharper as he climbed, until Tom reached what had to be a maintenance hut on the roof.

Its door was steel. Steel was good.

Pushing it open, he waited for shots.

All he got was cold air sweeping away the stench and a blizzard of snowflakes that dodged around him, suddenly free to swirl down the stairs behind. In the distance, the burning huts looked like campfires before battle, bright splashes against a wall of night. For a second that scene in *Andrei Rublev* with fires on the hillside filled his mind. Half believing the roof empty, Tom opened the door wider and stepped out.

His name arrived on the wind.

Her scream was as fierce as the wind that whipped at the tails of the shirt he'd lent Alex and buffeted her as she fought to balance on a low parapet. Her legs were bare, her toes curled to get purchase on the ice. General Dennisov had his pistol to her head, his other hand gripping her wrist. She was swaying dangerously.

'You've made me late,' General Dennisov said.

'For what?' Tom demanded.

'The future,' he said tightly.

'Let her go.'

'Are you sure?' His fingers began to open and Alex yelled.

Letting his empty pistol hang by his side, Tom held up his other hand in instant surrender.

'Very wise.' The general steadied Alex slightly. 'Now, let that drop.' The sound of Kyukov's sidearm falling was swallowed by snow.

'Your friends will be too late.'

'My friends?'

'That helicopter.'

There really was a helicopter? He'd thought the noise had been in his head, like the stink in the orphanage corridors and the sickening fury that slicked this building's floors and leached from its walls.

'I have the photographs.'

'Of course you do. As you can see, I have the girl.' There was nothing human in the general's smile. 'Kyukov is dead, I imagine?' General Dennisov shrugged. 'I can forgive that. You shouldn't have burned my huts, though. That's disrespectful . . .'

'I didn't,' Tom said.

'But you did kill Kyukov?'

'Call it a favour.'

Without warning, the general pushed Alex, grabbing her back before she could topple over the edge. Dragging her from the wall, he kicked the back of her knee and put his pistol to her head as she crumpled, the knuckle of his trigger finger whitening.

For a second, Tom believed he'd fire.

'Now look what you've made her do.'

Alex climbed back on to the parapet. She was crying.

Did Becca cry as she crashed? Could you see a tree well enough through tears to hit it at eighty? Maybe Caro was right. Maybe it really was an accident. Maybe Bec didn't kill herself after all . . . Below the level of Tom's fear, below the howling wind and burning huts, were deeper impulses, older hungers.

Inside his head, Tom offered the God of the Old Testament whatever he wanted. He didn't know if he was heard. There were days he was damn sure there was no one there to make the deal. All the same, the wind stilled slightly, the moon came out from behind cloud, and Alex stopped crying.

'General,' Tom said.

The Russian's eyes were fixed on the folder Tom pulled from his jacket.

'I take it this is the last set?'

Despite himself, the man nodded. 'We came together,' he said, 'to burn them after Stalin died. I kept copics. The commissar did the same. Gabashville . . .' The general glanced at the piss drying on Alex's legs and looked as if he might push her off the roof anyway. 'He didn't keep copies. He had fakes made, perfect right down to the thumbprints on the back. Fakes were what he brought to our ceremony. Fakes were what we toasted with that awful brandy of his.'

Tom could see Beziki enjoying making fools of them.

'When did you find out?'

'I didn't. The commissar wanted something from Gabashville. Gabashville revealed what he'd done and told him to go elsewhere. The little thief had grown a conscience . . .'

'About killing the boy in the chair?'

'There'd been a murder. We needed a murderer.'

'And when flayed bodies kept turning up?'

'What could they do? They were already implicated. Drench a knot in blood and it becomes impossible to unpick. Golubtsov's father was devastated, you know.' General Dennisov looked at Alex and his smile was a wasteland of desires. 'Poor Kyukov. The things he liked to do. And now he's dead.'

'That was me.'

'Well, it was hardly going to be her, was it?' The man shook Alex, like a terrier with its catch. 'I'm not sure why Sir Edward's so upset. She's not even his real daughter.'

'I think you'll find she might be.'

When Alex stiffened, Tom realized that her Russian had improved in the weeks she'd been away. Then he realized that it might have improved, and she might well have understood, but that wasn't what transfixed her.

Turning in a tight circle over the burning huts, a white helicopter shuddered in the sudden updraft. The pilot fought for control and then came in hard and low, straight at their building. The machine was squat and sharp-edged, and so quiet Tom could barely hear it. A searchlight flicked on and blinded him before he could look away.

After-glare burned his retina.

When he glanced back, the light was on Alex.

The general stopped pointing his pistol at her and aimed at the helicopter instead, ducking as a rattle of automatic fire put bullets through the hut behind him. It was an impressive piece of shooting.

'Step down,' General Dennisov ordered.

With his pistol to Alex's head, the general let himself be driven back by the copter's downdraught, which threw up such a blizzard it almost swept him off the roof. Edging closer, its searchlight filtered by dancing snow, the machine followed, until General Dennisov turned away, using Alex to shield him from its glare.

Very slowly, the helicopter positioned itself over the abattoir, never more than a few feet above its surface. Then it settled, skis spreading as they took the craft's full weight. As its engine died, and the only sound became the low chop of slowing blades, General Dennisov pushed his pistol under Alex's jaw.

'Turn off that shitting light,' he shouted.

The searchlight went off. Whoever did it changed his mind, and it flicked on again, but angled away from the general. A door slid back and a figure dropped to the roof, stumbling slightly under the weight of a rifle.

Pulling off a flying helmet, she shook out her hair.

General Dennisov looked in disgust from the burning huts to the girl in front of him. 'Fuck it,' he said. 'I should have known it was you.'

Ignoring her father, Yelena walked round to help the pilot from his seat. Metal leg dragging, Dennisov limped around the rear of the small helicopter, avoiding its tail rotor. His face was fierce with pain.

'Your wife came to my bar.' He stared at Tom. 'She told me about the deal you made. A woman like that . . . I'm not sure you deserve her.'

'Your father wants these.' Tom held up the photographs.

'Of course he does.' Dipping into his pocket, Dennisov threw across a gas lighter designed like a blowtorch. 'Burn them.'

In his eyes was certainty, and a fury so bitter his mouth twisted at its taste. This was an officer who killed his own CO for being crap at the job, who'd ridden a Ural motorbike out to a log cabin after being told he'd never ride again, who could barely stand for the pain of flying a copter.

'Do it,' Dennisov ordered.

His sister raised her weapon and it was Tom she pointed it at. When her father stepped forward, she waved him back. The general's eyes flared, but when Yelena twitched the rifle, he stopped where she indicated.

'The catch on the side . . .' Dennisov's voice was flat, his patience eaten away.

Blue flame danced from the lighter's nozzle.

'Wait,' Yelena said.

Tom waited.

'You.' She pointed at Alex. 'Describe them.'

Alex looked from Yelena to the general, who still gripped her arm. At a jerk of Yelena's rifle, Alex pulled free and went to stand beside Tom.

'A man on an old-fashioned motorbike.'

'Burn it,' Dennisov ordered.

Tom put the lighter to the photograph's corner and watched flames catch and cardboard curl. 'No,' Dennisov said, when he was about to let go.

Tom held it until he could feel his fingers singeing. When he looked over, the general was smiling. 'And the next,' Yelena said.

'Three young men in an old Mercedes.'

Tom burned that as he'd burned the last, holding it and the ones that came after for as long as he could manage. If he didn't hold them for as long as the first, Dennisov said nothing and didn't make him pick them up again.

'Two men with two girls.'

They joined the others as sprinkled ash on the snow.

'A girl in a bath,' Alex said. 'She's not wearing anything.'

'She's in the bath,' Yelena said. 'She wouldn't be.'

'A man tied to a chair.' Alex's voice faltered. 'He's trying to escape.'

'And on the back?' Dennisov asked.

'A fingerprint.'

'A thumbprint,' the general corrected her.

Describing the next few photographs, Alex simply said, 'He's been cut ... And again ... He's been cut some more ...' Her voice became flat and her eyes dead as she fought to keep her horror under control. Tom felt ashamed for forgetting how young she was.

'He's dead,' she said finally.

The last photograph Tom simply burned without giving Alex a chance to describe it. She had no need to see four children her own age, their heads twisted half off by wire as they hung from a tree.

'Come here,' General Dennisov ordered.

Alex returned to the parapet.

'If you kill her,' Tom said, 'my father-in-law will release files from our Administration in Berlin, files that mention you by name. All this will have been for nothing. Your reputation will be ruined.'

'Rumours,' the general said. 'Filthy propaganda, lies . . . What we'd expect from the West. Anyway, where's your proof now?'

'What files?' Dennisov asked.

'Kyukov flayed a girl,' Tom told him, 'the daughter of a German scientist who moved to Moscow. Your father framed the son of an NKVD general in his place, and persuaded his comrades to help kill the boy. Then he blamed his murder on four German teenagers and hung them from a tree. You've seen the photographs.'

'He didn't kill her himself?'

'Not that one.'

'There were others?'

'The girl at Patriarch's Ponds,' Tom said. 'The dead children in the ruined house. Beziki's sons. Who knows how many —'

'Nobodies.' The general's voice was brutal, his eyes dark with hate. God knows, Tom thought, he'd been bad enough as a parent. He could barely imagine what it must have been like to have this man for a father. 'And I don't flay them. What do you think I am?'

'Who shaved your head?' Yelena looked at Alex, naked but for Tom's shirt, hugging herself against the cold, her hair cropped to nothing.

Alex glanced at the general.

'You,' Yelena told Tom, 'stand beside her.'

Tom didn't recognize the woman Yelena had become.

Her face was harder, her cheekbones sharper. She stood, gripping the strange rifle as if she knew how to use it. One flare barrel, one shotgun, one that looked like it belonged on an SLR. Tom suddenly remembered where he'd seen it: propped in a corner of the commissar's study. It had been Sveta's husband's.

'So,' said Yelena, when Tom had climbed up, 'the truth. Do you really believe forgiveness of sins is possible?'

'Yes,' Tom replied, surprising himself.

'Even for what I'm about to do?'

'If you know you're going to it,' Tom said, 'and you know it's wrong, then you can stop yourself doing it.'

Even he knew it didn't really work like that.

'What if I can't?'

'Then you're forgiven.'

'Please,' Alex said.

'My mother was a nobody.' Yelena said. 'Please was a word she used often.'

'Do it or don't do it,' her brother said.

Yelena looked at Alex and the English girl's eyes widened.

Stepping down, she grabbed the general's wrist, locking him in place. The entire world shifted. Out on the edge, beyond the burning huts, a wolf howled and Tom felt a shiver akin to shock.

Swivelling to face her father, Yelena fired.

At the noise, the wolf at the wire turned for the trees.

It was old, and its haunches hurt, and one hip was sore from a wound that wouldn't heal. But habits learned young are hard to break, and here was where winter had taught it to

456

find food. In its childhood, bodies from inside had been dumped beyond the wire, always pointing away, so the guards could say they died escaping. The wolf knew now, because it was old enough to know these things, that no one ever escaped.

58

Banquet

Alex had a bath on the plane.

She hadn't known planes could have baths. This one had a bath and not just any bath. It was an iron bath held up on legs that ended in lion's claws. The plane also had a shower and two round basins side by side, in front of a real mirror, not one of those slabs of silvered glass you found screwed to the wall of lavatories in ordinary planes. She'd asked how long she could take. The Russian girl told her to take as long as she liked, and then glared at her brother and Major Tom from the embassy, daring them to disagree.

'Whose plane is it?'

'Everyone's,' her brother said. 'It belongs to the people.'

He said it in such a way, and with such a twist to his lips, that Alex didn't know if he was joking.

'Go,' the girl said.

Alex went and lay in hot water up to her chin for an hour.

She would have emptied the bath and run another if Major Fox hadn't knocked to tell her they'd soon be landing. He said that Yelena, who had to be the Russian girl, had found her something to wear, since she thought Alex wouldn't want to put back on the shirt she'd been wearing. She was right.

Alex wondered how Yelena knew.

Dismissing the thought, as she'd been dismissing all thoughts of what happened on the roof, Alex opened the bathroom door a little and found a neatly folded dressing gown outside.

So that was how she came to land in Sebastopol, wearing a man's silk dressing gown, heading down the steps from the plane with it flapping round her knees, while hard-eyed young men in smart uniforms stared straight ahead.

A long, low black car had been parked near the plane, with a chauffeur, or perhaps a soldier, waiting by the rear door. He opened it as Alex approached.

'I thought we were going home?' Alex said.

'We have something to do first,' Major Fox told her.

There was something affectionate in his gaze, as if he felt he knew Alex well, for all she didn't really know him. He might be an uncle she rarely saw, an old friend of her mother's, something like that. 'What?' she asked.

'We have to go to a banquet. Are you going to be all right?'

'You mean, can I manage to be quiet, not draw attention to myself, remember that I'm not meant to drink alcohol, and only speak when I'm spoken to?'

'Something like that.'

Alex rolled her eyes and wondered why he grinned.

The meal was in full swing when Tom stepped back to let Alex and Yelena enter. Dennisov waved Tom on and shut the door behind them all. From the look of the tables, with their platters of food, picked-at plates and dozens of guests wearing expressions that suggested they'd long since reached capacity, the eating part of the evening was nearly over.

The smoke from candles mixed with that from cigars, and from logs and pine cones smouldering in a fireplace far more modern than Tom had expected. He thought of dachas as wooden. Official ones being perhaps a little grander than private ones.

This one, from what he could see of it on arriving, was made of sandstone, possibly concrete, the National Theatre in London, if someone had welded circular balconies to one edge so that they hung in space like parked flying saucers.

'You all right?' Tom asked.

'I'm fine,' Alex replied.

Tom realized it might not be the first time he'd asked.

She wore a simple white dress, with complicated embroidery across the bust, also in white so it could only be seen when light caught it. Her shaved head was hidden beneath a blue scarf, tied at the back.

'A woman's waving,' she said.

Pushing back her chair, Wax Angel examined Dennisov crossly, nodded to Yelena and kissed Alex on both cheeks. 'Such a commotion you've caused.'

When Alex blushed, Wax Angel laughed.

'If you can't cause a commotion at your age, when can you?'

She indicated the seat beside her and Alex sat, Dennisov taking the place on Wax Angel's other side, leaving Yelena and Tom to take seats opposite. Food appeared instantly, helpings of lamb plov with rice, onions, carrots and spices. Looking up, Tom realized Dennisov's plate was untouched.

'I can't see Sveta,' he said.

'You go off to get yourself killed,' Wax Angel said. 'You take your sister instead of my granddaughter, your sister who has no training. And you expect Sveta to be here to greet you? Sveta refused to come.'

'She should be here.'

'Yes,' Wax Angel said angrily, 'she should. Instead she's in Moscow, for all you know crying herself stupid because she believes the idiot she loves is dead.'

'I'll telephone her.' Dennisov scraped back his chair.

The people at the tables nearby stilled and soldiers in smart greatcoats standing round the walls looked over. 'Sit,' Wax Angel said firmly.

Dennisov sat.

'I've telephoned already. She hates you. I'm to make sure you know that.'

Into the silence that followed, Alex said, 'Doesn't Gorbachev have a dacha near Moscow?' Yelena looked grateful.

'A small one,' said Wax Angel. 'Two storeys with a green roof, tin cupolas and a terrace overlooking the Moskva. Too small for a dinner this size.'

'You've been there?' Alex asked.

'Before it was his.' Wax Angel squinted at the tables overflowing with drunken, increasingly noisy guests. 'Still, I doubt that's the real reason we're here. The little dacha is where he goes to think, where he goes to feel safe. There are people here Gorbachev wouldn't want through his door. There are people here the devil wouldn't want.' Reaching for her glass, she downed a shot and sighed in satisfaction as Stolichnaya hit her throat and she inhaled the fumes.

'Don't let me get drunk,' she said.

'You're drunk already,' said Alex, then looked worried in case she'd been rude.

'That isn't drunk,' Dennisov said. 'That's barely started.'

Pushing aside her plate, Wax Angel reached into the middle of the table, snuffed out a white candle and removed it from its holder, smoke curling like a pig's tail from the wick as she put it carefully in front of her.

'You have a knife?'

She tested the blade of Tom's lock knife against her palm, then cut away an inch from the top of the candle where the wax was still warm. Closing her eyes for a second, she opened them again and began carving with practised ease, curls of wax filling her plate like wood shavings as she released the figure from its prison.

The sword took a while to appear, then an upraised arm,

461

followed by a woman's head and shoulders, her flowing hair and her other arm, which pointed down. Her body came next, barely hidden beneath her robes. She leaned slightly forward, pitched on the edge of movement, the muscles of her legs tensed, one foot angled to the ground.

Feathered and intricate, her wings were the last things Wax Angel carved. They were tight to her back and on the edge of being unfurled, the carving being circumscribed by the shape and thickness of the stolen candle.

'That,' said Wax Angel, 'is how she's meant to look.'

Those seated at the top table looked across to see why Alex and Dennisov had started clapping, and the commissar caught Wax Angel's eye across the room and smiled.

He'd been watching.

'We'll get you home tomorrow,' Tom promised Alex.

'Do my parents know?'

Tom wondered if Alex realized how she'd just referred to Anna and Sir Edward. 'Yes,' he said, 'the commissar telephoned them earlier.'

'How are they?'

'I'm told your mother cried.'

Alex bit her lip, and Wax Angel lifted a freshly filled vodka from Dennisov's fingers and put it in front of Alex, grinning when Dennisov opened his mouth to protest and Alex gasped as the alcohol hit her throat. 'Have another,' she suggested.

Tom shook his head and the old woman chuckled.

'What are you, her father?'

'She already has one of those.'

Alex looked across at him and there were tears in her eyes.

Their plates were taken away and sweetmeats were served. Tom imagined that they'd just skipped several courses, going from first to last and missing out those in the middle. He wasn't upset by that, and from the look of them neither were the others, although Alex tore at a bread roll with the quiet savagery of someone who'd gone without food for too long. Looking up, she found Tom watching.

'You all right?' she asked.

Tom nodded. He was too.

'Remember this,' Wax Angel told the girl.

The old woman stared round the room with a quiet intensity, almost as if trying to fix in her memory who was here, where they sat and what they were wearing.

The top table was full of old men, with one slightly younger man in the middle. The President's face had started appearing in newspapers in the West almost as frequently as it did in the Soviet Union. There were younger men at other tables. Men in uniform and men in suits. A few women. Not as many as Wax Angel would have liked, Tom suspected. Not as many as there should have been.

Alex said, 'Are you expecting something to happen?'

Wax Angel wrapped her arm round Alex, and after a moment's hesitation the girl leaned into her hug. 'No,' Wax Angel said, 'I'm not. That's the beauty of it. This is not the night Stalin fell ill. No one is expecting anything to happen at all.'

She raised her vodka glass.

'We have your Englishman to thank for that.'

59

Going Home

Sveta met them off their flight from Sebastopol, Dennisov walking straight into a slap so hard it echoed off the VIP section's tiled walls.

'How dare you not take me?'

Whatever he said in the fierce embrace that followed killed her fury, and when Sveta hugged Yelena in turn, it was more protective than anything else.

Wax Angel and the commissar simply smiled, turning their attention to Yelena when she said she wanted to go home. Sveta tried to insist that she travel with them, but Yelena was firm about taking the bus.

She intended to go food shopping before returning to the bar.

Wax Angel wished her luck with that.

Now Tom and Alex were in the back of a Zil, with Sveta up front and Dennisov stubbornly riding rearguard on a borrowed Ural behind. Their little cavalcade stopped twice. The first time at a Beryozka shop so Alex could buy *matryoshka* dolls for her mother, a carved wooden bear for her father, and a red scarf to hide her hair until it grew back. She was hoping to find one with a hammer and sickle in the corner.

Since Alex had no hard currency, Tom had to lend it to her. It was the kind of teenage lend where both sides knew the money was never coming back. Buying the presents had been his suggestion so that seemed entirely fair. And he was glad Alex had liked the idea, because he needed a few words with Sveta, and for that Alex needed to be out of the way.

'Did you know what Dennisov intended?'

'Who said he intended anything? My grandfather merely fixed the helicopter.'

'And the strange gun?'

'The commissar was shocked to find it missing.'

'I bet . . . So, why didn't he ever move against the general himself?'

He watched Sveta wonder if she should answer. 'You realize,' she said finally, 'that General Dennisov died after a long battle against cancer fought with the bravery you'd expect from a Soviet hero? TASS is preparing a broadcast to announce his death. As soon as that's done, Leningrad's Channel 5 will start work on a documentary for broadcast in his adopted city . . . His funeral will be televised. *Pravda* will run an obituary.'

'And London will block any of the Berlin reports that mention General Dennisov by name from being released under the forty-year rule.'

'I have your word?'

'Yes,' Tom said, hoping that Caro's father could deliver.

'It's complicated . . . The general had a letter Khrushchev sent to my father. The first line says, "I'm relying on you."' Sveta hesitated. 'It was written in late February 1953 and hand-delivered. My father met with General Dennisov first thing next morning.'

Tom felt the last bits of the puzzle slot into place.

Sveta nodded, her eyes on the driving mirror.

'Stalin went to a banquet the day after, watched a film, retired to his dacha at Kuntsavo and went to bed. That place is the size of a hotel. Beria was there, Khrushchev and Golubtsov too. All of them. Where you found Golubtsov *père*, you found Dennisov. No one dared disturb Stalin when he didn't appear for breakfast. My grandfather arrived that night, insisted on paying his respects and discovered the Boss on his bedroom floor, in a puddle of piss. No one can even agree whether he was alive or dead. It was three days before they announced that the Great Leader was no more.'

'How close did we just come to history repeating itself?'

'Very,' Sveta said. 'Only this man is a good man.'

'And your grandfather wouldn't give his permission?'

Sveta shrugged. 'Anything else?'

Tom checked that Alex wasn't on her way back.

'Who was really behind her abduction?'

'I think it went like this. Gorbachev wants to know whether the old guard will stand by him. My grandfather promises they will. Alex falls in love with one of Vedenin's staff. Vedenin doesn't know that, but his son, Vladimir, does . . . When General Dennisov finds out, he sees an opportunity. He objects to Gorbachev being given the top post. He objects to the suggestion that we negotiate with the West. He objects to anything that doesn't put one of his allies in the top job.'

Tom waited.

'Taking Alex muddied the waters and gave the general leverage when it came to protecting his reputation. Those Berlin papers were dangerous. Your friend Beziki messed everything up by grabbing the girl after Vladimir Vedenin died. He must have known what he was bringing on himself.'

'But he had the photographs.'

'In the end, they weren't enough. The general was dying. He hated how Russia was changing. And he wanted his reputation protected. Alex's father could provide that. I'm sure you've worked out that Sir Edward already knew exactly what the general and Kyukov were capable of . . .'

'Christ,' Tom said.

'Your God, not mine. Sir Edward is very English.'

Tom waited for her to say more.

'You don't like him,' Sveta added. 'We know that. But he's a good man, for an Englishman.' She shrugged. 'My grandfather considers him to be one anyway. Soon London will ask if he thinks our offer is a ruse.'

'What offer?'

'To begin to embrace democracy.'

'Is it a ruse?'

'I don't know.' Sveta looked briefly troubled. 'My grandfather says we can't afford to keep fighting the West. So we're going to do a terrible thing to you. We're going to take away your enemy, come in from the cold.' She shrugged. 'We tamed the tundra, defeated the Nazis almost singlehandedly and put the first satellite into space. I don't see why democracy should be so hard . . .'

'You know I'll report that?'

'I'm counting on it. We might have lost the Cold War. You know I'll deny saying that. We intend to win the thaw.'

'You never were Vnutrenniye Voiska were you?'

Turning, Sveta reached out to offer her hand. 'Colonel Milova,' she said, 'KGB. At your service.'

'Colonel?'

'There are some benefits to a happy outcome.'

'As well as a sense of pride in having done your duty to the state?'

'That too,' Sveta said.

The buildings of the Garden Ring swept by and the Zil passed through red lights with traffic police holding back the cars that would have gone on green. They were nearing the embassy when Tom remembered something. 'If you want your cassette back, Dennisov has it. Your books too.'

'You found the stuff in my wardrobe?'

'Yeah.'

'All of it?'

'Badges, cassettes, Davie's postcard, books, your poems . . .'

Alex groaned. 'No one else read them, did they?'

'Only your mother.'

'Tell me you're joking.' Alex drew up her knees, hugging them to her chest. She was chewing her lip as she stared past Sveta to the road beyond. 'You are joking. Aren't you?'

'I wouldn't worry.'

'Wouldn't *worry*!'

'She said no one who'd actually had sex could possibly have written them.'

Alex's expression passed through hurt, anger and outrage to eye-rolling contempt in seconds. 'Shows what she knows.'

Tom wasn't sure he was meant to hear that.

'Can I ask a question?' she said.

He nodded.

'What do I tell them?'

'What do you want to tell them?'

'Nothing,' she said firmly. 'They'll only fuss.'

'That's their job,' he told her and she made a face at him too.

Leaning forward, Tom asked Sveta to take a long way round.

So Sveta turned into a backstreet, weaved her way between parked cars and slowed in a little square, still white from that morning's snow. She brought the Zil to a halt outside a glass-fronted bakery that looked shut. Vanishing inside, she reappeared with a brown paper bag. 'Dennisov's favourites.'

Maybe she was going to call him that for ever.

'You can have one now.' Pulling a sticky pastry from the bag, Sveta handed it to Alex, who examined it doubtfully. Politeness won.

'Thank you,' she said.

'And one for him. Now I shut this.'

A glass wall rose inside the Zil and immediately descended for Sveta to add, 'So you can talk,' in case that wasn't obvious. As she pulled away, the Ural fell into position behind and Alex put her pastry on the seat beside her.

'You'll upset her if you don't eat it.'

With a sigh, the girl took a bite.

Drifts were piled up on both sides of the main road, and a snowplough stood abandoned in a slot reserved for traffic police. Well-wrapped women, with headscarves to protect them from the wind, and zinc scrapers with wooden handles, cleared pavements. Office workers went to their jobs. Night workers came home. A stall in a tiny park had a queue for hot tea. Children skated on a small lake watched by babushkas, Prokofiev blaring from speakers hung on the trees. The whole city moved like slightly faulty clockwork. And Tom realized that he'd grown to like the place.

'You're not listening,' Alex protested.

'I was thinking about Sveta's grandfather.'

'That's probably better than thinking about Sveta. Oh, don't look so shocked. It's obvious. Do you mind about . . .?'

'Dennisov? I think they'll be good together.'

'I loved him, you know. Well, I thought I did.'

They weren't talking about Dennisov now, obviously.

'Do you think he ever thinks about me?'

Tom thought of Kotik, burned to death in the warehouse, his hands wired behind his back and Alex's jade ring on his finger. The boy he'd seen at the New Year's Eve party watching over Vedenin.

'No,' Tom said firmly, 'I don't imagine he does.'

Alex bit her lip and stared out of the window.

'What should I do?'

Tom thought of all the things he could and should have said to Becca, and realized he should probably stop linking Alex and Becca in his head like this. Alex didn't need it and Becca deserved better.

'Be kind.'

She glanced at him.

'You're bright, talented, opinionated . . .' He liked that she didn't try to deny it, blush or nod in agreement. She simply waited, looking slightly watchful. Then she waited some more when he couldn't find the words. 'You can afford to be kind.'

'Be kind how?'

'Be the person they think you are. Just this once.'

She nodded to herself, then nodded to Tom and tapped on the glass screen as if Sveta were a real chauffeur rather than a Soviet officer with a grandfather in the Politburo. 'Could I go home now?'

Sveta grinned.

The huge wrought-iron gates on Maurice Thorez Embankment were already open. The Soviet guard outside came to attention and the British guard stepped back to let the black Zil enter, but Sveta drew up outside.

'Please,' Alex said. 'They'll want to meet you.'

'No,' said Sveta. 'It's not appropriate and this is better. This gives you time to check through your lies. It also gives them time to see you coming.' She inclined her head towards Sir Edward and Lady Anna, who stood awkwardly on the steps. 'What advice did he give you?'

'Be kind to them.'

Sveta shrugged. 'I've heard more stupid suggestions.'

Opening her own door, she climbed out and opened Alex's for her. Then she surprised Tom by hugging the girl and whispering something.

Alex stepped back.

'All right?' Sveta said.

'You think so?' Alex asked.

'I know so . . . Now, go.'

Sveta watched her head for the gate, then nodded for Tom to get back in the car and reversed slowly until they were in a position to watch the reunion. Tom didn't know what to expect. He wasn't even sure what he hoped for, other than that neither side said something stupid. He needn't have worried.

Alex looked at her mother and closed the gap between them at a run, wrapping her arms tightly around her. Anna Masterton's arms came up from instinct and tightened in turn as Alex leaned into her and the sobs took hold.

They stood locked together, Sir Edward looking on so awkwardly that he seemed almost grateful when Tom swung open his door and went over to him.

'I was asked to give you this, sir.'

Sir Edward took the very small, very ordinary envelope, which the commissar had handed Tom before saying his goodbyes, and extracted a sheet of yellowing paper, skimming it once, then reading it more slowly. His face was haunted and when he looked up Tom realized there were tears in his eyes.

'You've read it?'

'Of course not, sir.'

'It's a love letter.' He looked at Anna Masterton, then at Alex. 'Written a very long time ago, a very long time ago indeed.'

'In Berlin?'

'Yes, in Berlin.'

'You were in love with a German girl?'

The ambassador shook his head.

'A Russian girl?' Perhaps Tom sounded too surprised because Sir Edward glanced across at him and his mouth twisted. For a second, the sadness threatened to spill over and then he was in control again.

'Not a girl,' he said.

He said it so quietly he might have been saying it to himself.

Just inside the gate, Alex and Lady Masterton were locked in an embrace so tight it looked as if it could never be broken. Whatever they were saying to each other was private. They both seemed to be in tears.

'How's my daughter?'

'She'll be fine,' said Tom, wondering if Sir Edward realized what he'd just said. 'That is, I think she'll be fine. I'm sorry, sir, I hope I'm allowed to say . . . you might want to go easy on her for a while.'

'Did they . . .?'

Tom shook his head. 'She's been treated carefully.'

The 'treated carefully' bit was a lie and he imagined the man knew it. But it was up to Alex how much she wanted to tell them, how much she wanted to keep to herself.

'I'm told . . .' Sir Edward looked at Tom. 'London say you offered yourself as a swap.' When Tom didn't deny it, he nodded to himself. 'Who enticed her away?'

'The boy in question is dead.'

'Vedenin's son?'

'No, sir. A friend of his. It might be best not to . . .'

'Mention his death to my daughter?'

'Yes, sir.'

He was good at clipped, Sir Edward. At home with words stripped so bare all the meaning resided in the spaces. Tom was coming to realize there was more to the man than he first thought.

'Do I want to know who was behind it?'

'Probably not. Most of those implicated are dead.'

'Ever meet someone called Kyukov?'

'I killed him.'

Tom felt rather than saw Sir Edward glance at his daughter.

'I owe you,' the ambassador said.

Alex finally stepped back from her mother, and as Tom and Sir Edward watched, Lady Anna reached up to caress Alex's face. Sir Edward sighed. 'I'm going to have to let her go to that bloody school, aren't I?'

He grimaced.

'Well, aren't I?'

Sveta smiled as Tom climbed back into the Zil.

He had said his goodbyes to Alex's parents and received a firm shake from her father, a silently mouthed *Thank you* from her mother. Now it was done, he'd cross the city for his flight to London. There were things he needed to say to Caro.

The kind of things a man needs to say to a woman face to face. He wanted Caro to be able to see his eyes when he asked her for another go. His Aeroflot flight left from Sheremetyevo in an hour but he imagined they'd hold it for him if he hit traffic. Except that he wouldn't hit traffic. This was Moscow, and the Zil had its own bit of road.

Right down the middle.

Acknowledgements

Moskva is fiction and it goes without saying that no one in this book existed, except for the ones who did.

Thanks go to Jonny Geller of Curtis Brown for fixing the deal. To my editor at Penguin, Rowland White, for his sharp editorial eye and remorseless insistence that *if we just did . . .* (and endless cups of coffee). To Emad Akhtar, also at Penguin, for making a few but highly pertinent suggestions. My copy-editor, Emma Horton, who tweaked and trimmed and added *that*s, and stamped ruthlessly on repetition.

I owe a research debt to Antony Beevor's *Stalingrad* and *Berlin*, and Keith Lowe's *Savage Continent*, and an even bigger debt to Vasily Grossman's *Life and Fate*, which *Le Monde* called 'the greatest Russian novel of the twentieth century'. (They probably forgot Bulgakov's *Master and Margarita*.)

I'd like to tip my hat to Grigori Chukhrai's 1959 *Ballad of a Soldier*, made during the Khrushchev thaw. It won the Special Jury prize at Cannes in 1960, the same year that *La Dolce Vita* took the Palme d'Or: a perfect counterpoint of East and West. A tip of the hat also to those who shared their memories of living or working in 1980s Moscow. Tom Fox is an amalgam of two or three people.

You know who you are.

Finally, love and thanks to Sam Baker, my partner, who was writing her own novel and wrestling with setting up a company while I was off, holed up in garrets and hammering away at a laptop. Here's to still hanging round ley lines littered with sites of slaughter and canonization. I'm glad. *Kisses for Mayakovsky* is included for you.